New
TOEIC
第1次就考好

New
TOEIC
第1次就考好
文法

# 序

台灣近年來因應國際化之需求，職場上對於英語能力的要求有日漸提升的趨勢。多益考試的成績廣受全球企業所採用，其成績可作為招聘員工、內部升遷或遴選員工赴海外受訓等之標準，也因此報考多益考試的人口也愈來愈多。

New Toeic 測驗分「聽力測驗」和「閱讀測驗」兩大部分。文法在考題上主要分布在第二部份的閱讀測驗，特別是 Part 5「單句填空」和 Part 6「段落填空」。但嚴格說來，考生對於英文句法（syntax）的熟悉度不只影響了閱讀理解的能力，甚至也左右了第一部份聽力測驗的反應速度。

文法能力雖非一蹴可幾，但準備多益文法也不是沒有訣竅可言。《第一次就考好 New TOEIC 文法》針對多益考試常出現的文法概念，精選了 25 章多益必考文法課程，摒棄一般文法書生硬瑣碎的規範性解說，而以提綱挈領的方式讓讀者迅速掌握文法句型重點，減輕讀者學習文法的頭痛感。更可喜的是，每則文法概念均搭配實用的商務情境例句，這簡直是讀者的一大福音，因為多益考試的特色就是題目和商業主題息息相關，如果光有文法知識而對商務用字不熟悉，要拿到金色證書就顯得有困難了。

值得一提的是，每章文法課程後所附的模擬試題還分 450 和 650 兩級門檻，讓讀者在準備考試的過程能掌握自己的學習程度，按部就班累積文法實力。模擬試題的解析精闢，帶領讀者破解解題關鍵與考題陷阱，不是告訴讀者答案「是什麼」，而是讓讀者理解「為什麼」。這等於在練習的過程中強化了對句型的掌握及語意的理解，實際提升了溝通能力。近年來台灣學生在面對亞洲其他國家英語力的躍進程度，顯得有點焦慮與欠缺自信。在此也與讀者共勉，英語的實力是長期學習的累積，一次的考試成績不能代表一輩子的英語能力，但期望透過本書的學習，讓你第一次就考好多益文法，並得到貨真價實的英語力！

資深 Discovery 編譯
陳慧萍 Sophie Chen

—— 經歷：年代數位課程特約教學設計師
公立國中英語教師
國、高中教材編輯，教學節目錄製

# Contents 目錄

# Win Fox 文法必贏 使用說明
## 本書分成 25 單元文法課程＋5 回新多益實戰試題

該單元文法觀念概述。

商務英文和文法概念並重的教學設計。

單元文法必學的相關固定概念。

此固定概念的概述。

---

**Unit 01 名詞** 商務主題 會議

### 名詞的種類
- 名詞是用來表達「人」、「事」、「物」的名稱。依據其功能可分為普通名詞、集合名詞、物質名詞、專有名詞和抽象名詞。
- 有單複數之分的稱為「可數名詞」，只有普通名詞和集合名詞是可數名詞。物質名詞、專有名詞和抽象名詞是「不可數名詞」，沒有單複數之分。

用商務英文學多益句型 **名詞** 必考重點句

**How many/How much 的用法**

**How many representatives will you be sending to the conference?**
你要派多少位代表去參加會議？

詢問「可數名詞」的數量必須用 How many，而且該名詞要用「複數型態」。詢問「不可數名詞」的數量則必須用 How much。

⊃ A: How many **cookies** do you want?
B: Not too many. Just **a few**.
A：你想吃多少餅乾？
B：不要太多，一些就好。

⊃ A: How much **milk** do you want?
B: Not too much. Just **a little**.
A：你要喝多少牛奶？
B：不要太多，一些就好。

**定冠詞 the**

**The CEO was late to the meeting.**
總裁開會遲到了。

如果要表達「特定的」名詞，前面必須要加定冠詞 the。

⊃ The **beef** I ate yesterday was bad.

---

每一個文法單元都搭配一個商務主題。

搭配該單元商務情境及固定概念的商用句。

搭配此固定概念的日常生活例句。

---

答對以下 10 個問題就擁有多益 450 的實力！ **Level 1** 挑戰多益 *450*
請從 (A)、(B)、(C)、(D) 中選出一個最適合的答案。

答對以下 10 個問題就擁有多益 650 的實力！ **Level 2** 挑戰多益 *650*
請從 (A)、(B)、(C)、(D) 中選出一個最適合的答案。

每單元題目皆分為兩階段，循序漸進掌握學習。

---

Practice Test 1 **多益文法模擬考 第一回**

**單句填空▶**請從 (A)、(B)、(C)、(D) 中選出一個最適合的答案。

Practice Test 1 **單句填空** 試題解析

25 個文法單元後，還有多益文法模擬試題（共五回），核對解析，做最後衝刺。

### 名詞的種類

- 名詞是用來表達「人」、「事」、「物」的名稱。依據其功能可分為普通名詞、集合名詞、物質名詞、專有名詞和抽象名詞。
- 有單複數之分的稱為「可數名詞」，只有普通名詞和集合名詞是可數名詞。物質名詞、專有名詞和抽象名詞是「不可數名詞」，沒有單複數之分。

**用商務英文
學多益句型**

**名詞** 必考重點句

---

**How many/How much 的用法**

## How many representatives will you be sending to the conference?

### 你要派多少位代表去參加會議？

詢問「可數名詞」的數量必須用 How many，而且該名詞要用「複數型態」。
詢問「不可數名詞」的數量則必須用 How much。

⊃ A: **How many cookies** do you want?
　 B: Not too **many**. Just **a few**.
　 A：你想吃多少餅乾？
　 B：不要太多，一些就好。

⊃ A: **How much milk** do you want?
　 B: Not too **much**. Just **a little**.
　 A：你要喝多少牛奶？
　 B：不要太多，一些就好。

---

**定冠詞 the**

## The CEO was late to the meeting.

### 總裁開會遲到了。

如果要表達「特定的」名詞，前面必須要加定冠詞 the。

⊃ The **beef** I ate yesterday was bad.
　 我昨天吃的牛肉是壞掉的。

⊃ The **wind** blew from the west.
　 這陣風從西邊吹來。

⊃ The **tea** you bought was more expensive than mine.
　 你買的茶比我買的貴。

名詞的複數變化請看 p.454

名詞的複數變化請看 p.454

**單複數同形的名詞**

# Several new book series were discussed at the meeting.

**會議上討論了幾套新書。**

有些可數名詞是單複數同形，例如 series（系列）、species（種類）、deer（鹿）、fish（魚）、salmon（鮭魚）、bison（美洲野牛）、buffalo（水牛）、reindeer（馴鹿）、antelope（羚羊）、sheep（綿羊）。

fish 在此為複數

➲ **Fish are** cold-blooded.
　　魚是冷血動物。

species 在此為單數

➲ Pandas are **an** endangered **species**.
　　貓熊是瀕臨絕種的動物。

deer 在此為複數

➲ There **are** ten **deer** on the farm.
　　農場有十隻鹿。

**名詞單複數該用什麼動詞？**

# There are many items on the agenda for today.

**今天的議程上有很多項目。**

使用「可數名詞」時，動詞需要根據可數名詞的單複數變化，代名詞也會因為單、複數而有 it/they 的變化。

使用「不可數名詞」時，be 動詞要搭配 is/was，一般動詞則要做第三人稱單數的動詞變化，代名詞一律用 it。搭配複數的可數名詞，be 動詞要搭配 are/were，一般動詞則不需變化，代名詞用 they。

➲ There **is** a lot of **coffee**, but there **isn't** any **sugar**.
　　有許多咖啡，但是沒有糖。

➲ A: **Are** there any **dounts** left?
　　B: There **is** one left.
　　A：還有甜甜圈嗎？
　　B：還有一個。

➲ A: How do you like the **ice-cream**?
　　B: **It tastes** delicious.
　　A：你覺得這冰淇淋如何？
　　B：很好吃。

# Ron's team are specialists in their field.
### 榮恩的團隊是該領域的專家。

代表集合體的名詞稱為「集合名詞」。集合名詞指「整體」時要配單數動詞，指集合體的「組成份子」時要配複數動詞使用，且意思不同。

| 集合名詞 | 整體（搭配單數動詞） | 組成份子（搭配複數動詞） |
|---|---|---|
| family | 家庭 | 家人 |
| class | 班級 | 全班同學 |
| people | 民族 | 人 |
| team | 團隊 | 組員 |

➲ **My family is** small.
　　我家是小家庭。

➲ **David's family are** farmers.
　　大衛的家人都務農。

➲ There **are** only a few **families** in this village.
　　這村莊只有幾戶人家。

# Gold was the main topic of the investment conference.
### 黃金是這場投資大會的主要話題。

用來表示「材料」、「食材」、「飲料」、「化學名稱」、「自然物質」等的名詞，稱為「物質名詞」。物質名詞通常不需要加冠詞，是「不可數名詞」。

| | |
|---|---|
| 材料 | metal 金屬、brick 磚、glass 玻璃、cloth 布、paper 紙 |
| 食材 | food 食物、salt 鹽、chicken 雞肉、cheese 起士、wheat 小麥 |
| 飲料 | wine 酒、beer 啤酒、coffee 咖啡、milk 牛奶 |
| 化學名稱 | ice 冰、gold 金、gas 瓦斯、lead 鉛 |
| 自然物質 | air 空氣、wind 風、rain 雨、fire 火、smoke 煙 |

➲ **Air** is necessary to life.
　　空氣是生存所必備的。

➲ **Chicken** is more delicious than **beef**.
　　雞肉比牛肉美味。

➲ I prefer **beer** to **wine**.
　　我比較喜歡喝啤酒而不是紅酒。

### 不可數名詞：抽象名詞

# The manager gave a presentation about the importance of teamwork.

**經理發表了有關團隊合作重要性的談話。**

用來表示「性質」、「動作」、「狀態」、「疾病」、「學科」等抽象概念的名詞，稱為「抽象名詞」。抽象名詞通常不加冠詞，也沒有複數形。

| 性質 | kindness 仁慈、honesty 誠實、happiness 快樂 |
|------|------|
| 動作 | advice 建議、crime 犯罪、punishment 處罰、teamwork 團隊合作 |
| 狀態 | childhood 兒童期、youth 青年期、friendship 友誼 |
| 疾病 | cancer 癌症、chickenpox 水痘、diabetes 糖尿病 |
| 學科 | English 英文、geography 地理、chemistry 化學 |

⊃ **Honesty** is the best policy.
　誠實為上策。

⊃ Money doesn't bring you **happiness**, but love does.
　金錢不會帶給你快樂，但是愛會帶給你快樂。

⊃ I need your **advice**.
　我需要你的建議。

⊃ He suffers from **lung cancer**.
　他罹患肺癌。

⊃ **English** is much more interesting than **chemistry**.
　英文比化學有趣多了。

### 用量詞把不可數名詞變可數

# Everyone was given a sheet of paper to take notes.

**每個人都拿到一張紙做筆記。**

物質名詞可以用「容器」或「度量單位」來量化。

⊃ He had **a glass of <u>milk</u>** for breakfast.
　他早餐喝了一杯牛奶。

⊃ Let's have **a bottle of <u>beer</u>**.
　我們來喝一瓶啤酒吧！

⊃ I want **two pounds of <u>sugar</u>**.
　我要兩磅的糖。

# Level ① 挑戰多益 450

**請從 (A)、(B)、(C)、(D) 中選出一個最適合的答案。**

1. Do you know how _____ people can fit in that car?
   (A) much
   (B) much of
   (C) many
   (D) many of

2. I'd love to go with you, but I'm afraid I don't have _____ time.
   (A) many
   (B) a lot
   (C) much
   (D) lots

3. We have plenty of chili powder to use, but _____ much soy sauce left.
   (A) there isn't
   (B) there aren't
   (C) isn't
   (D) aren't

4. She wasn't too happy with the clothes she bought. _____ looked a lot better in the store.
   (A) It
   (B) Which
   (C) They
   (D) Those

5. I don't know what happened, but there _____ of water on the kitchen floor.
   (A) is lot
   (B) a lot
   (C) lots
   (D) is a lot

*1.* 你知道這輛車可以載多少人嗎？

解析 people 是集合名詞，恆為複數，詢問時要用 how many。how much 是用在不可數名詞。

- fit [fɪt] (v./adj.) 適合於；適合的
- fit [fɪt] (v./adj.) 適合於；適合的

---

*2.* 我想跟你去，但是我怕沒時間。

解析 time 是不可數名詞，用 much 來修飾，也可以用 a lot of time 或 lots of time。

- afraid [əˋfred] (adj.) 遺憾，恐怕（表婉轉語氣）；害怕的

---

*3.* 我們有許多辣椒粉可使用，但是沒有多少醬油了。

解析 soy sauce（醬油）是不可數名詞，前面用 much 修飾。要表示「有」可用 There is/are＋主詞。因為本句主詞 soy sauce 是不可數名詞，所以要用 there is。如果主詞是複數名詞，則用 there are。

- chili [ˋtʃɪlɪ] (n.) 辣椒
- powder [ˋpaʊdɚ] (n.) 粉，粉末
- soy sauce [ˋsɔɪˋsɔs] (n.) 醬油

---

*4.* 她對自己買到的衣服不太滿意，因為它們在店裡看起來漂亮許多。

解析 clothes 是恆複數的集合名詞，因此後面代名詞用 they。

- a lot 非常，頗

---

*5.* 我不知道發生了什麼事，但是廚房地板上有一大灘水。

解析 「有……」的英文用法可用「There is/are＋主詞」來表示。水是不可數名詞，所以用 There is water.「有水。」要形容水量很多，可以用 a lot of water 或 lots of water。因此本題選 (D)：There is a lot of water...（有很多水……）。

- happen [ˋhæpən] (v.) 發生

---

答案 1.(C) 2.(C) 3.(A) 4.(C) 5.(D)

6. _____ the same group of flowers which you took the photo of last year?
   (A) Aren't these
   (B) Aren't they
   (C) Isn't this
   (D) Isn't

7. This class of students _____ to spend more time practicing for the upcoming exam.
   (A) need
   (B) needs
   (C) is in need
   (D) needing

8. I admit I was nervous about meeting them, but your family _____ all very nice.
   (A) are
   (B) is
   (C) was
   (D) will

9. It gives me great _____ to introduce the president of our company, Harold Schumacher.
   (A) pleasure
   (B) please
   (C) pleasing
   (D) pleased

10. The necessities of life are food, water and _____.
    (A) breath
    (B) breathe
    (C) gas
    (D) air

**6.** 這些花不是跟你去年拍的是同一種花嗎？

解析 雖然 flowers 是「複數」，但是 a group of flowers 指一種類別的花，必須視為「單數」，因此動詞採用單數的 is。Isn't it...是以否定疑問來反問的用法。

**7.** 這個班級的學生必須花更多的時間準備即將到來的考試。

解析 主詞是 This class，而此處的 class 指的是「班上學生」，應視為複數，因此動詞用 need。

• upcoming [`ʌp͵kʌmɪŋ] (adj.) 即將來臨的

**8.** 我承認跟你的家人會面之前我很緊張，但是他們人都很好。

解析 主詞 your family 是指「你的家人」，因此須用複數動詞 are。注意前句用過去式，表示和對方家人見面是已經發生的事情，but 後面的句子用現在式，表示陳述事實。

• nervous [`nɝvəs] (adj.) 緊張的

**9.** 十分高興能介紹敝公司的總裁，哈洛舒曼茄。

解析 動詞 give（給予）後面必須接「名詞」作為受詞。pleasure 是名詞，表「愉悅；高興」，please 是動詞，意為「使高興」，pleasing 是形容詞，表「令人愉快的」，pleased 是形容詞，指「感到高興的」。

• introduce [͵ɪntrə`djus] (v.) 介紹　　　• president [`prɛzədənt] (n.) 總統；總裁

**10.** 食物、水和空氣是生存必備的要素。

解析 對等連接詞 and 所連接的詞性必須一致，和 food、water 對等的是 gas（瓦斯；汽油）及 air（空氣），依常理判斷，應當選空氣。

• necessity [nə`sɛsətɪ] (n.) 必需品

答案 6.(C) 7.(A) 8.(A) 9.(A) 10.(D)

請從 **(A)**、**(B)**、**(C)**、**(D)** 中選出一個最適合的答案。

**1.** She was worried when she realized she left a very important _____ on the bus.
(A) paper
(B) paged
(C) papers
(D) sheet

**2.** If you're not busy tonight, maybe we can meet up for a _____ of beer at Jeff's house.
(A) cup
(B) box
(C) bottle
(D) case

**3.** The only thing that matters to him is his own _____ and the _____ of his wife.
(A) happy ; happiness
(B) happiness ; happiness
(C) happy ; happy
(D) happiness ; happy

**4.** I'd thought they might have an argument, but it ended up being just a _____.
(A) fight
(B) discussion
(C) problem
(D) spat

**5.** Compared to _____, brick is a much stronger material for building houses.
(A) wood
(B) woods
(C) wooden
(D) woody

**1.** 當她發現自己把一份很重要的文件留在公車上時,她很擔心。

解析 名詞前面有冠詞 a,所以只能選單數的名詞 paper(文件)。sheet 是紙張的單位量詞,例如 a sheet of paper(一張紙)。paper 若當「紙張」解釋,前面無法直接加 a,若想量化時須借用「量詞」。

* realize [ˋrɪəˏlaɪz] (v.) 領悟,察覺到　　　　* important [ɪmˋpɔrtn̩t] (adj.) 重要的

---

**2.** 如果你今晚不忙的話,也許我們可以到傑夫的店碰面喝瓶啤酒。

解析 物質名詞可以用「容器」來量化,例如 a bottle of beer(一瓶啤酒)、a cup of tea(一杯茶)等,不同的物品有不同的容器量詞,cup 是「杯」,box 是「箱」,bottle 是「瓶」,要視情況使用。beer 啤酒的計量通常是 bottle(瓶)或 glass(玻璃杯),因此答案選 (C)。

* meet up 遇到,碰面

---

**3.** 對他而言,最重要的是他自己快樂,他妻子也快樂。

解析 英文中用來表達抽象概念的名詞稱為「抽象名詞」。以本題為例,happy 是形容詞,名詞是 happiness。在「所有格」後面必須要用名詞,在定冠詞 the 後面也必須用名詞,因此本題選 (B)。

* matter [ˋmætɚ] (v.) 有關係,要緊　　　　* happiness [ˋhæpɪnɪs] (n.) 快樂

---

**4.** 我還以為他們會吵架,但實際上只是在討論。

解析 argument 是「爭吵;辯論」的意思,之後有對等連接詞 but,表示語氣出現轉折,後面必須使用詞性、情境和 argument 相同,但意思不同的詞。選項 (A) fight 是「打架」,和爭吵差不多,選項 (C) problem是「問題」,和句意不合,選項 (D) spat 是 spit「吐口水」的過去式和過去分詞。只有選項 (B) discussion「討論」符合題意。

* argument [ˋɑrgjəmənt] (n.) 爭吵,辯論　●end up 結束(其後接 Ving 或 with/in＋N)

---

**5.** 和木頭相比,用磚塊來建房子是堅固多了。

解析 此題句意是物質名詞 brick 和空格做比較,因此空格用的也應該是物質名詞。(C)、(D) 選項都是形容詞,不可選。使用「物質名詞」時,不須加冠詞,字尾也不用加 s,答案選 (A)。如果 wood 加 s,是「森林」的意思,此時當普通名詞。brick 當作「物質名詞」是指「磚塊」,一樣不須加上冠詞,字尾也不用加上 s,但是如果當「普通名詞」使用時,a brick 是指「一塊磚」,bricks 是指「多塊磚」。

* compare [kəmˋpɛr] (v.) 比較　　　　　　* material [məˋtɪrɪəl] (n.) 材料;原料

答案 1.(A) 2.(C) 3.(B) 4.(B) 5.(A)

**6.** For the _____ class I'm taking, I need to submit one story per week.
- (A) short stories
- (B) short story
- (C) short storied
- (D) shorting story

**7.** The old man's _____ makes him a friend to everyone.
- (A) kind
- (B) kindly
- (C) kindness
- (D) kindred

**8.** The employees of this company all get _____ vacation every December.
- (A) a week
- (B) week
- (C) a week's
- (D) a weak

**9.** The children counted at least twenty _____ swimming in the aquarium. They were all goldfish.
- (A) fish
- (B) fishes
- (C) of fish
- (D) of fishes

**10.** I'm not sure where I read it, but I think it was in _____ newspaper.
- (A) yesterday's
- (B) yesterday
- (C) a day ago
- (D) a day's

*6.* 我正在上的短篇故事課每星期必須繳交一篇故事。

解析 這題的 class 前方必須放課程名稱,是單數的名詞片語,用來說明後方 class 的性
質、功能。因此答案選「短篇故事」的單數形 short story。

● submit [səb`mɪt] (v.) 繳交;呈遞　　　● per [pɚ] (prep.) 每

*7.* 那位老人家很仁慈,所以大家都把他當好朋友。

解析 所有格後面只能接名詞,例如 his sister、my friend 等。選項 (A) kind 是形容詞「仁
慈的」。選項 (B) kindly 可指形容詞「親切的」,或是副詞「親切地」。選項 (C)
kindness 是名詞「仁慈」。選項 (D) kindred 則是名詞「親屬」、「血緣關係」。
依句意,答案選 (C)。

*8.* 這家公司的員工每年十二月都可以放假一週。

解析 空格後方是單數的普通名詞 vacation,且句意沒有特指哪一個 vacation,可推測空
格可能是 a（＋形容詞）或是所有格,選項 (A)、(B) 不符。選項 (D) weak 是「虛
弱」的意思,和句意不符。(C) 為正確答案。要指某些無生命的東西時,也可以套
用人的所有格形式,例如 today's newspaper（今日的報紙）。本題則是 a week's
vacation（一週的假期）。

● employee [ɛm`plɔɪi] (n.) 受雇者,員工　　● vacation [ve`keʃən] (n.) 假期

*9.* 那些小朋友算過水族缸裡至少有二十條魚,全部都是金魚。

解析 fish 是單複數同形,一隻魚用 a fish,兩隻魚用 two fish。fishes 則是指「很多種類
的魚」,例如:There are a lot of fishes in the ocean.「海裡有很多種類的魚。」
本題因為後面有「全部都是金魚」,表示水族缸裡都是同一種魚類,因此要用 at
least twenty fish「至少二十隻魚。」

● count [kaʊnt] (v.) 計算,數　　　● aquarium [ə`kwɛrɪəm] (n.) 水族缸;水族館
● at least 至少

*10.* 我不確定是在哪裡看過它,我想應該是在昨天的報紙上看到的。

解析 空格後方是名詞 newspaper,前方要用形容詞或是所有格。(B)、(C) 皆是副詞,
不能選。某些無生命的東西也可以套用人的所有格形式,例如 a month's vacation
（一個月的假期）。本題的 (A) yesterday's newspaper（昨天的報紙）和 (D) a
day's newspaper（一天份的報紙）都是這種用法,但依句意 (A) 較正確。

● newspaper [`njus`pepɚ] (n.) 報紙

答案 6.(B) 7.(C) 8.(C) 9.(A) 10.(A)

# Unit 02 代名詞

## 代名詞種類

- **人稱代名詞**：用來代替已提過的人稱，有主格 (I/you/he...)、受格 (me/you/him...)、所有格 (my/your/his...)、所有代名詞 (mine/yours/his...)、反身代名詞 (myself/yourself/himself...) 等。
- **指示代名詞**：用來指明一定的人或事物。包括：this、that、these、those。
- **不定代名詞**：用來代替不特定的人或物。包括：all、few、much、many、most、several、none、some、any、everything、everyone、no one、nobody、nothing……等等。

**用商務英文學多益句型**

## 代名詞　必考重點句

### 人稱代名詞基本概念

所有人稱代名詞請看 p.454

**A: When can you finish the report?**
**B: I'll have it on your desk this afternoon.**

A：你何時可以完成這份報告？
B：我今天下午會把它交到你的桌上。

**it** 可代替前面單數的事物，**we/us** 可代替前面複數的人；**they/them** 可用以代替前面複數的人事物。

They（他們，主格），代替前面的 Many students

➲ **Many students** had food poisoning. **They** were sent to the hospital.
很多學生食物中毒。他們被送去醫院了。

it（它，受格），代替前面的 a cake

➲ I baked **a cake**. Do you want to taste **it**?
我烤了一個蛋糕。你要嚐嚐嗎？

### 以人稱代名詞來泛指某群人

**A lot of overtime is required, but you get used to it.**
很常要加班，不過會適應的。

代名詞 we、you、they 可以泛指一般人，we、you 常被用來指「人們，人類」。they 通常用以指某特定人群，以避免使用被動語態。

➲ **We** live in a rapidly changing world.
我們活在一個快速變遷的世界。

用 they 泛指 people in Nigeria

➲ Do **they** speak English in Nigeria? = Is English spoken in Nigeria?
奈及利亞的人說英文嗎？

### it 指時間、天氣、距離等

## It takes a minute for the printer to warm up.
**印表機暖機要一下子。**

it 可指時間、天氣、距離、季節……等，也可以代替前面已經提過的片語或子句。

指天氣
- ⊃ The weather report said it's going to be clear and sunny today.
  氣象報告說今天天氣晴朗無雲。

指距離
- ⊃ It's over 20 miles from downtown to the airport.
  市中心到機場的距離超過二十英里。

代替前面的子句
- ⊃ **We're supposed to finish the project by 5 p.m.**, but I don't think it's possible.
  我們得在下午五點前完成企畫，可是我覺得辦不到。

### 用 it 當虛主詞

## It is important that you answer customer inquiries promptly.
**迅速回覆顧客的詢問是重要的。**

it 當作虛主詞，代替後面較長的不定詞、動名詞、名詞子句。

代替後方的動名詞片
- ⊃ It is no use **crying over spilt milk**.
  覆水難收，後悔無濟於事。

代替後方的不定詞片
- ⊃ We found it impossible **to finish the work by 5 p.m.**
  我們發覺下午五點前要做完這個工作是不可能的。

### 指示代名詞

## Could you file these documents for me?
**你可以幫我把這些文件歸檔嗎？**

指示代名詞可以用來表達空間和時間上的相對距離感。this、these 一般用來指較近的人或事物，that、those 則用來指較遠的人或事物。

- ⊃ Do you have any free time this Saturday?
  你這週六有空嗎？

- ⊃ In those days, international calls were very expensive.
  在當時，國際電話是非常昂貴的。

所有不定代名詞單複數
判別請看 p.455

that/those of 的用法

## Women's salaries are lower than those of men.

女性的薪資比男性低。

that of... 和 those of... 可以代替前面已提到過的單數或複數名詞，以避免重複。

➲ The cost of electricity is more than **that of** gas.
電費比瓦斯費貴。

➲ Chinese exports exceed **those of** the United States.
中國的出口額超過美國。

**any/some 的用法**

## Are any of the printers working?

有能用的印表機嗎？

不定代名詞 some 和 any 皆可代替複數名詞（表示數）或單數名詞（表示量），或是當形容詞放在名詞前。some 常用在肯定句，泛指「一些，若干」；any 則常用於疑問、否定、條件句，泛指「一些，任一（事物）」。

some 指的是 my friends 中的「一些」，表示數

➲ I went shopping with **some** of my friends yesterday.
我昨天和我一些朋友去逛街。

any 指的是 the wine 中的「一些」，表示量

➲ Did you drink **any** of the wine in this glass? Yes, I had **some**.
你有喝這杯葡萄酒嗎？有，喝了一些。

any 指的是 the applications 中的「一些」，表示數

➲ Did you review **any** of the applications? Yes, I reviewed **some** of them.
你看過這些申請表了嗎？有，我看過一些了。

**something/anything/nobody 的用法**

## Someone left a message for you.

有人留言給你。

不定代名詞 some、any、no、every 與名詞 thing、body、one 結合成 **something**、**anything**、**nobody**、**everyone** 後，必須搭配單數動詞，且修飾這些字的形容詞須放在其後。

➲ **Something is** wrong.
事情不對勁。

else 是形容詞，必須放在 anybody 後方

➲ **Is** there **anybody** else home?
還有其他人在家嗎？

## either/neither 的用法

### The documents may be sent by either e-mail or fax.

這些文件可用電子郵件或傳真寄出。

either 和 neither 比較：

1. either 表示「兩者任何一個」，當單數用。若當連接詞用，常作 either... or...，句中動詞以其接近的名詞判斷單複數。

2. neither 表示「兩者皆非」，本身具否定意味，動詞通常用單數。當連接詞用時，常作 neither...nor...，句中動詞也以其接近的名詞判斷單複數。

➲ We can take the MRT or the bus. **Either is** convenient.
我們可以搭捷運或公車。任何一種都很方便。

➲ We have two children, but **neither lives** in Taiwan.
我有兩個孩子，但是都沒住在台灣。

➲ **Either** he or you **are** mistaken.
不是他判斷錯誤，就是你。

➲ **Neither** her mother **nor** her father **likes** her boyfriend.
她的爸媽都不喜歡她的男友。

*（左側旁註）*
her 是代名詞，後方用單數動詞。

ther 是代名詞，後用單數動詞。

詞 are 搭配最接近的詞 you

詞 likes 搭配最接近名詞 her father

## all/none 的用法

### None of the applicants are qualified for the position.
申請者中沒有人符合這個職缺的資格。

all 和 none 比較：

1. all 和 none 都用於三者以上

2. 代名詞 all 表示「一切，全部」，代名詞 none 表示「誰也沒有」。

3. all 可以當形容詞，none 不可當形容詞。

4. all 須搭配複數動詞，none 搭配的動詞則單複數皆可。

➲ **All** of the fans **were** so excited to see the superstar in Taiwan.
**All** the fans **were** so excited to see the superstar in Taiwan.
所有的粉絲都非常興奮可以在台灣見到這位超級巨星。

➲ **All** of the employees **have** to attend the seminar, but **none** of us **want** to.
全體員工必須參加研討會，但沒有一個人想去。

*（左側旁註）*
作代名詞

作形容詞

和 none 都作代名詞

## The managers are getting raises, and so are we.
**經理們都有加薪，我們也有。**

在肯定句中，so 可以用來代替前一句提過的事物，以避免重複。這時候 so 後方會接 be V／助動詞＋名詞／代名詞。so 在這裡的功能和代名詞很像，但因為代替的是「整件事」，所以是一個副詞。

⊃ He is on the baseball team, and **so am I**.
他是棒球隊的成員，我也是。

⊃ I graduated from this school, and **so did my brother**.
我是這個學校畢業的，我弟弟也是。

☐ **1.** Many of our friends will attend the party. _____ will probably arrive around 7 p.m.
(A) He
(B) They
(C) Us
(D) It

☐ **2.** This calculator is completely useless. Why did you buy _____ ?
(A) them
(B) that
(C) such
(D) it

☐ **3.** Do you know if _____ speak much English in Mexico?
(A) we
(B) they
(C) them
(D) it

☐ **4.** Today the weather is very nice, but tomorrow _____ will probably rain a little.
(A) it
(B) some
(C) that
(D) should

☐ **5.** _____ she or you should explain this case to the client.
(A) Both
(B) We
(C) If
(D) Either

**1.** 很多我們的朋友都會參加宴會，他們大概晚上七點會抵達。

解析 空格處需要主詞，用代名詞代替前面提過的名詞 many of our friends，指多數的他
者，故選 (B) They。

● attend [əˋtɛnd] (v.) 參加

**2.** 這個計算機一點用處也沒有，你怎麼會買它？

解析 動詞 buy 後面接受詞，需用代名詞代替前面提過的單數名詞 this calculator，故
選 (D) it。注意，such 可做形容詞，指「如此的」，如：Why did you buy such a
thing?「你怎麼會買這樣的東西？」。such 也可以做指示代名詞，指「如前所述的
人事物」，如：Such is his decision.「他的決定就是這樣。」

● calculator [ˋkælkjəˏletə] (n.) 計算機

**3.** 你知道墨西哥人常說英文嗎？

解析 泛指「一般人」時，代名詞可用 we、you、they。但是 we、you 這時候會包括說
話者本身，和本句的語境不符。本題是指他國的人民，是排除自己的某特定人群，
代名詞需用 they，故這題選 (B)。

● Mexico [ˋmɛksɪko] (n.) 墨西哥

**4.** 今天的天氣非常好，可是明天可能會下一點雨。

解析 對等連接詞 but 前後的主詞應一致，因此判斷空格要用和 the weather 對等的字
眼。代名詞 it 可用來指天氣，故選 (A)。

● probably [ˋprɑbəblɪ] (adv.) 或許

**5.** 應該去跟客戶解釋這個案子的不是你就是她。

解析 空格後出現 she or you，可以推測這裡句首的連接詞可能是 either 或是 neither。選
項中只有 (D) 為正確答案，either...or... 表示「A 或 B」其中之一。選項 (A) Both 後
方搭配的連接詞是 and，因此不是正確答案。

● client [ˋklaɪənt] (n.) 客戶

答案 1.(B) 2.(D) 3.(B) 4.(A) 5.(D)

6. After looking at it more closely, I realized it was my notebook and not _____ .
(A) you
(B) him
(C) yours
(D) their

7. We're all too busy this week for a get-together, so we decided to plan one later _____ month.
(A) one
(B) those
(C) that
(D) this

8. _____ of the baseball players must attend the training camp.
(A) All
(B) We
(C) Part
(D) Group

9. She is from Taichung, and so _____ .
(A) I am
(B) am I
(C) are us
(D) we are

10. The teacher asked again if _____ had any questions.
(A) all
(B) anyone
(C) student
(D) us

**6.** 在更詳細看過之後，我認出這是我的筆記本，不是你的。

解析 連接詞 and 前後需要兩個文法結構一致的字、片語或句子，這裡 my notebook 必須對應 your notebook，故須填入所有格代名詞 yours，答案為 (C)。

● notebook [`notbʊk] (n.) 筆記本；筆記型電腦

**7.** 我們這星期都太忙了，沒辦法聚會，所以決定這個月晚點再另外安排時間。

解析 前方句子說到這星期 (this week) 會處於忙錄的狀態，知道需要再找之後的時間聚會，只有 this month 可指未來的這個月，答案為 (D)。若選 (A) 形成的 one month 為非特定時間 (B) 選項的 those 後面須搭配複數名詞，選 (C) 形成 that month 指過去的時間，皆不正確。

● get-together [`gɛtə͵gɛðə] (n.) 聚會，聯歡會

**8.** 所有的棒球選手都必須參加訓練營。

解析 ...of the baseball players 必須以代名詞作為主詞，介系詞 of 前面不可用人稱代名詞，選項 (B) We 錯誤，只有選項 (A) All 正確，代表 the baseball players 的全體。另外，(C) Part 和 (D) Group 前面需要加上 a，形成 a part of（一部分的）或 a group of（一群）後面才可接複數可數名詞。

● training camp 訓練營

**9.** 她是台中人，我也是。

解析 以 so 代替前方說過的事情 (from Taichung) 後方的主詞與動詞必須倒裝，變成「and so＋動詞＋主詞」，故選 (B)。注意，(C) 的 are us 為「動詞＋受詞」，不可選。

**10.** 老師又問了一次，看有沒有人還有任何問題。

解析 if 子句缺少主詞，選項 (D) us 為受詞，不可選。選項 (C) student 需要冠詞，以表示特定對象的學生，也不對。選項 (A) all 雖然可以當主詞，但從句意上來判斷，老師應該是問有沒有「任何人」還有問題，故答案選 (B)。

答案 6.(C) 7.(D) 8.(A) 9.(B) 10.(B)

# Level 2　挑戰多益 650

請從 (A)、(B)、(C)、(D) 中選出一個最適合的答案。

1. She decided the dress was too large and went looking for a smaller _____ .
   (A) it
   (B) that
   (C) one
   (D) each

2. _____ rain _____ snow will keep the postmen from their appointed rounds.
   (A) Either ; or
   (B) Neither ; nor
   (C) Not ; or
   (D) All of the above

3. She did like the expensive coat, but she ended up deciding that she just couldn't afford _____ .
   (A) it
   (B) those
   (C) more
   (D) some

4. The fans in Boston are more excited than _____ in New York.
   (A) that
   (B) those
   (C) they
   (D) them

5. _____ of these overdue customers _____ very much from us.
   (A) No one ; buys
   (B) None ; buys
   (C) Not one ; buy
   (D) Neither ; buy

**1.** 她覺得那件洋裝太大了，所以又去找了一件比較小號的。

解析 a smaller... 後面需用單數名詞 dress，指不同的一件裙子。為了避免重複，dress 要以代名詞替換，只有 (C) one 正確。注意 it 和 that 都指和前面同一件的 large dress，不可選。(D) each 則指前面提過兩件以上的東西，與本題不符。

● look for... 尋找⋯

**2.** 無論是下雨還是下雪，郵差還是按照既定班次送信。

解析 選項 (A) 的 either...or 表示兩者之中，有一個是成立的。neither...nor 是兩者全否定，按照題意，答案應選 (B)，表示風雨無阻，郵差照樣會完成工作。動詞 keep... from＋N/Ving 的意思是「阻礙（人）不能（做某事）」。例：The heavy rain kept her from going mountain climbing.「大雨使得她無法爬山。」

● postman [`postmən] (n.) 郵差

**3.** 她的確喜歡那件很貴的外套，可是她最後認為自己買不起。

解析 but 前後指的是想買卻買不起的「同一件」東西，即 the expensive coat，所以需要代名詞 it，答案為 (A)。

● afford [ə`ford] (v.) 花費得起

**4.** 波士頓的粉絲比紐約的更興奮。

解析 than 前後比較的對象必須一致，這裡比較的是 the fans in Boston，和 the fans in New York。為避免重覆，要把後方的 the fans 改為複數代名詞 those（那些），故選 (B)。

● Boston [`bɔstən] (n.) 波士頓

**5.** 那些欠款未還客戶的消費都不是很高。

解析 第一空格要填入 none，作「一個也沒有」解釋，這是表示「全數否定」的不定代名詞，none 後面的動詞可用單數，也可用複數，選項 (B) 正確。選項 (D) Neither 表示「兩者皆非」，但由題意來看，overdue customers 應是兩者以上，且 neither 後方的動詞也要用單數的 buys。(A)、(C) 選項則是 No one 和 Not one 都不適合放在 of 前方，因此不可選。

● overdue [`ovə`du] (adj.) 欠款的，未還的

答案 1.(C) 2.(B) 3.(A) 4.(B) 5.(B)

6. I'm still not certain what it is, but _____ is wrong with this program.
   (A) anything
   (B) something
   (C) thing
   (D) this thing

7. Either one bear or several raccoons _____ going to live in this caged enclosure.
   (A) are
   (B) is
   (C) was
   (D) All of the above

8. The cost of fresh fish is generally more than _____ frozen fish.
   (A) that
   (B) those
   (C) that of
   (D) those of

9. I went to the seminar with _____ of the new books I'd purchased.
   (A) some
   (B) any
   (C) few
   (D) which

10. If you need any more water, just let me know and I'll bring you _____ .
    (A) it
    (B) that
    (C) glass
    (D) some

**6.** 我還不確定是什麼，不過這個計畫有問題。

> 解析 thing 這個字指的是具體的事情或物體，選項 (C) 或 (D) 不可選。而 anything 用在否定句和疑問句，如果用在肯定句泛指「任一（事物）」，語意不符。故答案為 (B)，something 指不甚明確的事物。something is wrong 意指「有事情或某部分出錯」，正好呼應前一句的 what it is 中的單數代名詞 it。

- program [ˋprogræm] (n.) 計畫，節目

**7.** 會被關在這個圍場的，不是一頭熊，就是幾隻浣熊。

> 解析 連接詞 either...or 用來連接兩個主詞 one bear 和 several raccoons，主詞一個是單數，另一個是複數，此時採「就近原則」：由最接近動詞的主詞來決定動詞該用單數還是複數。本題中，raccoons 距離動詞位置最近，所以動詞用複數，答案選 (A)。

- raccoon [ræˋkun] (n.) 浣熊
- enclosure [ɪnˋkloʒ⊅] (n.) 圍場，圈用地

**8.** 新鮮的魚一般來說比冷凍魚的價錢高。

> 解析 than 比較的兩種東西必須一致，由句子前面 the cost of fresh fish 知道比的是「價錢」，故後面也是要比 the cost of frozen fish，為避免重覆 the cost，單數的字須用 that 代替，但別忘了還有介系詞 of，答案為 (C)。

- generally [ˋdʒɛnərəlɪ] (adv.) 一般地；普遍地

**9.** 我帶著我買的一些新書去參加座談會。

> 解析 some 指「一些」，套入句子中符合句意，故答案為 (A)。注意，選項 (C) few 指「很少」，a few 才是「一些」的意思。選項 (B) any 主要用在疑問句與否定句，在本句不適合。選項（D）為關係代名詞，後方要接子句 (S + V)，也不是答案。

- seminar [ˋsɛmɪnə] (n.) 研討會；講習會

**10.** 如果你還需要更多水，請隨時跟我說，我會拿來給你。

> 解析 if 子句中 any more water 指更多「任何」其他的水，選項中只有 (D) some 可以代替非特定的東西，故答案選 (D)。選項 (C) glass 如果加上不定冠詞，形成 a glass，也正確。

- bring 人＋物 / bring 物 to 人：帶…給某人

答案 6.(B) 7.(A) 8.(C) 9.(A) 10.(D)

### 動詞的種類

- 動詞用來表達「行為」和「動作」。
- 動詞依據後方是否需要受詞,可分為「不及物動詞」與「及物動詞」。及物動詞後面需要受詞。不及物動詞不需要受詞,如果有需要受詞的情況,則要再加上介系詞。

用商務英文
學多益句型 | **及物、不及物動詞** | 必考重點句

---

**不及物動詞基本概念**

## The bank opens at 10:00.
**銀行十點開門。**

不及物動詞不需要受詞或補語,用「主詞+動詞」就足以表達句意。

⊃ Birds **fly**.
鳥飛。

⊃ The bus is **coming**.
公車來了。

⊃ The boy **tripped** and **fell**.
這男孩絆到跌倒了。

---

**不及物動詞怎麼接受詞**

## Please go to counter number six.
**請到六號櫃台。**

不及物動詞則需要「介系詞」來接受詞。

⊃ Please look **at the blackboard**, students.
同學們,請看黑板。

⊃ We're about to run **out of gas**. Let's look **for a gas station**.
我們的汽油快用光了,找間加油站吧。

⊃ The campers slept **in a tent**.
去露營的人睡在帳棚裡。

**及物動詞基本概念**

## I'd like to withdraw fifty dollars.
### 我想提款五十美元。

「及物動詞」不需介系詞，後面直接接受詞。

⊃ He **likes** <u>dogs</u> while she **likes** <u>cats</u>.
他喜歡狗，而她喜歡貓。

⊃ I don't **know** <u>what to do</u>.
我不知道該怎麼辦。

**授予動詞**

## The bank gave me a credit card with a $1,000 limit.
### 銀行發給我額度一千美元上限的信用卡。

需要兩個受詞的動詞稱為「授與動詞」。這兩個受詞一個是 indirect object（間接受詞），另一個是 direct object（直接受詞）。直接受詞以「物」為主，間接受詞以「人」為主。授與動詞的兩個受詞可以互換位置，但間接受詞前需要加上介系詞。

注意，若直接受詞為代名詞，則只能用和介系詞搭配的用法。例如：Give it to me. 不能說成 Give me it.。

**常用授與動詞與其搭配的介系詞**

| 搭配 to | give, bring, lend, show, send, write, sell, teach, tell |
|---|---|
| 搭配 for | buy, sing, make |
| 搭配 of | ask |

⊃ He **lent** <u>me</u> fifty dollars.
= He **lent** fifty dollars **to** <u>me</u>.
他借我五萬元。

⊃ The boy **writes** <u>her</u> a letter every day.
= The boy **writes** a letter **to** <u>her</u> every day.
那男孩每天寫一封信給她。

⊃ Could you **sing** <u>me</u> a song?
= Could you **sing** a song **for** <u>me</u>?
你可以唱一首歌給我聽嗎？

# Level ❶ 挑戰多益 *450*

**請從 (A)、(B)、(C)、(D) 中選出一個最適合的答案。**

**1.** You really should _____ the person to whom you're speaking.
(A) look
(B) look at
(C) looking at
(D) looking

**2.** My real name is Jeremy, but you're welcome to call _____ Jerry.
(A) me
(B) I
(C) my
(D) mine

**3.** Can you _____ some money right now?
(A) lent us
(B) lend me
(C) borrow me
(D) borrowed me

**4.** The contract _____ effective on June 1st.
(A) are
(B) starts
(C) becomes
(D) begins

**5.** You must have been working overtime. You look _____ .
(A) happy
(B) tired
(C) excited
(D) ready

**1.** 你說話時眼睛應該要看著對方。

解析 should（應當）後面要用原形動詞，不能用進行式。look 當作「看，注視」時是不及物動詞，與受詞之間必須加上介系詞 at。

● person [`pɜsən] (n.) 人

**2.** 我的本名是傑瑞米，但你也可以叫我傑瑞。

解析 動詞 call 可作「打電話給……；喊叫；稱呼」解釋。根據題意，這裡應該是「稱呼，把……叫做」的意思，為及物動詞。但後面光接受詞意思還不完整，必須補上受詞補語。用法為：call＋受詞＋補語，如：call me Jerry（叫我傑瑞）。類似用法還有 name 一字，如：name him Peter（把他命名為彼得）。

● real [ril] (adj.) 真實的

**3.** 你現在能借點錢給我嗎？

解析 lend 和 borrow 中文都翻譯成「借」，但 lend 指的是「借出」，表示把東西出借給他人，而 borrow 指的是「借入」，向他人借東西。這裡句意指的是「借出」，且前方有助動詞 can，動詞要還原成 lend，所以答案選 (B)。如果把「借」的方向調換一下，用 borrow，則句子可改寫如下：Can I borrow some money from you?「我可以跟你借點錢嗎？」使用 borrow，後面必須搭配介系詞 from，之後再接「借錢的對象」。

**4.** 合約六月一日起生效。

解析 become 意思是「變成，開始變得」，後面需加形容詞。become effective 指法律或合約「開始生效」，注意不要受中文影響而用 starts/begins effective，這兩個動詞後面都不能接形容詞。

● effective [ɪ`fɛktɪv] (adj.) 有效的；（法律等）生效的

**5.** 你一定一直在加班。你看起來很累。

解析 must have been working overtime（一定一直在加班）是說話者根據對方面容所做的推測，可知對方樣子一定看起來很「疲憊」，故選 tired。look 意思是「看起來……」，後面接形容詞。

● overtime [`ovɚ͵taɪm] (adv.) 加班

答案 1.(B) 2.(A) 3.(B) 4.(C) 5.(B)

**6.** Can you _____ a glass of water?
(A) get to
(B) get me
(C) get for me
(D) get you

**7.** Please _____ this letter to the director.
(A) take
(B) deliver
(C) give
(D) All of the above

**8.** Please show _____ to your teacher.
(A) me
(B) my note
(C) they
(D) I

**9.** I _____ a letter a month ago, but I haven't heard back from her yet.
(A) wrote Mom
(B) wrote to Mom
(C) sent to Mom
(D) All of the above

**10.** Her father didn't give _____ to her.
(A) them
(B) it
(C) the money
(D) All of the above

**6.** 你可以拿杯水給我嗎？

解析 動詞 get 作「拿來；取來」解釋，如果後面是間接受詞（人），中間就不需要介系詞，直接用「get＋人＋物」，故答案選 (B)。如果本句 get 後面是直接受詞（物），就要用到介系詞，再接表人的間接受詞，句型為「get＋物＋for＋人」。如：Can you get a glass of water for me? 注意介系詞用 for，表示「給，供……」。

---

**7.** 請把這封信交給主管。

解析 動詞 take/deliver/give 都可以表示把「東西」轉交給「他人」。這裡的直接受詞是 this letter，間接受詞是 the director。注意 the director 前面的介系詞是 to，常和表示「交付東西給他人」的動詞連用。

● director [dɪˋrɛktɚ] (n.) 主管；導演

---

**8.** 請帶我去找你的老師。

解析 在「show＋人＋to/into 地點」的句型中，動詞 show 作「指引、帶領（某人到……）」解釋，空格內應填入受詞，所以答案選 (A)。選項 (C) 的 they 如果改成受格的 them，就可選。注意，to your teacher 指的是「到你的老師所在位置」，因為這裡的 to 引導出來的是「方向、方位」。例：The waiter showed me to the door.「服務人員送我到門口。」

---

**9.** 我一個月前寫了封信給媽媽，但我還沒有收到她的回信。

解析 授與動詞 write 和 send 的句型為「write/send＋人＋物」，間接受詞（人）和直接受詞（物）a letter 中間不需要介系詞，故答案選 (A)。如果 write 後面先接直接受詞（物），才需要在間接受詞（人）前面放介系詞 to，句型為「write/send＋物＋to＋人」，如：I wrote a letter to Mom.

● hear from＋某人：得知、收到（某人消息）

---

**10.** 她的父親不把它們給她。

解析 (A)、(B)、(C) 三個選項都對，都是表示「物」的直接受詞。特別注意：授與動詞的受詞一般有兩種位置，但直接受詞如果是代名詞 it/them，則必須直接跟在動詞後面，所以 give it/them to her 是唯一的位置。如果直接受詞是一般名詞，例如 money，位置可前可後，所以 give the money to her ＝ give her the money。另外，動詞 give 習慣上與介系詞 to 搭配。

答案 6.(B) 7.(D) 8.(A) 9.(A) 10.(D)

# Level ② 挑戰多益 *650*

**請從 (A)、(B)、(C)、(D) 中選出一個最適合的答案。**

1. May I _____ a favor _____ you?
   (A) borrow ; from
   (B) lend ; to
   (C) request ; for
   (D) ask ; of

2. Your proposal _____ very interesting, but I'm afraid our investors won't accept it.
   (A) sounds
   (B) hears
   (C) listens
   (D) talks

3. Could you _____ how _____ this printer?
   (A) tell ; to use
   (B) teach me ; I use
   (C) show me ; to use
   (D) tell me ; use

4. Did you _____ that the CEO is going to sell off the company to an undisclosed buyer?
   (A) listen
   (B) find
   (C) hear
   (D) see

5. Our food products are mouth-watering. Our customers really _____ them delicious.
   (A) eat
   (B) look
   (C) taste
   (D) find

**1.** 我可以請你幫個忙嗎？

解析 「ask a favor of＋某人」表示「請（某人）幫忙……」，本片語介系詞固定用 of。選項 (C) 的動詞 request 意思和 ask 近似，搭配的介系詞也一樣，所以 for 如果改成 of，就是正確答案。另外，ask 如果作「向（某人）提出問題」解釋時，習慣上也是與 of 搭配，句型為「ask＋問題＋of＋人」。例：He asked a question of me.＝He asked me a question.「他問我一個問題。」

● favor [`fevɚ] (n.) 幫助；贊同

**2.** 你的提案聽起來很有趣，但是我們的投資人恐怕不會接受。

解析 sound、hear、listen 三字都有「聽」之意，但只有 sound（聽起來）後面能加形容詞，句型為「sound＋形容詞（聽起來……）」或「sound like＋名詞（聽起來像……）」。而 hear（聽見）後面必須接受詞，listen（注意聽）則必須接介系詞 to，才能接受詞。

● interesting [`ɪntərɪstɪŋ] (adj.) 有趣的        ● I'm afraid＋that 子句：恐怕…

**3.** 可以請你教我如何使用這台印表機嗎？

解析 動詞如果用 tell（告訴），後面需要受詞「人」，受詞之後再接不定詞。選項 (A) 的 tell 後面缺少受詞，所以不能選；選項 (D) 的 tell 後面有受詞，但第二個答案必須改成不定詞 to use。選項 (B) 的第一個答案 teach me 是正確的，但是第二個答案要改成 to use 才可以。故答案選 (C)，show 作「指示；引導」解釋，帶有教導的意思。

● printer [`prɪntɚ] (n.) 印表機

**4.** 你有聽說執行長將把公司賣給一個秘密的買家嗎？

解析 「聽說」某傳聞必須用 hear 一字，後面接 that 子句當受詞，也可用「hear of/about＋名詞」來表達「聽說；得知」某事，如：I didn't hear about his injury.「我沒聽說他受傷的事。」listen 則是「注意聽；聽從」的意思，後面須接介系詞 to，才能接受詞。

● CEO = chief executive officer 執行長，行政總裁
● undisclosed [ˌʌndɪs`klozd] (adj.) 未公開的；秘密的

**5.** 我們的食品令人垂涎三尺。我們的顧客真的覺得它們很好吃。

解析 空格後接了受詞，又馬上接了一個形容詞當受詞補語，可知空格應為 believe/consider/suppose/think 這一類的動詞，(D) 為正確答案。選項 (B) 和 (C) 後方都要直接接形容詞或「like＋名詞」，選項 (A) 則是直接接受詞即可。

● mouth-watering [`mauθˋwɑtərɪŋ] (adj.) 令人垂涎的
● delicious [dɪ`lɪʃəs] (adj.) 美味的

答案 1.(D) 2.(A) 3.(C) 4.(C) 5.(D)

**6.** Did you see the boss _____ to Susan in his office? I think she's going to get a promotion.
(A) talked
(B) will talk
(C) can talk
(D) talking

**7.** I heard that your proposal _____ the attention of the CEO at the last meeting.
(A) caught
(B) will catch
(C) catches
(D) can catch

**8.** To learn Japanese so quickly, Janice devoted _____ to studying it daily for a year.
(A) she
(B) herself
(C) her
(D) her own

**9.** Please _____ this check _____ the director for me.
(A) give ; to
(B) give ; for
(C) giving ; to
(D) giving ; for

**10.** If you _____ the secret code word, I'll _____ the treasure map.
(A) tell ; show
(B) tell me ; show you
(C) tell to me ; show to you
(D) tell me ; show to you

**6.** 你有看見老闆在他辦公室裡跟蘇珊說話嗎？我想她要得到升遷了。

解析 及物動詞 see（看見）的句型為「see＋受詞＋原形動詞／現在分詞」，因此本題選 (D) talking。see 後面接現在分詞時，是強調看到動作「正在進行」，如果接原形動詞，則是強調「事實」或是表示看見「動作的全部過程」，如：I saw him fall off his bike.「我看見他從腳踏車上摔下來。」

● promotion [prə`moʃən] (n.) 升遷；晉級；促銷

**7.** 我聽說你的提案在上次會議中得到總裁的注意。

解析 hear 後面接 that 子句時，子句中的動詞時態要依據事件發生的時間決定。本句中事件發生於 last meeting（上次會議），屬過去時間，因此動詞用過去簡單式 caught。

● catch one's attention 得到某人的注意

**8.** 為了快速學好日文，珍妮絲花一整年每天專心學習。

解析 devote（專心於某事），後面經常接 oneself、time 或是 energy，表示將大部分的時間、精力用在某事上面。devote 後面如果要接人稱受詞，只能用反身代名詞，句型為「devotes oneself to＋某事」。

● devote [dɪ`vot] (v.) 專心於；將⋯奉獻給

**9.** 請幫我把這張支票交給主管。

解析 本句句首的 Please 須與祈使句搭配，表示禮貌的請求或命令。祈使句以原形動詞起首，所以空格要填入原形動詞 give，而介系詞應該要用 to，表示「給予（某人）」，故答案選 (A)。

**10.** 如果你告訴我密碼，我會把藏寶圖拿給你看。

解析 授與動詞 tell 和 show，後面必須有表「人」的間接受詞，後面表「物」的直接受詞才能存在，故答案選 (B)，不選 (A)。如果把「物」移到「人」之前，則必須加上介系詞 to，本句也可改寫成 If you tell the secret code word to me, I'll show the treasure map to you.

答案 6.(D) 7.(A) 8.(B) 9.(A) 10.(B)

# 感官、連綴、使役動詞

商務主題
投資理財

## 感官、連綴、使役動詞概略

- 感官動詞：指的是與五官知覺相關的動詞，包括：look、sound、smell、taste、feel、see、watch、look at、hear、listen to 等等。

- 連綴動詞：用來連接主詞與補語，說明主詞的特質、狀態等，後面可接「形容詞」或「(like)＋名詞」作為補語。常見的連綴動詞有 be 動詞、become、get、turn、grow、fall、keep、seem 等等。

- 使役動詞：包括 have、make、let 和 get，表示「命令、允許、要求、交代」某人做某事，後方會接「下令」或「要求」的對象，再接要求做的動作（原形動詞／to＋原形動詞）。

用商務英文
學多益句型

## 感官、連綴、使役動詞　必考重點句

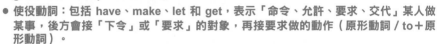

**感官動詞＋原形動詞**

### During the bull market, we watched our portfolio grow.

**股市上漲時，我們看著我們的投資組合增值。**

感官動詞 see（看見）、watch（注視；觀察）、look at（看著）、hear（聽見）、listen to（注意聽）、feel（感覺到）當及物動詞，後面需要受詞。受詞後面接原形動詞，強調「動作發生的事實」。

➲ I **saw** the boy **enter** the building.
　我看到那個小男孩進了那棟建築物。

➲ He **heard** someone **break** a window at Mrs. Wang's house last night.
　他昨晚聽到有人打破王太太家的窗戶。

**感官動詞＋Ving**

### We saw interest rates falling and decided to buy a house.

**我們看到利率下降，決定買房子。**

感官動詞當及物動詞，受詞後面接 Ving，強調「動作正在進行」，表主動。受詞後若接過去分詞 p.p.，強調受詞處於被動地位。

現在分詞 shaking 表示動作正在進行

➲ We **felt** the house **shaking**.
　我們覺得房子在震動。

過去分詞 called 表示受詞 the name 是「被」呼喚的

➲ I **heard** my name **called**.
我聽到有人叫我的名字。

### 連綴動詞基本用法

## Gold is a very popular investment.
### 黃金是很受歡迎的投資。

連綴動詞皆以下列方式表現：「主詞＋連綴動詞＋形容詞／(like)＋名詞」。大部分的連綴動詞後方均接形容詞作補語，但也有少部分的連綴動詞則可接形容詞、也可接名詞，最典型的代表即為 be 動詞。

形容詞 late 當主詞 I 的補語

➲ I **was** **late** for work yesterday.
我昨天上班遲到了。

名詞片語 a marketing manager 當主詞 He 的補語

➲ He **is** **a marketing manager**.
他是個行銷經理。

### 連綴／感官動詞 look/sound/smell/taste/feel＋形容詞

## Investing in futures sounds risky.
### 投資期貨聽起來很有風險。

感官動詞 look（看起來）、sound（聽起來）、smell（聞起來）、taste（嚐起來）、feel（感覺上；摸起來）等用來強調個人的知覺與感受，用法同屬於連綴動詞。這一類感官動詞是不及物動詞，它們後方不需要受詞，須接上形容詞當補語。

➲ The flower **smells** **sweet**.
這朵花聞起來香香的。

➲ Your job **sounds** **very interesting**.
你的工作聽起來很有趣。

### 連綴／感官動詞 look/sound/smell/taste/feel＋like＋名詞

## That mutual fund sounds like a good investment.
### 那支共同基金聽起來像是不錯的投資。

look、sound、smell、taste、feel 後面如果要接名詞，必須先接上介系詞 like，再接名詞。

➲ The man **looks like** **a thief**.
那個人看起來像小偷。

⊃ The milk **smells like** <u>rotten fish</u>.
　　這牛奶聞起來像臭掉的魚。

⊃ The coffee **tastes like** <u>dishwater</u>.
　　這杯咖啡喝起來像洗碗水。

## Mortgages are getting harder to obtain.
**抵押借款愈來愈難了。**

連綴動詞 **become**、**get**、**turn**、**grow**、**fall** 表示「變成，變得」。這類動詞強調變化的過程，或狀態的轉變，所以也常用進行式表現。

⊃ The days **are becoming** shorter.
　　白天變得愈來愈短。

⊃ Everyone **is growing** older every day.
　　每個人都在一天天的逐漸老去。

⊃ The weather **has** suddenly **turned** cold.
　　天氣突然變冷了。

⊃ Tim often **falls** asleep in class.
　　提姆在課堂上常常睡著。

## The cost of living keeps rising.
**生活費用持續攀升。**

連綴動詞 **keep** 表示「維持，持續」，後方常接形容詞。

⊃ Please **keep** <u>quiet</u> because the baby is sleeping.
　　小嬰兒在睡覺，請保持安靜。

⊃ I like to **keep** <u>busy</u>.
　　我喜歡保持忙碌。

**表「似乎」的連綴動詞**

# Bonds seem to be an attractive investment choice.

**債券似乎是個具有吸引力的投資選擇。**

連綴動詞 **seem**、**appear** 可表示「似乎；看起來好像」，後方可接形容詞 / (to be) 名詞。注意，其他的連綴動詞都可以用進行式表現，只有 seem 和 appear 不可以。

➲ He **seems happy**.
　　他看起來很開心。

➲ He **seems (to be) a nice man**.
　　他看起來像個好人。

> 大部分「seem to be＋名詞」的句子是不可省略 to be 的，如：He seems to be the boss. 但在強調主觀感受時會將 to be 省略，通常名詞前會有描述性的形容詞，如上面例句中的 nice。

➲ He **appears younger** than he really is.
　　他看起來比實際年紀還小。

**使役動詞＋原形動詞**

# Sally's parents made her save part of her allowance each month.

**莎莉的父母要她每個月存下一部分的零用錢。**

使役動詞 **make/have/let** 後方接了受詞後，要接原形動詞。其中以 make 的語氣最強烈，有「逼迫，迫使」之意，have 指「命令，交代」，let 則表「允許」。此外，make 後方接了受詞後，也可接形容詞，作「使⋯⋯變得」解釋。

➲ I **made** him **tell** the truth.
　　我逼他說出實話。

➲ Tom's boss **let** him **take** the day off from work.
　　湯姆的老板允許他請假一天不用上班。

➲ Don't **make** the problem even **worse**.
　　別讓問題變得更糟。

使役動詞 **get** 後方接了受詞後，則接 to＋原形動詞。意思為「使得，命令」某人做某事。

➲ I **got** Tom **to repair** my bicycle.
　　我要湯姆修理我的腳踏車。

（左側邊註）
形容詞 happy 當主詞 He 的補語

名詞片語 a nice man 當主詞 He 的補語

形容詞比較級 younger 當主詞 He 的補語

## We had our house appraised by a real estate agent.

**我們請不動產仲介替我們的房子估了價。**

使役動詞的受詞為「物」時，受詞後接過去分詞 p.p.，強調「命令某事被完成」。

⊃ I **had** my passport **renewed**.
　　我把護照更換了。

⊃ Could you **get** it **done** by Friday?
　　你可以讓它在周五前完成嗎？

## Kelly asked her husband to open an investment account.

**凱莉請她丈夫開個投資帳戶。**

還有一類動詞語意與使役動詞相近，但本身並非使役動詞，如 **ask/tell/want/need** 等，這類動詞後方接了受詞後，要接「to＋原形動詞」。

⊃ Our teacher **asked/told** us **to clean** the classroom.
　　我們的老師交代我們要打掃教室。

## My investment advisor helped me (to) set up a portfolio.

**我的投資顧問幫我建立投資組合。**

help「幫忙」的用法也與使役動詞類似，help 後方接受詞後，再接 (to) 原形動詞表示「幫忙某人做某事」，to 通常省略。

⊃ The man **helped** me **(to) carry** the luggage.
　　那位先生幫我提行李。

⊃ I **helped** him **(to) find** the watch.
　　我幫他找到了手錶。

# Level 1　挑戰多益 450

**請從 (A)、(B)、(C)、(D) 中選出一個最適合的答案。**

☐ **1.** Absence _____ the heart grow fonder.
(A) makes
(B) seems
(C) feels
(D) causes

☐ **2.** This cake _____ delicious.
(A) looks
(B) smells
(C) tastes
(D) All of the above

☐ **3.** The Corpse Flower—the stinkiest plant on earth—_____ rotted flesh.
(A) smells
(B) smells like
(C) stinks
(D) tastes

☐ **4.** Honey, you _____ great in that dress!
(A) look
(B) see
(C) look like
(D) seem

☐ **5.** Do you _____ that book on the shelf? Could you hand it to me?
(A) watch
(B) see
(C) have
(D) read

**1.** 離別增情意。

解析 空格後有受詞 the heart，後方再接原形動詞 grow，所以只有選項 (A) 和 (C) 可以考慮，句型分別為「(make) 使役動詞＋受詞＋原形動詞」與「(feel) 感官動詞＋受詞＋原形動詞」。根據題意，應選 (A)。這裡的 grow fonder 指「變得更有情意」，放在使役動詞 make 後面作受詞 the heart 的補語。選項 (B) seems 是連綴動詞，後面必須接形容詞，選項 (D) cause「造成，使得」後面的受詞則必須接不定詞（to V）作為受詞補語。

- absence [`æbsəns] (n.) 缺席，不在

**2.** 這塊蛋糕看起來／聞起來／嚐起來很好吃。

解析 空格後面是形容詞 delicious，前三個選項都是感官動詞，後面可接形容詞，且文意皆合，因此三個選項都為正確答案。

- delicious [dɪ`lɪʃəs] (adj.) 美味的

**3.** 「屍花」是地球上最臭的植物，聞起來像腐臭的肉。

解析 空格後面是名詞，所以答案只能選 (B)，因為只有介系詞 like 後面可以接名詞。句型：連綴動詞（smell/look/taste/sound）＋like＋名詞。選項 (A)、(D) 後面應接形容詞，選項 (C) stink 意為「發出惡臭」，為不及物動詞，後面不會再接受詞。

- stinky [`stɪnkɪ] (adj.) 臭的
- flesh [flɛʃ] (n.)（人或動物的）肉

**4.** 親愛的，妳穿這件衣服看起來真漂亮！

解析 空格後面有形容詞 great「出色的」，所以只有選項 (A) 和 (D) 可以考慮。選 (D) 與句意不合，因為 seem「看起來」表示推測與不肯定，中文作「似乎」解釋。選 (A) 才符合句意，look「看起來」指的是外表看來如何，後面接形容詞。選項 (B) 是「看見」，選項 (C) 是「看起來像」，兩者後方均須接名詞當受詞。

**5.** 你看到架上那本書嗎？可以麻煩你把那本書遞給我嗎？

解析 空格後面的受詞是 that book，所以選項 (B) 與 (D) 都是可能答案，必須參看第二句，才能確定空格應填入哪個動詞。hand 在這裡當動詞，作「把……遞給」解。如果選 (D)，與句意不合，因為 read 表示「閱讀」，故答案選 (B)。see 指的是視覺能力，表示「看見，看到」。

- shelf [ʃɛlf] (n.) 架子

答案 1.(A) 2.(D) 3.(B) 4.(A) 5.(B)

6. Edward's eyes widened when he _____ Olivia's new miniskirt.
   (A) saw
   (B) watched
   (C) looked
   (D) had seen

7. Why don't you _____ the kids have some ice cream?
   (A) have
   (B) make
   (C) let
   (D) allow

8. The teacher asked the class _____ down immediately.
   (A) sit
   (B) sits
   (C) to sit
   (D) to sat

9. The soldiers _____ the driver get out of the vehicle.
   (A) asked
   (B) made
   (C) told
   (D) All of the above

10. Her parents never _____ her go out on dates.
    (A) make
    (B) allow
    (C) have
    (D) let

**6.** 當愛德華看到奧莉薇亞新的迷你裙時，他眼睛睜得好大。

解析 空格後面的受詞是 miniskirt「迷你裙」，動詞應搭配具有「看見、瞥見」字義的選項，故選 (A) saw「看見」。如果要選 (C)，還要加介系詞 at，形成 look at＋N（被看的對象）。(D) 則應改為過去式 saw 才對。

● widen [`waɪdən] (v.) 放寬，擴大

**7.** 你為什麼不讓孩子們吃一點冰淇淋呢？

解析 選項 (A)、(B)、(C) 均為使役動詞，受詞後面接原形動詞。但 have 與 make 皆表示命令，與句意不合。故答案選 (C)，句型為「let＋受詞＋原形動詞」。選項 (D) 的 allow 雖然也可以作「讓……」解釋，但受詞之後必須接不定詞，換言之，have some ice cream 的 have「吃」要改成 to have 才行。

**8.** 老師要求全班立刻坐下。

解析 本題中，動詞 ask 表示「要求；命令」，後面接被要求的對象，也就是 the class，之後必須接不定詞，故選 (C)。

● immediately [ɪ`midɪɪtlɪ] (adv.) 立即地

**9.** 這些軍人逼司機下車。

解析 從受詞 the driver 後面使用原形動詞片語 get out of「從……離開」可知，答案應該選使役動詞，故選 (B)。如果選 (A) 或 (C)，後面必須改成不定詞 to get out of 才行。

● soldier [`soldʒɚ] (n.) 軍人　　　　● vehicle [`viək!] (n.) 交通工具，車輛

**10.** 她的父母從不讓她出去約會。

解析 空格之後的動詞片語 go out 是原形，所以應選使役動詞。根據句意判斷，答案應選 (D) let，表示「准許」某人做某事。(A) make 和 (C) have 則有「逼迫、命令」之意。如果要選 (B)，後面要改成不定詞 to go out 才行。

● on dates 約會

答案 6.(A) 7.(C) 8.(C) 9.(B) 10.(D)

# Level 2 挑戰多益 650

**請從 (A)、(B)、(C)、(D) 中選出一個最適合的答案。**

1. Be quiet and _____ the orchestra! The music _____ beautiful.
   (A) hear ; sounds
   (B) listen ; hears
   (C) listen to ; sounds
   (D) notice ; seems

2. What _____ so good? It's making me _____ terribly hungry.
   (A) tastes ; feel
   (B) smells ; feel
   (C) smelled ; feel like
   (D) smells ; have

3. If you take the pants over to that counter, you can _____ the girl adjust them for you.
   (A) have
   (B) let
   (C) make
   (D) help

4. In case you hadn't _____ , Paul and I have been together for several months.
   (A) looked
   (B) seemed
   (C) noticed
   (D) watched

5. It is important _____ students _____ comfortable making mistakes when speaking English.
   (A) to let ; feel
   (B) to have ; feel
   (C) to make ; feel
   (D) All of the above

**1.** 安靜聽交響樂團演奏！這音樂聽起來很優美。

解析 「聽音樂」的動詞要用「listen to＋聽的對象」，表示非常「用心、專注」地聆聽。hear 作「聽見，聽到」解釋，指的是聽到某聲音但不刻意留意聲音的內容。要表示音樂或聲音「聽起來」的感覺要用 sound。故答案選 (C)。

● orchestra [`ɔrkɪstrə] (n.) 交響樂

**2.** 什麼東西聞起來這麼香？這味道讓我覺得肚子快餓扁了。

解析 從第二句的 hungry「飢餓的」可推斷說話者還沒吃東西，所以第一空格應該選的感官動詞是 smell「聞起來」，而非 taste「嚐起來」；因為還沒吃過東西，所以用現在式。從第二空格後面的 hungry 可知應填入的動詞是 feel。terribly 是副詞，修飾形容詞 hungry。句中的 make 是使役動詞，作「令人……，使得……」，後面必須接原形動詞 feel。

**3.** 如果你把這件褲子拿到櫃檯那邊，可以請那裡的女生幫你修改。

解析 由原形動詞 adjust 可推斷前面的空格必須使用使役動詞。前三個選項都是使役動詞，但只有選項 (A) 的 have 有「請託」的意思。選項 (B) 的 let 表示「允許、准許」，選項 (C) 有「逼迫」的意思，故選 (A)。

● counter [`kauntɚ] (n.) 櫃臺　　　　● adjust [ə`dʒʌst] (v.) 調整

**4.** 你可能還沒注意到吧，保羅和我已經交往幾個月了。

解析 in case 是連接詞，表示「如果，假設」。在這個由 in case 引導的從屬子句中，使用的時態是過去完成式，表虛擬語氣。四個選項的動詞都與眼睛感官有關，但只有選項 (C) noticed 具有「注意，察覺」之意，故答案選 (C)。此外，選項 (D) watched 後面通常需要受詞。選項 (A) looked 和 (B) seemed 後面要接形容詞當補語，因此都不是答案。

**5.** 讓學生講英語犯錯時不會覺得不自在，這是很重要的。

解析 由虛主詞（本身沒有意義，只有主詞的功能）引導的句型「It is＋形容詞＋to V」中，意義上真正的主詞是不定詞這個部分。let/have/make 三者皆用來表示「使人……，令人……」，後面必須接原形動詞，選項 (A)、(B) 或 (C) 皆可，故選 (D)。

● comfortable [`kʌmftəbl] (adj.) 自在的，舒適的

答案 1.(C) 2.(B) 3.(A) 4.(C) 5.(D)

☐ **6.** Why don't you _____ TV or _____ a book?

(A) see ; read

(B) look ; watch

(C) watch ; read

(D) watch ; see

☐ **7.** He _____ his little sister _____ him her lunch money.

(A) asked ; give

(B) made ; give

(C) made ; to give

(D) made ; gave

☐ **8.** You've been drinking. Why don't you _____ me drive tonight?

(A) make

(B) have

(C) let

(D) All of the above

☐ **9.** _____ ! You can _____ the ocean from here.

(A) Watch out ; look at

(B) Listen ; hear

(C) Look ; see

(D) All of the above

☐ **10.** Teresa enjoyed going up to the roof at night to _____ the starry sky.

(A) watch

(B) look

(C) stare at

(D) All of the above

**6.** 你為什麼不看看電視或看看書呢？

解析 感官動詞中與眼睛有關的字，中文統稱為「看」，但其英文字意是有差別的。see 指的是「看得到」，read 指的是「閱讀書面文字」，watch 指的是「觀看動態表演」，例如球賽、節目等等。look 當「看」解釋時，後面必須接介系詞 at，再接「被看的物體」。look at 指的是「盯著某物或某人看」。第一空格後面的受詞是 TV，應搭配 watch，第二個受詞是 a book，應搭配 read，所以答案選 (C)。

**7.** 他逼他妹妹把她午餐的錢給他。

解析 第一空格用 asked 或 made 皆可，後面再接受詞（被逼迫或要求的對象）。如果用 asked，受詞後面要用不定詞 to give。如果用 made，受詞後面要用原形動詞，所以答案選 (B)。
- lunch money 午餐費用

**8.** 你喝了酒，今天晚上讓我開車，如何？

解析 「Why don't you（Why not）＋原形動詞？」這個句型表示「提議、勸誘」，作「為什麼不……？」解。空格應填入原形動詞，依照句意，應選 (C)。因為 make 和 have 都有「命令」的意味在裡面，只有 let 表「允許；准許」之意。let 的受詞 me 後面要接原形動詞 drive。
- drink [drɪŋk] (v.) 飲酒

**9.** 你聽！從這裡可以聽到海的聲音。／你看！從這裡可以看到海洋。

解析 注意第一空格後面有驚嘆號。以動詞或動詞片語起首的驚嘆用語，目的在吸引對方的注意力。例如：Look!「你看！」／ Listen!「你聽！」／ Watch out!「當心！」／ Be careful!「小心！」等。按照句意，選項 (A)、(B) 或 (C) 皆可，故選 (D)。
- ocean [oˋʃən] (n.) 海洋

**10.** 泰瑞莎喜歡晚上爬上屋頂去欣賞滿天星空。

解析 動詞 enjoy 後面必須接 Ving (going up)。空格前面有 to，表示有待填入動詞以形成不定詞，答案可選 (A)，watch 表示「觀賞、觀看」；(B) 若改成 look at 表示「注視某物或人」也可選。(C) stare at 則語意不符，故答案選 (A)。
- starry [ˋstɛrɪ] (adj.) 佈滿星星的

答案 6.(C) 7.(B) 8.(C) 9.(D) 10.(A)

# Unit 05 現在式

## 現在式的種類

- 現在式可以分為「現在簡單式」、「現在進行式」、「現在完成式」及「現在完成進行式」四種。
- 現在簡單式：表達真理、經常發生的動作或狀態、以及現在的事實或狀態。
- 現在進行式：表達說話此時正在發生的事情。
- 現在完成式：表達從過去一直持續到現在的狀況、曾有的經驗，或剛完成的動作。
- 現在完成進行式：表達已發生一段時間且持續進行中的動作。

**用商務英文學多益句型**

## 現在式 必考重點句

### 現在式 be 動詞變化

## Our team is responsible for the advertising campaign.

**我們團隊負責廣告宣傳活動。**

「現在簡單式」中若使用 be 動詞，必須跟隨主詞變化，即 I am、you are、he is 等。非人稱的主詞，若是單數時，be 動詞使用 **is**，複數則使用 **are**。

➲ **This job is** important to me.
這份工作對我很重要。

➲ **The new employees** are due to start work next week.
新員工預計下星期開始上班。

### 現在式一般動詞變化

第三人稱單數動詞字尾變化規則請看 **p.456**

## The company uses TV commercials to promote its products.

**這家公司用電視廣告促銷它的產品。**

在「現在簡單式」中，如果主詞是第三人稱單數，動詞字尾需要加上 s 或 es，或因為拼字關係，去掉 y，加上 ies。

動詞後面加上 s

➲ He **rides** his bicycle every weekend.
他每個週末騎他的腳踏車。

以 ch、sh、s、z、x、o 結尾的字，加上 es。

➲ The fly **buzzes** around my head.
蒼蠅一直在我頭頂上發出嗡嗡聲。

以「子音＋y」結尾的字，去掉 y，加上 ies。

➲ My mother always **worries** about me.
我媽媽一直很擔心我。

何時用現在簡單式？

## The customer is always right.
**顧客永遠是對的。**

「現在簡單式」用法有三種：表達真理、經常發生的動作或狀態、以及現在的
事實或狀態。

示真理

➲ The earth **is** round.
　地球是圓的。

常發生的動作或狀態

➲ He usually **gets up** late.
　他經常晚起。

在的事實或狀態

➲ My knee **hurts**.
　我膝蓋很痛。

現在簡單式助動詞

## Do you think lowering prices will increase market share?
**你認為降低價格可以增加市佔率嗎？**

「現在簡單式」在疑問句或否定句中使用助動詞 **do** 和 **does**（僅第三人稱單數
使用），助動詞之後的動詞一律用原形。

➲ **Does** she <u>like</u> to swim? No, she **doesn't**.
　她喜歡游泳嗎？ 不，她不喜歡。

➲ I **don't** <u>want</u> to live without you.
　我不希望生命中沒有你。

現在進行式

字尾變化規則請看
6

## Our company is conducting a market survey.
**我們公司正在進行一項市場調查。**

表達現在正在發生的事情，可以用「現在進行式」。現在進行式的動詞要改為
**be＋Ving**。

詞是複數，動詞用
＋Ving。

➲ The children **are playing** in the park.
　孩子們正在公園裡玩。

詞是第三人稱單數，
用 is＋Ving。

➲ Mom **is cooking** in the kitchen.
　媽媽正在廚房煮飯。

句直接將 be 動詞
主詞前

➲ Is the baby **sleeping** now?
　寶寶正在睡覺嗎？

過去分詞字尾變化規則
請看 p.457

## 用現在完成式表「持續狀況」

# Sales have increased for three quarters in a row.
### 銷售量一連三季成長。

「現在完成式」用來表達從過去一直持續到現在的狀況，動詞部份要改為 have/has + p.p.。p.p. 即過去分詞，也就是動詞的第三態變化。

for＋一段時間，表示「已經（多久）了」。

since＋過去時間 / 過去式，表示「從……開始」。

○ I **have studied** English for six years.
我學英文已經六年了。

○ My brother **has played** basketball since he was little.
我哥哥從小就開始打籃球了。

## 用現在完成式表「經驗」

# Have you worked in marketing before?
### 你以前有行銷的經驗嗎？

「現在完成式」也可表達曾有過的「經驗」。

○ **Have** you **seen** *An Inconvenient Truth*? No, I **haven't**.
你看過《不願面對的真相》嗎？不，我沒看過。

○ **Has** Lisa ever **been** to Japan? Yes, she **has been** there twice.
麗莎去過日本嗎？是的，她去過兩次。

## 用現在完成式表「已完成的動作」

# The retailer has just opened a new store.
### 這家零售商剛開了新店面。

「現在完成式」的第三種用法則是表示「剛完成的動作」，經常和副詞 just（剛）、already（已經）、yet（還；尚未）連用。

○ The shipment **has** just **arrived**.
貨品剛運到。

○ John **has** already **finished** his homework.
約翰已經完成作業。

## The company has been looking for new ways to attract prospective clients.

**這家公司一直都在尋求吸引顧客的新方式。**

「現在完成進行式」所表達的意涵是「最近發生且持續進行中」的動作，用來強調「動作持續進行的狀態」，動詞型態為 have/has been＋Ving。「現在完成式」相較之下則是表示事實和經驗，動詞型態為 have/has＋p.p.。

現在完成進行式，強調動作進行中。

➲ She **has been writing** the report for two hours.
　她已經寫那份報告寫了兩小時。

現在完成式，說明事實。

➲ She **has written** the report.
　她把報告寫好了。

現在完成式，說明經驗。

➲ A: **I have** only **flown** in an airplane once. I'm a little scared.
　A: 我只搭過一次飛機，我有點害怕。

現在完成進行式，強調動作持續進行，表示搭飛機很安全。

　B: Don't worry. **I have been flying** for years. It's nothing to be scared of.
　B：別擔心，我搭飛機很多年了，沒什麼好怕的。

# Level ❶ 挑戰多益 *450*

**請從 (A)、(B)、(C)、(D) 中選出一個最適合的答案。**

**1.** Sam _____ want to go to the meeting this afternoon.
(A) is
(B) doesn't
(C) wasn't
(D) was

**2.** Lisa usually _____ at the office at 8:00 am.
(A) arrives
(B) arrival
(C) arriving
(D) arrive

**3.** Franklin _____ played the piano since he was ten years old.
(A) is
(B) will
(C) does
(D) has

**4.** Peter _____ for our company for two years.
(A) works
(B) has worked
(C) has working
(D) working

**5.** Helen, _____ you finished typing that report up yet?
(A) did
(B) have
(C) will
(D) can

**1.** 山姆今天下午不想去開會。

解析 want（想要）為一般動詞，本題為現在簡單式，當主詞為第三人稱單數時，want 字尾原本應加 s，但此處卻為原形動詞，可知本題應為否定句，動詞前應填入否定助動詞 doesn't。

● want [wɑnt] (v.) 想要　　　　　　● meeting [`mɪtɪŋ] (n.) 會議

---

**2.** 麗莎通常上午八點抵達辦公室。

解析 usually（經常，通常）為頻率副詞，與現在簡單式連用，表某事發生的次數或頻率。主詞 Lisa 為第三人稱單數，因此動詞字尾須加 s。其他頻率副詞還有 always（總是）、often（時常）、sometimes（有時）、never（從未）等字。

● arrive [ə`raɪv] (v.) 抵達，到達

---

**3.** 富蘭克林從十歲開始彈鋼琴。

解析 since（自從）這個連接詞經常和現在完成式「have/has＋過去分詞」連用，表示某動作從過去某時間即已開始持續到現在。動詞 played 在此為動詞的第三態變化（過去分詞），前面應加上完成式的助動詞 has。注意，since 子句的動詞用過去式，代表過去時間起點。

● play＋the＋樂器：彈奏…樂器

---

**4.** 彼得已經為我們公司工作兩年了。

解析 「for＋一段時間」須與現在完成式「have/has＋過去分詞」連用，表示某動作或狀態從過去持續到現在已經一段時間。也可代換成「since＋過去時間起點」，如：for two years（已經兩年了）＝ since two years ago（自從兩年前起）。

● company [`kʌmpənɪ] (n.) 公司

---

**5.** 海倫，你那份報告已經打完了沒有？

解析 yet 用於疑問句時意思是「已經……了嗎？」，與現在完成式「have/has＋過去分詞」連用，用來詢問某事是否已經完成。答句則經常搭配 already（已經）、just（剛剛）或 not...yet（尚未）等副詞。

● type [taɪp] (v.) 打字　　　　　　● report [rɪ`port] (n.) 報告

---

答案 1.(B) 2.(A) 3.(D) 4.(B) 5.(B)

**6.** Please hold on a minute. Ms. Patrick _____ talking on another line now.
(A) was
(B) is
(C) can
(D) am

**7.** A: Do you like our products, Mr. Li?
B: Yes, I _____.
(A) do
(B) like
(C) will
(D) did

**8.** The secretary _____ contacting our suppliers right now.
(A) has
(B) is
(C) will
(D) are

**9.** Will you hurry up? You _____ talking on the phone for 20 minutes!
(A) has been
(B) will
(C) are
(D) have been

**10.** Mr. Collins, _____ to Japan before?
(A) will you go
(B) are you going
(C) have you been
(D) can you go

**6.** 請等一下。派翠克小姐正在講另一線電話。

解析 本句為電話用語，句尾的 now 指出時間為「現在」，且題目中已有現在分詞 talking 一字，因此動詞須使用現在進行式「be＋現在分詞」。Ms. Patrick 為女性 (she)，故 be 動詞選 is。
- hold on 等一下
- line [laɪn] (n.) 線；電話線

**7.** A: 李先生，你喜歡我們的產品嗎？

B: 我喜歡。

解析 本題為現在簡單式的疑問句，以助動詞 Do 引導。簡答時，應以相同的助動詞回答。肯定簡答說 Yes, I do.，否定簡答則說 No, I don't.；若要詳答則應說 Yes, I like them.，其中的 like 為及物動詞，後面一定要接受詞，不可以說 Yes, I like.。
- product [`prɑdəkt] (n.) 產品

**8.** 秘書現在正在聯繫我們的供應商。

解析 right now 意思是「就是現在」，指出本句的時間，因此動詞須使用現在進行式「be＋現在分詞」，題目中已有現在分詞 contacting 一字，故選 be 動詞 is。
- contact [kən`tækt] (n.) 聯繫；接觸
- supplier [sə`plaɪɚ] (n.) 供應商

**9.** 你可以快一點嗎？你已經講電話講了二十分鐘啦！

解析 「for＋一段時間」與現在完成式連用，表示某動作或狀態從過去持續到現在已經一段時間。如果要強調動作的持續性，或是表達說話者對此一持續狀態的情緒，則可用現在完成進行式「have/has been＋現在分詞」，本句主詞是 you，助動詞應搭配 have。 have been talking for 20 minutes 即表示說話者等得不耐煩了。
- hurry up 趕快

**10.** 柯林先生，你以前去過日本嗎？

解析 現在完成式可用來詢問從過去到現在為止的經驗，經常搭配 ever（曾經）、before（以前）等副詞。要問人「是否去過某地」須說 have you been to...，不可說 have you gone to...。
- have/has been to... 曾經去過…
- before [bɪ`for] (adv.) 以前

答案 6.(B) 7.(A) 8.(B) 9.(D) 10.(C)

# Level ❷　挑戰多益 *650*

**請從 (A)、(B)、(C)、(D) 中選出一個最適合的答案。**

**1.** We _____ been trying to call the bank for over an hour, but the line is still busy!
(A) has
(B) have
(C) had
(D) are

**2.** Our tour of the facilities has been delayed because it _____ .
(A) rain
(B) rains
(C) is raining
(D) might not rain

**3.** I've _____ my photography portfolio online, but I'm not finished yet.
(A) put
(B) putted
(C) been putting
(D) been put

**4.** Jason _____ the password, so he can't log into his email account.
(A) has forgotten
(B) hasn't remember
(C) remembered
(D) have forgot

**5.** We've _____ a dog _____ about five years.
(A) own ; for
(B) having ; since
(C) gotten ; in
(D) had ; for

*1.* 我們試著打電話給銀行超過一小時了，但是仍然忙線中。

**解析** 看到 been（be 動詞過去分詞），就知道要用完成式。後句的 the line is still busy 表示電話依舊忙線中，可知打電話的動作仍然持續進行中。因此應當使用現在完成進行式「have/has been＋現在分詞」，來強調動作持續進行的狀態。主詞是 We，因此完成式的助動詞用 have。

● line [laɪn] (n.) 電話線路

---

*2.* 我們參觀設施的行程因為下雨而被延遲。

**解析** 現在完成式 has been delayed 表參觀行程被延後且狀態持續到現在，可推知「目前還在下雨」，因此表原因的 because 子句的動詞應用現在進行式 is raining。

● facility [fə`sɪlɪtɪ] (n.) 設施，設備　　● delay [dɪ`le] (v.) 延誤，耽擱

---

*3.* 我正在把我的攝影作品放到網路上，但還沒放完。

**解析** 句首的 I've 是 I have 的縮寫，後面可接現在完成式，也可接現在完成進行式。由後句 but I'm not finished yet 可知攝影作品集正「持續上傳」到網路上，還沒結束。此時，用強調「還繼續在進行」的現在完成進行式，比用表示「已經完成」的現在完成式來得貼切，故選 (C)。

● photography [fə`tɑgrəfɪ] (n.) 攝影　　● portfolio [pɔrt`folɪo] (n.) 作品；公事包

---

*4.* 傑森已經忘了密碼，所以無法登入自己的電子郵件信箱。

**解析** Jason 無法登入自己的電子郵件信箱，可知他「忘了」密碼，空格應該填入現在完成式的動詞 has forgotten，答案選 (A)。選項 (B) 如果把 remember 改成過去分詞 remembered，也是正確答案。

● password [pæs`wɜd] (n.) 密碼　　● account [ə`kaunt] (n.) 帳戶
● log into 登入

---

*5.* 我們養狗大約有五年了。

**解析** 本題測驗現在完成式與介系詞 for/since 的搭配。第一個空格一定要填入過去分詞，才能與前面的 We've (We have) 形成現在完成式，因此只有選項 (C) 和 (D) 可考慮。第二個空格後面有 five years，這是表一段時間的複數名詞，介系詞要用 for，因此正確答案是 (D)。選項 (A) 的 own 應改成 owned；選項 (B) 的 having 應改成 had，但 since 後面須搭配 five years ago，表示從五年前開始養狗；選項 (C) 的 in 則應改成 for。

**答案** 1.(B) 2.(C) 3.(C) 4.(A) 5.(D)

6. Sarah _____ her dinner, so she can't have any dessert.
   (A) hasn't finished
   (B) wasn't eaten
   (C) hadn't had
   (D) hasn't ate

7. Randy _____ found the map, so we _____ start the adventure.
   (A) has ; can
   (B) hadn't ; couldn't
   (C) have ; can
   (D) had ; can

8. I have _____ that band before, but I can't remember their style.
   (A) heard
   (B) been hearing
   (C) hear of
   (D) hearing

9. Doris _____ a letter to her sister, but hasn't _____ it.
   (A) write ; mailed
   (B) has written ; sent
   (C) wrote ; send
   (D) had written ; sent

10. We _____ a relationship with that company since 2004.
    (A) were having
    (B) will have
    (C) are having
    (D) have had

**6.** 莎拉還沒吃完晚餐，所以她不可以吃甜點。

解析 由後句的 she can't have any dessert 可推知莎拉應該是「還沒有吃完晚餐」，所以不可以吃甜點。動詞應用現在完成式 hasn't finished，故選 (A)。選項 (D) 若改成 hasn't eaten 也是正確答案。選項 (B) 的被動式不合邏輯，因為主詞是人 Sarah。選項 (C) 的過去完成式（had＋p.p.）應用來與另一過去動作或事件做比較。先發生的動作或事件用過去完成式，後發生的動作或事件用過去簡單式，以區隔兩個過去事件的先後。

**7.** 蘭迪已經找到地圖了，所以我們可以展開冒險之旅了。

解析 本題測驗現在完成式與助動詞用法。第一空格後面是 find 的過去分詞，主詞 Randy 是第三人稱單數，所以空格要填入 has 或 had。但從句意判斷，並沒有線索指示整句話的時間是在「過去」，所以不用 had。句中使用連接詞 so 連結前後兩個句子，表「因果關係」。從文法和句意來看，只有選項 (A) 正確。

● adventure [æd`vɛntʃə] (n.) 冒險

**8.** 我曾聽說過那支樂團，但已經不記得他們的風格了。

解析 空格內必須填入過去分詞 p.p.，與前面的 have 形成現在完成式。hear 作「聽聞，得知」解釋，也可以用 hear of 表示同樣意思，所以選項 (A) heard 或 (C) heard of 皆是正確答案。

**9.** 朵莉絲已經寫了一封信要給她妹妹，但還沒寄。

解析 第二個空格前面有 hasn't，可知空格應當填入過去分詞 mailed 或 sent，表現在完成式。第一個空格則可填入現在完成式 has written，也可以填入 wrote，表示「信寫完了，寫信的動作結束了」。現在完成式強調「過去與現在的關係」：表示信雖寫好了，但「到現在為止」還沒寄出（hasn't sent）。故答案選 (B)。

**10.** 我們從二○○四年起就跟那家公司有聯繫。

解析 since 意思是「自從……起」，接過去時間起點，表示動作或狀態從過去某時間起持續到現在，主要子句須與現在完成式「have/has＋過去分詞」連用。本句主詞為 We，故答案選 have had。其中的 have 為現在完成式助動詞，而 had 則為動詞 "have" a relationship 的過去分詞。

● relationship [rɪ`leʃənˌʃɪp] (n.) 關係，關聯

答案 6.(A) 7.(A) 8.(A) 9.(B) 10.(D)

# Unit 06 過去式

## 過去式的種類

- 過去式常用的形式可分為「過去簡單式」、「過去進行式」、「過去完成式」。
- 過去簡單式：表達過去的經驗、狀態，和習慣的動作。
- 過去進行式：表達過去某一時間點正在進行的動作。
- 過去完成式：表達過去某時間前持續發生的狀態，或已經完成的事情。

**用商務英文學多益句型**　**過去式**　必考重點句

### 過去式 be 動詞變化

## The business plan was four pages long.
**那份營運計劃書只有四頁。**

「過去簡單式」表示過去的經驗、狀態，和習慣的動作，常會搭配表示過去的時間副詞。過去式若使用 be 動詞，須跟隨主詞做變化，即 I was、you were、he was 等。非人稱的主詞，若是單數時，be 動詞使用 **was**，複數則使用 **were**。

- ⊃ I **was** a student **last year**, but now I'm a teacher.
  我去年還是學生，但現在是老師了。

- ⊃ The products **were** available in retail stores.
  在零售門市可以買到那些產品。

### 過去式一般動詞變化

## The retail chain decided to put its plans for expansion on hold.
**這家零售連鎖店決定暫緩擴點計畫。**

在「過去簡單式」中，若動詞為一般動詞，則必須用動詞的過去式。過去式分規則與不規則兩種變化，規則變為在動詞字尾加上 d 或 ed，或因為拼字關係，去掉 y，加上 ied。

- ⊃ I **spoke** to the CEO an hour ago.
  我一小時前跟總裁說過話。

- ⊃ Last week, I **stayed** up late studying every night.
  上個禮拜我每晚都在熬夜讀書。

- ⊃ I **tried on** the skirt in the store.
  我在店裡試穿過那件裙子，並決定買。

動詞三態變化請看 p.457

常見的不規則動詞變化請看 p.458

speak 的過去式為不規則變化 spoke

stay 的過去式為規則變化，字尾加 ed

try 的字尾為「子音＋y」，過去式要去 y 加 **ied**

過去式助動詞

# Did the sales forecast prove accurate?
**銷售預測的結果準確嗎？**

「過去簡單式」用 **did** 開頭可形成疑問句。否定句將 **did not/didn't** 放在動詞前。助動詞後一律使用原形動詞。

疑問句中第一個 Did 為助動詞，第二個 do 為動詞「做，表現」；答句中的 did 為動詞過去式。

➲ A: **Did** John **do** well on his exam?
　 B: Yes, he **did** well.
　　 A：約翰考得好嗎？
　　 B：是的，他考得不錯。

➲ A: **Did** they **have** anything to drink after dinner?
　 B: No, they **didn't**. They drank nothing.
　　 A：晚餐後他們有喝什麼嗎？
　　 B：不，他們沒喝。他們什麼都沒喝。

易混淆片語：used to/be used to

# The company used to make its products locally, but now it manufactures them overseas.
**過去這間公司於國內製造產品，但現在則是海外製造。**

「**used to**＋原形動詞」表示過去的習慣，現在沒有這樣的習慣了；「**be/get used to**＋Ving/N」則表示已養成的習慣。

➲ I **used to** **work out** when I had free time.
　 我以前有空時都會去健身。

➲ **Are** you **used to** **the hot weather** here yet?
　 你習慣這裡炎熱的天氣嗎？

過去進行式

# The company was considering expanding its operations.
**公司當時正考慮要擴大營運。**

「過去式」著重在事實，「過去進行式」則著重在過去當下正在進行的動作。過去進行式的動詞型態為 **was/were＋Ving**。

去式 called 著重於實、短暫的動作；過進行式 was having nner 則是表示當下正進行的動作。

➲ When you called, I **was having dinner**.
　 你打電話來時我正在吃晚餐。

○ I broke my arm while I **was playing** tennis.
我打網球時，手臂骨折了。

○ I **was playing** in the park yesterday afternoon.
我昨天下午在公園玩。

過去完成式

# Sales had been slow before the company implemented a new business plan.
**在公司實行新的營運計畫之前，銷售狀況一直不佳。**

1. 「過去完成式」用來描述過去某個時間點之前持續發生的狀態，或是已經完成的事情，其動詞型態為 had＋p.p.。

2. 「過去完成式」經常與另一個「過去簡單式」的句子連用，先發生的動作用過去完成式，後發生的動作用過去簡單式，以區隔兩個過去事件的先後。

過去完成式 I had lost my wallet 發生的時間早於過去式 I didn't have any money。

○ I didn't have any money because I **had lost** my wallet.
我沒有錢，因為我丟了我的皮包。

○ They **had packed** their suitcases several days ahead of their vacation.
他們在假期來臨前幾天就打包好了行李。

○ They **had forgotten** to buy plane tickets, so they had to stay in Taiwan.
他們忘記買機票，所以只得留在台灣。

○ He enjoyed seeing his old friends last night, because he **hadn't seen** them in a long time.
他昨晚跟老朋友見面很愉快，因為他們已經很久沒見面了。

○ By the time he arrived at the airport, the plane **had** already **taken off**.
他到達機場的時候，飛機已經起飛了。

# Level ① 挑戰多益 *450*

請從 (A)、(B)、(C)、(D) 中選出一個最適合的答案。

**1.** Helen was writing her thesis _____ morning when you saw her at the library.
(A) tomorrow
(B) yesterday
(C) last
(D) the

**2.** I _____ send the payment to Mr. Wang yesterday, so he is very upset.
(A) did
(B) well
(C) didn't
(D) can't

**3.** A: Did your presentation at the meeting go well?
B: Yes, _____.
(A) it didn't
(B) it was
(C) it went
(D) it did

**4.** Jerry _____ the clients to tour the factory yesterday.
(A) took
(B) will take
(C) takes
(D) can take

**5.** A: Did you talk with our agent Mr. Sanderson yesterday?
B: _____
(A) Yes, I talked.
(B) Yes, I will.
(C) Yes, I did.
(D) No, I won't.

*1.* 你昨天上午在圖書館看到海倫時，她正在寫論文。

解析 動詞時態是過去進行式 was writing，因此只能選表「過去」的時間副詞，昨天上午用 yesterday morning，不能用 last morning。如果要講今天早上，可以用 this morning 或 in the morning。

- thesis [`θisɪs] (n.) 論文

*2.* 我昨天沒有寄費用給王先生，所以他很生氣。

解析 前半句的時間為 yesterday，因此動詞時態應用過去簡單式。根據後半句 so he is very upset 的句意可推知主詞「沒有」寄費用給王先生，所以本題應用否定句，故應加入否定助動詞 didn't。

- payment [`pemənt] (n.) 費用，款項
- upset [ʌp`sɛt] (adj.) 不高興；失望

*3.* A：你在會議中的簡報進行得順利嗎？

B：是的，很順利。

解析 本題問話的人用的是過去簡單式疑問句，以助動詞 Did 引導。答句的 Yes 代表此處為肯定簡答，所以應說 Yes, it did.。至於 Yes, it was. 則用來回答 be 動詞引導的過去式問句，如：Was his presentation interesting? Yes, it was.「他的簡報有趣嗎？是的，很有趣。」

- presentation [ˌprizɛn`teʃən] (n.) 展示，演示；簡報
- go well 進行順利

*4.* 傑瑞昨天帶客戶參觀工廠。

解析 本句時間為 yesterday，時態應用過去式。動詞 take 的過去式為不規則變化 took。

- client [`klaɪənt] (n.) 客戶
- tour [tʊr] (v./n.) 旅行，遊覽；參觀

*5.* A：你昨天有跟我們的代理商山德森先生談過嗎？

B：是的，我有。

解析 本題問話的人用的是過去簡單式疑問句，以助動詞 Did 引導。簡答時，應以相同的助動詞回答，如：Yes, I did. 或 No, I didn't.。若要詳答則應說 Yes, I talked with him yesterday.，不可以只說 Yes, I talked.。

- agent [`edʒənt] (n.) 代理商；仲介

答案 1.(B) 2.(C) 3.(D) 4.(A) 5.(C)

**6.** Are you looking for Mary? I _____ in the meeting room a few minutes
ago.
(A) see him
(B) saw him
(C) will see her
(D) saw her

**7.** I'm sorry I wasn't in the office when you came. I _____ a meeting with
our suppliers.
(A) am having
(B) was having
(C) were having
(D) are having

**8.** A: Did you take notes during the presentation yesterday?
B: _____
(A) No, I wasn't.
(B) Yes, I could.
(C) No, I didn't.
(D) Yes, I will.

**9.** Can you tell me what your previous job _____?
(A) was
(B) is
(C) will be
(D) were

**10.** Before I started working in sales, I _____ a computer programmer.
(A) were
(B) was
(C) am
(D) will be

**6.** 你在找瑪莉嗎？我幾分鐘前在會議室裡看到她。

解析 「一段時間＋ago」意思為「……時間以前」，屬於過去時間副詞，因此動詞應用過去簡單式。動詞 see 的過去式為不規則變化 saw，Mary 為女性，代名詞受格要用 her，故選 (D)。

● look for 尋找　　　　　　　　　● ago [ə`go] (adv.) 在…以前

---

**7.** 抱歉你來的時候我不在辦公室。我正好在跟我們的廠商開會。

解析 本題的時間是上一句的 when you came（當你來的時候），而當時主詞正在開會，因此動詞應用過去進行式「was/were＋現在分詞」，表示「在過去的某一個時間點，某一個動作正在進行」。

● I'm sorry＋that 子句：抱歉，不好意思…

---

**8.** A：昨天簡報時你有做筆記嗎？

　　B：不，我沒有。

解析 本題為過去簡單式的疑問句，以助動詞 Did 引導。肯定簡答時應說 Yes, I did.，否定簡答則說 No, I didn't.。

● take notes 做筆記　　　　　　● during [`dʊərɪŋ] (prep.) 在…期間

---

**9.** 可以告訴我你的上一份工作是什麼嗎？

解析 本句的 what 問句併入 Can you tell me...? 的結構中作為受詞，這種用法稱為「間接問句」，句型為「wh-疑問詞＋主詞＋動詞」。此外，previous job 意思為「上一份工作」，根據其字義可知動詞應用過去簡單式，所以間接問句應寫成 what your previous job was。

● previous [`priviəs] (adj.) 先前的

---

**10.** 開始做業務之前，我是個電腦程式師。

解析 Before（在……以前）所引導的子句為表「時間」的從屬子句。從屬子句中的動詞 started 為過去簡單式，故主要子句的動詞也須用過去簡單式。主詞為 I，be 動詞須搭配 was。

● sales [selz] (n.) 業務；銷售　　● computer programmer 電腦程式師

---

答案 6.(D) 7.(B) 8.(C) 9.(A) 10.(B)

請從 (A)、(B)、(C)、(D) 中選出一個最適合的答案。

1. Because of the robbery, we _____ call the police and our insurance company.
   (A) have
   (B) had to
   (C) would
   (D) could

2. After all of the guests _____ seated, the announcer began to introduce the speaker.
   (A) had been
   (B) have
   (C) has to
   (D) have been

3. I didn't realize that the Lions had won the game until I heard on the radio that they _____.
   (A) are
   (B) were
   (C) had
   (D) should

4. Mindy was talking loudly during the meeting, so I _____ hear what Jack said.
   (A) wasn't
   (B) can't
   (C) didn't
   (D) won't

5. Don't worry. Before the shipment was sent, Mary _____ payment.
   (A) will receive
   (B) can receive
   (C) had received
   (D) should receive

*1.* 由於發生了搶案，我們必須打電話給警察和保險公司。

解析 文法上選項 (B)、(C)、(D) 皆可考慮，但就句義上 (C) would 表「意願」，(D) could 表「推測，許可」皆不恰當，以 (B) 最符合句意。助動詞 have to 是「必須」的意思，過去式是 had to。

● robbery [`rɑbərɪ] (n.) 搶劫；搶劫案　　● insurance [ɪn`ʃurəns] (n.) 保險

*2.* 所有的賓客就座之後，司儀開始介紹演講者。

解析 seat 當動詞「坐下，就座」解釋時，必須用被動語態 be seated 或反身代名詞 seat oneself。began（begin 的過去式）表示是過去發生的事，而「賓客就座」發生在「介紹演講者」之前，因此要用過去完成式，故選 (A)。

● seat [sit] (v.) 使就座　　● announcer [ə`naunsə] (n.) 宣告者；司儀

*3.* 直到聽到廣播，我才知道獅隊贏了比賽。

解析 not...until... 是「直到……才……」的意思。前面用到 the Lions had won the game（獅隊贏得了比賽），所以後面應當是 until I heard on the radio that they had won the game（直到我聽到廣播說他們贏得了比賽），重複用字可省略，因此只要留下 they had 就行了。

● realize [rɪə`laɪz] (v.) 知道

*4.* 明蒂開會時講話很大聲，所以我沒聽到傑克說的話。

解析 前半句的 was talking 為過去進行式，表示「過去某一時刻正在發生的事」。根據句意，當時明蒂正在大聲講話，所以說話者無法聽見傑克所說的話。動詞 hear（聽見）沒有進行式的用法，故此處須用過去簡單式否定用法 didn't hear。

● loudly [`laudlɪ] (adv.) 大聲地

*5.* 別擔心。在貨物送出前，瑪莉就已經收到貨款了。

解析 本句中有兩個動作，一個是 the shipment was sent（貨物送出），另一個是 received payment（收到貨款），兩個動作皆發生在過去，但「收到貨款」的動作在「貨物送出」前已經完成，因此先發生的動作須用過去完成式「had＋過去分詞」，寫成 had received payment。

● receive [rɪ`siv] (v.) 收到，接到

答案 1.(B)　2.(A)　3.(C)　4.(C)　5.(C)

**6.** When Stuart arrived in Hamburg, he realized he _____ the documents.
(A) has forgotten
(B) had forgotten
(C) will have forgotten
(D) will forget

**7.** That interview was hard! Thank goodness I _____ for it ahead of time.
(A) had prepared
(B) prepare
(C) should prepare
(D) will prepare

**8.** Fox and his new wife had their wedding on a secluded island last month. They _____ only dated for two weeks before they _____ the knot.
(A) have ; have tied
(B) had ; tied
(C) had ; have tied
(D) have ; tied

**9.** Fox's wife _____ romantically involved with several Hollywood actors before they got married.
(A) has been
(B) was
(C) had
(D) had been

**10.** Fox told reporters that two of them _____ actually met many years ago, but it wasn't until recently that they _____ a soul mate in each other.
(A) have ; find
(B) had ; find
(C) had ; found
(D) have ; find

**6.** 當史都華抵達漢堡時，他才知道他忘了帶文件。

解析 本句中主詞「抵達漢堡」時才發現到他「忘了帶文件」，要表示「過去某一動作之前已經發生的事」，須用過去完成式。本句「忘了帶文件」的動作發生在前，因此須用過去完成式 had forgotten。

● realize [`rɪə͵laɪz] (v.) 領悟，了解；實現

**7.** 那場面試好難！謝天謝地我有提前準備。

解析 本句中「準備面試」的動作發生在面試之前，而以動詞 was 判斷面試發生的時間在過去，因此空格的動詞須用過去完成式 had prepared。Thank goodness 是「謝天謝地」的意思，可單獨使用也可接子句，其他說法還有 Thank god 或 Thank heavens 等。

● interview [`ɪntə͵vju] (n.) 面試　　　　　● prepare [prɪ`pɛr] (v.) 準備
● ahead of time 提前；提早

**8.** 福克斯與新婚妻子上個月於一處隱密島嶼舉行婚禮。他們僅交往兩週即步入禮堂。

解析 從第一句得知兩人結婚已是上個月的事情，而兩人交往是在結婚前，且又持續一段時間，故先發生的動作「交往」要用過去完成式 had dated，而後發生的動作「結婚」要用過去簡單式 tied the knot，故答案選 (B)。

● secluded [sɪ`kludɪd] (adj.) 隱密的　　　● tie the knot 結為連理

**9.** 福克斯的妻子在婚前曾和數名好萊塢男演員傳出緋聞。

解析 這裡指的是婚前就已發生的事情，所以主要子句要用過去完成式。「涉入，捲入……」的用法是 be involved with...，因此 had 後必須要再加上 been，答案為 (D)。

● romantically [rə`mæntɪklɪ] (adv.) 浪漫地，小說般地

**10.** 福克斯告訴記者，其實兩人多年前已結識，但直到最近才發現彼此為心靈伴侶。

解析 此句的「結識」是在「發現彼此為心靈伴侶」這個過去事件多年之前就已經發生的事，因此應用過去完成式 had met 來描述。而後發生的動作 found a soul mate in each other 則用過去簡單式，答案選 (C)。此外，「直到最近才……」的句型是「it wasn't until recently that＋過去簡單式子句」，也可寫成「主詞＋didn't V until recently」。

● soul mate 心靈伴侶

答案 6.(B)　7.(A)　8.(B)　9.(D)　10.(C)

## 未來式的種類
- 未來式常用的形式可分為「未來簡單式」、「未來進行式」、「未來完成式」。
- 未來簡單式：表達未來的狀態、事實，以及在不久的未來將會去做的事。
- 未來進行式：表達未來某時間正在進行、或持續一段時間的動作。
- 未來完成式：表達在未來的某個時間點或期限之前，將已完成的事情。

**用商務英文 學多益句型**　**未來式**　必考重點句

---

**未來簡單式：will＋原形動詞**

## All employees will receive a Christmas bonus.
**所有員工都會收到聖誕節獎金。**

「未來簡單式」用來指未來會發生的事情，例如計畫、意圖、可能的狀況、未來的行程等，動詞的部份為 will ＋原形動詞。

⊃ I **will study** hard.
　我會努力讀書。

⊃ A: **Will** you **go** biking with me this Saturday?
　B: Sorry, I won't have time.
　A：你星期六要跟我去騎腳踏車嗎？
　B：抱歉，我沒有時間。

---

**未來簡單式：be going to＋原形動詞**

## Are we going to get raises this year?
**我們今年會加薪嗎？**

「未來簡單式」的另一種型態是 be going to＋原形動詞。be going to 和 will 差別在於 be going to 用來表達「事先決定的意圖」，will 則表示「未經事先考慮好的意圖」。此外，will 還表達「意願或決心」，be going to 則無此意。

用 will 表示臨時決定的事

⊃ I'm sorry. I forgot to pay the bill. I **will** do it tomorrow.
　很抱歉，我忘記繳帳單了。我明天會去繳。

用 be going to 來表示事先決定好的事

⊃ He **is going to** change jobs next month.
　他打算下個月換工作。

用 will 表示意願或決心

⊃ I **will** be a manager one day.
　我總有一天會當上經理的。

現在簡單式代替未來式

# Performance evaluations begin on Monday.
## 績效考核星期一開始。

可以用「現在簡單式」來表達「預先計畫好」或「肯定將要發生的事」。

➲ I **leave** for Japan on the fifth.
　　我五號要出發日本。

➲ The fall semester **starts** next week.
　　秋季學期下個星期開始。

現在進行式代替未來式

# Are you going on the company trip next week?
## 你下周要參加公司旅遊嗎？

「現在進行式」也可用來表達未來時態，不過僅限於少數「來去動詞」go、come、leave、start、arrive、return 等。

➲ **Are** you **returning** to Taitung during Chinese New Year?
　　你農曆過年時會回台東嗎？

➲ My friends **are coming** to my house tomorrow night.
　　我朋友明晚會來我家。

未來進行式

# Where will we be staying on the business trip?
## 出差時我們會住在哪裡？

意：本句型不能用 be
ʝing to＋be＋Ving。

「未來進行式」所要表達的是「未來某明確時間正在做某事」，該動作為持續發生的狀態。動詞部分為 will be ＋ Ving。

➲ A: What **will** you **be doing** tomorrow morning?
　　B: I **will be working**.
　　A：你明天上午要做什麼？
　　B：我要上班。

➲ At this time tomorrow, I**'ll be flying** to Hawaii.
　　我明天此時會飛往夏威夷。

➲ Don't call us between 8:00 and 9:00—we**'ll be watching** our favorite show then.
　　八點到九點之間不要打電話給我們，我們這個時候會在看最愛的節目。

## The new employees will have completed the training course by next Friday.

**新進員工下周五以前將完成訓練課程。**

「未來完成式」表達「現在到未來之間的一段時間將會發生某事」，動詞部分為 will have＋pp。

表示現在到五點之間，瑪麗會做完家事。

➲ Mary **will have finished** her housework by five o'clock.
瑪麗五點前會做完家事。

預估自己未來的行程

➲ I **will have cleaned the house** when you arrive.
你到的時候，我會打掃好房子了。

表示到六月底為止，羅伯就已在這裡工作十年。

➲ Robert **will have worked** here for 10 years at the end of June.
羅伯到六月底就已在這裡工作十年了。

## Level 1　挑戰多益 450

**請從 (A)、(B)、(C)、(D) 中選出一個最適合的答案。**

**1.** The tour bus will be _____ the hotel this evening at nine o'clock.
(A) returning
(B) returning to
(C) return
(D) return to

**2.** A: Have you decided what to tell them?
B: Yes. I _____ them the truth.
(A) will tell
(B) am going to tell
(C) plan to tell
(D) All of the above

**3.** When _____ your bedroom? I'm tired of seeing this mess every day!
(A) are you cleaning
(B) are you going to clean
(C) did you clean
(D) will you have cleaned

**4.** Who do you think _____ the next president?
(A) is
(B) is going to be
(C) going to be
(D) to be

**5.** Look out! _____ your head on the doorway!
(A) You hit
(B) You're hitting
(C) You're going to hit
(D) You were hitting

*1.* 遊覽車今晚九點會回到旅館。

解析 本句已經有 will be，表示應使用「未來進行式」，指未來某時間進行的動作。動詞 return 是「回到（某地）」的意思，後面要接介系詞 to，再接地點，所以選 (B)。

• tour bus 遊覽車

*2.* A：你決定好要跟他們說什麼了嗎？
B：決定了。我要跟他們說實話。

解析 此句題意表達「未來會做某事」，「be going to、will、plan to＋原形動詞」都能表達類似的意義，故答案選 (D)。

• decide [dɪˋsaɪd] (v.) 決定

*3.* 你何時要整理房間？我受不了每天看這一團亂！

解析 本題說話者問對方何時計劃清理房間，be going to 有「未來計劃做某事」之意，故選 (B)。

*4.* 你覺得誰會是下一屆總統？

解析 在問句句尾看到 the next president（下一屆總統），可以判斷本句要表達的是對未來事件的「預測」，因此空格應該要用未來式 will be 或是 is going to be，答案選 (B)。

• president [ˋprɛsədənt] (n.) 總統，主席

*5.* 小心！你的頭要撞到門口了！

解析 此題意為「小心！你的頭快撞到門口了！」，用 be going to 可表「眼前即將發生之事」，故選 (C)。

• doorway [ˋdɔrˏwe] (n.) 門口

答案 1.(B) 2.(D) 3.(B) 4.(B) 5.(C)

**6.** _____ to the play tomorrow evening?
(A) Do you go
(B) Are you going
(C) Have you gone
(D) Were you going

**7.** _____ to Tokyo tomorrow on business.
(A) I'll flying
(B) I have flown
(C) I fly
(D) I'm flying

**8.** A new hairstyle _____ make you feel much better.
(A) will
(B) will always
(C) will have
(D) Either a or b

**9.** She _____ by the time we get there.
(A) is leaving
(B) leaves
(C) will have left
(D) will leave

**10.** The company _____ an outing the Saturday after next.
(A) is to go on
(B) is going on
(C) will going on
(D) goes on

**6.** 你明天晚上要去看戲嗎？

解析 問句的句尾出現了未來時間 tomorrow evening，因此本句應用未來式。本句的動詞 go 屬於「來去動詞」，可以直接用進行式來表示即將發生之事，因此答案選 (B)。

**7.** 我明天要飛到東京出差。

解析 此句出現了表示未來的時間副詞 tomorrow， 可判斷應用未來式。此句的動詞 fly 也屬於「來去動詞」的一種，因此可以用現在進行式代替未來式，故選 (D)。

● on business 出差

**8.** 新髮型總能讓你心情大好。

解析 此題 will 帶有承諾或建議之意涵，加 always 表強調，語氣更重。(A) 或 (B) 均可，故選 (D)。

● hairstyle [`hɛr͵staɪl] (n.) 髮型

**9.** 我們到那之前她就會離開了。

解析 在句尾看到 by the time we get there（我們到那之前）表示「現在到未來之間的一段時間」，可以推測句子的時態應為「未來完成式」will have＋p.p.，表示這段時間內主詞 she 就會完成的事情，因此答案選 (C)。

**10.** 公司下下星期六要舉辦員工旅遊。

解析 本題的時間副詞 the Saturday after next（下下星期六）表示未來時間，句子應該用未來式。本句的動詞 go 屬於「來去動詞」，可直接以現在進行式代替未來式，故選 (B)。

● outing [`autɪŋ] (n.) 出外遊玩，遠足

**答案** 6.(B) 7.(D) 8.(D) 9.(C) 10.(B)

# Level ② 挑戰多益 650

請從 (A)、(B)、(C)、(D) 中選出一個最適合的答案。

1. Don't worry about me. I _____ packing my suitcase when we leave for the bus station.
   (A) finished
   (B) finish
   (C) will have finished
   (D) will be finishing

2. I _____ give my mother flowers for her birthday. She _____ be so surprised.
   (A) will ; will
   (B) will ; is going to
   (C) am going to ; will
   (D) am going to ; is going

3. You forgot to submit the form, so you _____ to fax it to us immediately.
   (A) will have
   (B) are going
   (C) will
   (D) None of the above

4. James _____ his girlfriend for three years at the end of the month.
   (A) will have known
   (B) have known
   (C) will know
   (D) will be knowing

5. If we use this strategy, the project _____ very successful.
   (A) will be
   (B) will being
   (C) was
   (D) is

**1.** 不用擔心我，當我們前往公車站時，我會事先打包好我的行李。

解析 從 when we leave for the bus station（當我們前往公車站時）的語氣，可以知道這是「未來」的時間，因此應當用未來式，所以只能選 (C) 或 (D)。使用「未來完成式」可表達「未來某時間點前將已完成的事」，故選 (C)。「未來進行式」則表達「未來某時間點正在進行的事」，如果說話者到出發時還正在打包行李，顯然會來不及，與前一句 Don't worry about me. 的語意不合，因此不可選 (D)。

● suitcase [`sutkes] (n.) 行李箱，小型旅行箱

**2.** 我要送花給我媽當生日禮物。她會嚇一大跳。

解析 be going to 和 will 均可表未來式，但前者通常用來表達「事先計劃好要做的事」，所以「打算、計劃」送花給媽媽宜用 be going to；而後句則表示對未來狀況的「預測」，可用 be going to，也可用 will，故答案選 (C)。

● surprised [sə`praɪzd] (adj.) 驚訝的

**3.** 你忘了交那份表格，所以你必須立刻傳真給我們。

解析 此題說話者提出「未來必須做某事」，應選 (A)，have to 意思是「必須」，will have to 則表未來的義務。選項 (B) 是陳述事實，無建議意味。選項 (C) will 之後不可直接加 to，須加原形動詞。

● submit [səb`mɪt] (v.) 提交　　　　● immediately [i`mɪdɪətlɪ] (adv.) 立即地

**4.** 到了這個月底，詹姆斯將已和他的女友認識滿三年。

解析 表達「將已……」就要用未來完成式：主詞＋will have p.p. 的句型，答案選 (A)。本句中的「這個月底」就是一個未來時間點，到了月底才滿三年，所以前面的介系詞要用 at 而不是 by。by 表示的是期限，指在某個時間點之前就已……。

**5.** 如果我們採用這個策略，這個計畫將會非常成功。

解析 此為條件句，表「如果我們……，就會……」，通常用 will 表示。這裡的 will 亦帶有承諾意涵，承諾或預期如果做了什麼事就會得到如何的結果，故選 (A)。

● strategy [`strætədʒɪ] (n.) 策略　　　● project [`prɑdʒɛkt] (n.) 計畫，方案

答案 1.(C) 2.(C) 3.(A) 4.(A) 5.(A)

**6.** _____ for her when her flight arrives tonight?

(A) Will you wait

(B) Will you be waiting

(C) Are you waiting

(D) Do you wait

**7.** We're selling our house because _____ to Philadelphia.

(A) we're moving

(B) we move

(C) we'll move

(D) we'll have moved

**8.** Don't lose this ticket. _____ need it to pick up your laundry.

(A) You'd

(B) You've

(C) You'll

(D) You would

**9.** By this time next year, we _____ the experiment.

(A) will have started

(B) have started

(C) will start

(D) are starting

**10.** _____ meeting with Mr. Wilson at 1:00 p.m. tomorrow, so can I schedule an appointment with you for later in the day?

(A) I can

(B) I will

(C) I will be

(D) I'm to

**6.** 她的班機抵達時你會在等她嗎？

解析 此題要表達的是「當她班機抵達」這個短暫動作的同時，進行長時間等待的這個動作。when 子句中可用現在式代替未來式，因此可以推知 tonight 是未來時間，主要子句要用未來進行式 will be＋Ving，故答案選 (B)。

● flight [`flaɪt] (n.) 班機

---

**7.** 我們正在賣房子，因為我們要搬到費城去了。

解析 此題有表未來計畫的意味，用現在進行式或 be going to 均可表達此意，故 (A)。will 則用於表達沒有事先計劃，而在說話當時才臨時做出的決定，與本題賣房子的語境不合，故不可選 (C)。

● move to 搬到某處

---

**8.** 這張票別搞丟了，你需要用它來領洗好的衣物。

解析 此題用 will 表未來須做之事，選 (C)。

● pick up 收拾，整理

---

**9.** 明年此時，我們就已經展開實驗了。

解析 by 指「到某一時刻為止」，用在未來時態須與「未來完成式」連用，指該時間點以前將已經完成的事。未來完成式表達對未來動作或事件的預測，動詞部分要用 will have＋p.p.，答案選 (A)。

● experiment [ɪk`spɛrəmənt] (n.) 實驗

---

**10.** 我明天下午一點會跟威爾森先生碰面，所以我可以跟你約明天晚一點的時間嗎？

解析 本句時間點為 1:00 p.m. tomorrow，要表示「未來某一時刻正在進行的事」，須用未來進行式「will be＋現在分詞」。未來進行式除用來表示「確信」或「預測」某事會發生之外，也可用來表達「委婉的語氣」，特別是在詢問他人的安排時，如：When will you be seeing Peter? 就比 When will you see Peter? 來得客氣。

● schedule [`skɛdʒʊl] (v.) 將…排入時間表　　● appointment [ə`pɔɪntmənt] (n.) 約會

---

答案 6.(B) 7.(A) 8.(C) 9.(A) 10.(C)

# 被動語態

**主動與被動語態概略**

● 當句子的主詞和動作的關係是主動的，這樣的動詞稱為「主動語態」，一般句子多屬此類。如果主詞是動作的承受者，稱之為「被動語態」。

用商務英文
學多益句型

被動語態 必考重點句

**什麼時候用被動語態？**

## I was interviewed two times before I was offered a position.

我在得到工作之前被面試了兩次。

主詞不確定或不重要時，會使用被動語態。被動語態句型為： S＋be動詞＋p.p.。

主動語態 ⊃ In the Philippines, people **eat** meals with rice.
在菲律賓，人們以米飯為主食。

被動語態 In the Philippines, meals **are eaten** with rice.

描述「狗已經被餵過」比知道是誰餵了狗還重要時，使用被動語態

⊃ The dog **has been fed**.
= Somebody has fed the dog.
有人餵過狗了。

**by＋執行者 / with＋工具**

## The job candidates were interviewed by the manager.

工作應徵者都被經理面試過了。

在被動語態中，如果提及執行動作的人，要在人的前方加上介系詞 **by**。若執行動作的是工具，則要用介系詞 **with**。

⊃ The song was composed by **Jay Chou**.
這首歌是周杰倫譜曲的。

⊃ The victim was stabbed with **a knife**.
被害人被刀子刺傷。

⊃ The photo was shot with **a digital camera**.
這張相片是用數位相機拍攝的。

## We will inform you when a decision is made.
做好決定時我們會通知你。

英文中幾乎所有時態都可以形成被動語態。現在簡單式的句子換成被動式時，只要把動詞改為：be 動詞＋p.p.。過去簡單式則把 be 動詞換成過去式的 was/were 即可。

主動語態　⊃ The company **hires** new employees each month.
　　　　　公司每月都會雇用新員工。

被動語態　New employees **are hired** (by the company) each month.

主動語態　⊃ Johnny's parents **gave** him lots of presents on his birthday.
　　　　　強尼的爸媽在他生日那天送他許多禮物。

被動語態　Johnny **was given** lots of presents (by his parents) on his birthday.

進行式的被動語態

## Your application is being reviewed by the HR department.
你的申請案件正由人資部審核中。

現在進行式換成被動式時，把原本的 be 動詞＋Ving 改為：be 動詞＋being＋p.p.。過去式進行式則把 be 動詞換成過去式的 was/were 即可。

主動語態　⊃ The guests **are congratulating** the bride and the groom.
　　　　　賓客們正在祝福新郎和新娘。

被動語態　The bride and the groom **are being congratulated** (by the guests).

主動語態　⊃ The maid **was cleaning** the bathroom.
　　　　　女僕正在清理浴室。

被動語態　The bathroom **was being cleaned** (by the maid).

## You have been chosen for the sales position.
你已獲選擔任業務一職。

現在完成式 have/has＋p.p. 換成被動式 → **have/has been＋p.p.**。

過去完成式 had＋p.p. 換成被動式 → **had been＋p.p.**。

主動語態    ⊃ The government **has built** a new road.
政府已經建造了新道路。

被動語態    A new road **has been** built (by the government).

主動語態    ⊃ The police **had arrested** the suspect for speeding.
警方已經逮捕了超速的嫌犯。

被動語態    The suspect **had been arrested** (by the police) for speeding.

## Applicants will be hired based on their qualifications and experience.
申請者將依其資格與經驗錄用。

未來式 will＋原形動詞 換成被動式 → **will＋be＋p.p.**。

主動語態    ⊃ The teacher **will collect** the exams at the end of the class.
老師在下課前會收考卷。

被動語態    The exams **will be collected** (by the teacher) at the end of the class.

## Résumés can be sent by e-mail or fax.
履歷可用電子郵件或傳真寄送。

若動詞組合為助動詞＋原形動詞換成被動式 → **助動詞＋be＋p.p.**。

主動語態    ⊃ The applicant **must sign** each page of the form.
申請人必須在每頁上都簽名。

被動語態    Each page of the form **must be signed** (by the applicant).

**有被動意義的形容詞**

# We are pleased to inform you that you've been selected for the position.

**很高興通知您，您已被錄用擔任本職。**

有一類形容詞是由「過去分詞」轉化而成的，兼具「被動」的意義（即 be 動詞＋過去分詞）與形容詞的功用，都用來描述「狀態」或「情況」，亦即可單純視為「形容詞」。

⊃ My little sister **is scared**.
　我的小妹妹很害怕。

⊃ The department store **is located** downtown.
　那間百貨公司位於市中心。

# Level ① 挑戰多益 *450*

請從 (A)、(B)、(C)、(D) 中選出一個最適合的答案。

**1.** This book I found _____ in 1533.
  (A) is written
  (B) was written
  (C) was writing
  (D) was wrote

**2.** The president _____ an assassin.
  (A) was killed by
  (B) be killed by
  (C) killed by
  (D) None of the above

**3.** In whose name was this letter _____?
  (A) writing
  (B) written
  (C) wrote
  (D) been written

**4.** A: Did you break this window?
  B: No. It _____ before I got here.
  (A) broke
  (B) was broke
  (C) was broken
  (D) broken

**5.** A: Did Lionel pay for the meal?
  B: Yes. The meal _____ for by Lionel.
  (A) has been paid
  (B) was pay
  (C) did be paid
  (D) was paid

*1.* 我找到的這本書是 1533 年寫的。

解析 主詞是 this book，後面的 I found 是省略了關係代名詞 that 的形容詞子句，this book (that) I found 意思是「我找到的這本書」。本書完成的時間是過去：1533 年，所以被動語態應該用過去式，答案選 (B)。

*2.* 總統遭刺客暗殺。

解析 本題的 kill 為及物動詞「殺害」，主詞是 the president，選項中均有介系詞 by，所以空格應該填入被動語態，表示「被殺害」，答案選 (A)。by 後方的 assassin 則是暗殺動作的執行者。選項 (B) 的問題在 be 動詞用了原形動詞，這是不需要的，除非前面有助動詞（can/will/may）等等。

● president [ˋprɛsədənt] (n.) 總統　　　● assassin [əˋsæsṇ] (n.) 刺客

*3.* 這封信是以誰的名義寫的？

解析 whose 的意思是「誰的」，是 who 的所有格。「in one's name = in the name of ＋某人／組織」，表示「以……名義」。例：The letter was written in Brown's name.「這封信是以布朗的名義寫的。」如果不知道是以誰的名義寫的，就用疑問句 In whose name... 發問。空格內應填入過去分詞，和句中的 was 形成被動語態。

*4.* A：窗戶是你弄破的嗎？

　B：不是我，我到這裡之前，窗戶就已經破了。

解析 第二句中的 It 代替前面的 this window。在第一句中當受詞的 this window 換到第二句當主詞，因此空格內要填入被動語態「be 動詞＋p.p.」。選項 (A) 是主動語態。(B) 用錯動詞，broke 是過去式，不是過去分詞。(D) 少了 be 動詞，只有 (C) 是時態和形式都完全正確的答案。此被動語態 The window was broken. 可表示動作「被弄破了」，也可形容狀態「已經破掉了」。

*5.* A：這頓飯是羅內爾付的錢嗎？

　B：是的。這頓飯是羅內爾付的。

解析 「pay for＋N」表示「付錢（買……）」。本題答句的主詞為 the meal，空格內應填入被動語態 be paid。問句的時態使用過去式，答句中動詞同樣也要使用過去式，故答案選 (D)。

● meal [mil] (n.) 餐

答案 1.(B) 2.(A) 3.(B) 4.(C) 5.(D)

6. A: Did Fred take the car or the truck?
   B: He _____ the car.
   (A) has taken by
   (B) did taken
   (C) took
   (D) was taken by

7. This photo was taken _____ a friend of mine.
   (A) of
   (B) on
   (C) than
   (D) by

8. A: Open the safe and give me all the money!
   B: But the safe can't _____ until tomorrow morning.
   (A) open
   (B) opened
   (C) be opened
   (D) be opening

9. My wallet _____ stolen.
   (A) is
   (B) was been
   (C) has been
   (D) be

10. Rain _____ for the next three days.
    (A) is expecting
    (B) is expected
    (C) expects
    (D) will expect

*6.* A：弗萊德買了汽車還是卡車？

B：他買了汽車。

解析 動詞 take 作「買」解釋。空格前面的主詞是 He，後面的 the car 是受詞，故判斷本句用主動語態即可，答案選 (C)。

● truck [trʌk] (n.) 卡車

---

*7.* 這張照片是我一個朋友拍的。

解析 「take a picture/photo of＋N」表示「幫（某人或某物）拍照」。本句主詞是無生命的 this photo，所以使用被動語態 was taken。空格須填入的介系詞是 by，後面加動作執行者（a friend of mine）。take a photo（of＋N）其中 of 後面接的是「拍照的對象」，但 of＋N 不一定要提及，本題即為一例。

---

*8.* A：把保險櫃打開，把錢全拿給我！

B：但是保險櫃要到明天早上才打得開。

解析 主詞是無生命的 safe（保險櫃），可知應該使用被動語態，空格前面有助動詞 can't，所以後面使用「原形 be 動詞＋p.p.」，答案選 (C)。句中的 until 是「介系詞」，作「直到……為止」解釋。

● safe [sef] (n./adj.) 保險櫃，安全的

---

*9.* 我的錢包被偷了。

解析 空格後面是動詞 steal 的過去分詞 stolen，前方搭配 be 動詞表被動語態。按時間邏輯推斷，東西被偷是發生過的事情，所以選項 (A) 的現在式不適合。空格前沒有助動詞，所以 (D) 選項也不正確。選項 (B) 如果改成 was 可以是正確答案，單純表示「錢包被偷」此一過去事件。(C) 是正確答案，現在完成式強調此一事件與現在的關聯，表示錢包之前被偷了，現在還沒找到。

---

*10.* 接下來三天預計都會下雨。

解析 動詞 expect 作「預期，期待」解釋。本句主詞是無生命的 rain，所以空格應該填入被動語態，答案選 (B)。其他選項都是主動語態，不可選。被動語態的動作執行者（by＋N），因為不是重點，所以往往不需要提出來，本題即是一例。

---

答案 6.(C) 7.(D) 8.(C) 9.(C) 10.(B)

# Level ② 挑戰多益 *650*

**請從 (A)、(B)、(C)、(D) 中選出一個最適合的答案。**

1. The new program _____ explained to the students by the principal right now.
   (A) is
   (B) being
   (C) was
   (D) is being

2. _____ we _____ in euros or dollars?
   (A) Do ; get paid
   (B) Are ; paid
   (C) Will ; be paid
   (D) All of the above

3. When the police arrived at the accident scene, it was clear to them that she _____ instantly.
   (A) had been killed
   (B) was killed
   (C) die
   (D) had die

4. A: Who should sign the application?
   B: The person asking for the loan should _____ the application.
   (A) sign
   (B) been signed
   (C) be signing
   (D) be signed

5. The tower _____ being _____ by a Japanese construction company.
   (A) is ; built
   (B) has ; built
   (C) will ; building
   (D) None of the above

**1.** 校長正在向學生們解釋新課程。

解析 時間副詞是 right now（現在），表示應當使用「現在進行式」。本題若用主動語態表示為 The principal is explaining the new program to the students right now.，現在進行式改成被動語態，會變成 be＋being＋p.p.，故要用 is being explained。

• principal [`prɪnsəpl] (n.) 校長，首長

**2.** 他們會付我們歐元還是美元？

解析 選項 (A)、(B)、(C) 都是正確答案，皆是被動語態，但意思不太一樣。選項 (A) 的「get＋p.p.」的被動語態比較強調動作。「be 動詞＋p.p.」的被動語態，則既可以表示動作，又可以表示狀態。雖然選項 (B)、(C) 都是被動語態，但是前者用現在式表達事實，後者用未來式表示未來將發生的事。未來式後面必須用原形動詞 be，再接過去分詞 p.p.。

• euros [juroz] (n.) 歐元

**3.** 當警察抵達事故現場時，她顯然早已斷氣。

解析 要比較兩個發生在過去的事件時，先發生的事件用「過去完成式」，後發生的事件用「過去簡單式」。以本題而言，當事人死亡的時間比較早，故應用過去完成式，而且主詞 she 應該是「被殺害」，所以還要搭配被動式 had been killed，答案選 (A)。注意，動詞 die「死亡」一字為瞬間動作，沒有持續性。要表達已死亡多時，必須用形容詞 dead，「死亡的」來描述此一狀態。

• accident scene 事故現場　　　　　• sth. be clear to sb. …對某人來說是顯而易見的

**4.** A：誰應該在這份申請書上簽名？

B：申請貸款的人應該要在申請書上簽名。

解析 本句主詞是 the person，asking for the loan 是分詞片語的一種（現在分詞表主動），修飾前面的 the person，指「申請貸款的人」。空格內應該填入動詞，用主動語態即可，助動詞 should 後加原形動詞，故答案選 (A)。

• loan [lon] (n.) 貸款　　　　　• application [`æplə`keʃən] (n.) 申請書

**5.** 這座塔樓由一家日本建築公司興建當中。

解析 主詞是 the tower，by 引導出的 a Japanese construction company 是動作的執行者，可知空格應該填入動詞的被動語態。由兩空格中間所夾的 being 一字可知此處應用被動語態的現在進行式「be 動詞＋being＋p.p.」，強調動作正在進行當中。第一空格應填入第三人稱單數 is，第二空格應填入 build 的過去分詞 built，故選 (A)。選項 (B) 中間則應該搭配 been，has been built 可表示「已經被興建」完成。

• construction [kəns`trʌkʃən] (n.) 建築；建造

答案 1.(D) 2.(D) 3.(A) 4.(A) 5.(A)

6. Our products _____ to China if we go through all the necessary channels.
   (A) can be exported
   (B) can be imported
   (C) should be bought
   (D) can be selling

7. I'm sorry, Mr. Jones. The contract has already _____, and it's too late to change it.
   (A) to sign
   (B) been signed
   (C) be signed
   (D) been sign

8. The product promotion at the Orion Department Store was _____ by Richard.
   (A) arranged
   (B) setting up
   (C) been arranged
   (D) to arrange

9. The products _____ inspected by trained experts.
   (A) have been
   (B) have being
   (C) should to
   (D) will

10. After an all-night session, the promotional video for the exhibition _____ completed by the Media Team.
    (A) be
    (B) are
    (C) was
    (D) has

**6.** 如果我們通過所有必須的管道,我們的產品就可以出口到中國。

解析 export...to... 指「出口……到……」,import...from... 則指「從……進口……」,根據本題句意應選 can be exported,也可代換為 can be sold。
- export [ɪks`port] (v.) 出口
- import [ɪm`port] (v.) 進口
- channel [`tʃænl] (n.) 管道;頻道

---

**7.** 很抱歉,瓊斯先生。合約已經簽了,要改已經來不及了。

解析 動詞 sign(簽訂;簽字)的行為者應為「人」,而本題是以「物」the contract 當主詞,故動詞應使用「被動語態」。本句的時態為完成式,所以被動語態寫成 has been signed。
- too...to... 太…而不能…

---

**8.** 獵戶百貨公司的產品促銷是由理查安排的。

解析 本題的主詞為「物」the product promotion,所以動詞應用「被動語態」was arranged,也可代換為 was set up(此 set 為過去分詞)。若用選項 (C) 空格前方應改為 has,has been arranged 表示「已經被安排好了」。
- arrange [ə`rendʒ] (v.) 安排,籌備
- set up 設置;安排,策劃

---

**9.** 這些產品已經由受過訓練的專家檢查過。

解析 主詞為「物」the products,所以動詞應用「被動語態」have been inspected。(B) 選項是錯誤的被動與態,要改成 have been 表示「完成」或是 is/was being「表示正在進行」。其它選項則應修改為:(C) should be inspected(應該被檢查);(D) will be inspected(將會被檢查)。
- inspect [ɪn`spɛkt] (v.) 檢查,視察

---

**10.** 經過一整晚的討論,展覽的宣傳錄影帶由媒體團隊完成了。

解析 主詞為「物」the promotional video,所以動詞應用「被動語態」。主詞為單數,故 be 動詞搭配 was。
- promotional [prə`moʃənl] (adj.) 宣傳的
- exhibition [ˌɛksə`bɪʃən] (n.) 展覽
- session [`sɛʃən] (n.) 一節、一場、一段時間;會議

答案 6.(A) 7.(B) 8.(A) 9.(A) 10.(C)

# 情態助動詞

**助動詞的種類**

● 時態助動詞（如 do、did、have、has、will 等）是沒有詞義的。而有詞義的（如 can、may、should、must 等）稱之為「情態助動詞」，後面加原形動詞。

用商務英文
學多益句型

**情態助動詞** 必考重點句

**表「建議或請求」**

## Could you tell everybody about the training seminar on Friday?

**能麻煩你告訴大家周五的訓練研討會的事情嗎？**

情態助動詞可用來表示「客氣、婉轉的建議或請求」，例如 could、would、may 或 shall（用在第一人稱）。

○ **Could** you do me a favor?
　你可以幫我忙嗎？

○ **Would** you close the window?
　你可以關上窗戶嗎？

○ **May** I come in?
　我可以進來嗎？

○ **Shall** we dance?
　我們跳舞好嗎？

**表「可能性」**

## We may have to reschedule the sales training course.

**我們可能須重新排定業務訓練課程的時間。**

情態助動詞可以表達「可能性」，例如：may 或 might。might 實踐的可能性較 may 低。

○ I **may** go to see that movie tomorrow.
　我可能明天會去看那部電影。

○ Alice **might** study abroad this fall.
　愛麗絲今年秋天可能會出國讀書。

表「確定性」

## All employees can benefit from on-the-job training.

**所有員工皆能於在職訓練中受益。**

情態助動詞可以表達「確定性」，這類助動詞有 can（過去式 could）、will（過去式 would）及 be able to（可用在過去式、現在式和未來式）。

⊃ I **can** finish the project in ten days.
　我十天內可以把案子做完。

⊃ If temperatures continue to rise, the Polar Ice Cap **will** melt.
　如果氣溫愈來愈高，北極冰帽將會融化。

⊃ Ted **couldn't** go to work yesterday because he was sick.
　泰德昨日無法上班，因為他生病了。

⊃ I'm afraid I won't **be able to** have dinner with you tonight.
　恐怕我今晚無法和你共進晚餐。

表「提供建議」

## We should hire a consultant to help set up an employee training program.

**我們應該聘請一名顧問協助策劃員工訓練。**

情態助動詞也可以用來「提供建議」。例如：should/ought to 或 had better（注意：had 不是過去式，沒有 have better 或 has better 的用法，否定用 had better not）。

⊃ We **should** think carefully before taking any action.
　我們採取行動之前應該仔細思考。

⊃ You **ought to** be more careful.
　你應該要小心一點。

⊃ You **had better** leave now or you'll miss your bus.
　你最好現在出發，不然就趕不上公車了。

## New sales reps have to complete the sales training program.

**新進業務代表必須完成業務訓練課程。**

表達「義務」的情態助動詞是 **must** 和 **have to**，表示現階段應盡、或是設想到的義務。表示在未來的時態下「應該、得做……」，則用未來式 **will have to**。若表示在過去時態下「應該……」，則要用 **had to** 表示。

⊃ You **must** study harder.
　你必須更用功。

⊃ My son had a high fever, so I **had to** call the doctor in the middle of the night.
　我兒子發高燒了，所以我必須半夜打電話給醫生。

⊃ They **have to** finish the report by July 31st.
　他們必須在七月三十一日前完成報告。

⊃ I **will have to** borrow money to pay the rent for next month.
　我得向朋友借錢來付下個月房租了。

**will have to** 表示在未來的某個時間點必須要做這件事，若用 **have to** 語意則是指說話當下設想的計畫。

## Computer training may increase employee productivity.

**電腦培訓可能會增加員工產值。**

表達「推測」的情態助動詞可以用 **can**、**could**、**may**、**might** 或 **must**。肯定推測以 must 的語氣最強烈（注意不能以 mustn't 表否定推測，mustn't 意為「不准」，表「禁止」）；否定推測則以 can't 的語氣最強烈。

⊃ A: **Can** it be true?
　B: No, it **can't** be true
　A：這是真的嗎？
　B：不，不可能是真的。

⊃ A: **Could** he be Mr. Right?
　B: Maybe.
　A：他會是白馬王子嗎？
　B：或許是。

⊃ You **may** be right.
　或許你是對的。

might 的可能性較
may 小

○ If you were older, you **might** understand.
如果你年紀大一點，或許就會明白了。

○ You **must** be tired after such a long trip.
這麼遠的旅程，你一定累壞了。

表「過去推測」

## Better safety training might have prevented the accident.
較好的安全訓練或許能防止這場意外。

「推測」過去發生過的事情，要用 may/must/might/could + have p.p.。推
測語氣的強弱依助動詞而定。

must have＋p.p.
是強烈肯定的推測

○ It **must have rained** last night.
昨晚一定下過雨。

might have＋p.p.
表示可能性較低的猜測

○ It's no use thinking about what **might have been**.
猜想當初怎樣，現在可能會如何，是沒有用的。

may have＋p.p.
較 might have＋p.p.
可能性高

○ The injury **may have caused** brain damage.
這傷勢可能會造成腦部損傷。

○ They played baseball in the rain. They **could have caught** a bad cold.
他們在雨中打棒球，他們可能會得重感冒。

表「惋惜、後悔」

## The company should have provided better training for its customer service staff.
公司應該要提供客服人員更好的訓練才是。

should have＋p.p. 是用來表示「過去應當做而未做的事」，通常是一種惋惜
與後悔的語氣。

○ He only slept for three hours. He **should have slept** longer.
他只睡了三小時，他應該睡久一點才對。

○ He only won second prize. He **should have practiced** more.
他只拿到第二名，他應該多多練習才是。

○ She failed the English exam. She **should have studied** harder.
她英文考試不及格，她應該要更用功才是。

# Level 1 挑戰多益 *450*

**請從 (A)、(B)、(C)、(D) 中選出一個最適合的答案。**

1. I _____ want to be in his shoes.
   (A) wouldn't
   (B) couldn't
   (C) hadn't
   (D) would've

2. I'm busy right now. _____ you answer the door for me?
   (A) Should
   (B) Might
   (C) Could
   (D) May

3. We looked hard, but _____ find your new apartment.
   (A) might not
   (B) weren't able to
   (C) wouldn't
   (D) shouldn't

4. I look tired because I _____ sleep last night.
   (A) can't
   (B) couldn't
   (C) shouldn't
   (D) wouldn't

5. The Joneses said that they _____ come, but not to expect them.
   (A) mustn't
   (B) must
   (C) might
   (D) would

**1.** 我不會想要落入他的處境。

解析 本題表說話者意願，應用助動詞 woudn't，意為「不想」，故選 (A)。in one's shoes
表示「站在某人的立場，處在某人的狀況」。

**2.** 我現在很忙。你可以去幫我開門嗎？

解析 本題為客氣詢問對方意願的用法，應用助動詞 could，故選 (C)。may 或 might 則
較常搭配主詞 I，用來請求許可，如：May I use your telephone?「我可以借用你的
電話嗎？」

● answer [ˋænsə] (v.) 接電話，應門

**3.** 我們很努力找，但無法幫你找到新公寓。

解析 本題表「能力」，應用助動詞 weren't able to，表示「無法達成某事」，故選 (B)。
此為過去式用法，等同 couldn't。

● apartment [əˋpɑrtmənt] (n.) 公寓

**4.** 我看起來很累，因為我昨晚無法好好睡。

解析 本題時間明確指出為昨天晚上，而 couldn't 在此為 can't 的過去式，表示「無法達
成某事」，故選 (B)。shouldn't 表否定「建議」，wouldn't 表否定「意願」，均不
可選。

● tired [taɪrd] (adj.) 疲倦的

**5.** 瓊納斯一家人說他們可能會來，但不必特意等他們。

解析 此句為過去式用法，(C) 和 (D) 均有可能。由後半句的 not to expect them 可推知瓊
斯一家人有可能會來，但不太確定。might 表「可能」，故選 (C)。would 則表「意
願」，與句意不合。

● expect [ɪksˋpɛkt] (v.) 指望，預料

答案 1.(A) 2.(C) 3.(B) 4.(B) 5.(C)

**6.** If you want to get a promotion, you _____ spend more time learning new skills.
(A) could
(B) should
(C) would
(D) may

**7.** Be careful, or the dog _____ bite you.
(A) must
(B) would
(C) should
(D) might

**8.** _____ I borrow your stapler?
(A) Will
(B) Would
(C) Shall
(D) Could

**9.** Excuse me, Miss. _____ I trouble you for a glass of water?
(A) Might
(B) May not
(C) Should
(D) Shall

**10.** We're all packed now. _____ we go then?
(A) Maybe
(B) Shall
(C) Might
(D) Mustn't

**6.** 如果你想要升遷，你應該多花一點時間學新技能。

解析 本句是對想升遷者表達「建議」，故選情態助動詞 should（應該）最貼切。其他選項 could 和 may 則表「可以；許可；可能」，而 would 表「意願」。

● spend＋時間＋Ving：花時間做…

**7.** 請小心，不然那條狗可能會咬你。

解析 此句為含蓄的推測用法，應用 might 表「可能」，故選 (D)。

● bite [baɪt] (v.) 咬

**8.** 我可以跟你借釘書機嗎？

解析 could 為禮貌且含蓄的詢問用語，表「是否可以」，故選 (D)。would 也可用來客氣詢問對方的意願，與主詞 you 搭配，如：Would you lend me your stapler?「你可以借我你的釘書機嗎？」

● stapler [`steplɚ] (n.) 訂書機

**9.** 小姐，不好意思。能麻煩妳給我一杯水嗎？

解析 此句題意為說話者想麻煩別人做某事，故用肯定疑問句。Might 用以客氣詢問「是否可以」，故選 (A)。選項 (B) 若改為 May 也是正確用語。

● a glass of... 一杯…

**10.** 我們現在都打包好了。可以出發了嗎？

解析 本句為徵求對方意見，應搭配表「建議做某事」的助動詞 shall，故選 (B)。shall 一般用於第一人稱 I/we，意思是詢問對方「……好嗎？要不要……？」

● pack [pæk] (v.) 收拾，包裝

答案 6.(B) 7.(D) 8.(D) 9.(A) 10.(B)

# Level 2 挑戰多益 650

請從 (A)、(B)、(C)、(D) 中選出一個最適合的答案。

**1.** We've analyzed the company's current situation, and we think it _____ be time to diversify.
(A) was
(B) might
(C) wasn't
(D) have

**2.** Our agent just called from China to thank you. You _____ done a good job on your trip there.
(A) must have
(B) did have
(C) have never
(D) could have

**3.** The advertising agency lost the bid for the contract to their rivals. They _____ prepared more for it.
(A) might have
(B) could have
(C) should have
(D) will have

**4.** We'll have to increase profit margins soon, or else we'll _____ lay off more employees.
(A) haven't
(B) have
(C) have to
(D) must

**5.** I forgot to bring my money, so I _____ buy groceries on the way home.
(A) hadn't
(B) wouldn't
(C) couldn't
(D) shouldn't

**1.** 我們已經分析了公司目前的狀況，我們想現在可能是多樣化經營的時候了。

解析 「It's time to ＋原形動詞」意思是「該是做……的時候了」，本句中 be 動詞以原形
呈現，可推知前面須加上情態助動詞，而 might 意思是「可能」，是一種委婉的表
達方式。

- analyze [ˋænˌaɪz] (v.) 分析
- diversify [daɪˋvɝsəfaɪ] (v.) 使多樣化，增加產品的種類以擴大（業務）

---

**2.** 我們的代理商剛從中國打電話來謝謝你。你在那裡出差時一定表現得很好。

解析 「must＋原形動詞」可用來表示現在的「義務」或對現在事件的「推測」；「must
have＋過去分詞」則用來表示對過去事件的推測，意思是「一定（有做了某
事）」。根據第一句句意「代理商打電話來道謝」，可推知說話者「推測對方先前
一定做了好事」，故用 must have done a good job。

- do a good job 表現得好

---

**3.** 廣告公司標案時輸給了對手。他們該多做一些準備才是。

解析 「might/could/should have＋過去分詞」用來表示對過去事件的「遺憾、責備」
之意，代表「某事該做卻未做」或「不該做卻做了」。本題說 They should have
prepared more for it. 言下之意就是「事實上他們的準備不週」。

- advertising agency 廣告公司
- rival [ˋraɪvl] (n.) 對手
- bid [bɪd] (n.) 投標，出價

---

**4.** 我們必須馬上增加利潤率，否則我們將必須解聘更多員工。

解析 「have to＋原形動詞」意思是「必須」，與 must 同義，但語氣上 must 則比較強
烈。注意 have to 屬一般動詞片語，疑問或否定句須搭配助動詞 do，也可搭配其他
情態助動詞，如本句的 we'll have to...（我們將必須……），但 must 則已是情態助
動詞，不能再與 will 連用。

- increase [ɪnˋkris] (v.) 增加
- or else 否則，要不然
- profit margin 利潤率，利潤的百分比
- lay off 解雇

---

**5.** 我忘了帶錢，所以沒辦法在回家路上順道去買菜。

解析 前句說「忘了帶錢」，因此可確定導出後句「無法買菜」的結果。助動詞應用
couldn't（can't 的過去式），表「無法做某事」，故選 (C)。

- grocery [ˋgrosərɪ] (n.) 食品雜貨店，食品雜貨（複數）

---

答案 1.(B) 2.(A) 3.(C) 4.(C) 5.(C)

6. That's impossible! Sean _____ have the password to that account.
   (A) mustn't
   (B) might
   (C) couldn't
   (D) might not

7. The market is so unstable now that it's hard to say what will happen. Prices _____ go up, or they _____ go down.
   (A) can ; can't
   (B) may ; may not
   (C) may ; may
   (D) will ; won't

8. You _____ put on your glasses or you_____ be able to read the fine print.
   (A) could ; wouldn't
   (B) should ; might not
   (C) would ; might
   (D) should ; may

9. Her parents don't think _____ get married so young.
   (A) she should
   (B) she can
   (C) she could
   (D) she might

10. I never have any money. I knew I _____ bought that car!
    (A) shouldn't have
    (B) couldn't have
    (C) might not have
    (D) wouldn't have

**6.** 不可能！西恩不可能會有那個帳戶的密碼。

解析 本題前句已說明 impossible，表「不可能」，故後者必須用否定句。mustn't 是 must not 的縮小，表強烈禁止，與句義不符，couldn't 有「不可能」之意，選 (C)。

- password [pæs`wɜd] (n.) 密碼
- account [ə`kaunt] (n.) 帳戶

**7.** 市場如此不穩定，很難說會發生什麼事。價格可能上漲，也可能下跌。

解析 前句說「很難說會發生什麼事」，可推知後句中的價格「上漲」或「下跌」均有可能，因此兩個情態助動詞均選肯定的 may。

- so...that＋子句：如此⋯以至於⋯
- unstable [ʌn`stebl̩] (adj.) 不穩定的

**8.** 你該戴上眼鏡，不然可能會看不見印得很小的字。

解析 句中的連接詞 or 作「否則」解，此句型有「你應該⋯⋯；否則你可能無法⋯⋯」之意。第一空格應填入為表「建議」的 should，第二空格則應填入表含蓄推測「無法達成某事」的might not，故選 (B)。

- put on... 戴上⋯

**9.** 她的父母認為她不該這麼年輕就結婚。

解析 should 表「應該做某事」之意，選 (A)。

- married [`mærɪd] (adj.) 已婚的，結婚的

**10.** 我一直沒什麼錢。我就知道我當初不該買那輛車！

解析 shouldn't 表「不應該做某事」之意，後面加上完成式用法，表「不該做某事但已經做了」，選 (A)。

答案 6.(C) 7.(C) 8.(B) 9.(A) 10.(A)

# 附加問句

**附加問句概述**

● 附加問句是附在「直述句」之後的簡短問句,用來徵求對方的同意或確認,類似中文「對不對?」或「不是嗎?」等說法。

用商務英文
學多益句型

**附加問句** 必考重點句

### 肯定句後的附加問句

## You're going to the concert this Saturday, aren't you?

**你這星期六要去聽演唱會,不是嗎?**

如果前面的直述句是肯定句,附加問句便用「否定句」的縮略語:否定助動詞 / be 動詞＋主詞。注意,附加問句中的動詞型態與時態,必須和前面的直述句一致;主詞也都要換成代名詞。

it 代替前句的 novel

➲ **The novel is** interesting, **isn't it**?
這本小說很有趣,不是嗎?

they 代替前句的 All children

➲ **All children like** candy, **don't they**?
所有的小朋友都喜歡吃糖果,不是嗎?

she 即為前句的 Helena

➲ **Helena has lived** in London for ten years, **hasn't she**?
海蓮娜已經在倫敦住了十年,對吧?

### 否定句後的附加問句

## You haven't been to the new amusement park, have you?

**你還沒有去過那個新的遊樂園,對吧?**

如果前面的直述句是否定句,或是含有否定意義的字詞 never/no/nothing/nobody 等時,附加問句便用肯定句:助動詞 / be 動詞＋主詞。

➲ **Andrew isn't** your boss, **is he**?
安德魯不是你的老闆,對吧?

➲ **You won't** forget me, **will you**?
你不會忘記我,對吧?

⊃ **Tom hasn't** lost weight, **has he**?
  湯姆還沒變瘦，不是嗎？

⊃ **Dale** seldom **goes** to the movies, **does he**?
  岱爾很少看電影，對吧？

**直述句是 There is/There are... 的附加問句**

## There are lots of good shows on TV tonight, aren't there?
### 今晚電視上有很多好節目可看，對吧？

There is/There are... 作「有……」解釋，表達一種「存在的狀態」。在這類句子中，附加問句皆為 be 動詞＋there。

⊃ **There are** five people in your family, **aren't there**?
  你家有五個人，對吧？

本身具有否定意味

⊃ **There is** no one in the room, **is there**?
  房內沒有人，不是嗎？

⊃ **There was** a fire downtown yesterday, **wasn't there**?
  昨天市區發生了一場火災，不是嗎？

**各種祈使句的附加問句**

## Let's see a play this weekend, shall we?
### 我們這週末來看齣戲，好嗎？

以原形動詞起首的句子稱作祈使句，用來向對方提出請求、下命令、邀約或建議，所以後面的附加問句也有所不同。

1. 表示請求對方幫忙的祈使句，附加問句用 will you？

2. 表示邀請對方做某事的祈使句，附加問句用 won't you？

3.「Let's＋原形動詞」表示勸誘，附加問句用 shall we？

在祈使句中，受話的一方是「第二人稱 you（你；你們）」，you 是句中隱含的主詞，這就是為什麼附加問句的主詞都是 you。

示請求對方幫忙

⊃ Close the door, **will you**?
  把門關上，好嗎？

示邀請對方做某事

⊃ Stay for dinner, **won't you**?
  留下來吃晚餐，好嗎？

勸誘

⊃ Let's take a break, **shall we**?
  我們休息一下，好嗎？

**A: You bought tickets for the performance, didn't you?**

**B: Yes, I did.**

**A：你買了那場表演的門票，不是嗎？**

**B：是的，我買了。**

附加問句的回答方式，和一般 yes/no 的問句一樣，只須針對主要子句狀況簡答不須考慮附加問句的肯定與否。

只針對 Elaine 是不是好朋友而回答 yes 或 no

⊃ A: Elaine is your best friend, isn't she?

  B: **Yes, she is.**

  A：伊蓮是你最要好的朋友，不是嗎？

  B：沒錯，她是。

只針對 Barry 喜不喜歡喝茶來回答 yes 或 no

⊃ A: Barry doesn't like tea, does he?

  B: **No, he doesn't.**

  A：貝瑞不喜歡喝茶，對吧？

  B：沒錯，他不喜歡。

# Level 1  挑戰多益 450

請從 (A)、(B)、(C)、(D) 中選出一個最適合的答案。

☐ **1.** Carla has been working on that document for a long time, _____ ?
(A) hasn't she
(B) will she
(C) did she
(D) had she

☐ **2.** Yvonne _____ drive, _____ she?
(A) can ; can not
(B) can ; can't
(C) can ; cannot
(D) can't ; can't

☐ **3.** Your teacher is over 40, _____ ?
(A) isn't she
(B) doesn't she
(C) she isn't
(D) will she

☐ **4.** They _____ to New York, haven't they?
(A) went
(B) have to go
(C) have gone
(D) haven't been

☐ **5.** She plays the violin in the orchestra, _____ she?
(A) can
(B) doesn't
(C) is
(D) All of the above

*1.* 卡拉已經做那份文件做好久了，不是嗎？

解析 附加問句是附在陳述句後面的簡短問句，與中文的「對不對、是不是」雷同，是用
來詢問或請求確認資訊。基本用法為「肯定句＋否定附加問句」與「否定句＋肯定
附加問句」。附加問句的時態與助動詞須與陳述句一致，本句陳述句為現在完成式
肯定句，因此附加問句須寫成否定的 hasn't she?。
● document [`dɑkjəmənt] (n.) 文件

*2.* 伊芳會開車，不是嗎？

解析 本題測驗重點：附加問句中有助動詞 can。在附加問句的表達中，如果前方的直述
句是肯定，附加問句就用否定，且 can not 應縮寫成 can't，故答案選 (B)。代名詞
she 是代替前面直述句的 Yvonne。
● drive [draɪv] (v.) 開車，駕駛

*3.* 你的老師四十多歲了，不是嗎？

解析 附加問句的基本句型為「肯定句＋否定附加問句」與「否定句＋肯定附加問句」。
本題前面為肯定敘述，而且用的是 be 動詞的現在式敘述句，因此附加問句也用
現在式的否定縮寫 isn't she。這裡的 she 代替的是前面的 the teacher，故答案選
(D)。

*4.* 他們已經去紐約了，不是嗎？

解析 附加問句用現在完成式 haven't they，直述句的動詞也應使用現在完成式，且用肯
定句，故選 (C)。「S＋has/have gone to＋地點」表示「人已經到了某地」，gone
是動詞 go 的過去分詞。(B) 選項的 have to 是一般動詞，助動詞應該搭配 do，正
確的附加問句型態應該是 don't they。

*5.* 她在管絃樂團拉小提琴，不是嗎？

解析 本題測驗重點：一般動詞的附加問句。直述句是肯定語氣，所以附加問句要用否
定。因為 play 是一般動詞，所以否定句必須使用助動詞 doesn't/don't。主詞是
she，所以助動詞用 doesn't，答案選 (B)。
● violin [vaɪə`lɪn] (n.) 小提琴　　　● orchestra [`ɔrkɪstrə] (n.) 管絃樂團

**答案** 1.(A) 2.(B) 3.(A) 4.(C) 5.(B)

6. That is Mrs. Henderson's husband, isn't _____ ?
   (A) he
   (B) she
   (C) it
   (D) that

7. Those are the dogs' towels, aren't _____ ?
   (A) those
   (B) them
   (C) they
   (D) these

8. Let's dance, _____ we?
   (A) will
   (B) can
   (C) could
   (D) shall

9. Don't forget, _____ you?
   (A) will
   (B) won't
   (C) would
   (D) do

10. Please, come in and sit down, _____ you?
    (A) will
    (B) won't
    (C) would
    (D) wouldn't

**6.** 那是安德森太太的先生，不是嗎？

解析 附加問句一律得以代名詞代替原主詞，但不要因為直述句提到 Mrs. Henderson's husband，就填入代名詞 he。本句主詞不是 Mrs. Henderson's husband，而是指示代名詞 that，所以附加問句的主詞用 it，不可用 that，答案選 (C)。只要直述句是「That/This is＋N」，附加問句的主詞一律用 it。

● husband [`hʌsbənd] (n.) 丈夫

---

**7.** 那些是狗兒用的毛巾，不是嗎？

解析 本題使用指示代名詞 those 當主詞。只要直述句是「Those/These are＋N」，附加問句的主詞一律用複數的 they，所以答案選 (C)。

● towel [`tauəl] (n.) 毛巾

---

**8.** 咱們來跳舞好嗎？

解析 本題測驗重點：祈使句的附加問句。遇到表示勸誘的「Let's＋原形動詞」，附加問句一律用 shall we，故選 (D)。

● dance [dæns] (v.) 跳舞

---

**9.** 不要忘了，好嗎？

解析 本題測驗重點：祈使句的附加問句。本題的祈使句屬於「請求對方幫忙、下令」的一種，附加問句一律用 will you?，所以答案選 (A)。

● forget [fɚˋgɛt] (v.) 忘記

---

**10.** 請進來坐，好嗎？

解析 本題測驗重點：祈使句的附加問句。本題的祈使句屬於「邀請對方做某事」的一種，附加問句一律用 won't you?，所以答案選 (B)。

● come in 進來

答案 6.(C) 7.(C) 8.(D) 9.(A) 10.(B)

# Level ② 挑戰多益 *650*

請從 (A)、(B)、(C)、(D) 中選出一個最適合的答案。

☐ **1.** Hey, you over there. Try to be a little quieter, _____ you?
(A) won't
(B) will
(C) can
(D) could

☐ **2.** Your mother-in-law _____ move in with you, _____ she?
(A) has ; hasn't
(B) won't ; will
(C) will not ; won't
(D) None of the above

☐ **3.** The people who live in Tokyo _____ really angry about it, _____ ?
(A) aren't ; are they not
(B) are ; aren't they
(C) are not ; are them
(D) were; were they

☐ **4.** There _____ left to do, _____ there?
(A) is nothing ; is
(B) isn't anything ; is
(C) are no tasks ; are
(D) All of the above

☐ **5.** A: Humans aren't the same species as gorillas, are they?
B:_____, they _____.
(A) Yes ; aren't
(B) Yes ; not
(C) No ; aren't
(D) No ; are

**1.** 喂，那邊的人安靜一點，可不可以？

解析 祈使句的形式有很多種，遇到請求對方幫忙或下令的祈使句，附加問句用 will you?，故答案選 (B)。

● quiet [`kwaɪət] (adj.) 安靜的

**2.** 你婆婆不會和你們一起搬進去吧？

解析 從空格後面的原形動詞 move 可知，直述句的時態與完成式無關，空格應該填入未來式助動詞 will，後面才會接原形動詞。選項 (C) 的兩個答案都是否定的，不可選，故答案選 (B)。代名詞 she 代替前面的 your mother-in-law。

● mother-in-law 婆婆，岳母

**3.** 那些住在東京的人對此真的很生氣，是吧？

解析 第一空格要填入 be 動詞，主詞是 the people，所以空格應填入 are。直述句為肯定句，所以第二空格要填入否定的附加問句，答案選 (B)，they 代替前面的 the people。選項 (A) 的問題出在兩個答案都是否定。選項 (C) 的問題出在第二個答案，are 後面必須用主格 they，而不是受格 them。選項 (D) 則是兩個答案都是肯定，也不能選。

● be angry about＋N：對……感到生氣

**4.** 接下來沒什麼要做的，對吧？

解析 本題測驗重點：there is/are... 的附加問句。句型「There is/are＋N」作「有……」解釋，表達一種「存在的狀態」。動詞的單複數由後面的名詞，也就是主詞來決定。選項 (A)、(B)、(C) 都是正確答案，而且有個共通點：第一個答案都讓直述句形成否定句。選項 (A) 的不定代名詞 nothing 是單數，be 動詞用 is；因為 nothing 本身帶有否定意義，形同否定句；選項 (B) 的不定代名詞 anything 也是單數，be 動詞的否定式 isn't；選項 (C) 中 no tasks 的 no 是否定用字。所以，這三個選項的附加問句全須用肯定句，答案為 (D) 皆可。

● task [tæsk] (n.) 任務

**5.** A：人類和大猩猩不是同一物種吧？

B：沒錯，他們不是。

解析 本題考的是附加問句的回答方式。附加問句的回答與一般 Yes/No 問句無異，本題動詞為 be 動詞，肯定回答為 Yes, they are.，否定回答為 No, they aren't.，所以答案選 (C)。

● human [`hjumən] (n.) 人類　　　● gorilla [gə`rɪlə] (n.) 大猩猩

答案 1.(B) 2.(B) 3.(B) 4.(D) 5.(C)

☐ **6.** A yard _____ three feet, _____ ?
   (A) is ; isn't it
   (B) isn't ; is it not
   (C) isn't ; isn't it
   (D) isn't ; are they

☐ **7.** You _____ a few dollars you could lend me, _____ you?
   (A) have ; haven't
   (B) haven't ; do
   (C) don't have ; do
   (D) don't have ; haven't

☐ **8.** Nobody saw the prisoner escape, _____ ?
   (A) didn't they
   (B) did they
   (C) didn't he
   (D) did he

☐ **9.** Someone has taken the money, _____ ?
   (A) has they
   (B) hasn't they
   (C) have they
   (D) haven't they

☐ **10.** You had a successful business trip to Hong Kong, _____ ?
   (A) had you
   (B) didn't you
   (C) were you
   (D) hadn't you

**6.** 一碼等於三英尺，是嗎？

解析 在附加問句的句型中，前面的直述句用否定，後面就要用肯定；前面用否定句，後面就用肯定，因此 (B)、(C) 明顯不是答案。(D) 選項的附加問句動詞並沒有對應到前句的主詞 a yard，因此也不能選，只有 (A) 是正確答案。

- yard [jɑrd] (n.) 碼，院子
- inch [ɪntʃ] (n.) 吋

**7.** 你沒有錢可以借我，對吧？

解析 第一空格要填入意思與「擁有」相關的動詞。選項 (C) 的 don't have 是動詞 have 的否定型態，因為 have 是一般動詞，所以附加問句要用助動詞 do，(C) 即為正確答案。選項 (A) 的問題出在第二個答案：haven't 要改成 don't。(B) 是用現在完成式的助動詞 haven't 作為混淆的選項，因此不能選。(D) 選項中前方直述句用的是否定的 don't have，後方的附加問句應該用 do you，因此也非正確答案。

- lend [lɛnd] (v.) 借出

**8.** 沒人看到犯人脫逃，對吧？

解析 如果直述句的主詞是不定代名詞 nothing/nobody/someone/somebody/everyone 等等，附加問句的人稱代名詞一律用 they。本句主詞是 nobody，本身具否定意義，附加問句要用肯定，答案選 (B)。

- prisoner [`prɪsənə] (n.) 犯人，囚犯
- escape [əˋskep] (v.) 脫逃

**9.** 有人把錢拿走了，對吧？

解析 本句主詞 someone 是不定代名詞，所以附加問句的主詞必須用 they。直述句的動詞用現在完成式 has taken，附加問句也要用完成式，因為 they 為複數人稱，故助動詞要用 have 而不用 has，答案選 (D)

- take [tek] (v.) 拿走

**10.** 你到香港談生意很成功，不是嗎？

解析 附加問句的基本句型為「肯定句＋否定附加問句」與「否定句＋肯定附加問句」。由動詞 had 可看出本句為過去式肯定句，因此附加問句須寫成過去式否定句 didn't you？。

- have a business trip 出差
- successful [səkˋsɛsfəl] (adj.) 成功的

答案 6.(A) 7.(C) 8.(B) 9.(D) 10.(B)

129

# Unit 11 不定詞

商務主題
**訂單送貨**

## 不定詞概述

● 不定詞的型態是「to＋原形動詞」。不定詞不是句子，而是作為名詞、形容詞或副詞，主要用來表達「目的、意願、尚未完成的事」。

**用商務英文學多益句型**

## 不定詞　必考重點句

### 不定詞基本用法

## I told them to send the package to my business address.
**我叫他們把包裹寄到我公司地址。**

不定詞最常見有「受詞」、「補語」、及「受詞補語」三種用法。另外，不定詞偶爾也可以當「主詞」用，但是較舊式的用法。

不定詞當 like 的受詞

➲ Do you like **to play video games**?
　 你喜歡打電動嗎？

不定詞 to believe in yourself 當主詞 The most important thing 的補語

➲ The most important thing is **to believe in yourself**.
　 最重要的是你要相信自己。

不定詞當受詞 me 的補語

➲ She told me **not to cry**.
　 她叫我不要哭。

To know her 是本句的主詞

➲ **To know her** is to love her.
　 瞭解她就是愛她。

### 接不定詞當受詞的動詞

## Would you like us to send your order COD?
**你希望貨到付款嗎？**

want、need、would like、plan、hope、expect、decide、agree、refuse 等動詞，若後方要接另一個動詞，一定要用不定詞 to＋原形動詞的型態。

➲ I plan **to study** physics in university.
　 我計畫在大學念物理學。

➲ Which movie did you decide **to see**?
　 你決定要看哪一部電影？

## Would it be possible to send my order by airmail?
**我的訂單可以用空運寄送嗎？**

不定詞可以當「主詞」使用，但經常用虛主詞 it 代替，不定詞則移到句尾，it
之後也可加上「for＋人」，表示「對……而言」。

meet people from other<br>untries 是真主詞

➲ **It** is interesting **to meet people from other countries**.
認識各國不同的人很有趣。

express your feelings<br>真主詞，for you 是做<br>定詞動作的人。

➲ Is **it** difficult **for you** to express your feelings?
表達感覺對你來說困難嗎？

不定詞當副詞用

## If your order is damaged, we'll be glad to replace it at no cost.
**若貨物受損，我們樂意免費換貨給您。**

不定詞可以當「副詞」使用，用來修飾動詞或形容詞，意思是「為了……」。

ve 修飾動詞 eat，to<br>修飾動詞 live。

➲ We eat **to live**, not live **to eat**.
我們吃飯是為了活著，而活著不是為了吃飯。

stay healthy 修飾動<br>exercise

➲ I exercise every day **to stay healthy**.
我每天運動以保持健康。

other you 修飾形容<br>orry

➲ I'm sorry **to bother you**.
很抱歉打擾你。

不定詞當形容詞用

## We have lots of packages to ship.
**我們有很多包裹要運送。**

不定詞也可以當作「形容詞」，用來修飾名詞或代名詞。

y 修飾代名詞<br>hing

➲ Do you have anything **to say**?
你有什麼話想說嗎？

e in 修飾名詞<br>tment

➲ I'm looking for an apartment **to live in**.
我在找一間公寓住。

## We reserve the right not to ship orders with incorrect billing addresses.

帳單地址不正確的訂單，我們保留不出貨的權利。

不定詞的否定型態是 not + V。

⊃ My father told me **not to goof around**.
　我父親叫我不要遊手好閒。

⊃ She gets up early in order **not to miss** the school bus.
　她早起趕搭校車。

## The invoice states the amount owed and where to send payment.

發貨單上載明應付金額以及付款地址。

不定詞可以和疑問詞（如：who、what、how、why、where 等）或連接詞 whether 連用，構成不定詞片語。

what to do 當動詞 know 的受詞

⊃ I don't know **what to do**.
　我不知道該怎麼辦。

when to quit 當動詞 know 的間接受詞

⊃ Some people don't know **when to quit**.
　有些人不懂得什麼時候該放棄。

whether to have the chicken or the fish 當動詞 wonder 的受詞

⊃ I'm wondering **whether to have** the chicken or the fish.
　我在考慮要吃雞肉還是魚。

## This product is too heavy to ship by airmail.
這個產品太重無法空運。

too + adj./adv. + to V 的句型是「太……所以不能……」的意思。本句型也可以用 so + adj./adv. + that... 改寫。

⊃ She is **too young to go** to school.
　= She is **so young that** she can't go to school.
　她年紀太小，所以不能去上學。

⊃ He ran **too slowly to win** a prize.
　= He ran **so slowly that** he didn't win a prize.
　他跑太慢了，無法贏得獎品。

## Level 1   挑戰多益 *450*

請從 (A)、(B)、(C)、(D) 中選出一個最適合的答案。

☐ **1.** Do you want _____ it or not?
(A) do
(B) to do
(C) doing
(D) to doing

☐ **2.** Harold _____ move to Hawaii.
(A) plans to
(B) plans
(C) has plans
(D) is planning

☐ **3.** The teacher said that _____ good grades one must work very hard.
(A) get
(B) to get
(C) getting
(D) gotten

☐ **4.** When he asked her if she likes _____ movies, she said that she does.
(A) watch
(B) watched
(C) will watch
(D) to watch

☐ **5.** It's often stated that to see is _____.
(A) believing
(B) to believe
(C) believable
(D) to be believed

*1.* 你要做還是不做？

解析 動詞 want 後面出現另一個動詞時，要將動詞轉為不定詞 to V 作為其受詞，故答案選 (B)。

*2.* 哈洛德打算搬去夏威夷。

解析 句子裡已經有一個動詞 move，前面空格要填的動詞 plan 用法必須為「plan＋to V」，不定詞 to move 作為 plan 的受詞，故答案選 (A)。
● move to＋地點：搬到某處

*3.* 老師說想得到好成績就必須非常努力用功。

解析 不定詞和動名詞的差別在於，不定詞有「為了……」表目的的意涵，而動名詞的意思則偏於「動詞的名詞化」。根據語氣，本題應當用 to get good grades（為了要得到好成績）。
● grade [ɡred] (n.) 成績

*4.* 他問她是否喜歡看電影時，她回答她喜歡。

解析 like＋to V 是「喜歡……」的意思，也可以用 like＋Ving，不定詞和動名詞都可以當 like 的受詞，故答案為 (D) to watch。
● quiet [`kwaɪət] (adj.) 安靜的

*5.* 常言道：眼見為憑。

解析 To see is to believe. 等於 Seeing is Believing. 主詞與補語必須是對稱的，to see 要和 to believe 對稱，seeing 則與 believing 對稱，故此題選 (B)。
● state [stet] (v.) 陳述，說明　　　　　● believe [bɪ`liv] (v.) 相信

答案 1.(B) 2.(A) 3.(B) 4.(D) 5.(B)

6. _____ yourself is the highest achievement in life.
   (A) Know
   (B) To know
   (C) Knowledge
   (D) All of the above

7. I think it is quite difficult _____ French.
   (A) learns
   (B) to learn
   (C) learning
   (D) for learning

8. It is easy _____ me to write an English e-mail.
   (A) to
   (B) with
   (C) on
   (D) for

9. The post is too _____ into that hole.
   (A) big to fit
   (B) big a fit
   (C) big to fitting
   (D) big that to fit

10. The computer system has crashed again! Didn't I tell you _____ open suspicious e-mails?
    (A) not
    (B) not to
    (C) no
    (D) can't

**6.** 了解自己是生命中最大的成就。

解析 本句動詞為 is，反身代名詞 yourself 不可作為主詞，故需要選項 (B) 的不定詞 To know 形成不定詞片語，作為主詞。

● achievement [ə`tʃivmənt] (n.) 成就

**7.** 我覺得學法文蠻難的。

解析 「it is＋形容詞＋ to V」的句型中，it 作為虛主詞，用來代替後面的不定詞，故答案選 (B)，指「學法文」這件事很困難。

● quite [kwaɪt] (adv.) 頗　　　　　　● difficult [`dɪfɪkəlt] (adj.) 困難的

**8.** 寫一封英文電子郵件對我來說是很簡單的。

解析 在「it is＋形容詞＋to V」的虛主詞句型中，若要加上「對……來說」，介系詞要用「for＋人」，且要放在不定詞前方，故答案選 (D)。

● easy [`izɪ] (adj.) 簡單的

**9.** 這竿子太大放不進那個洞。

解析 too...to V 用法為 too＋adj./adv.＋to V，故答案選 (A)。

● post [pɔst] (n.) 竿子；郵件　　　● hole [hol] (n.) 洞

**10.** 電腦系統又壞掉了！我不是跟你說不要開可疑的電子郵件嗎？

解析 前句說到電腦壞了，表示後句應該是說之前有強調「不要去做某事」。在英文中，「不要去做」就會用 not to V 的寫法，因此答案選 (B)「不要去開可疑的電子郵件」。can't 是助動詞，不會出現在這個位置。

● suspicious [sə`spɪʃəs] (a.) 可疑的

答案 6.(B) 7.(B) 8.(D) 9.(A) 10.(B)

# Level ② 挑戰多益 *650*

**請從 (A)、(B)、(C)、(D) 中選出一個最適合的答案。**

☐ **1.** She was embarrassed to tell her new friend that she doesn't know how _____ a bicycle.
(A) to ride
(B) ride
(C) riding
(D) will ride

☐ **2.** The problem is just that your English is _____ to take this beginning class with us.
(A) good
(B) best
(C) better
(D) too good

☐ **3.** We are not convinced that you are experienced _____ to take this position.
(A) a lot
(B) more
(C) very
(D) enough

☐ **4.** Don't worry. I'll remind you when _____ time to leave for the meeting.
(A) its
(B) it
(C) it's
(D) it has

☐ **5.** Because he has lived in Tokyo for a month, Hector is the best person _____ our guide.
(A) to be
(B) to have been
(C) for
(D) with

*1.* 她很尷尬地告訴她的新朋友，說她不知道如何騎腳踏車。

解析 how to do sth.（如何做）、what to do（做什麼）、where to go（去哪裡）等是常用的「疑問詞＋不定詞」形成的片語。本句的 how to ride a bicycle 作為動詞 know 的受詞，故選 (A)。

● embarrassed [ɪm`bærəst] (adj.) 尷尬的；困窘的

---

*2.* 問題是你的英文太好了，不能跟我們一起上初級課程。

解析 problem 一字暗示出後面應該接帶有否定意味的敘述。too... to... 是「太……所以不能……」的意思，例如 too short to slam dunk（太矮所以不能灌籃），故選 (D)。反之，enough to V 則是「夠……而可以……」的意思，如：your English is good enough to take the advanced class（你的英文夠好，可以上進階課程）。

● adj./adv.＋enough＋to V：夠…而可以…

---

*3.* 我們不相信你的經驗足以擔任這項職務。

解析 enough to 是「足夠……」的意思。experienced 當作形容詞，指「有經驗的」。enough當作副詞修飾形容詞、動詞或副詞時，必須要放在被修飾詞的後面。故選 (D)。

● convince [kən`vɪns] (adj.) 確定的

---

*4.* 別擔心，開會的時間到了，我會提醒你。

解析 看到句子後方有 time to leave for the meeting，可推知前方應是用虛主詞的句型 it's time to V 表示「做某事的時間到了」，答案選 (C)。

● remind [rɪ`maɪnd] (v.) 提醒　　　　　● leave for＋地方：前往某地

---

*5.* 因為海克特在東京已經住一個月了，所以他是我們最佳的導遊人選。

解析 空格內應填入不定詞 to V，作形容詞用，修飾 the best person；to be... 有「使成為……」的意思，答案選 (A)。注意：不定詞是由「to＋原形動詞」所組成，所以 to be 中的 be 不能改為 am/is/are 等。

● guide [gaɪd] (n.) 嚮導

---

答案 1.(A) 2.(D) 3.(D) 4.(C) 5.(A)

**6.** Because Bernice wasn't flexible _____ to compromise, she lost the bid to someone else.
(A) well
(B) enough
(C) much
(D) very

**7.** We review the material frequently in order _____ forget what we've learned.
(A) to
(B) not
(C) not to
(D) don't

**8.** It was _____ that we decided to stay indoors all day long.
(A) hot
(B) very hot
(C) so hot
(D) hotter that

**9.** The purpose of the mask is _____ the eyes and face.
(A) protect
(B) for protect
(C) to protect
(D) All of the above

**10.** It is better _____ anything than _____ stupid.
(A) not to say ; to sound
(B) to not say ; sounding
(C) not saying ; sounding
(D) None of the above

**6.** 因為班尼司在協調上不夠有彈性,所以她失去了她的出價標的,讓別人拿走了。

解析 後一句說她「失去了」她的標的,表示前一句應該是說她「不夠」有彈性,應該選 enough。well「好地」和 much「很多」都修飾不可數名詞,very「非常」則修飾形容詞,這三個選項都不合適。

- compromise [`kɑmprə,maɪz] (n./v.) 妥協,讓步
- bid [bɪd] (v./n.) 命令,喊價;出價,投標

---

**7.** 我們時常複習這些資料,以免忘記我們曾學過的東西。

解析 in order to 是「為了……」,否定時把 not 放在不定詞 to V 的前面即可,有「以免」的意思。

- material [mə`tɪrɪəl] (n.) 素材,資料
- frequently [`frikwəntlɪ] (adv.) 頻繁地,屢次地

---

**8.** 天氣好熱,所以我們決定一整天都待在室內。

解析 so...that... 是「如此……以致於……」的意思,故選 (C)。選項 (A) hot 或 (B) very hot 後面不會接 that 子句,可接表「因果關係」的連接詞 so,如:It was very hot, so we decided to stay indoors all day long. 但這種表達方式語意上則沒有 so... that... 來得強烈。

- indoors [ɪn`dɔrz] (adv.) 在室內
- all day long 整天

---

**9.** 面罩的目的是要保護眼睛和臉。

解析 本句的主詞為 the purpose of the mask,動詞為 is,而 protect 也是動詞,所以必須以不定詞呈現,作為補語之用,故答案為 (C)。

- purpose [`pɝpəs] (n.) 意圖,目的
- mask [mæsk] (n.) 面罩

---

**10.** 與其說出蠢話,不如什麼都不說。

解析 這題考的是特殊句型 It is better＋to V,以句子的語意來判斷,第一空格的不定詞應用否定詞 not to V。另外,遇到連接詞 than 作比較的時候,前後兩個結構應該一致,前面用不定詞,後面的動詞 (sound...) 也一定要用不定詞 to sound。故答案選 (A)。

- better [`bɛtɚ] (adj.) 最好

答案 6.(B) 7.(C) 8.(C) 9.(C) 10.(A)

# Unit 12 動名詞

**動名詞概述**

● 動名詞的形式是 Ving，亦即，在動詞後面加上 ing。

● 動名詞是名詞，不是動詞，可以當句中的主詞、補語、受詞等等。

**用商務英文 學多益句型**

## 動名詞　必考重點句

### 動名詞當主詞用

## Purchasing an extended warranty is a good idea.
**購買延長保固是個好主意。**

動名詞可以當主詞：此時主詞當成「一件事」，故動詞必須用單數。

○ **Drinking too much coffee is** bad for your health.
咖啡喝太多有害身體健康。

○ **Writing letters takes** too much time.
寫信太花時間了。

letters 是複數，但動詞不會因此用複數，因為 letters 只是主詞的一部分。本句的主詞是 writing letters（寫信）這一件事，視為單數。

### 動名詞當主詞補語

## The most difficult task was negotiating the contract.
**最困難的任務是協議合約內容。**

動名詞可以放在 be 動詞後當主詞補語，修飾或補充說明主詞。

○ My hobby **is collecting stamps**.
我的嗜好是集郵。

○ My favorite leisure activity **is playing tennis**.
我最喜歡的休閒活動是打網球。

○ The only sport he's good at **is swimming**.
他唯一擅長的運動是游泳。

**動名詞當受詞**

## The lawyer spent several days drafting the contract.
律師花了幾天草擬合約。

有些動詞後面不可接不定詞 (to V)，只能接動名詞 (Ving) 當受詞，例如：enjoy（喜歡）、stop（停止）、quit（戒除）、practice（練習）、finish（完成）、mind（在意）、avoid（避免）、spend（花費）等等。

➲ He **quit/stopped** gambling.
他已經戒賭了。

➲ Jessie **practices** playing the piano every day.
傑西每天練習彈鋼琴。

➲ Andy **finished** writing his essay and then went to bed.
安迪寫完作文便上床睡覺。

➲ Would you **mind** opening the window?
你介意把窗戶打開嗎？

**動名詞當介系詞的受詞**

## Do you plan on accepting the employment contract?
你打算接受這份聘雇合約嗎？

在介系詞（片語）後方若要接一個動詞，必須將它換成動名詞。

e fond of＋N/Ving
示「喜歡…」

➲ He is fond **of** going out at night.
他喜歡晚上出去玩。

e good at＋N/Ving
示「擅長於…」

➲ She is good **at** baking cookies.
她很會烤餅乾。

e worth＋N/Ving
示「值得…」

➲ The book is **worth** reading.
這本書值得讀一讀。

eam of＋N/Ving
示「夢想…」

➲ He dreams **of** traveling around the world someday.
他夢想有一天可以環遊世界。

e interested in＋N/Ving
示「對…感興趣」

➲ He's interested **in** building models.
他對做模型很感興趣。

系詞 by＋N/Ving
示「方法，途徑」

➲ Mr. Huang earns his living **by** teaching.
黃先生以教書為生。

接動名詞 / 不定詞意義相同的動詞

## The salesman began explaining/to explain the warranty terms.

**業務員開始解釋保固條款。**

有些動詞後面可接動名詞 (Ving) 或不定詞當受詞，意義皆同。這一類的動詞有 like、love、hate、continue、start、begin、stand 等。

➲ I **like/love** **swimming**. = I **like/love** **to swim**.
　我喜歡游泳。

➲ She **hates** **making** mistakes. = She **hates** **to make** mistakes.
　她討厭犯錯。

➲ He **continued** **telling** the story. = He **continued** **to tell** the story.
　他繼續說故事。

➲ The baby **began/started** **crying**. = The baby **began/started** **to cry**.
　小嬰兒開始哭了起來。

➲ I can't **stand** **waiting** in line. = I can't **stand** **to wait** in line.
　我受不了排隊。

接動名詞 / 不定詞後意義不同的動詞

## I forgot sending/to send the warranty card to the manufacturer.

**我忘了已寄過 / 要寄保證卡給製造商。**

另外有一些動詞後面可以接「動名詞」也可以接「不定詞」當作受詞，但是兩者意思不同。這一類動詞有：try、stop、forget、remember 等。

Ving 表示「已經聊過天了」，接在 forget 後方表示「忘記了這件事」。

➲ I **forgot** **chatting** with her at the bus stop.
　我忘記曾經和她在公車站牌聊天。

to V 表示「還沒說」，接在 forget 後方指的是「之後（不要忘記）說」。

➲ Don't **forget** **to say** good night to your parents before going to bed.
　別忘了上床前要跟父母道晚安。

停止抽菸的動作；也就是說「原本在抽菸」。

➲ He **stopped** **smoking** when the teacher came.
　當老師來的時候，他停止抽菸。

停止原本手邊在做的事，開始抽菸；也就是說「還沒抽菸」。

➲ He **stopped** **to smoke**.
　他停下來抽菸。

# Level 1  挑戰多益 *450*

**請從 (A)、(B)、(C)、(D) 中選出一個最適合的答案。**

1. The moment the window broke the little infant started _____.
   (A) cry
   (B) crying
   (C) cried
   (D) cries

2. Are you interested _____ a puppet show?
   (A) to seeing
   (B) in seeing
   (C) of going to see
   (D) to go see

3. _____ healthily is especially important for pregnant women.
   (A) Eating
   (B) Will eat
   (C) Eat
   (D) By eating

4. You can get to Gimpo Airport _____ the subway from downtown Seoul.
   (A) in taking
   (B) by take
   (C) to take
   (D) by taking

5. We should stop _____ some gas before we get on the freeway.
   (A) buying
   (B) to buy
   (C) buy
   (D) bought

**1.** 窗戶破掉的那一剎那，小嬰兒哭了起來。

> 解析 動詞 start 後面可能接不定詞（to V）或動名詞（Ving），意思皆同。答案選 (B)。
> 注意：the moment 連接詞相當於 when。

● infant [`ɪnfənt] (n.) 嬰兒

**2.** 你對木偶戲感興趣嗎？

> 解析 片語 be interested in 表示「對……感興趣；喜歡……」。介系詞 in 後面只能接名
> 詞或動名詞，故答案選 (B)。

● puppet [`pʌpɪt] (n.) 木偶

**3.** 健康的飲食對孕婦特別重要。

> 解析 本題已有動詞 is，所以句首的動詞 eat 必須改為動名詞當主詞，答案選 (A)，不
> 可選 (C)。動名詞當主詞視為一件事，用來陳述事實，動詞用單數 is。選 (B) 表未
> 來，不合句意。選項 (D) 的介系詞 by 表示「藉由（方法）」，介系詞片語無法當
> 主詞。

● pregnant [`prɛgnənt] (adj.) 懷孕的

**4.** 你從首爾市中心搭地鐵可以到達金浦機場。

> 解析 「get to＋地點」的意思是「到達……」。搭乘交通工具用 by 表示「方法；手
> 段」。因為 by 是介系詞，後面只能接名詞（交通工具名稱）；如果要接動詞，動
> 詞一定要變成動名詞，所以答案選 (D)。注意：用「by＋交通工具」時，交通工具
> 前面不需要定冠詞 the。例：I go to work by subway every day.「我每天搭地鐵上
> 班。」

● subway [`sʌbˌwe] (n.) 地下鐵　　　　● downtown [`daʊn`taʊn] (n.) 市中心

**5.** 我們上高速公路之前應該停車加點油。

> 解析 stop 是這一句的主要動詞，後方不可能再接動詞，因此不能選 (C)、(D)。stop 後
> 方接 to V 和 Ving 文法都通，但是意義不同，因此必須根據句意來判斷。stop to V
> 是「停止現在手邊的事，去進行 to V 這件事」；stop Ving 則是「停止目前正在進
> 行的事」。根據句意，上高速公路前應該是要「停車去加油」，因此答案要選 (B)
> to buy。

● gas [gæs] (n.) 汽油；瓦斯　　　　● freeway [`friwe] (n.) 高速公路

答案 1.(B) 2.(B) 3.(A) 4.(D) 5.(B)

**6.** Thank you _____ me with my homework.
- (A) for help
- (B) for helping
- (C) for helped
- (D) helping

**7.** _____ is definitely not easy.
- (A) Quitting smoking
- (B) To quit smoke
- (C) Quit smoking
- (D) Quitting smoke

**8.** Robert doesn't _____ well, but James is good at _____ .
- (A) singing ; it
- (B) sing ; sing
- (C) sing ; singing
- (D) sings ; singing

**9.** If you're free tonight, how about _____ a movie?
- (A) seeing
- (B) go see
- (C) going
- (D) see

**10.** His worst habit, _____ his nails, totally drives me crazy!
- (A) biting
- (B) to bite
- (C) is biting
- (D) was biting

**6.** 謝謝你協助我的作業。

解析 句型「Thank＋人＋for＋N/Ving」表示「為了……謝謝某人」。介系詞 for 後面只能名詞或動名詞，所以答案選 (B)。

● help 人 with 物：協助某人…

---

**7.** 戒菸真的很不容易。

解析 本句缺少主詞。選項 (A)、(D) 動名詞或選項 (B) 不定詞均有可能當主詞。動詞 quit 作「戒除、停止（某種習慣）」解釋，這個字後面只能接名詞或動名詞，故選 (A)。

● definitely [`dɛfənətlɪ] (adv.) 著實地；確切地

---

**8.** 羅伯特歌唱得不是很好，但詹姆士很會唱歌。

解析 第一空格前面是 doesn't，所以後面空格必須填入原形動詞 sing。第二空格是介系詞 at 的受詞，介系詞後面要接動名詞 singing，故選 (C)。「be good at＋N/Ving」表示「對……很擅長」，例：Tina is good at playing chess.「蒂娜很會下棋。」

● be good at... 擅長於…

---

**9.** 如果你今天晚上有空，我們去看場電影好不好？

解析 「how about＋N/Ving」表示「提議（做某事）」。因為 about 是介系詞，所以後面必須接名詞或動名詞，選項 (A) 的 seeing 為正確答案。選項 (C) 如果改成 going to 也是正確答案。「看電影」可用 see a movie、go to a movie、go to the movies 等片語表達。

● free [fri] (adj.) 有空的；免費的

---

**10.** 他有個習慣非常糟糕——咬指甲，真是讓我抓狂！

解析 本句主詞是 His worst habit，動詞是 drives，drive 作「逼使、迫使（人）……」解釋，後面需要人作受詞，再接形容詞 (crazy) 作受詞補語，用來說明受詞 me 處於什麼狀態。兩個逗號所夾的字表「同位語」，與主詞 His worst habit 指同一件事，所以應將動詞 bite 名詞化，轉為動名詞 biting，故選 (A)。

● nail [nel] (n.) 指甲　　　　　● drive sb. crazy 使人抓狂

答案 6.(B) 7.(A) 8.(C) 9.(A) 10.(A)

請從 **(A)**、**(B)**、**(C)**、**(D)** 中選出一個最適合的答案。

☐ **1.** In order to prepare for the trip to Mexico, she and I _____ several months learning Spanish.

(A) used

(B) took

(C) spent

(D) cost

☐ **2.** _____ the door, she saw that her apartment had been robbed.

(A) Upon opening

(B) When she open

(C) Was opening

(D) When opened

☐ **3.** I really don't _____ cleaning the apartment today, as I have other things to do.

(A) want to

(B) want

(C) feeling like

(D) feel like

☐ **4.** I can't talk to him _____ angry.

(A) without get

(B) not to get

(C) without getting

(D) not getting

☐ **5.** I can't stand _____ so long to be served at a restaurant.

(A) have to wait

(B) having to wait

(C) having waiting

(D) to have waiting

*1.* 為了準備墨西哥之旅，我和她花了好幾個月學習西班牙文。

解析 表示「花費了……時間」，若主詞是人 (she and I)，動詞必須用 spend（過去式和過去分詞皆為 spent），句型是「人＋spend＋時間＋Ving」（某人花了某時間做某事），spend 後面的動詞一律用 Ving，故本題選 (C)。(A) used 是「使用」，後面不會接時間，通常是接「實體的物品」或是「手段」，因此不能選。

● prepare [prɪ`pɛr] (v.) 準備

---

*2.* 一打開門，她就發現她的公寓被洗劫了。

解析 介系詞 upon 指「在……時間後立即」，後面應接名詞或動名詞，故選 (A)。upon opening the door 意指「在打開門的那一刻」。選項 (B) 由連接詞 when 引導，動詞應改成過去式 opened。

● rob [rɑb] (v.) 搶劫

---

*3.* 我今天很不想打掃公寓，因為我有其他事情要做。

解析 空格後是動名詞 cleaning，因此答案要選一個後方可以接 Ving 的動詞。選項中只有 feel like（想要）後面要接名詞或動名詞，另外因為空格前方有助動詞的否定式 don't，因此後方要選原型動詞的選項，故選 (D)。

● apartment [ə`pɑrtmənt] (n.) 公寓

---

*4.* 我每次跟他說話一定會生氣。

解析 本句要配合選項先釐清句意，(B) 是不定詞的否定式，表示「不要……」，前方的句子應是表示建議的語意：I told him not to get angry. 因此不能選 (B)。其它選項則是在考 not/never...without 雙重否定的句型，用來強調「每……必……」之意。介系詞 without 後面要接名詞或動名詞，所以選 (C)。

● participate [pɑr`tɪsəpet] (v.) 參加，參與

---

*5.* 我無法忍受在餐廳裡必須等這麼久才有人服務。

解析 stand 是「忍受」的意思。stand＋to V/Ving 是「忍受某事」的意思，選項 (A) 即不符合此用法。stand 後面可接不定詞與動名詞，選項 (B) 將 have to 變化為動名詞 having to，後面接原形動詞表「必須（做某事）」，故 (B) 為正解，而 (C) having 後應改成不定詞。選項 (D) 雖用了不定詞，但 to 後面應該直接接上不能忍受的動作：to wait。

● serve [sɝv] (v.) 上菜；服務

---

答案 1.(C) 2.(A) 3.(D) 4.(C) 5.(B)

6. It is fun _____ games, but sometimes _____ hard is necessary.
   (A) playing ; to work
   (B) playing ; working
   (C) playing ; work
   (D) to play ; work

7. I don't mind _____ your stories, but don't expect me _____ them.
   (A) listening ; believing
   (B) to listening ; believe
   (C) listening to ; to believe
   (D) to listen ; to believe

8. You could make some money _____ selling that car you never _____ .
   (A) by ; drive
   (B) for ; driving
   (C) by ; driving
   (D) for ; drive

9. _____ drugs _____ a good way to land yourself in jail.
   (A) Selling ; are
   (B) Sell ; is
   (C) To sell ; are
   (D) Selling ; is

10. Jordan's parents _____ about _____ him a car for his sixteenth birthday.
   (A) thought ; getting
   (B) think ; get
   (C) are thinking ; to get
   (D) thinking ; getting

**6.** 玩遊戲是很有趣，但有時候努力工作也是必要的。

> [解析] 句型「It is fun＋to V/Ving」表示「（做）……是很有趣的」。fun「樂趣」是名詞，第一空格可填入不定詞 to play 或動名詞 playing。第二空格後面的動詞是單數 is，空格處欠缺主詞，可填入不定詞或動名詞，但應與前句一致，故答案選 (B)。

- necessary [`nɛsəˏsɛrɪ] (adj.) 必要的

---

**7.** 我不介意聽聽你的故事，但不要期待我會相信。

> [解析] 動詞 mind 作「介意；在乎」解釋，這個字後面只能接動名詞。動詞 expect 作「期待，指望」解釋，後面必須接不定詞。所以答案選 (C)。注意「listen to＋某人 / 某事」，一定要介系詞 to，才能接聆聽的對象（受詞）。

- mind [maɪnd] (v.) 介意
- expect [ɪks`pɛkt] (v.) 期待

---

**8.** 你可以把你那輛從不開的車子賣了，賺一點錢。

> [解析] 依照句意，第一空格要填入介系詞 by。by 表示「方法，途徑」，後面只能接名詞或動名詞，如空格後面的動名詞 selling。第二空格缺少一般動詞，因為「that car you never...」是關係子句修飾前面名詞的結構，其中主詞是 you，後面必須接動詞，that car you never drive 意思是「你從不開的車子」，故答案選 (A)。

---

**9.** 販賣毒品只會讓你快一點進監牢。

> [解析] 本句缺少主詞和動詞。第一空格要填入動名詞或不定詞當主詞，不管是動名詞或是不定詞當主詞，都當成一件事情看待，所以動詞一定用單數的 is。故答案選 (D)，選項 (C) 則須將動詞改為單數的 is。

- drug [drʌg] (n.) 毒品；藥品
- jail [dʒel] (n.) 監獄

---

**10.** 喬丹的父母考慮買一輛汽車給他當作十六歲的生日禮物。

> [解析] 本句缺少動詞。第一空格無論填入過去式 thought，還是現在進行式 are thinking 皆可。第二空格前面是介系詞 about，所以後面要接動名詞 getting。故選項 (A) 是正確答案。「think about＋N/Ving」作「考慮，打算」解釋。

- get 人＋物：給某人…

---

[答案] 6.(B) 7.(C) 8.(A) 9.(D) 10.(A)

# 分詞當形容詞

## 分詞的種類

- 分詞有兩種：現在分詞的型態是 Ving，過去分詞簡稱 p.p.。分詞主要的功能為表示不同的動詞時態。

- 分詞常當作情緒形容詞使用。「過去分詞」表示被動，用來修飾「被引起情緒者」，通常是有生命的「人」。「現在分詞」表示主動，通常用來修飾「引起情緒者」，通常是無生命的「物」。

**用商務英文學多益句型** | **分詞當形容詞** 必考重點句

### 分詞修飾名詞

## We had to cancel our scheduled business dinner.
**我們必須取消預定的商務晚餐。**

分詞形態的形容詞與一般形容詞一樣，可置於名詞前面修飾名詞，或置於 be 動詞與連綴動詞之後作為補語。現在分詞 (Ving) 作形容詞時，表示所修飾的名詞是「主動」進行該動作者；過去分詞 (p.p.) 作形容詞時，則表示所修飾的名詞是「被動」承受該動作者。

石頭主動落下，用 Ving 當形容詞。

⊃ Watch out for **falling** rocks along the road
　小心沿路的落石。

窗戶是被打破的，用 p.p. 當形容詞。

⊃ Could you get someone to fix the **broken** window?
　你可以請人修理破掉的窗戶嗎？

### 現在分詞 Ving 當情緒形容詞

## The president gave an interesting speech at the company dinner.
**董事長在公司餐會上發表了一段有趣的演說。**

情緒動詞 bore/excite/interest/surprise 表示「使無聊 / 使興奮 / 使感興趣 / 使驚訝」，這些動詞也可以換成分詞型態變成情緒形容詞。轉為現在分詞 (Ving) 時，表示主詞是「令人感到……的」，後方的介系詞會用 to。

⊃ This news is **surprising** **to** us.
　這個消息對我們而言很意外。

⊃ The ending of the movie was a little **confusing**.
　那部電影的結尾有點令人困惑。

過去分詞 p.p. 當情緒形容詞

## Chuck was surprised at winning the raffle at the year-end dinner.

查克贏得尾牙摸彩大獎很驚訝。

情緒動詞轉為過去分詞 (p.p.) 時，可以用來形容「人（對某事）感到……」，後方搭配的介系詞會因字而異。

| 對……感到無趣 | be bored **with**... |
| 對……感到興奮 | be excited **about**... |
| 對……感到興趣 | be interested **in**... |
| 對……感到驚訝 | be surprised **at**... |
| 對……感到厭倦 | be tired **of**... |
| 對……感到感動 | be touched **by**... |
| 對……感到驚嚇 | be scared **of**... |
| 對……感到困惑 | be confused **by/about**... |
| 對……感到麻煩 | be troubled **by**... |
| 對……感到尷尬 | be embarrassed **about**... |
| 對……感到滿意 | be satisfied **with**... |
| 對……感到高興 | be pleased **with**... |

➲ His mother was **touched by** the card he made.
他母親被他做的卡片感動了。

➲ They're **tired of** eating frozen food.
他們已經對冷凍食物感到厭倦了。

➲ The little girl is **scared of** spiders.
小女孩很怕蜘蛛。

➲ Michael is **interested in** comics.
麥可對漫畫很感興趣。

## Don't forget to have reservations made for the company dinner next Friday.

**不要忘記要把下禮拜五的公司晚宴先預定好。**

分詞可以當作動詞（get、make、have、keep、leave、feel 等等）的補語，句型為「動詞＋受詞＋Ving/p.p.」。Ving 表示受詞是「主動地進行」這件事，p.p. 則表示受詞是「被動地」接受這個動作，且有「完成」意味。

受詞 leaky roof 是「被」修理的，用 p.p. 表被動。

➲ You should **get** that leaky roof **fixed**.
你應該把那漏水的屋頂修好。

受詞 picture 是「被」拍的，用 p.p. 表被動。

➲ She doesn't like to **have** her picture **taken**.
她不喜歡被拍照。

受詞 him 主動進行「跑」這件事，用 Ving 表主動。

➲ I **saw** him **running** in the rain.
我看見他正在雨中奔跑。

# Level **1**　挑戰多益 *450*

**請從 (A)、(B)、(C)、(D) 中選出一個最適合的答案。**

**1.** Tell me what you are _____.
(A) interesting
(B) interested in
(C) interested
(D) interesting in

**2.** Nobody likes me. I think I must be too _____.
(A) bored
(B) boring
(C) bore
(D) boredom

**3.** Mary _____ by the news of her father's illness.
(A) was troubling
(B) is trouble
(C) was troubled
(D) troubled

**4.** A: Is it serious, Doctor?
B: Well, these test results do look _____.
(A) trouble
(B) troubled
(C) troubling
(D) as trouble

**5.** Are you _____ with your meal, sir?
(A) satisfaction
(B) satisfy
(C) satisfied
(D) satisfying

**1.** 告訴我你對什麼有興趣。

解析 情緒動詞 interest 的過去分詞 interested 表「（人）感到有興趣的」，現在分詞 interesting 則表「（物）令人感到有趣的」。此處修飾的是人（you），故應用 interested。另外，特別要注意，名詞子句的 what 為受詞，故必須使用介系詞 in，答案為 (B)。

● interested [`ɪntrəstɪd] (adj.) 感興趣的

**2.** 沒有人喜歡我，我想我一定是太無趣了。

解析 這題要特別注意，雖然主詞為人（I），但他是引起別人覺得無趣的人，故應用現在分詞 boring 來修飾，答案為 (B)。

● boredom [`bɔrdəm] (n.) 厭煩，厭倦

**3.** 瑪莉為她父親生病的消息而心神不寧。

解析 由 by 一字可推知本題應用被動，情緒動詞 trouble 的被動用法為「人＋be 動詞＋troubled by＋物」，故選 (C)。

● illness [`ɪlnɪs] (n.) 疾病，病

**4.** A：很嚴重嗎，醫生？

B：嗯，這些檢查結果看起來確實令人擔憂。

解析 題目的動詞為感官動詞 look「看起來⋯⋯」，後面應接形容詞，只有 troubled 或 troubling 可考慮。此處修飾的是物（test results），故用 troubling（令人心煩的）。此外，前面的 do 為強調用法，意思是「確實」。

● result [rɪ`zʌlt] (n.) 結果

**5.** 您滿意您的餐點嗎，先生？

解析 情緒動詞 satisfy 意思是「使⋯⋯滿意」，修飾人時的句型為「人＋be 動詞＋satisfied with＋物」，故答案為選項 (C)。

● meal [mil] (n.) 餐點

答案 1.(B) 2.(B) 3.(C) 4.(C) 5.(C)

6. Don't you ever get _____ that stupid video game?
   (A) tired of
   (B) tire with
   (C) tiring of
   (D) tired

7. I'm very _____ about the exam next week.
   (A) worried
   (B) worry
   (C) worrying
   (D) worries

8. Army life is very _____.
   (A) tiring
   (B) tired
   (C) tire
   (D) tired of

9. Getting lost in the wilderness was a _____ experience.
   (A) terrify
   (B) terrifying
   (C) terrified
   (D) terrifies

10. The girl's parents were _____ by the news that she was safe.
    (A) relieve
    (B) relief
    (C) relieving
    (D) relieved

6. 你難道從來不會對那個蠢透了的電動玩具感到厭倦嗎？

解析 情緒動詞 tire 意思是「使厭倦；使疲倦」，修飾人時的句型為「人＋be/get tired of/with＋物」，與介系詞 of 連用指「（心理上）感到厭倦」，與介系詞 with 連用時指「（生理上）感到疲倦」，故答案為選項 (A)。

● video game 電動玩具

---

7. 我非常擔心下週的考試。

解析 情緒動詞 worry 意思是「使擔憂」，修飾人時的句型為「人＋be 動詞＋worried about＋物」的用法，答案為選項 (A)。

● worried [ˋwɝɪd] (adj.) 擔心的

---

8. 從軍生涯非常累人。

解析 本題主詞是物（army life），應用現在分詞 tiring（累人的）來修飾，故答案為選項 (A)。

● army [ˋɑrmɪ] (n.) 陸軍部隊

---

9. 在野外迷路是個恐怖的經驗。

解析 主詞是 getting lost 這件事情，後方應用現在分詞來修飾此經驗是「令人覺得恐怖的」，答案為 (B)。

● wilderness [ˋwɪldɚnɪs] (n.) 荒野

---

10. 女孩的父母得知她平安後鬆了一口氣。

解析 主詞是 the girl's parents，by 後面的事件「讓」他們感到鬆一口氣，要用過去分詞來修飾主詞被引起的情緒，答案為 (D)。

● relieve [rɪˋliv] (v.) 緩和，減輕（痛苦、負擔）

答案 6.(A) 7.(A) 8.(A) 9.(B) 10.(D)

# Level 2  挑戰多益 *650*

請從 (A)、(B)、(C)、(D) 中選出一個最適合的答案。

☐ **1.** Aren't you _____ going to the dance without a date?
(A) embarrassed to
(B) embarrassed about
(C) embarrassing to
(D) embarrassing

☐ **2.** The players were all very _____ because it was their first time playing in a foreign country.
(A) excite
(B) exciting
(C) excited
(D) excitement

☐ **3.** Laurence of Arabia _____ everyone by marching his army across the Arabian Desert.
(A) surprised
(B) was surprising to
(C) was surprised
(D) surprising

☐ **4.** This grammar is _____ to me. I keep getting things _____.
(A) confused ; confusing
(B) confused ; confused
(C) confusing ; confusing
(D) confusing ; confused

☐ **5.** When Darryl quit his job last month, his co-workers were sorry _____ him go.
(A) to see
(B) seeing
(C) saw
(D) seen

**1.** 沒有攜伴參加舞會你不會難為情嗎？

解析 情緒動詞 embarrass 的過去分詞 embarrassed 表「（人）感到難為情的」，現在分詞 embarrassing 則表「（物）令人感到難為情的」。此處修飾的是人（you），故應用 embarrassed。其句型為「人＋be動詞＋embarrassed about/at＋物」的用法，故答案為選項 (B)。

● date [det] (n.) 約會對象

**2.** 選手們全都非常興奮，因為那是他們第一次在外國比賽。

解析 情緒動詞 excite 的過去分詞 excited 表「（人）感到興奮的」，現在分詞 exciting 則表「（物）令人感到刺激的」。此處修飾的是人（the players），故應用 excited，故答案選 (C)。

● foreign [`fɔrɪn] (adj.) 國外的

**3.** 阿拉伯的勞倫斯行軍橫跨阿拉伯沙漠，震驚了每個人。

解析 本句缺少動詞，從語意上瞭解，勞倫斯是做出壯舉之人，而且句中又有介系詞 by ＋marching...（藉由……）作為副詞修飾動詞用，故空格應填入動詞 surprised（surprise 的過去式），答案為選項 (A)。

● march [mɑrtʃ] (v.) 行軍

**4.** 這個文法對我來說太令人混淆了，我一直把事情搞混了。

解析 第一句情緒動詞的用法為「物＋be 動詞＋現在分詞＋to＋人」；第二句用法為「人＋get＋物＋過去分詞」，這裡的 get 是「使……（成某種狀態）」之意。

● keep＋Ving：持續地…

**5.** 上個月達利爾辭職時，他的同事都對他離去感到遺憾。

解析 非分詞型態的情緒形容詞修飾人時的句型為「人＋be 動詞＋sorry to V」故答案為選項 (A)。

● quit [kwɪt] (v.) 停止，戒掉　　● co-worker [`ko,wɝkɚ] (n.) 同事，共事者

答案 1.(B) 2.(C) 3.(A) 4.(D) 5.(A)

**6.** The woman wore a very _____ dress.
(A) reveal
(B) revealed
(C) revealing
(D) reveals

**7.** You look _____ about something. What's the matter?
(A) trouble
(B) troubled
(C) troubling
(D) troubles

**8.** The driver said the accident occurred because he _____ the brake and the gas pedals.
(A) confuses
(B) confused
(C) confusing
(D) confuse

**9.** What a _____ it is to see you! This is so _____ because I'm only here for a day.
(A) surprising ; surprised
(B) surprised ; surprising
(C) surprise ; surprising
(D) surprise ; surprise

**10.** The teacher is _____ the slow progress of his students.
(A) frustrating
(B) frustrate
(C) frustrated by
(D) frustrated for

**6.** 這個女人穿著一件非常暴露的洋裝。

解析 此處欠缺的是形容詞。一般動詞的現在分詞當形容詞表「主動、進行」，過去分詞則表「被動、完成」。現在分詞 revealing 指衣服露出許多身體部位，意為「暴露的，袒胸露肩的」，屬主動用法，故選 (C)。

- revealing [rɪˋvilɪŋ] (adj.) 暴露的

**7.** 你看起來為某事所苦，怎麼了？

解析 題目的動詞為感官動詞 look「看起來……」，後面應接形容詞，只有 troubled 或 troubling 可考慮。此處修飾的是人（you），故用 troubled（感到心煩的），句型為「人＋look troubled about＋物」。

- What`s the matter? 怎麼了？

**8.** 該名駕駛說意外之所以發生是因為他把煞車和加油踏板搞混了。

解析 because 引導子句，需要主詞（he）和動詞，故空格需要填入動詞 confused（confuse 的過去式），答案為 (B)。

- brake [brek] (n.) 煞車
- pedal [ˋpɛdl] (n.) 加油踏板

**9.** 見到你真是個驚喜！這真是一個驚喜啊，因為我只來這裡一天而已。

解析 「What a＋名詞＋it is...」為驚嘆句的用法，故第一空格應選名詞 surprise。第二空格應填入現在分詞修飾主詞 this，指「這件事令人驚喜」，句型為「物＋be 動詞＋surprising」，故答案為選項 (C)。

- for＋一段時間：長達…的時間

**10.** 這位老師對他的學生進步緩慢感到挫折。

解析 由空格前後的 be 動詞與 by 可推知本題應用被動，情緒動詞 frustrate 的被動用法為「人＋be 動詞＋frustrated by＋物」，答案為選項 (C)。

- progress [ˋprɑgrɛs] (n.) 進步

答案 6.(C) 7.(B) 8.(B) 9.(C) 10.(C)

# 形容詞

## 形容詞概述

- 形容詞用來說明事物的性質或特徵，例如 beautiful、fluent、exciting、handsome...，其「比較級」和「最高級」變化會在下一個章節一併介紹。
- 「基數」和「序數」也是形容詞的一種。基數詞是 one、two、three「一、二、三」等等，序數詞是 first、second、third「第一、第二、第三」等等。
- 形容詞一般可置於名詞前或 be 動詞後，但有些敘述性的形容詞只能放在 be 動詞之後當作補語，例如 afraid、alone、asleep、alive、awake、unable 等等。

**用商務英文
學多益句型**

## 形容詞　必考重點句

### 形容詞的基本用法

**If the product is defective, it can be returned for a refund.**

**如果產品有瑕疵，可以退費。**

形容詞用來修飾名詞，一般放置於名詞之前。它也可放在 be 動詞或連綴動詞後方，此時形容詞為「補語」。

形容詞置於名詞前

➲ The **beautiful girl** can speak fluent **English**.
那位漂亮的女孩會說流利的英文。

➲ It's an **exciting game**.
那是場令人興奮的比賽。

形容詞放在 be 動詞後，
修飾主詞。

➲ The groom is **handsome** and the bride is **beautiful**.
新郎帥，新娘美。

➲ My dream finally came **true**.
我的夢想終於成真。

### 冠詞、形容詞、名詞的排序

**The two large new factories will begin production next month.**

**這兩家大型新工廠下個月開工。**

若有一串形容詞用來修飾名詞時，排列順序通常為：

冠詞→數量→大小→長短→性質→顏色→國籍出處→材料→名詞。

⊃ I bought **an expensive brown leather coat**.
　我買了一件貴重的棕色皮夾克外套。

⊃ **Those ten run-down old red brick houses** will be torn down next month.
　那十間破舊的老紅磚屋將於下個月拆除。

---

英文的序數與基數

## Every tenth product on the assembly line is inspected for quality.
### 裝配線上每十件產品即品管檢測一次。

基數詞要變化成序數詞一般字尾加上 **th** 即可，但是部分序數詞有固定拼法，並且會依據字尾產生變化。變化方式如下表：

| | 基數 | 序數 | | 基數 | 序數 |
|---|---|---|---|---|---|
| 1 | one | **first** | 11 | eleven | eleven**th** |
| 2 | two | **second** | 12 | twelve | twel**fth** |
| 3 | three | **third** | 13 | thirteen | thirteen**th** |
| 4 | four | four**th** | 20 | twenty | twent**ieth** |
| 5 | five | fi**fth** | 21 | twenty-one | twenty-**first** |
| 6 | six | six**th** | 30 | thirty | thirt**ieth** |
| 7 | seven | seven**th** | 100 | one hundred | one hundred**th** |
| 8 | eight | eigh**th** | 101 | one hundred and one | one hundred and **first** |
| 9 | nine | nin**th** | | | |
| 10 | ten | ten**th** | 1000 | one thousand | one thousand**th** |

⊃ There are **three** cars over there; the **second** one is mine.
　那邊有三輛車，第二輛是我的。

⊃ The **two** girls are from Japan. The **first** is from Tokyo and the **second** is from Osaka.
　那兩個女孩來自日本。第一個是東京人，第二個是大阪人。

⊃ **One third** of our products are exported to Europe.
　我們三分之一的產品出口到歐洲。

數詞＋序數詞」
形成「分數」，例
one third（三分之
、two thirds（三分
之）。

## Hundreds of cars roll off the production line every day.

生產線上每天生產數百輛汽車。

hundreds of... 是「數以百計的……」，thousands of... 是「數以千計的……」，「數以萬計的」則用 tens of thousands of...。

⊃ **Millions of** Africans live in poverty.
　上百萬的非洲人生活在貧窮之中。

⊃ **Thousands of** factory workers have been laid off.
　數千名員工被解雇。

## The manufacturer was able to improve product quality.

製造商可以改進產品品質。

有些形容詞沒有比較級的變化，只能當作補語，放在 be 動詞或連綴動詞後面，不能放在名詞前面。這類的形容詞有 **afraid**、**alone**、**asleep**、**alive**、**awake**、**unable** 等等。

⊃ I'm **afraid** of the dark.
　我怕黑。

⊃ He couldn't fall **asleep**, and lay **awake** in bed all night.
　他睡不著，整晚醒著躺在床上。

⊃ I was **unable** to afford a car.
　我養不起車子。

## Strict standards ensure the quality of Swiss watches.

嚴格的標準保證瑞士錶的品質。

專有名詞形成的形容詞，以大寫字母開頭。例如 **English**、**French**、**American**、**Greek**、**Japanese**、**Taipei** 等。

⊃ Alex is an **English** teacher.
　艾力克斯是英文教師。

⊃ I like **Japanese** food very much.
我很喜歡日本料理。

⊃ How can I get to **Taipei** Station?
我要怎麼到台北車站？

**物質名詞演變成的形容詞**

## The plastic toys are assembled at a factory in China.
**這些塑膠玩具是在中國的工廠組裝的。**

物質名詞直接當形容詞用時，沒有比較級的變化。例如：**stone**、**brick**、**gold**、**silver**、**iron**、**wood** 等。從物質名詞演化而來的形容詞也沒有比較級的變化。例如：**sunny**、**rainy**、**windy**、**wooden**、**golden**、**stony** 等。

⊃ She sat on a **stone** wall.
她坐在石牆上。

⊃ The little pig lived in a **brick** house, while his brothers lived in a **wood** house and a **straw** house.
小豬住在磚屋，而他的哥哥們住在木屋和稻草屋。

⊃ I don't like **rainy** days; I prefer **sunny** ones.
我不喜歡雨天，我比較喜歡晴天。

**複合形容詞**

## New labor-saving robots were installed on the assembly line.
**裝配線上安裝了新型的省力機器人。**

兩個字以上結合而成的形容詞為「複合形容詞」，通常以現在分詞與過去分詞的型態出現，形成規則如下：

+ Ving
詞＋現在分詞）

⊃ We enjoyed the **breathtaking** mountain scenery.
我們觀賞令人嘆為觀止的山景。

+ Ving
容詞＋現在分詞）

⊃ His brother is a **good-looking** guy.
他的哥哥長得很好看。

+ Ving
詞＋現在分詞）

⊃ We painted the room with **quick-drying** paint.
我們用快乾漆油漆房間。

| | |
|---|---|
| N + p.p.<br>（名詞＋過去分詞） | ⊃ My grandfather is **bed-ridden**.<br>我爺爺臥病在床。 |
| | |
| adj. + p.p.<br>（形容詞＋過去分詞） | ⊃ She sells cheap **ready-made** clothes at a local market.<br>她在本地市場裡賣便宜的成衣。 |
| | |
| adv. + p.p.<br>（副詞＋過去分詞） | ⊃ He was impressed by the **well-planned** project.<br>他提出一個周詳的企劃案。 |
| | |
| p.p. + prep.<br>（過去分詞＋介系詞） | ⊃ He threw away the **torn-up** letter.<br>他丟掉那張撕裂的信紙。 |
| | |
| adj. + N-ed<br>（形容詞＋字尾加上 ed<br>的名詞） | ⊃ She fell in love with a **good-mannered** gentleman.<br>她愛上那位風度翩翩的紳士。 |

**the＋形容詞：表某類的人或事物**

## The Japanese make good luxury cars, but the best are made by the Germans.
日產的豪華轎車品質良好，但德國產的才是世界第一。

「the＋形容詞」或「指示代名詞＋形容詞」可用來表示某類的人或事物。

⊃ **The wounded** were rushed to the hospital for treatment.
傷者被緊急送到醫院治療。

⊃ Robin Hood took from **the rich** and gave to **the poor**.
羅賓漢劫富濟貧。

⊃ Many of **those invited** are under eighteen.
許多受邀的人還不滿十八歲。

# Level 1　挑戰多益 *450*

**請從 (A)、(B)、(C)、(D) 中選出一個最適合的答案。**

☐ **1.** Several _____ people were in line to buy tickets for the new movie.
(A) groups
(B) few
(C) dozen
(D) ten

☐ **2.** At least _____ of the cars here were made in Japan.
(A) one third
(B) one
(C) some
(D) all

☐ **3.** We figured they were probably _____ by looking at their clothes.
(A) German
(B) Europe
(C) Mandarin
(D) Spain

☐ **4.** He asked the _____ girl what she wanted for her birthday.
(A) ten
(B) ten year
(C) ten years old
(D) ten-year-old

☐ **5.** The _____ woman is married to the man in the blue suit.
(A) good looks
(B) good-looking
(C) looking good
(D) look-good

*1.* 好幾十人排隊買票要看新的電影。

解析 空格內應填入形容詞，修飾後面的 people。選項 (B) groups 後面如果有介系詞
of，就可選。選項 (B) 的 few 可當形容詞，但性質與 several 重複，若去掉其中之
一即可。選項 (C) dozen 原意為「一打，十二個」，當形容詞可作「十幾個」解
釋，several dozen 或 a few dozen 意思是「數十個」，故選 (C)。

● in line 排成一排

*2.* 這裡至少有三分之一的車是日本製的。

解析 at least 是「至少」的意思，後面應該接一個明確的量，如選項 (A) one third（三分
之一）。注意，這裡的 one third 是分數的用法，為「基數／序數」，整個可以視
作代名詞。選項 (B) one 雖是明確的量，但因為後面動詞用 were，所以不能選。選
項 (C) some 因為不明確，也不能選。選項 (D) all 會和 At least 矛盾，沒有「至少
全部」這種講法。

● at least 至少

*3.* 看他們的衣著，我們覺得他們可能是德國人。

解析 表國籍的字可當名詞，也可當形容詞。如選項 (A) German 可指「德國人」或「德國
籍的」，在本題中作形容詞用，因此字尾不加 s。選項 (B) Europe 是歐洲，「歐洲
人」要用 European。選項 (C) Mandarin 是中文。選項 (D) Spain 則是西班牙，「西
班牙人」要用 Spanish。

● probably [ˋprɑbəblɪ] (adv.) 或許

*4.* 他問那個十歲的女孩想要什麼生日禮物。

解析 十歲是 ten years old，但如果要把這個詞當作形容詞用，必須使用連字號，形成「複
合形容詞」：ten-year-old，注意中間的 year 必須要用單數，不能用 years。

*5.* 那位美麗的女子嫁給了穿藍色西裝的男子。

解析 複合形容詞的形成法有許多種，本題用的是「形容詞＋現在分詞」：good-looking
（好看的）。the man in the blue suit 是指「穿藍色西裝的男子」的意思。

● be married to... 和某人結婚

答案 1.(C) 2.(A) 3.(A) 4.(D) 5.(B)

**6.** The police knew the problem was serious when _____ of people called to complain.

(A) ten

(B) couple

(C) many

(D) hundreds

**7.** This picture frame looks _____, but I think it's actually made of plastic.

(A) wood

(B) woods

(C) woody

(D) wooden

**8.** The medic's job is to attend to those _____ in battle.

(A) wound

(B) wounds

(C) wounded

(D) wounding

**9.** One-fifth of the products were damaged during shipment, which is 20 _____.

(A) percentage

(B) hundred

(C) percents

(D) percent

**10.** The shipment left Keelong today and will arrive a week later on _____.

(A) fifteen

(B) the fifteenth

(C) the fifteen

(D) fifteenth

6. 數百名群眾打電話來抱怨，警方才知道問題嚴重了。

解析 常見的數量形容詞有 hundreds of（好幾百的；數以百計的）、thousands of（好幾千的）、many（許多的）。因為題目中已經有了 of，所以不能選 (A) ten 或 (C) many（只能用 ten people、many people）。選項 (B) couple 是「一對；兩個」的意思，經常以 a couple of＋N 來表現，在 couple 之前必須加冠詞才行。

- complain [kəm`plen] (v.) 抱怨

7. 那相框看起來是木頭做的，但是我認為其實是塑膠。

解析 「木頭製的」有兩種講法，可以用 be made of wood 或直接用形容詞 wooden。本題用到動詞 look（看起來……），後面要直接加形容詞，因此選 wooden。

- frame [frem] (n.) 框架，骨架

8. 軍醫的工作是照顧那些戰場上的傷兵。

解析 「指示代名詞＋形容詞＝名詞」。wounded 當形容詞是「受傷的」的意思，這裡用 those wounded 表示「受傷的人」。

- medic [`mɛdɪk] (n.) 軍醫
- attend to... 照料…

9. 五分之一的產品在運送過程中受損，也就是百分之二十。

解析 one-fifth 是「五分之一」，也就等於 twenty percent。注意：percent 前面的數字不管是多少，percent 都不加 s。

- percent [pɚ`sɛnt] (n.) 百分之一

10. 貨物今天由基隆運出，將於一週後抵達，也就是十五號。

解析 日期的表示方式應用「the＋序數」表示。選項中只有 (B) 符合，the fifteenth 即是「十五號」。

- 一段時間＋later/ago：（…時間）之後／以前

答案 6.(D) 7.(D) 8.(C) 9.(D) 10.(B)

## Level ② 挑戰多益 650

**請從 (A)、(B)、(C)、(D) 中選出一個最適合的答案。**

☐ **1.** He was given a prize for being the _____ person to shop at the new store.
- (A) one hundred
- (B) hundreds
- (C) hundred
- (D) hundredth

☐ **2.** She noticed that every day she studied, the foreign language became more and more _____.
- (A) understand
- (B) understanding
- (C) understood
- (D) understandable

☐ **3.** It may not have been your sweater, but I did see something _____ in the back of the car.
- (A) clothes
- (B) wear
- (C) yours
- (D) red

☐ **4.** All the salesmen in our company want to date Shirley because she is such a _____ woman.
- (A) fund-raising
- (B) good-looking
- (C) hair-raising
- (D) hot-headed

☐ **5.** The two songs are in foreign languages; _____ is in German, and _____ is in Spanish.
- (A) one ; two
- (B) the first ; the second
- (C) first ; second
- (D) the one ; the other

*1.* 他是第一百個在那家新開幕商店消費的人，因而得到一個獎品。

解析 一個人不可能成為一百個人，只能成為「第一百個人」，所以本題選 (D) hundredth
（第一百的）。

● prize [praɪz] (n.) 獎品，獎項

*2.* 她發現每天學習，外語就會變得愈來愈容易理解。

解析 more and more... 是「愈來愈……」的意思，這是形容詞的用法，因此本題只能
選「形容詞」，understand 是動詞，所以不能選。現在分詞 understanding 是「瞭
解的」，過去分詞 understood 是「被瞭解的」，而 understandable 是「可瞭解
的」。根據文意，應當選 (D)。

● notice [`notɪs] (v.) 注意　　　　　　● language [`læŋgwɪdʒ] (n.) 語言

*3.* 那可能不是你的毛衣，但是我確實在車子後座看到某件紅色的東西。

解析 要形容 something、anything、nothing 等，形容詞必須放在這些詞的後面，例如
something red、nothing difficult 等。

● sweater [`swɛtɚ] (n.) 毛衣

*4.* 我們公司裡所有的業務都想跟雪莉約會，因為她是如此漂亮的女人。

解析 複合形容詞通常不難判斷其意思，由「名詞／形容詞＋現在分詞」組成的形容詞
代表「主動」，如：a hair-raising movie（令人毛骨悚然的電影）；而由「名詞／
形容詞＋過去分詞」組成的形容詞則代表「被動」，如：man-made shoes（手工
鞋）。這一題根據句意應選 (B) good-looking（好看的）。

● date [det] (v./n.) 與…約會；約會（的對象）
● good-looking [`gʊd`lʊkɪŋ] (adj.) 外表好看的

*5.* 那兩首歌是外文歌，第一首是德文歌，第二首是西班牙文歌。

解析 前句提到兩首歌，空格必須填入序數 the first（第一）及 the second（第二），不能
只用基數 one 和 two。若要用不定代名詞，則用 one（其中之一）及 the other（另
一個）。

● foreign [`fɔrən] (a.) 外文的　　　　　● German [`dʒɝmən] (a.) 德語的，德國的

答案 1.(D) 2.(D) 3.(D) 4.(B) 5.(B)

☐ **6.** The company manufactures _____ car mirrors at its factory in China and exports them to The United States and Canada.

(A) round small metal

(B) small round metal

(C) metal small round

(D) small metal round

☐ **7.** Your incompetence has resulted in the loss of _____ of dollars of company money.

(A) thousand

(B) 10 thousand

(C) tens

(D) thousands

☐ **8.** I've been to Hong Kong on business _____ of times.

(A) dozen

(B) a dozen

(C) two dozens

(D) dozens

☐ **9.** Nearly _____ the people on the _____ island live below the poverty line.

(A) a half ; dense population

(B) half of ; densely-populated

(C) half ; dense-populated

(D) one half ; population density

☐ **10.** More than _____ of our company's employees are over the age of 50.

(A) a third

(B) third

(C) the third

(D) one out three

**6.** 這間公司在中國廠生產鐵製汽車小圓鏡，並出口到美國和加拿大。

解析 本句有一串形容詞修飾名詞 car mirrors，排列順序為：大小 (small) → 形狀 (round) → 材料 (metal)，答案應選 (B)。

- manufacture [`mænjə`fæktʃə] (v.) 生產
- export [ɪk`spɔrt] (v.) 出口

---

**7.** 你的無能已經造成本公司好幾千美元的金錢損失。

解析 thousand 是「千」，前面加數字時 thousand 不可加 s，如：ten thousand dollars （一萬美元）；若要表示「好幾千」則說 thousands of，前面不可再加數字。

- incompetence [ɪn`kɑmpətəns] (n.) 無能力；不適任

---

**8.** 我已經去香港出差過許多次。

解析 dozen 是「十二個，一打」，要表達「幾打⋯⋯」應用「數字＋dozen＋複數名詞」，如：one dozen eggs、two dozen eggs，不管是幾打，dozen 均不加 s，這種用法同 hundred 和 thousand。而 dozens of 則是指「好幾打的；許多的」。

- on business 出差
- dozen [`dʌzn̩] (n.) 一打，十二個；十來個

---

**9.** 在這個人口密度極高的島嶼上，幾乎有一半的人生活在貧困線下。

解析 第一個空格後有 the people，前方不能再放分數形式的代名詞 (a half/one half)，必須用所有格用法 (B) half of 或是指示形容詞的用法 (C) half the people。另外，複合形容詞中 populated 是過去分詞「居住的」，要修飾這個動作前方應該要用副詞 densely，因此答案選 (B)。

- poverty line 貧困線
- densely-populated [`dɛnzlɪ `pɑpjəletɪd] (adj.) 密度極高的

**10.** 本公司三分之一以上的員工超過五十歲。

解析 「幾分之幾」的表達方式為「分子為基數，分母為序數」，如：one third（三分之一）、two thirds（三分之二）。其他像 a half（二分之一）則為固定的用法，而 one fourth（四分之一）或 three fourths（四分之三）也可用 a quarter 或 three quarters 表示。

- employee [ɛm`plɔɪi] (n.) 雇員，員工

答案 6.(B) 7.(D) 8.(D) 9.(B) 10.(A)

## 副詞的種類

- 用來修飾「動詞」、「形容詞」和「副詞」的詞是「副詞」。
- 副詞依詞彙意義可大略分為「地點副詞」、「時間副詞」、「情狀副詞」、「程度副詞」、「頻率副詞」以及其他不屬於這五類的副詞。

用商務英文
學多益句型

**副詞**　必考重點句

時間副詞的時態

### The R&D department will unveil the new product next month.
**研發部下個月將公開新產品。**

時間副詞可用於表達「將要發生」、「過去發生的事」或「經常發生的事」。根據不同的時間副詞，會搭配未來式、過去式或現在式。常見的時間副詞與時態搭配如下：

| 現在式 | 過去式 | 未來式 |
|---|---|---|
| now | yesterday | tomorrow |
| every day | last night | tonight |
| most days | before | someday/some day/one day |
| still | the day before yesterday | next month |
| currently | | later |
| | | soon |

- ➲ **Are** you going **to watch** TV **tonight**?
  你今晚要看電視嗎？

- ➲ **Will** you be a doctor **someday**?
  你將來要當醫生嗎？

- ➲ I **was** a student **before**, but I **am** a teacher **now**.
  我以前是學生，但現在是老師。

表達常態時，無須特別加上時間副詞。

- ➲ Tom **is** **usually** late for work.
  湯姆上班常遲到。

- ➲ It **is/was** cold **this morning**.
  今天早上很冷。

**ago、since、和 still**

## The engineers haven't finished developing the product yet.

**工程師還沒有完成產品的開發。**

1. 表達「在……之前」的時間副詞有 ago 和 before，常與「過去簡單式」連用，但 ago 前面會加上時間，而 before 則不加時間。

2. 表達「自從……」的時間副詞有 since，常與「完成式」連用。用於完成式中表示「已經」的副詞，則有肯定語氣的 already 和否定、疑問語氣的 yet。

3. still 是「仍然」，常用於 be 動詞後或一般動詞前，表示動作的持續。

⊃ My father **died** two years ago.
我爸爸兩年前過世。

⊃ He **was** often late for school **before**.
他以前上學經常遲到。

⊃ She **graduated** three years ago, and **has worked** as a flight attendant **since then**.
她三年前畢業，從那時開始到現在都當空姐。

t 用於疑問句中指
已經」，用於否定句中
指「還（沒）」。

⊃ A: **Have** you **finished** your work yet?
B: No, not **yet**.
A：你已經把工作做完了嗎？
B：不，還沒。

⊃ She has **already** gone to the book fair.
她已經去逛書展了。

⊃ He is **still** eating his dinner.
他還在吃他的晚餐。

**用地點副詞表達動作發生的地方**

## Several new appliances are being developed here at company headquarters.

**幾項新設備正在總公司這裡研發當中。**

地點副詞多放在句尾，或是放在動詞後面來修飾動詞。常見的地點副詞有 here、there、inside、outside、nearby、home 等，或以介系詞 in、at、on、under 等加上場所，也會形成地點副詞。

⊃ The kids are playing **under** the tree.
孩子們正在樹下玩耍。

為The bus comes here.
的倒裝

⊃ **Here <u>comes</u>** the bus.
公車來了。

⊃ I've been looking for you **everywhere**.
我到處找你。

⊃ It was raining heavily **outside** that day.
那天外面雨下得很大。

home 本身可以當作副
詞,前可不加介系詞,
表示「在家」、「回
家」、「到家」和「回
國」等意思。

⊃ Allen will take an airplane **home**.
艾倫會搭機回國。

⊃ My parents live **nearby**, so I don't need to cook at home. Instead, I always go to their house for dinner.
我父母住附近,所以我在家不用煮飯。我反而都去他們家吃晚餐。

**程度副詞**

## The new car is almost ready to go into production.
**新車差不多準備好要量產了。**

「程度副詞」用來表達程度多寡,例如 very、much、so、almost、enough 等。
修飾「形容詞」或「副詞」時,一般會放在所修飾的詞之前,但 enough 須放
在所修飾的詞之後。

⊃ She is **very** tall, while her sister is **very** short.
她很高,但她妹妹很矮。

⊃ My grandfather is **almost** 90 years old.
我祖父快九十歲了。

⊃ It's **so** hot today.
今天真熱。

⊃ My brother isn't <u>**old**</u> **enough** to understand what I'm talking about.
我的弟弟年紀不夠大,不懂我說什麼。

**具否定意義的程度副詞**

## Hardly any of the prototypes were approved for production.
**幾乎沒有一個樣品可以批准生產。**

hardly 是「幾乎不」,scarcely 是「幾乎不」、「決不」等意思,barely
是「僅僅」、「幾乎沒有」的意思。這些程度副詞本身就帶有否定的意思。

➲ I can **hardly** believe my eyes.
我幾乎不敢相信我的眼睛。

➲ There was **scarcely** any traffic on the road.
路上幾乎沒有車。

➲ He **barely** has any money left.
他幾乎一毛錢不剩。

**頻率副詞**

## The company usually introduces a new product line once every two years.
**這間公司通常每兩年推出一條新產品線。**

表達頻率的修飾詞為「頻率副詞」，例如 always、usually 等，用來修飾「動詞」，通常放於一般動詞之後，be 動詞之前。

表示次數的頻率副詞則放在動詞後面，例如一次是 once，兩次是 twice，三次以上用「數字＋times」，即 three times、four times 等。次數後面也可以加上一段時間單位，例如 three times a week（一週三次）、once a month（一個月一次）等。詢問頻率時用 How often...?；詢問次數時則用 How many times... in a week (month/year)?

常用的頻率副詞依照頻率多寡可排列為：

| | |
|---|---|
| always | 總是 |
| usually | 常常，經常 |
| often | 時常，通常 |
| seldom | 不常，很少 |
| rarely | 很少 |
| never | 從不 |

➲ We **always** go to school five days a week.
我們一星期都上課五天。

➲ My father **often** helps me with my homework.
我爸爸常常協助我寫作業。

➲ Many students go to cram school **three times** a week.
許多學生一星期去補習班三次。

○ We have a class reunion **once** a year.
　我們一年開一次同學會。

○ A: **How often** do you exercise?
　B: About **twice** a week.
　Ａ：你多久運動一次？
　Ｂ：大概一星期兩次。

副詞的形成規則請看
p.458

**情狀副詞**

## The software developers tested the program carefully for bugs.
**軟體開發人員仔細測試程式找出錯誤。**

用來描述動作狀態的副詞叫做「情狀副詞」，例如 **carefully**、**happily** 等，通常放在動詞之後。許多情狀副詞都是由「形容詞加上 ly」演變而來。情狀副詞 **honestly**、**frankly**、**obviously** 等通常可以單獨放在句首，用來修飾整個句子。

○ The children **played** happily in the park.
　每個人孩子在公園裡都玩得很開心。

○ Don't **take** it seriously. I'm just kidding.
　別太在意。我只是開玩笑而已。

○ **Obviously**, he didn't understand what I was talking about.
　很明顯，他並不知道我剛剛在說些什麼。

**表達因果的副詞**

## We've increased our R&D staff, and consequently are able to develop products more quickly.
**我們已增加研發成員，因此可以增快研發產品的速度。**

用來表達因果的副詞有：therefore（因此）、consequently（結果；因此）、thus（因此）和 as a result（因而）。

注意，therefore 是副詞，不能連接兩句，必須要用連接詞 and 或另起一句。

分號具有連接詞的功用

○ The laptop is light **and** therefore convenient to carry.
　這台筆電很輕，因此攜帶很方便。

○ The teacher spoke very fast; **as a result**, many students couldn't understand what she was saying.
　那老師說話很快，因此許多學生都不懂她說什麼。

## We are developing a new tablet computer, and so is our competitor.
**我們正在研發一款新的平板電腦，我們的對手也是。**

表示「也」的副詞有 also、too、either、so 等。too 放在肯定「附和句」句尾，either 放在否定「附和句」句尾。附和句也可以「倒裝句」呈現，so 用在肯定倒裝句，neither 用在否定倒裝句。

⊃ He can speak English, and he can **also** speak French.
= He can speak English, and he can speak French, **too**.
他會說英文，也會說法文。

⊃ Ted can't come. Nina **also** can't come.
= Ted can't come. Nina can't come, **either**.
泰德不能來，妮娜也不行。

裝附和句的 be 動詞隨著後面的主詞做變

⊃ I'm a student, and **so** <u>is he</u>.
= I am a student, and he is, **too**.
我是學生，他也是。

裝附和句的助動詞需著後面的主詞做變化

⊃ I don't like coffee, and **neither** <u>**does my husband**</u>.
= I don't like coffee, and my husband doesn't, **either**.
我不喜歡咖啡，我先生也不喜歡。

# Level ① 挑戰多益 *450*

請從 (A)、(B)、(C)、(D) 中選出一個最適合的答案。

**1.** Look how _____ that dog sits and waits for its owner to return.
(A) nice
(B) nicely
(C) proper
(D) very nice

**2.** _____ have you been to the beach this summer?
(A) How
(B) How often
(C) How many times
(D) How many times will

3. _____, the exam wasn't _____ difficult.
(A) Luckily ; terrible
(B) Luckily ; very
(C) Fortunate ; terribly
(D) Lucky ; too

**4.** I was very _____ for school because I woke up _____.
(A) lately ; late
(B) late ; lately
(C) early ; late
(D) late ; late

**5.** Gracie got fired because she doesn't work _____ enough.
(A) fast
(B) fastly
(C) slowly
(D) faster

**1.** 你看那隻狗坐得多好，等牠主人回來。

解析 空格前面的 how 表感嘆，作「多麼的……」解釋，有強調的意味。how 後面可接
副詞或形容詞，至於該選哪一個，關鍵在於句中使用的是一般動詞還是 be 動詞。
本句使用一般動詞 sits，所以答案選 (B)，用副詞 nicely 來修飾動詞。

● owner [`onɚ] (n.) 物主，所有人

**2.** 你這個夏天已經去了海邊幾次？

解析 詢問狀況用 How，但是本題問的並非狀況。How often 是「多常……」，用來問頻
率，答案應選詢問次數的 How many times，have 在句中是表完成式的助動詞，後
面不能再加上 will，故選 (C)。

● beach [bitʃ] (n.) 海灘

**3.** 幸好，考試不會太難。

解析 第一空格應該填入副詞，放在句首來修飾整個句子。第二空格後有形容詞 difficult，
修飾形容詞必須用副詞，very 就是表示「程度」的副詞，故答案選 (B)。

● difficult [`dɪfɪˌkʌlt] (adj.) 困難的

**4.** 我很晚才到學校上課，因為我很晚才起床。

解析 第一空格前有 be 動詞，所以應填入形容詞。第二空格前面是動詞 woke up（原形
為 wake up），所以應填入副詞。early 和 late 的副詞與形容詞均同形，從詞性來
看，選項 (C) 和 (D) 均可考慮，但是 because 所連結的兩個句子應互為因果，(C)
的句意不合，故答案應選 (D)。另外，要注意 lately 也是副詞，意思是「近來，最
近」，與「遲到」無關。

**5.** 葛雷絲被開除了因為她工作不夠快。

解析 這題要選修飾動詞 work 的副詞，按照句意，應該是「工作不夠快」才會「被開
除」，所以 slowly「慢地」與句意不符。fast 的形容詞和副詞同形，答案選 (A)。

● get fired 被開除

答案 1.(B) 2.(C) 3.(B) 4.(D) 5.(A)

**6.** We _____ appreciate your efforts to correct the problem in a timely manner.

(A) very

(B) much

(C) very much

(D) much very

**7.** He _____ didn't want to spend the money, as he kept coming up with excuses.

(A) obviously

(B) nearly

(C) unlikely

(D) practically

**8.** The house is _____ located near the Shilin MRT station.

(A) properly

(B) conveniently

(C) gladly

(D) None of the above

**9.** She'd like to continue walking to work, but her new apartment is too _____ away from her office.

(A) close

(B) far

(C) distant

(D) removed

**10.** I can't play baseball very _____, but I'm good at basketball.

(A) good

(B) better

(C) well

(D) nicely

6. 我們非常感謝你及時糾正錯誤。

解析 very 用來修飾「形容詞原級」或「副詞原級」，much 用來修飾「形容詞比較級」或「副詞原級」。而修飾「動詞」則必須用 very much。appreciate 是動詞，所以用 very much 修飾，位置可放在動詞前，也可放在動詞（＋受詞）後。

- appreciate [əˋpriʃɪet] (v.) 感激；欣賞　　• timely [ˋtaɪmlɪ] (adj.) 及時的；適時的

---

7. 他顯然不想花那筆錢，因為他不斷找藉口。

解析 四個選項都是副詞，obviously 是「明顯地」，nearly 是「幾乎」，unlikely 是「不可能地」，practically 是「實際上」。根據題意，應當選 obviously。

- come up with（針對問題）想出；提供

---

8. 這棟房子位於士林捷運站附近，很方便。

解析 當動詞 locate 作「位於……」解釋時，經常以被動語態表現，且主詞一定是表示地點的名詞，句型為「S＋be located in/at/on/near＋地點」。至於地點前面該用什麼介系詞，依照情況而定，原則上：in＋大地點；at＋小地點；on 指「在……之上」，如馬路、土地、岸……等。本題前三個選項都是副詞，但以句意而言，(B) 才是正確答案。conveniently 用來說明動詞 be located 的狀況很便利。

- conveniently [kənˋvinɪəntlɪ] (adv.) 方便地，便利地

---

9. 她想要繼續走路上班，但是她的新公寓離她的辦公室太遠了。

解析 對等連接詞 but（但是）所連接的是意思相反的兩個句子，故選 (B)。句型「A be far away from B」意為「A 離 B 很遠」，相反的表達方式為「A be close to B」，指「A 離 B 很近」。

- apartment [əˋpɑrtmənt] (n.) 公寓

---

10. 我棒球打得不太好，但我對籃球很在行。

解析 空格應填入副詞，用以說明動詞 play 的狀態。選項 (A) 是形容詞，無法修飾動詞。選項 (B) 是比較級，無法用 very 來修飾。選項 (D) 指「漂亮地；和善地」，不合句意，故選 (C)。well 可指「表現出色；滿意地」。

- S＋be good at＋N：對…很擅長

---

答案 6.(C) 7.(A) 8.(B) 9.(B) 10.(C)

# Level ② 挑戰多益 650

**請從 (A)、(B)、(C)、(D) 中選出一個最適合的答案。**

1. Jack frequently moves into a lower tax bracket because she _____ donates to charity and can therefore deduct that amount from her income.
   (A) often
   (B) never
   (C) likes to
   (D) seldom

2. _____, the bus was a few minutes late, so we were able to catch it.
   (A) Lucky
   (B) Luckily
   (C) Unlucky
   (D) Likely

3. This dish is delicious and nutritious. But _____, it's very easy to make.
   (A) better
   (B) best
   (C) better than all
   (D) best of all

4. We have to keep a close eye on the stock market because stock prices fluctuate quite _____.
   (A) often
   (B) always
   (C) frequent
   (D) many

5. I stayed up very late _____ night, and that's why I'm so tired today.
   (A) this
   (B) that
   (C) some
   (D) last

**1.** 傑克常常可以有較低的稅率等級，因為她常常捐錢給慈善機構，因此得以從她的所得中扣除。

> 解析 前半句說的「可以有較低的稅率等級」，表示她應該是「常常」捐錢才能扣除所得。never（從未），seldom（很少），與句意不符。likes to 後面應加原形動詞，但題目為 donates。所以答案選 (A) often（常常）。

- tax bracket 稅率等級
- deduct [dɪˋdʌkt] (v.) 扣除，減除

---

**2.** 幸好公車晚到了幾分鐘，我們才能趕上。

> 解析 空格應填入副詞，副詞置於句首用來修飾整個句子。從後面的句意判斷，答案應選 (B)。「S＋be able to＋原形動詞」表示「能夠（做某事）」，able 是形容詞，作「能夠的」解釋。

- catch [kætʃ] (v./n.) 追趕；趕上

---

**3.** 這盤小菜好吃又營養，但最棒的是它很容易做。

> 解析 從空格後面有逗點可知此處應填入可修飾全句的副詞（片語），故選 (D)。

- nutritious [njuˋtrɪʃəs] (adj.) 有營養的

---

**4.** 我們必須緊盯著股市，因為股價波動非常頻繁。

> 解析 這題要選擇修飾 fluctuate「波動」的副詞，且句意應該是說很頻繁，因為答案前有 quite，表「頗、滿」的意思。always 之前加上 quite 文意不順，many 修飾可數複數名詞，frequent「頻繁的」為形容詞，須加上 ly。答案選 (A)。

- keep a close eye 緊盯⋯
- fluctuate [ˋflʌktʃʊ͵et] (v.) 波動，變動

---

**5.** 我昨晚熬到夜深，這就是我今天會這麼累的原因。

> 解析 要用來表達過去的晚上有 that night（那晚）、one night（某一個晚上）和 last night（昨晚），根據後半句的 I'm so tired today，可推知前半句應該用 last night。

- stay up 熬夜

答案 1.(A) 2.(B) 3.(D) 4.(A) 5.(D)

**6.** The secretary called to ask if we would be _____ to the meeting this afternoon.

(A) go

(B) going

(C) gone

(D) went

---

**7.** I've never invested in the futures market, and _____ has my partner.

(A) always

(B) either

(C) ever

(D) neither

---

**8.** His family moved from Germany to Portugal about twenty years _____.

(A) since

(B) anew

(C) ago

(D) hence

---

**9.** Because Bernice wasn't flexible _____ to compromise, she lost the bid to someone else.

(A) well

(B) enough

(C) much

(D) very

---

**10.** I could _____ believe it when you told me that you'd won the lottery.

(A) hardly

(B) justly

(C) likely

(D) unlikely

**6.** 秘書打電話來問我們今天下午是否會去開會。

解析 秘書打電話是「過去」發生的事情，this afternoon 對祕書而言尚未到來，是「未來」會發生的事情，這時就要用「在過去式中描述未來」的方式，即「would be going to V」或「would be Ving」。

- secretary [`sɛkrə͵tɛrɪ] (n.) 秘書

---

**7.** 我從未投資過期貨市場，我的合夥人也是。

解析 本題為否定的「附和句」，指「主詞 A 不……，主詞 B 也不……」，可搭配 either 或 neither 兩種句型。either 須放句尾，如：I've never invested..., and my partner has never, either.；而 neither 則必須倒裝，如：I've never invested..., and neither has my partner.。注意：neither 本身已是否定副詞，故不須再搭配 never。

- futures market 期貨市場

---

**8.** 他家大概是二十年前從德國搬到葡萄牙。

解析 時態用的是過去簡單式，所以時間副詞用 twenty years ago（二十年前）。選項中表時間的副詞還有 since，指「此後，從那時起到現在」，通常與完成式連用；而 hence 則指「從此；因此」。

- Germany [`dʒɜmənɪ] (n.) 德國　　　　　　 • Portugal [`pɔrtʃʊgl] (n.) 葡萄牙

---

**9.** 因為柏妮絲在協調上不夠有彈性，所以她失去了她的出價標的，讓別人拿走了。

解析 後一句說她「失去了」她的標的，表示前一句應該是說她「不夠」有彈性，應該選 enough。well「好地」和 much「很多」都修飾不可數名詞，very「非常」則修飾形容詞，這三個選項都不合適。

- compromise [`kɑmprə͵maɪz] (n./v.) 妥協　　 • bid [bɪd] (v./n.) 喊價；出價

---

**10.** 你告訴我你中樂透時，我幾乎不敢相信。

解析 hardly 是「幾乎不，簡直不」的意思。justly 是「公正地」。likely 是「很可能地」，unlikely 是「不太可能地」。依據題意，應當選 (A)。

- lottery [`lɑtərɪ] (n.) 彩券，摸彩

答案 6.(B) 7.(D) 8.(C) 9.(B) 10.(A)

# 比較級與最高級

## 以形容詞或副詞做比較時的變化

● 比較的形式根據程度上的差異，可分成原級、比較級、最高級三種變化。

● 原級不和他物比較，維持形容詞／副詞的原形；比較級通常為兩者之間的比較，表達其中一者比另一者程度更深之意；最高級用於三者以上的比較，表達群體中程度最深者。

**用商務英文
學多益句型**　　**比較級與最高級**　　必考重點句

副詞、形容詞比較級與
最高級的字尾變化請看
**p.459**

### 形容詞比較級的用法

## This supplier offers lower prices than that one.
**這家供貨商提供的價碼比那家低。**

較短的原級（單音節的字）多數於字尾加了 er 之後，就成為比較級，較長的原級（雙音節或多音節的字）若要成為比較級，則必須在字前加 more；比較級之後常接 than。在兩者之間做比較時，常用 A ＋ be 動詞＋形容詞比較級＋ than B。

○ I am older **than** you.
　　我年紀比你大。

○ She is **more beautiful than** Mary.
　　她比瑪莉漂亮。

### 形容詞最高級的用法

## Which of these products is the cheapest?
**這些產品中哪一項最便宜？**

較短的原級（單音節的字）於字尾加了 est 之後，就成為最高級；較長的原級（雙音節或多音節的字）若要成為比較級，則必須在字前加 most。最高級之前常加 the。

○ I am **the oldest** student in my class.
　　我是班上年紀最大的學生。

○ She is **the most beautiful** girl at the party.
　　她是派對裡最漂亮的女孩。

**副詞比較級與最高級的用法**

## They deliver their products faster than any of their competitors.
**他們的送貨速度比競爭同業都快。**

副詞的比較級與最高級用法與形容詞相似。副詞比較級的基本句型為：A＋動詞＋副詞比較級＋than B；副詞最高級的基本句型為：A＋動詞＋副詞最高級＋in/of＋範圍。

⊃ I get up **earlier** than my sister.
　　我比我妹妹早起床。

⊃ He runs (the) **fastest** in the school.
　　他是全校跑最快的人。

**不規則的比較級與最高級變化**

## The purchaser asked the supplier for a better price.
**採購員要供貨商提供更好的價格。**

以下形容詞／副詞的比較級與最高級為不規則變化形。

| 詞性 | 原級 | 比較級 | 最高級 |
|---|---|---|---|
| 形容詞 | good | better | best |
| | bad | worse | worst |
| | many | more | most |
| | much | more | most |
| | little | less | least |
| | far | farther/further | farthest/furthest |
| 副　詞 | well | better | best |
| | badly | worse | worst |
| | far | farther/further | farthest/furthest |

⊃ You look **better** when you shave.
　　你刮鬍子之後好多了。

⊃ Try to do it **better** next time.
　　下次試著做好一點。

⊃ He is **the best** student in our class.
他是我們班上最優秀的學生。

⊃ The patient's fever is **worse** today.
病人今天發燒得更嚴重了。

⊃ **Of all the articles** in the magazine, this one is **the worst**.
雜誌所有的文章裡，這篇寫得最糟。

**原級比較用法：as 形容詞 / 副詞原級 as**

## Many commodities aren't as cheap as they used to be.

**許多商品都不像以前那樣便宜。**

形容詞原級的比較句型為：A+be 動詞＋as 形容詞 as＋B，副詞原級的比較句型為：A+be 動詞＋as 副詞 as＋B，其中副詞用來修飾句中的動詞。

⊃ Tom is almost **as tall as** his older brother.
湯姆跟他哥哥差不多高。

⊃ Give me your answer **as soon as** possible.
盡快把你的答案告訴我。

# Level 1  挑戰多益 *450*

請從 (A)、(B)、(C)、(D) 中選出一個最適合的答案。

**1.** She's well known for always doing _____ to please the customers.
(A) her good
(B) her utmost
(C) most
(D) best

**2.** How could rubies possibly cost _____ diamonds?
(A) as much as
(B) as little as
(C) less than
(D) more expensive than

**3.** The longer I wait, _____ difficult it becomes.
(A) the more
(B) the most
(C) more and more
(D) more

**4.** The first band was terrible, but this one is even _____.
(A) as bad as
(B) worst
(C) the worse
(D) worse

**5.** I must say, your English has gotten _____.
(A) more good
(B) well
(C) the best
(D) much better

*1.* 大家都知道她一直盡力滿足客戶需求。

**解析** 片語 do one's best 和 do one's utmost 都是「竭盡全力」的意思，故選 (B)。形容詞 well know 亦作 well-know，是「出名的，為人所知的」之意，經常以 be known for＋N 來表現。

- please [pliz] (v.) 討好

*2.* 紅寶石怎麼可能跟鑽石一樣貴？

**解析** as...as 表「和……一樣」之意，(A) cost as much as 意為「和……一樣貴」，搭配此選項可產生「紅寶石怎麼可能和鑽石一樣貴？」這種驚嘆質疑的語氣，故選 (A)。(B) as little as 指「和……一樣便宜」，但珠寶皆為高價產品，此選項不合語意。(C) less than 指「比……還便宜」，但此句有驚嘆質疑的語氣，若選 (C) 則失去此意，畢竟常理中紅寶石本來就比鑽石便宜，故不會問：「紅寶石怎麼可能會比鑽石便宜」。(D) more expensive than 應該搭配 be 動詞，非原句中的 cost。

*3.* 我等得愈久，情況就變得愈棘手。

**解析** 「the＋比較級，the＋比較級」表「愈……，就愈……」，為固定用法，故選 (A)。
- difficult [`dɪfɪˌkʌlt] (adj.) 困難的

*4.* 第一個樂團很爛，但這個更糟。

**解析** 題目中的 even 有「更、甚」之意，用來強調比較級，表後者比前者更糟，故選 (D) worse，為 bad 的比較級。(A) as bad as 為「和……一樣差」，屬原級比較，本句應說 This band is as bad as the first one.。(B) worst 為最高級，此句只有兩者在比較，故不適合。(C) the worse 是指「兩者中較差的一方」，屬於名詞詞性，不能放在 even 後方，因此也不能選。

- terrible [`tɛrəbəl] (adj.) 嚇人的，糟糕的

*5.* 我必須承認，你的英文比以前好多了。

**解析** get 為連綴動詞，意思為「變得」，後面應接形容詞。(B) well 為副詞，不可選。(A) 應改為 better，是 good 的比較級。get better 意思是變得比較好，比較級之前可加 much，表示強調。much better 有「好多了」之意，故選 (D)。本題是拿現在和過去相比，故用比較級，不用 (C) 最高級。

**答案** 1.(B) 2.(A) 3.(A) 4.(D) 5.(D)

6. John is the youngest person in our class, so you must be _____ than him.
   (A) younger
   (B) much younger
   (C) older
   (D) more older

7. Your bed looks more _____ mine.
   (A) softly than
   (B) comfortable than
   (C) harder than
   (D) or less than

8. Their house is about three times _____ as ours.
   (A) as big
   (B) more expensive
   (C) less expensive
   (D) bigger

9. John gets his substantial height from his father, who is much _____ his wife.
   (A) higher than
   (B) taller
   (C) the taller
   (D) taller than

10. I've never skied farther than that field. That field is _____ I've ever skied.
    (A) further
    (B) farther
    (C) the farthest
    (D) farthest

**6.** 約翰是我們班上年紀最小的人，所以你的年紀一定比他大。

解析 依照語意，John 已是班上最年輕的，其他的任何人應該都是比他年長，故選 (C)。
(A)、(B) 均不合語意，(D) 應改為 much older 才合文法。

**7.** 你的床看起來比我的舒服。

解析 句中的 look 指「看起來」，後面應加形容詞，故選 (B)。(A) 為副詞，應改為softer
than。(C) harder已是比較級，前面不應再加 more。(D) more or less為片語，
表「或多或少」之意，在此不合用法。

● comfortable [`kʌmfətəbl] (adj.) 舒適的

**8.** 他們的房子大約是我們的三倍大。

解析 times 在此表「倍數」，原句意思為「是……的三倍大」，有兩種句型可以表示：
(1) 數字＋times as＋形容詞＋as；(2) 數字＋times＋形容詞比較級＋than。題目
中已有 as 一字，故應套入第一種句型：three times as big as ours = three times
bigger than ours，故選 (A)。

**9.** 約翰的高個子遺傳自父親，他父親比太太高多了。

解析 「much ＋比較級」表強調比較之程度，故選 (D)。形容人的身高多用 tall，(A) 選項
的 high 適用於形容建築物、山等等。

● substantial [səb`stænʃəl] (adj.) 驚人的，真實的
● height [haɪt] (n.) 身高，高度，海拔

**10.** 我滑雪從未超出那片滑雪場的範圍。那片場地是我所滑過最遠的。

解析 前句的 never...farther than 雖為比較級句型，但實質涵義為最高級。從未滑超出
那片滑雪場的範圍，意即那片場地是「最遠的」，答案必定為最高級，故不選 (A)
或 (B)。far 的最高級為 farthest 或 furthest，且最高級之前要加定冠詞 the，故選
(C)。

● ski [ski] (v./n.) 滑雪；滑雪板

答案 6.(C) 7.(B) 8.(A) 9.(D) 10.(C)

# Level 2　挑戰多益 650

請從 (A)、(B)、(C)、(D) 中選出一個最適合的答案。

**1.** Living in the country is _____ than living in the city.
(A) healthier
(B) more quietly
(C) just as good as
(D) more healthier

**2.** To become a world-class athlete, you must always keep trying _____ harder.
(A) hard and
(B) hard by
(C) hardest and
(D) harder and

**3.** This painting looks almost _____ that one.
(A) worse as
(B) the same as
(C) as different than
(D) simpler as

**4.** He was asked to attend to the problem _____ as possible.
(A) as quick
(B) quicker
(C) as quickly
(D) more quick

**5.** We both have dark brown eyes. Your eyes are _____ as mine.
(A) dark
(B) as darkly
(C) as darker
(D) just as dark

*1.* 住在鄉下比住在城市裡健康。

解析 由 than 一字可推知此句為比較級用法，故選 (A) healthier，為 healthy 的比較級。
(B) be 動詞後面應加形容詞，用來形容 "living in the country" 這件事，不是副詞。
(C) as good as 為「和……一樣」之意，屬原級比較，後面不應接 than。(D) more
後面要加原級，但 healthier 為 healthy 的比較級。

*2.* 想成為世界級運動員，就必須不斷努力。

解析 「比較級 and 比較級」表「愈來愈……」之意，為比較級的強調用法，故選 (D)。
● world-class [wɜld klæs] (adj.) 世界級的　　● athlete [`æθlit] (n.) 運動員，體育家

*3.* 這幅畫看起來幾乎跟那幅一模一樣。

解析 比較級常用句型為「A＋be動詞＋比較級＋than B」或「A＋be動詞＋as＋原級
＋as B」。(A) worse 為比較級，後面應加 than。(D) 應改為 as simple as。(B)
的 the same 和 (C) 的 different 各有固定搭配的句型，the same as 表「和……一
樣」，需注意 same 通常與 the 連用，這裡的 the 和最高級前面的 the 意思不同；
be different from 指「與……不同」。故選 (B)。

*4.* 他被要求要盡快去解決問題。

解析 從空格後面的 as possible 可推知答案應選 (C)，as...as possible 是「盡可能」的意
思。兩個 as 中間應該用副詞 quickly 修飾動詞 attend to the problem 這個動作，因
此答案選 (C)。
● attend [ə`tɛnd] (v.) 專注處理某事（常作 attend to＋N）

*5.* 我們倆都有深棕色的眼睛。你眼睛的顏色就跟我的一樣深。

解析 題目中 mine 之前有 as，可知為「as＋原級＋as」的句型，因此 (A)、(C) 不可選。
空格處的原級用來修飾主詞 your eyes，詞性必須為形容詞，因此答案選 (D)。just
用來強調，表示「恰好一樣深」。
● dark [dɑrk] (adj./n.) 深色的；黑暗

答案 1.(A) 2.(D) 3.(B) 4.(C) 5.(D)

**6.** You don't know them _____ I do because they are my cousins.
(A) more than
(B) as well as
(C) well than
(D) much as

**7.** Please write letters to us as _____ as you can.
(A) often
(B) busy
(C) little
(D) frequent

**8.** You can donate as much or _____ money as you like.
(A) as little
(B) as few
(C) the most
(D) as often

**9.** Robert didn't spend much money, but Susan spent _____.
(A) more than him
(B) as much as him
(C) the least of all
(D) less than

**10.** She saves more money than you because she is _____ you.
(A) more thriftily than
(B) thriftier than
(C) less wastefully than
(D) as thrifty as

**6.** 你沒我那麼了解他們，因為他們是我的表親。

解析 原句為「你不像我一樣了解他們」，know 後面接副詞，well 在此當副詞用，「和⋯⋯
一樣」為 as...as 句型，故選 (B)。選項 (A) 看似文法無誤，但是在英文中，「了解某
人」副詞通常會用 well，比較級則要用 better，因此 (A) 為錯誤選項。

● cousin [ˋkʌzn̩] (n.) 堂 / 表兄弟姊妹

---

**7.** 請儘量常寫信給我們。

解析 as...as 句型應用原級，而動詞 write 之後應接副詞，often 在此為頻率副詞，表「常
寫信」，故選 (A)。(B) busy為形容詞，且不合語意。(C) little雖可當副詞，但不合
語意。(D) 應改為副詞 frequently。

---

**8.** 你的捐款或多或少都隨意。

解析 連接詞 or 前後所連接的字應為相同的詞性或結構，句中的 or 前面有 as much，為
as much money as you like 的省略，故 or 後方也應搭配 as...as 句型，中間加形容
詞原級，而 money 不可數，故用 as little，選 (A)。(B) as few 後面應加可數名詞。
(C) the most 為最高級，不合文法。(D) often 為副詞，不可用來修飾名詞 money。

● donate [ˋdonet] (v.) 捐贈，捐獻

---

**9.** 羅伯特沒花太多錢，但蘇珊花得最少。

解析 按照語意，原句想表達「Robert 沒花很多錢，但 Susan 是所有人之中花最少錢的
人」，故選 (C)。least 是 little 的最高級，比較級則為 less。than 後方必須要有比
較的對象，(D) 若改為 less than him 也是正確答案。(A) 和 (B) 都和語意不合。

---

**10.** 她存的錢比你多，因為她比你節省。

解析 thrifty 為形容詞原級，表「節儉的」。此句有 be 動詞 is，可知答案要找形容詞比
較級，故選 (B)。(A)、(C) 均使用副詞 thriftily，故不符。 (D) as...as 為「和⋯⋯一
樣」之意，在此不合語意。（編註：形容詞比較級字尾變化請參照 P. 459）

● thrifty [ˋθrɪftɪ] (adj.) 節儉的，簡約的

答案 6.(B) 7.(A) 8.(A) 9.(C) 10.(B)

### 介系詞的種類

- 介系詞是一種虛詞，不能單獨存在，必須與其他詞類，如：動詞、名詞等等，一同構成「介系詞片語」。
- 常見的介系詞種類有地點介系詞和時間介系詞，介系詞的意思不同，語意也跟著不同。除了時間介系詞和地點介系詞之外，介系詞也可能表示「手段 / 方法」、「帶有 / 包含 / 屬於」等等其他意涵。

**用商務英文學多益句型**　　**介系詞**　必考重點句

**表「地點」**

## The production manager spends most of his time at the factory.
**生產部經理大部分的時間都待在工廠裡。**

一般來說，表達地點時，較小的地方（如車站、餐廳、醫院）用 at，較大的地方（如國家、城市）用 in，但地點的大小常會依個人的觀感而有不同，因此相同的地點名詞可能會搭配不同的介系詞。比較簡單的區分方式是：at 強調「在某地點」，in 則表「在某空間之內」，例如 at home（在家）、in my room（在我的房間裡面），兩者強調的重點不一樣。

⊃ We live **at** 19 Park Road.
　我們住在公園路 19 號。

⊃ We live **in** Boston.
　我們住在波士頓。

⊃ Taipei 101 used to be the tallest building **in** the world.
　臺北 101 曾是世界第一高樓。

⊃ Let's meet **at** the airport. There is a nice café **in** the airport.
　我們在機場碰面吧。機場裡有家不錯的咖啡廳。

at 強調的是機場這個「地點」，in 指的是在機場的「空間裡面」。

**表「上下前後位置」**

# The manager read the new safety rules in front of the workers.

**經理在工作人員面前宣讀新的安全規則。**

地點介系詞可表達上下前後等位置關係，常見的介系詞如下：

| on | 在上面，有接觸面 | on the table 桌子上 |
|---|---|---|
| beneath | 在下面，多數是有接觸面 | beneath the earth 地底下 |
| under | 在正下方，在某範圍內 | under the tree 在樹下 |
| over | 在正上方，在某範圍內 | over the sea 海上 |
| above | 泛指所有的上方 | above the clouds 雲上 |
| below | 泛指所有的下方 | below the surface 水平面之下 |
| in front of | 在前面 | in front of the house 房子前面 |
| behind | 在後面；在背後 | behind the curtain 幕後 |
| in back of | 在後面 | in back of the school 學校後面 |
| between | 在兩者之間 | between Ted and Tom 泰德和湯姆之間 |
| across from | 在對面 | across from the post office 郵局對面 |
| next to/by | 在隔壁 | next to/by the hospital 醫院隔壁 |
| among | 在三者（或以上）之中 | among his classmates 同學之中 |
| around | 環繞；在四周 | around the corner 在街角 |
| near | 在附近 | near the door 在門附近 |

⊃ The old men played Chinese chess **under** the tree.
那些老人在樹下玩象棋。

⊃ The campers slept **beneath** the stars.
那些露營者露宿在星空之下。

⊃ Hundreds of people protested **in front of** City Hall.
好幾百人在市政府前示威。

⊃ This mountain bike is popular **among** the top riders.
這輛登山車在單車好手中很受歡迎。

# The manager walked along the assembly line observing the workers.

**經理沿著裝配線邊走邊監督工作人員。**

有些介系詞可以表示出「方向性」，此類常見的介系詞如下：

| into | 進入 | into the swimming pool 進入游泳池 |
|------|------|------|
| out of | 出來 | out of the swimming pool 出游泳池 |
| along | 沿著 | along the river 沿著河 |
| across | 橫越 | across the river 橫越河 |
| through | 貫穿 | through the city 穿越城市 |
| to | 前往；到達 | to London 去倫敦；到達倫敦 |
| toward | 朝向 | toward the gate 朝門的方向 |
| for | 向；前往 | for New York 前往紐約 |
| from | 從 | from here 從這裡 |

⊃ The kids sneaked **into** the movie theater.
孩子們偷偷跑進電影院。

⊃ The road runs **through** the city center.
那條道路貫穿市中心。

⊃ They drove **toward** Taipei.
他們朝著臺北行駛。

⊃ The car drove **across** the bridge.
那輛車開過那座橋。

# Workers at the factory punch in at 8:00 in the morning.

**工廠的員工早上八點打卡。**

表達年、月、日和時刻可用介系詞 in/on/at 等，列表如下：

| at | 時刻、某一點 | at three o'clock 三點、at noon 正午 |
|------|------|------|
| on | 某日、特定的一天 | on Monday 星期一、on his birthday 他生日 |
| in | 上下午、週、月、年 | in the morning 上午、in May 五月、in spring 春天 |

⊃ I usually eat lunch **at** noon.
我通常中午十二點吃午餐。

⊃ We're going to the mall **on** Saturday.
我們星期六要去購物中心。

⊃ They're going to get married **in** June.
他們打算在六月結婚。

定的日子，介系詞要
on。

**表「時間前後、期間」**

## Factory workers are required to punch in before they start their shifts.
**工廠的員工上班前必須打卡。**

描述時間的前後關係、或期間內外，以及時間起始的介系詞列表如下：

| before | 在……之前 | before leaving 在離開之前 |
|---|---|---|
| after | 在……之後 | after work 下班後 |
| in+時間 | 在……時間內／後 | in three hours 在三小時內／後 |
| within＋時間 | 在……時間內 | within three days 三天之內 |
| by＋時間 | 到……時間之前 | by 4 o'clock 到四點之前 |
| until＋時間 | 直到（……時間） | until 10 o'clock 直到十點 |
| from | 從 | from eight to ten 從八點到十點 |
| since | 自從 | since yesterday 從昨天開始 |
| for | 達……之久 | for 10 years 達十年 |
| during | 在……之間 | during summer vacation 暑假之中 |
| through | 在整個期間 | Monday through Friday 週一到週五 |

⊃ You should always wash your hands **before** you eat.
吃東西前一定要洗手。

⊃ He can finish the job **within** three days.
他三天內可以完成工作。

⊃ Can you wait for me **until** I come back?
你可以等我回來嗎？

⊃ I've lived in Canada **since** I was five.
我從五歲起就住在加拿大。

# Workers at the factory are paid by the hour.
**工廠的員工按時計薪。**

1. 介系詞中，常用 with、in 或 by 表示「手段」及「方法」。其中 with 亦有歸屬的意涵，用 with 表示「有」、相反詞 without 則表示「沒有」。

2. like 當作介系詞是「像……一樣」，as 則是「作為……」、「以……身分」、「如同」等意思。介系詞 against 則常用來表示「靠著」、「對抗」或「不利於」。

⊃ The boy **with** the short brown hair is my brother.
　那個有著棕色短髮的男孩是我弟弟。

⊃ They paid **in** cash, but I paid **with** my credit card.
　他們用現金付帳，但是我用信用卡付帳。

⊃ I go to school **by** bus, but my brother goes **by** subway.
　我搭公車上學，但我哥哥搭地鐵上學。

⊃ She leaned **against** the wall.
　她靠在牆上。

⊃ He's **like** a second father to me.
　對我而言，他就像是第二個父親。

⊃ Kevin works **as** a bartender.
　凱文的工作是酒保。

使用 in 時，後面加上「物質名詞」；使用 with 時，後面用「普通名詞」。

搭乘交通工具，用「by ＋交通工具」來表達。

# All the manufacturer's products are made from biodegradable materials.
**該製造商的所有產品都是用可分解物質製成的。**

1. of 是「屬於」，A of B 的意思即是「B 的 A」。from 是「來自……」，後方接來源地。

2. 另外，be made of 和 be made from 是常混淆的片語。它們都是「由……所製成的」，差別在於 be made of 表示從產品還可以知道材料為何，材料本質不變，屬於物理變化；be made from 則無法一眼看出材料為何，材料的本質已經改變了，屬於化學變化。

⊃ He is a friend **of** mine.
　他是我的一個朋友。

➲ I am **from** Taiwan. Where are you **from**?
我是台灣人，你是哪裡人？

➲ The bottle is **made of** plastic.
那個瓶子是塑膠做的。

➲ Paper is **made from** trees.
紙是用樹做成的。

### 介系詞片語

常見介系詞片語
請看 p.460~462

## The assembly line was shut down for inspection when the defect was discovered.
**該瑕疵被發現之後，裝配線就被關閉以進行檢查。**

介系詞和其他詞類可形成片語，例如：由「動詞＋介系詞」形成的片語，即為「動詞片語」；與形容詞結合成為「形容詞＋介系詞」的「形容詞片語」；還有以「介系詞＋名詞」所形成的片語，常當作「副詞」或「形容詞」使用。

➲ Alice **gets along with** everybody.
愛麗絲和每個人都處得很好。

➲ We **ran out of** soybean sauce.
我們醬油用完了。

➲ She is **good at** math.
她數學很好。

➲ He is a man **of courage**.
他是個有勇氣的人。

# Level ① 挑戰多益 *450*

**請從 (A)、(B)、(C)、(D) 中選出一個最適合的答案。**

**1.** I thought he lived downtown, but apparently he's living somewhere else _____ the city.
(A) at
(B) on
(C) in
(D) from

**2.** She wanted to take a class _____ the art school, but she did not register early enough.
(A) of
(B) to
(C) at
(D) on

**3.** How long does it take to drive _____ the tunnel?
(A) through
(B) in
(C) between
(D) on

**4.** We looked all _____ the playground but could not find the girl's earring anywhere.
(A) on
(B) within
(C) over
(D) under

**5.** We need to leave _____ the meeting in the next ten minutes, otherwise we'll certainly be late.
(A) for
(B) to
(C) at
(D) with

1. 我以為他住在鬧區,但他似乎住在城裡其他地方。

   解析 此題要選的是地點介系詞,小地方通常使用 at,比較大的地方通常用 in。例如 at the station(在車站)、at No. 7 Park Road(在公園路 7 號)、in Taipei(在臺北)等等。本題地點是 city,因此選擇介系詞 in。

   ● apparently [ə`pærəntlɪ] (adv.) 似乎;顯然地

2. 她想要在這所藝術學校上課,但是她沒有及時註冊。

   解析 此題句意是「在藝術學校上課」,此時介系詞會用 at,若用 in 則表示單純在「學校這個空間」,沒有上課的意涵,故選 (C)。

   ● register [`rɛdʒɪstɚ] (v.) 註冊;登記

3. 開車通過隧道要多久呢?

   解析 地點介系詞,tunnel 隧道是要從中穿越的,故選 (A)。

   ● tunnel [`tʌnl] (n.) 隧道

4. 我們在操場四處尋找,就是找不到那女孩的耳環。

   解析 空格前有 all,搭配句意應該要選表示「到處」的介系詞片語,故答案選 (C)。

   ● earring [`ɪr͵rɪŋ] (n.) 耳環

5. 我們再過十分鐘就得去開會,不然一定會遲到。

   解析 leave for 是動詞片語,表示「前往某地」。in＋時間表示「在……時間之內/後」,此題為後者,in the next ten minutes 是「再過十分鐘」的意思。

   ● certainly [`sɝtənlɪ] (adv.) 無疑地,必定

答案 1.(C) 2.(C) 3.(A) 4.(C) 5.(A)

6. Maurice likes to exercise _____ the early morning.
   (A) at
   (B) in
   (C) on
   (D) to

7. The rest of the group will have to wait _____ the leader returns.
   (A) until
   (B) before
   (C) on
   (D) upon

8. _____ a self-employed person, Jake works only for himself.
   (A) At
   (B) An
   (C) As
   (D) After

9. The new product was so dazzling, we could only sit and stare _____.
   (A) on that
   (B) at it
   (C) to this
   (D) on it

10. Norman was able to attract so many potential customers _____ making phone calls constantly.
   (A) by
   (B) for
   (C) to
   (D) of

*6.* 莫理斯喜歡在清晨運動。

解析 在早上用 in the morning，在下午用 in the afternoon，時間介系詞在較長一段時間通常用 in，在較短的時刻用 at。

*7.* 團隊其他成員將必須等到領隊回來為止。

解析 空格後有主詞與動詞，必須用「連接詞」來連接兩個句子，因此選項 (C)、(D) 都不能選。until（直到）和 before（在……之前）都可當連接詞與介系詞，根據語意，應選 wait until（等到……為止）。

*8.* 傑克自己當老闆，只為自己工作。

解析 介系詞 as 是「作為；以……身分」的意思。本題也可以寫成 Jake works only for himself as a self-employed person.
● self-employed [sɛlf ɪm`plɔɪd] (adj.) 自己經營的；自由業的；雇用自己的

*9.* 這個新產品實在太閃耀了，我們只能坐著然後盯著它看。

解析 這題要了解 stare「盯著看」，後面加上的介系詞是 at，所以答案要選 (B)。
● dazzling 眼花撩亂的，令人炫目的

*10.* 諾曼藉由不斷地打電話招引到許多潛在客戶。

解析 諾曼可以吸引客戶，應該是「藉由」不斷地打電話。表「藉由」的介系詞是 by，用法是「by＋Ving」，也就是題目中的 making phone calls constantly，因此答案選 (A)。
● be able to V 能夠去做…

答案 6.(B) 7.(A) 8.(C) 9.(B) 10.(A)

# Level ❷    挑戰多益 *650*

請從 (A)、(B)、(C)、(D) 中選出一個最適合的答案。

1. Police found the stolen painting _____ the man's van.
   (A) back
   (B) in back of
   (C) in the back
   (D) in the back of

2. _____ his friends, Joshua has a reputation for being very funny and outgoing.
   (A) Among
   (B) About
   (C) Across
   (D) After

3. Mr. Wilson will be out of his meeting _____ ten minutes. Would you like to have some coffee while you wait, Ms. Peters?
   (A) for
   (B) in
   (C) from
   (D) at

4. The client said he needed the product delivered _____ seven days.
   (A) with
   (B) within
   (C) without
   (D) for

5. She asked for two large coffees; one _____ cream and sugar, and one _____.
   (A) within ; without
   (B) with ; without
   (C) without ; for
   (D) for ; without

***1.*** 警方在該名男子的小貨車後車廂發現被偷的畫。

　**解析** in back of 是「在某物後面」，例如：in back of the post office（在郵局後面），in the back of 則是指「在某物內部的後面」，例如 in the back of the classroom（在教室裡的後面）。根據題意，畫是在車子裡，應當用 in the back of the man's van。

　● van [væn] (n.) 小貨車

***2.*** 他的朋友當中，約書亞的風趣和外向是出了名的。

　**解析** 本題指的是「在一群人當中」，介系詞應用 among，表三者以上的「在……之中」，故選 (A) among his friends（在他朋友之中）。

　● outgoing [ˋaʊtˎgoɪŋ] (adj.) 外向的　　　● reputation [ˎrɛpjəˋteʃən] (n.) 名譽，名聲

***3.*** 威爾森先生十分鐘後會開完會。彼得，你要在等候的時間喝杯咖啡嗎？

　**解析** 「in＋一段時間」表示「……時間之後」，「for＋一段時間」表示「持續……時間」。本題由句意可知 Peter 正在等 Mr. Wilson 十分鐘後開完會，因此介系詞應選 in。

　● while [waɪl] (conj.) 當…的時候

***4.*** 客戶表示產品必須在七天內送達。

　**解析** 四個選項中只有 (B)、(D) 可放在時間之前。「for＋時間」表示這個動作持續了一段時間，和句意對不上，(B) within 是正確答案，within seven days 就是「七天之內」的意思，也就是七天中的任何一天都可以，但是最後期限是第七天。

　● client [ˋklaɪənt] (n.) 委託人，客戶　　　● in seven days 七天之後，但不得遲於第七天

***5.*** 她要了兩杯大杯咖啡，一杯加奶精和糖，一杯沒加。

　**解析** 本題用 one...one... 來描述兩杯咖啡，一杯有糖和奶精，一杯則沒有。加了糖和奶精的咖啡，介系詞 with 有歸屬的意涵，表「含有」之意，相反詞則是 without。

**答案** 1.(D)　2.(A)　3.(B)　4.(B)　5.(B)

6. The doctor was able to identify the bacteria _____ his microscope.
   (A) with
   (B) by
   (C) toward
   (D) about

7. She motioned _____ the door and suggested that it was getting very late.
   (A) toward
   (B) across
   (C) about
   (D) without

8. The air conditioning is broken, so it's very hot _____ the office. Employees are therefore allowed to wear shorts and T-shirts.
   (A) around
   (B) through
   (C) in
   (D) outside

9. I was very surprised to hear that the old man is quite _____ singing.
   (A) best
   (B) best at
   (C) good
   (D) good at

10. After nearly a week in bed, I finally _____ my terrible cold.
    (A) got
    (B) got on
    (C) got over
    (D) got rid

**6.** 醫生能用顯微鏡來判斷是何種細菌。

解析 with 常用來表示「手段」及「方法」，例如：We Chinese eat with chopsticks while Westerns eat with fork and knife.「中國人用筷子吃飯，西方人則用刀叉。」此題的意思是「使用某種工具」，故選擇 (A) with。

- identify [aɪ`dɛntə͵faɪ] (v.) 確認，鑑定，驗明

**7.** 她朝著門比出手勢，提醒說天色已晚。

解析 motion 當作動詞是「打手勢；搖頭或點頭示意」的意思，要「往」門那邊看，才會知道天色已晚，所以選擇表示方向性的介系詞 toward（朝向）。

- motion [`moʃən] (v.) 打手勢，搖頭或點頭示意
- suggest [sə`dʒɛst] (v.) 建議，暗示

**8.** 空調壞了，所以現在辦公室裡面很熱。員工們因此可以穿著短褲和 T 恤工作。

解析 題目說「空調壞了」，可以推測「辦公室裡面很熱」，所以「員工們因此可以穿著短褲和T恤工作」。around the office 是「在辦公室周圍」；through 有「貫穿」的意思，through the office 是「從辦公室一邊到另一邊」；in the office 是「在辦公室裡面」；outside the office「在辦公室外面」，與後文文意不搭。答案為 (C)。

- air conditioning = ac 空調，冷氣　　　　● be allowed (to do sth.) 被允許做…

**9.** 聽說那老人家唱歌很好聽，我很訝異。

解析 be good at... 為介系詞片語，是「擅長於……」的意思，相反詞則是 be bad/poor at...（不擅於……）。介系詞 at 接名詞或動名詞，例如本題的 singing。

**10.** 在床上躺了近一星期，我的重感冒終於好了。

解析 get over 為固定用法，表示「康復；克服……」。get over one's cold 就是「感冒好了」的意思。(D) 選項如果改成 got rid of（擺脫……）也可選。

答案 6.(A) 7.(A) 8.(C) 9.(D) 10.(C)

# 對等連接詞

### 對等連接詞的種類

● 對等連接詞（and、or、but 等等）可連接詞性、結構相同的單字、片語或獨立句子。
● 對等連接詞所連接的單字或片語，詞性和功能必須一致。

用商務英文
學多益句型

## 對等連接詞　必考重點句

連接同詞性的單字 / 片語

**Make sure your passport and boarding pass are ready for inspection.**
**請準備好您的護照和登機證以供檢查。**

對等連接詞如：and（而且）、but（但是）、or（或者），或是由兩個字以上的詞組所形成的連接詞，如：both A and B（A 和 B 都）、either A or B（不是 A 就是 B）等等，其所連接的單字或片語，詞性和功能必須一致。

除了連接詞的意思之外，還要特別注意後方搭配的動詞單複數：

| 主詞 | 動詞使用 |
|---|---|
| A and B | 複數 |
| A or B | 和 B 一致 |
| both A and B | 複數 |
| A as well as B | 和 A 一致 |
| not only A, but (also) B | 和 B 一致 |
| either A or B | 和 B 一致 |
| neither A nor B | 和 B 一致 |

➲ This alley is **narrow**, **dark**, **and dangerous**.
這條巷子很窄、很暗，而且很危險。

動詞須和 Charlie 一致

➲ I don't think John **or** Charlie **has** time.
我不認為約翰或查理有空。

⊃ **Both** he **and** his wife **love** dogs.
他和他太太都喜歡狗。

⊃ **Neither** my mother **nor** my father **has** a university degree.
我爸爸和我媽媽都沒有大學學歷。

### 連接獨立的句子

## Can I take this bag as a carry-on, or do I need to check it?
**這個袋子能當隨機行李，還是必須拖運？**

and、but、or 常用來連接獨立的句子，前面通常以逗點隔開，時態與人稱須與連接句的主詞一致。其中 and 連接的兩個句子需同樣為肯定或同樣為否定，but 連接的句子則是一個肯定、一個否定。

⊃ He plays the piano, **and** she sings.
他彈鋼琴，她唱歌。

⊃ I like the car, **but** it's too expensive.
我喜歡這部車，可是太貴了。

⊃ Do they have to leave, **or** can they stay?
他們必須離開，或者他們可以留下？

### not only...but also... 的用法

## Not only first-class passengers, but also families with children are allowed to board first.
**不僅頭等艙的乘客可優先登機，有孩童隨行的家庭也可以。**

對等連接詞 not only...but also... 表示「不僅……也……」，連接兩個句子時，動詞與後面的主詞一致。若 not only 位於句首，第一個子句要倒裝，即助動詞或 be 動詞移到主詞前面，also 則必須置於動詞前。

⊃ He **not only** received a promotion, **but also** got a raise.
他不僅獲得升遷，還加薪了。

⊃ **Not only** Steve, **but also his brothers** are coming on the trip.
不只史提夫，他的兄弟們也會參加旅行。

⊃ **Not only did the star** sing, **but she also** played the piano.
這位明星不只唱歌，還彈了鋼琴。

## Flight status as well as gate information is displayed on the departure board.

**班機狀態以及登機門資訊都顯示在班機起飛時間看板上。**

用 as well as 表達兩者狀態一致時，強調的是前者，所以動詞須與前面的名詞一致。as well as 只可連接名詞和形容詞，無法用在動詞上的對稱。

A as well as B 的句型中，強調的部分是 A，動詞與 A 一致。

➲ The **mother** as well as her daughters is beautiful.
那位母親和她的女兒們一樣美麗。

➲ **Friends** as well as family **are** important to me.
朋友和家人對我來說都很重要。

## Knifes aren't permitted on flights, and scissors aren't either.

**禁止攜帶刀子上機，剪刀也是。**

用對等連接詞 and 來連接句子時，若第二個子句要表達「……也 / 也不」，則句尾要再搭配 too/either。這時候因為第二個子句的動詞會和第一個子句相同，所以後句的動詞為避免重複會以助動詞代替。

➲ Jane **took** a shower, **and** I **did**, **too**.
珍洗過澡了，我也是。

➲ They **aren't** here, **and** Peter **isn't**, **either**.
他們不在這裡，彼得也不在。

## You may check in either online or at the airport.

**你可以在線上或在機場辦理登機手續。**

either...or... 表示「不是……就是……」兩者其一；neither...nor... 表示「既不是……也不是……」兩者皆非。either...or... 和 neither...nor... 都可以用來連接單字、片語或子句，句中的動詞則跟隨最接近的名詞作單複數變化。若用 neither...nor... 引導兩個句子，兩個句子都要倒裝。

➲ **Either** George **or** Mary **is** responsible for the accident.
不是喬治就是瑪莉要為這場意外負責。

➲ **Neither** **was she sick** nor **was there** a traffic jam. She overslept.
她既不是生病也不是遇上塞車。她睡過頭了。

**for 和 so 的用法**

## We checked in online, so we don't need to wait in a long line at the airport.
我們已經辦理了線上登機手續，所以不必在機場大排長龍。

for 和 so 只能連接句子，不能連接單字或片語。連接時前面通常加上逗號，for（因為）表示推測的理由；so（所以）表示結果，不可放在句首。

○ He does not feel nervous, **for** he is well-prepared.
他不覺得緊張，因為他有萬全準備。

○ We've done it, **so** you won't have to.
我們已經做了，所以你不必做了。

請從 (A)、(B)、(C)、(D) 中選出一個最適合的答案。

**1.** Isabel _____ Doris are going to drive there together.
(A) or
(B) and
(C) with
(D) but

**2.** I would love to go to the party, _____ I have other plans that night.
(A) and
(B) or
(C) but
(D) if

**3.** _____ my brother, _____ my three sisters, caught a flu last winter.
(A) Both ; and
(B) Either ; or
(C) Not only ; but also
(D) Not only ; and

**4.** Don't worry. I will help you solve the problem, and _____.
(A) Jack will solve, too
(B) Jack won't, either
(C) Jack will, too
(D) Jack won't help, either

**5.** _____ Ella _____ Josie will sing the lead, but not both.
(A) either ; or
(B) neither ; nor
(C) both ; and
(D) Not ; but

*1.* 伊莎貝爾和朵莉絲要一起開車去那裡。

解析 兩個人名之後的 be 動詞為複數形 (are)，所以需要的連接詞是 and，答案為選項 (B)。

*2.* 我很想參加宴會，但是我那天晚上有別的計畫。

解析 四個選項都可以作連接詞，但從語意上判斷，前句與後句有彼此矛盾之意，故應選 but（但是）來表示語氣的轉折。

• plan [plæn] (n.) 計畫，打算，方案

*3.* 不只我的弟弟，還有我的三個妹妹去年冬天都得了流行性感冒。

解析 選項 (A) Both A and B 和選項 (B) Either A or B 的用法只限於主詞是「兩者」的時候使用，故皆非答案。Not only...but also 意思為「不僅……而且……」，作連接詞用，答案為 (C)。

• flu [flu] (n.) 流行性感冒

*4.* 別擔心。我會協助你解決問題，傑克也會。

解析 這一題考的是連接詞 and 搭配 too/either 表示「也是 / 也不是……」的用法。and 前方是肯定句，所以後方應該是表示「也是」的語氣，只有 (A)、(C) 選項可以考慮。在這樣的表達中，因為後句的動詞提的是和前句一樣的事情，所以只要用助動詞代替前方的動作即可，答案選 (C)。

• solve [sɑlv] (v.) 解決

*5.* 艾拉或是裘西其中一人會擔任主唱，不是兩個人都唱。

解析 由句尾的 but not both 可知只有一人會擔任主唱，所以只有選項 (A) either...or... 符合語意，為正確答案。(B) neither...nor... 表「兩者皆非」，(C) both...and... 表「兩者皆是」，均與語意不符。(D) not A but B 表示「不是 A 而是 B」，但根據句意，尚未決定主唱是哪一位，與語意不符。

• lead [lid] (n.) 主唱，主演

答案 1.(B) 2.(C) 3.(C) 4.(C) 5.(A)

**6.** The water in the pool is perfect; it's _____ too hot nor too cold.
(A) either
(B) neither
(C) both
(D) usually

**7.** I really want to go out with you, _____ I have to finish my assignment first.
(A) and
(B) or
(C) and
(D) but

**8.** It would be wise to invest in this company, _____ it has always been very profitable.
(A) for
(B) so
(C) then
(D) in order

**9.** I've already called Jim about the order, _____ you don't need to.
(A) and
(B) so
(C) for
(D) neither

**10.** The coach, _____ the team _____ ready for the game.
(A) as well as ; is
(B) as well as ; are
(C) as well ; is
(D) also ; was

**6.** 池裡的水溫剛剛好；不會太熱也不會太冷。

解析 兩個形容詞 hot 和 cold 之間有連接詞 nor，故應選 (B)。neither...nor... 的意思
是「既非……也非……」。

---

**7.** 我真的很想跟你出去，但我必須先完成我的作業。

解析 根據語意，前後句有語氣轉折，空格需填入「但是」意思的連接詞，一般常用
but，表「可是，不過」，故答案為 (D)。

● assignment [əˋsaɪnmənt] (n.) 作業，工作，分派工作

---

**8.** 投資這家公司很明智，因為它一直都相當賺錢。

解析 兩個句子用逗號相隔，中間需要連接詞，只有 (A) for 和 (B) so 是可能答案。從語
意上判斷，後面的句子應是表「原因」，故選 for，答案為 (A)。

● profitable [ˋprɑfɪtəbl] (adj.) 賺錢的；有利可圖的

---

**9.** 我已經打給吉米問過訂單的事，所以你不必打了。

解析 兩個句子用逗號相隔，中間需要連接詞，只有 (A)、(B) 和 (C) 是可能的答案。從語
意上判斷，後面的句子表示「結果」，故選 so，答案為 (B)。

● order [ˋɔrdə] (n./v.) 訂單；訂貨

---

**10.** 教練和隊員已準備好要比賽了。

解析 這一句考的是連接詞的判別，以及後方要搭配的動詞。表示「A 和 B」，除了用
and 之外，還可以用 as well as 當連接詞，但用 as well as 動詞的判別要依據其前
方的主詞 The coach，因此答案選 (A)。

● nervous [ˋnɝvəs] (adj.) 緊張不安的

答案 6.(B) 7.(D) 8.(A) 9.(B) 10.(A)

請從 **(A)**、**(B)**、**(C)**、**(D)** 中選出一個最適合的答案。

**1.** The coach said _____ Carl _____ Justin would start in tomorrow's game.
(A) either ; nor
(B) both ; or
(C) neither ; but
(D) neither ; nor

**2.** He has asked friends _____ family to help him move all his belongings into his new house.
(A) also
(B) as well as
(C) and with
(D) along

**3.** Their team has not yet won a game, _____ do I think they ever will.
(A) and
(B) nor
(C) so
(D) which

**4.** I don't think you or Charlie _____ the truth.
(A) knows
(B) will know
(C) know
(D) known

**5.** A super idol must be good at both singing and _____.
(A) dancer
(B) danced
(C) dancing
(D) dance

*1.* 教練說卡爾和賈斯汀明天比賽都不會擔任先發。

解析 主要動詞 said 後面是省略了 that 的名詞子句，子句中的主詞 Carl 和 Justin 之間需要連接詞，只有 (D) 選項的連接詞的搭配是正確用法，故選 (D)。(A) 若改為 either...or... 則表示「兩人之一」會先發，也是正確答案。

● coach [kotʃ] (n.) 教練

---

*2.* 他已經請親朋好友幫他把所有東西都搬進新家了。

解析 動詞 ask sb. to V 表示「請某人做某事」，friends 和 family 均為受詞，中間需要連接詞，選項中只有 (B) as well as 正確，意思等於 and。

● belonging [bə`lɔŋɪŋ] (n.) 所有物；財產；行李

---

*3.* 他們的隊伍一場比賽都沒贏過，我也不認為他們將來會贏。

解析 逗號後面的句子為倒裝句，即「助動詞＋主詞＋動詞」，只有 (B) nor 或 (C) so 可能為答案。但是前句有表否定的 not yet，故不可選 so，只可選 nor，答案為 (B)。

---

*4.* 我不認為你或查理知道真相。

解析 用 or 連接的句子，動詞根據最接近的主詞作變化，此句最接近的主詞為 Charlie，故動詞用 knows。

● truth [truθ] (n.) 事實；真理；真相

---

*5.* 超級偶像必須能唱又能跳。

解析 both...and... 為對等連接詞，在本題中須連結兩個詞性相同的單字，前面已出現 singing，故答案為 (C) dancing。

● idol [`aɪdl] (n.) 偶像

答案 1.(D) 2.(B) 3.(B) 4.(A) 5.(C)

6. I'm not going home until the report is completed, _____ is Patricia.
   (A) neither
   (B) not
   (C) and neither
   (D) and nor

7. It has not happened yet, _____ I don't think it will, _____.
   (A) and ; neither
   (B) but ; either
   (C) but ; neither
   (D) and ; either

8. Either Simon or you _____ to clean the classroom tomorrow.
   (A) has
   (B) had
   (C) have
   (D) having

9. He neither knows nor _____ what has happened.
   (A) care
   (B) caring
   (C) cares
   (D) cared

10. We decide _____ to drive a car _____ to take a taxi. We'll take the MRT.
   (A) neither ; nor
   (B) both ; and
   (C) either ; or
   (D) not ; and

**6.** 報告完成我才會回家,派翠西亞也一樣。

解析 neither...nor 的 neither 是副詞,不能當連接詞用。nor 是連接詞,但其後的句子必須倒裝。not 沒有前兩者的功用。本題空格若用 neither,需和 and 一起用,其後的句子也必須倒裝。若用 nor,則前方不需要 and,因為 nor 本身即為連接詞。正確答案為 (C)。

● complete [kəm`plit] (v.) 完成

---

**7.** 事情還沒發生,我也不認為會發生。

解析 這個題目的前後都是表達否定「不會發生」,因此應該用 and 連接的兩個同樣語氣的子句;若用 but,前後的子句應該是矛盾的關係,在這裡不符合句意,不選 (B)、(C)。兩句都否定時,表達「也不」時句尾應搭配 either,故答案為 (D)。

---

**8.** 明天不是賽門就是你要打掃教室。

解析 either...or... 連接兩名詞作主詞時,動詞跟較接近的主詞一致,本題較接近的主詞為 you,故應搭配 have 作動詞。

---

**9.** 他既不知道也不在乎發生了什麼事。

解析 用 neither...nor... 連接的單字或片語,其詞性和功能必須一致,本題 neither...nor 中間為現在簡單式第三人稱單數動詞 knows,故 nor 後面應該選擇 cares。

---

**10.** 我們決定不開車也不搭計程車。我們要搭捷運。

解析 後句說 We'll take the MRT.,前方的句子應該表達兩者皆非,neither...nor... 表示「既不是……也不是……」,根據語意應選 (A)。若選 (C) 則意思是開車或計程車兩者擇一,(B) 則是又開車又搭計程車,與後句語意不符。(D) 選項若改成 not to drive a car or take taxi 也有一樣的意思。

---

答案 6.(C) 7.(D) 8.(C) 9.(C) 10.(A)

231

### 從屬連接詞的種類

- 引導從屬子句和主要子句結合在一起的連接詞，即從屬連接詞。
- 從屬連接詞根據功能，可以引導三種子句：名詞子句（that/whether）、形容詞子句（that/who/which）、副詞子句（because/although/when/before/after/if）。
- 從屬連接詞連接的是從屬子句，語意不能獨立，必須仰賴主要子句。

用商務英文
學多益句型

從屬連接詞 ｜ 必考重點句

#### 用 that 引導名詞子句

**The manual says that the sewing machine should be oiled once a year.**

使用手冊上說縫紉機必須每年上油一次。

陳述一件事實時，會用 that 來引導名詞子句。名詞子句即子句作為名詞，可放在主詞、受詞或補語的位置，that 子句作為主詞時，常被放在句尾，並在句首加上虛主詞 it；that 子句作為受詞時，that 經常被省略。

that 子句作主詞

⊃ **That he didn't apologize is unacceptable.**
**It** is unacceptable **that he didn't apologize.**
他沒道歉令人難以接受。

作為 admit 的受詞，that 常被省略。

⊃ You have to **admit** (that) he's a responsible person.
你必須承認他是個有責任感的人。

作為 demand 的受詞，that 常被省略。

⊃ The lawyer **demanded** (that) his client be released immediately.
該律師要求立刻釋放他的當事人。

> demand 後面的 that 子句動詞須用原形 = his client (should) be released...

that 子句作為 announcement 的同位語

⊃ The **announcement** that a garbage dump was to be built **nearby** aroused opposition.
附近要蓋一座垃圾場的公告引發了抗議。

**用 whether 與疑問詞引導的名詞子句**

# I'm not sure whether the transmission needs to be replaced or not.

**我不確定變速箱需不需要更換。**

用 whether...or not 引導名詞子句，表示「是否」之意。whether...or not 的 or not 可省略，whether...or not 可以用 if 代替，但 if 後面不跟著 or not。

➲ We don't care **whether** you make a lot of money **(or not)**.
= We don't care **if** you make a lot of money.
我們並不在乎你是否賺很多錢。

➲ **Whether** you succeed **or** fail doesn't matter. At least you tried.
成功或失敗都沒有關係，至少你試過了。

➲ The boss wants to know **who** **is to blame**.
老闆想知道該歸咎於誰。

➲ Women don't like to be asked **how old** **they are**.
女人不喜歡被問她們幾歲。

詞子句作主詞時，只
用 whether 引導，不
用 if。

**形容詞子句的從屬連接詞**

# We want to hire a mechanic who can repair foreign cars.

**我們想聘請一位會修外國車的技師。**

形容詞子句的從屬連接詞常見的有二種：關係代名詞（who/which/whose/that 等），和關係副詞（when/where/why/how）。形容詞子句的位置必須放在被修飾的名詞或代名詞後面。

y 子句修飾名詞
son

➲ The **reason** why he quit is not clear.
他離職的原因不明。

➲ Patrick wants to study in a **country** where English is spoken.
派屈克想要去說英語的國家就讀。

## Remember to turn off the air conditioner when you leave the room.

離開房間時記得關冷氣。

副詞子句顧名思義，即引導的子句具副詞功能，用來修飾動詞、形容詞、副詞和主要句子。用 when/before/after/as soon as 等等從屬連接詞引領的子句，為表達時間的副詞子句。

➲ When **he saw Sophie**, he waved to her.
當他看到蘇菲時，他向她揮手。

➲ Don't forget to brush your teeth before **you go to bed**.
上床之前別忘了刷牙。

➲ We can watch a movie together after **I finish my homework**.
我寫完作業之後，我們可以一起看部電影。

➲ Tell him to call me as soon as **he comes back**.
他一回來就叫他打電話給我。

## The washing machine doesn't work, even though it's less than a year old.

這台洗衣機雖然還用不到一年，卻已經壞掉了。

從屬連接詞 although (= though)「雖然」、even though (= even if)「即使；就算」引導的副詞子句有讓步的意思。although/even though 還可以置於句首，當副詞子句放在句首時，與主要子句一定要用逗號隔開。

➲ **Although** we like the house, we can't afford it.
= We can't afford the house although we like it.
雖然我們喜歡這間房子，可是我們買不起。

➲ **Even though** Sean studies hard, he can't catch up with his classmates.
= Sean can't catch up with his classmates even though he studies hard.
就算尚恩再怎麼努力，他還是跟不上同學。

**because/since 引導表「原因」的副詞子句**

## We didn't get the microwave fixed because it was cheaper to buy a new one.

我們沒請人修理微波爐,因為買一台新的還比較便宜。

1. because 意指「因為」,所帶出的原因是說話者認為聽者還不知道的; since 意指「因為;既然」,所帶出的原由是說話者認為聽者已經知道的。

2. because 子句有時可改寫為: because of＋N/Ving。特別注意英文中不可同時出現 because 和 so 兩個連接詞,兩者必須擇其一。當副詞子句放在句首時,與主要子句一定要用逗號隔開。

➲ **Because** he was poor, he couldn't afford to buy a house.
= He couldn't afford to buy a house **because** he was poor.
因為他很窮,所以買不起房子。

➲ **Since** you're here, you might as well stay for dinner.
既然你在這裡,不妨留下來吃個晚餐。

➲ **Because** of the accident, I was stuck in traffic for two hours.
因為那起車禍,我在路上塞了兩個小時。

**so that/in order that 表目的的用法**

## The appliance must be assembled according to the instructions in order that it function properly.

這器具必須遵照說明指示來組裝,它才能夠正常運作。

in order that/so that 表示「因此」,其中的 in order/so 可以省略,成為 that 子句,意思皆是「為了;以便」。要特別注意的是,「so＋adj./adv.＋ that...」句型表示「結果」,意思為「如此……以致於」,不要和 so that 混淆。

that 表示「因此」

➲ They went to the museum early **so that** they could avoid the crowd.
他們很早到博物館是為了要避開人潮。

adj. that 表示「如
·以致於」

➲ The puppy was **so** cute **that** Nancy asked her mother if she could keep it.
小狗實在太可愛了,所以南西請求媽媽把牠留下來養。

## The power light will remain on as long as the machine is plugged in.

只要機器插上插頭，電源指示燈就會一直亮著。

if「如果」、unless (= if...not)「除非」、as long as (= so long as)「只要」
等從屬連接詞，可引導具有條件的副詞子句來修飾主要句子。

○ **If** you give up, you'll regret.
   你如果放棄，你會後悔。

○ **Unless** he apologizes, she won't forgive him.
   = **If** he doesn't apologize, she won't forgive him.
   除非他道歉，否則她不會原諒他。

○ **As long as** it doesn't rain, we will go.
   = **If** it doesn't rain, we will go.
   只要不下雨，我就去。

答對以下 10 個問題就擁有多益 450 的實力！

# Level 1　挑戰多益 450

**請從 (A)、(B)、(C)、(D) 中選出一個最適合的答案。**

**1.** All _____ need to do is make a small deposit.
(A) you can
(B) that you
(C) which you
(D) what you

**2.** _____ I ate breakfast, I quickly brushed my teeth and ran out the door.
(A) After
(B) When
(C) Before
(D) As soon as

**3.** _____ she walked into the room, she saw a mouse.
(A) As well as
(B) As soon as
(C) Where
(D) Because

**4.** _____ the storm, the ship couldn't sail for two days.
(A) Because of
(B) In spite of
(C) So
(D) Unless

**5.** _____ his wife died last week, he refuses to take time off.
(A) Though
(B) Because
(C) Unless
(D) So

**1.** 你必須做的就只是存一小筆錢。

解析 本句需要名詞子句作為主要子句的主詞,名詞子句需要以 that 引導,故答案為選項 (B),其中子句裡的 make a deposit 是「存款」的意思。

● deposit [dɪˋpɑzɪt] (n./v.) 存款;放置

---

**2.** 吃了早餐以後,我很快刷了牙然後跑出門。

解析 這題的四個選項都可以引導表「時間」的副詞子句,但只有 (A) 符合語意。若要選 (D) as soon as「一……就……」,應將句子修改為 As soon as I finished breakfast...,指「一吃完早餐就……」。

● brush one's teeth 刷牙

---

**3.** 她一走進房間就看到一隻老鼠。

解析 根據語意,應選表「時間」的從屬連接詞,選項中只有 (B) As soon as「一……就……」為正確答案。

● mouse [maʊs] (n.) 老鼠;滑鼠

---

**4.** 因為暴風雨的緣故,這艘船兩天無法航行。

解析 選項 (C) 和 (D) 為對等連接詞,須連接子句,不可選。選項 (A) 的 Because of(因為)和選項 (B) In spite of(儘管)皆為介系詞,後面可以接名詞(the storm),從語意上判斷,選項 (A) 最為正確。

● sail [sel] (v.) 航行

---

**5.** 雖然他太太上星期過世了,他還是拒絕請假。

解析 四個選項都可以用來連接副詞子句,因此需從語意上判斷。從屬子句的「太太過世」和主要子句的「拒絕請假」彼此有矛盾的關係,因此應選 (A) Though「雖然」。

● refuse [rɪˋfjuz] (v.) 拒絕

---

答案 1.(B) 2.(A) 3.(B) 4.(A) 5.(A)

**6.** We made an appointment _____ avoid having to wait.
- (A) so
- (B) so as
- (C) so as to
- (D) so that

**7.** As _____ as I get my computer set up, I'll send you an e-mail.
- (A) often
- (B) quickly
- (C) fast
- (D) soon

**8.** Our concern is just _____ or not you'll be able to finish the project by next month.
- (A) if
- (B) When
- (C) Such
- (D) whether

**9.** You can't have any dessert _____ you finish all your vegetables and rice.
- (A) as long as
- (B) so that
- (C) unless
- (D) in order that

**10.** I was feeling tired, _____ I didn't want to drive. _____ I took the bus, I was late for work.
- (A) because ; Because
- (B) because ; So
- (C) so ; Because
- (D) so ; So

**6.** 我們事先有預約，以避免久候。

解析 空格前有完整句子，後面並非子句，因此刪除連接詞 (A)。只有選項 (C) so as to 後面接原形動詞，so as to 的意思是「為了……」，相當於 in order to，因此為正確答案。注意，選項 (C) so as 是錯誤用法。另外類似的用法為 so that＋子句，這裡的 so as to avoid having to wait = so that we could avoid having a to wait.。

- appointment [əˋpɔɪntmənt] (n.) 約會　　● make an appointment 預約

---

**7.** 我的電腦一組裝好，就寄電子郵件給你。

解析 連接詞 as soon as 意指「一……就……」，為一固定用法，答案為選項 (D)。

- set up 組裝好

---

**8.** 我們只是擔心你下個月之前是不是能夠完成這個案子。

解析 just 後面整段為主要句子的主詞補語，故連接詞 if, when, whether 可能為答案，又因為空格後有 or not，故答案只能選 (D)：whether。

- concern [kənˋsɝn] (n.) 顧慮

---

**9.** 除非你把所有飯菜都吃完，否則你不可以吃任何甜點。

解析 四個選項都可以連接副詞子句，從語意上判斷，you finish all your vegetables and rice 為吃甜點的條件，故表「條件」的選項 (C) unless（除非）最正確。

---

**10.** 我覺得很累，所以不想開車。因為我搭了公車，上班才遲到。

解析 這題有兩個句子，第一個句子中，I was feeling tired 表「原因」，後面需要表「結果」的連接詞 so。第二個句子的 I was late for work 表「結果」，前面需要表「原因」的連接詞 Because，所以正確答案為 (C)。

答案 6.(C) 7.(D) 8.(D) 9.(C) 10.(C)

# Level 2　挑戰多益 *650*

請從 (A)、(B)、(C)、(D) 中選出一個最適合的答案。

**1.** The test was _____ difficult _____ only a few students passed it.
(A) very ; although
(B) so ; that
(C) enough ; because
(D) very ; but

**2.** _____ all of the players are here now, we can begin the game.
(A) When
(B) Once
(C) That
(D) Since

**3.** Call me _____ you get to the airport. I'll be waiting for your call!
(A) as soon as
(B) because
(C) until
(D) even

**4.** I don't know _____ Louis has finished _____ not.
(A) if ; and
(B) when ; or
(C) whether ; or
(D) that ; but

**5.** _____ you were able to understand his terrible handwriting is a miracle to me.
(A) This
(B) That
(C) These
(D) Those

**1.** 考試很難,所以只有一些學生通過。

解析 第一空格後的 difficult 應該是造成 only a few students passed it 的原因,所以應搭配程度副詞 so 與 that 子句,以句型「so+adj./adv.+that+子句」來表示「如此……以致於……」,答案為選項 (B)。

- difficult [ˋdɪfɪˏkʌlt] (adj.) 困難的

**2.** 現在既然所有的選手都到了,我們可以開始比賽了。

解析 前句「所有的選手都到了」明顯是後句「我們可以開始比賽了」的原因,因此空格內須填入表示「原因」的附屬連接詞,故選 (D) Since。

**3.** 你一到機場就打電話給我。我會等你的電話!

解析 由於後面的句子 I'll be waiting your call! 表示說話者預期對方的來電,所以空格填入 (A) as soon as「一……就……」最符合語意。選項 (C) 也是表「時間」的連接詞,意思是「直到」,指某動作持續到某時,若搭配本題的 call 則表示要對方一直打電話到他到機場為止,不合語意,故不可選。

- airport [ˋɛrˏport] (n.) 機場;航空站

**4.** 我不知道路易斯完成了沒有。

解析 主要動詞 know 後面需要有名詞子句,只有選項 (C) whether...(or not) 是正確的用法,也符合語意,為正確答案。這裡的 or not 也可以省略,或將 whether...or not 替換為 if。

**5.** 你看得懂他潦草的字跡,我覺得真是奇蹟。

解析 從空格到 his terrible handwriting 整段為主要句子的主詞,只有 (B) That 可以引導子句,作名詞用,故為答案。

- miracle [ˋmɪrək!] (n.) 奇蹟;奇事

答案 1.(B) 2.(D) 3.(A) 4.(C) 5.(B)

6. Do you know _____ to change this file into the new format?
(A) which
(B) Whose
(C) how
(D) if

7. The family expects _____ it will be in San Jose for the next three months.
(A) so
(B) such
(C) for
(D) that

8. _____ you give up the job offer, you'll regret.
(A) When
(B) Whether
(C) If
(D) That

9. _____ he apologizes, she won't talk to him again.
(A) Unless
(B) Since
(C) Because
(D) For

10. _____ your attempt failed, you did not lost too much.
(A) Even though
(B) Because
(C) Since
(D) Whether

**6.** 你知道要如何把這個檔案改成新格式嗎？

解析 know sth. 意思是「知道某事」，從空格到 the new format 整段為名詞子句，而且少了主詞，故淘汰 (D)：if。又因為空格後有不定詞 to change，故只可選 (C)：how，形成 how to change，為 how I can change... 的簡化。

● awkward [ˋɔkwəd] (adj.) 笨重的；笨拙，不熟練的

---

**7.** 這家人希望往後三個月都可以待在聖荷西。

解析 主要動詞 expects 後面需要名詞當受詞，只有 (D) that 可以引導名詞子句，故為正確答案。

● expect [ɪsˋkpɛkt] (v./n.) 期待，希望；預料

---

**8.** 你如果放棄這個工作機會，你會後悔。

解析 用從屬連接詞 if 表示「條件、理由」，且符合句意，故選 (C)。

● regret [rɪˋgrɛt] (v.) 後悔；感到遺憾 (n.) 後悔

---

**9.** 除非他道歉，否則她不會跟他說話。

解析 只有選項 (A) 符合語意。unless = if not，本句也可改成 If he doesn't apologize, she won't talk to him again.。

● apologize [əˋpɑləˌdʒaɪz] (v.) 道歉

---

**10.** 儘管你的努力未果，你也沒有太大損失。

解析 even though「即使，雖然」是 though 的強調；because 和 since 則表原因；whether 表「是否」。根據句意，答案應為 (A)。此外，even though 和 even if 意思相近，但 even though 強調「事實上已發生的事，非期待的結果」，而 even if 則指「即使未來可能會發生某事，或某事可能是事實，也不影響結果」。如：Even if it rains, he'll still come on time.「即使下雨，他還是會準時來。」

● attempt [əˋtɛmpt] (n./v.) 嘗試；企圖

答案 6.(C) 7.(D) 8.(C) 9.(A) 10.(A)

### 假設語氣的種類

● 假設的事情結局與事實不符，或與實際狀態相反，稱為假設句。

● 用 if、wish 引導子句稱假設子句，其動詞用的時態要比欲假設的時間往回退一步。譬如欲對「現在」狀況做假設，假設子句的動詞就要用「過去式」。

| 用商務英文學多益句型 | **假設語氣** 必考重點句 |
| --- | --- |

**對未來事件的預測或推論**

## If they don't agree to our terms, we won't do business with them.
### 如果他們不同意我們的條件，我們就不跟他們做生意。

if 子句在句首時，與主要子句之間須以逗號隔開。而 if 引導的假設子句以及主要句子的動詞變化，會因表達的時態不同而變化。對「未來可能發生的事」作推論時，假設子句須用「現在式」，主要子句則用「未來式」：

If＋S＋現在式動詞，S＋will/can/may＋原形動詞

> 對未來的假設，if 子句的動詞使用現在式，主要子句的動詞則用未來式。

❍ If it **rains** tomorrow, we'**ll** cancel the field trip.
　如果明天下雨，我們就取消校外教學。

❍ We'**ll** make it to the airport in time **if** traffic **is** light.
　如果交通順暢，我們就可以趕上火車。

**和現在事實不符的假設**

## If I were you, I would accept the company's offer.
### 如果我是你，我就會接受這公司的報價。

與「現在事實」相反的假設子句，動詞用「過去式」：

If＋S＋were/Ved，S＋should/would/could/might＋原形動詞。

含 be 動詞 were 的假設句裡，也可以把 if 去掉，were 放句首，為較文言的說法。

> 對現在事實的假設，與現在事實相反（事實上我不是你），假設句動詞使用過去式。

> 與現在事實相反（事實上我沒有足夠的錢）。

❍ If I **were** a bird, I **could** fly freely in the sky.
　＝ **Were** I a bird, I **could** fly freely in the sky.
　如果我是一隻鳥，我就可以自由地在天上飛。

❍ If I **had** enough money, I **would** buy the car.
　如果我有足夠的錢，我會買車。

### 和過去事實不符的假設

## If the sales manager had been at the meeting, he wouldn't have agreed to those terms.
**行銷經理要是有參加會議，他不會同意那些條款。**

與「過去事實」相反的假設子句，動詞用「過去完成式」：

If＋S＋had p.p., S＋should/would/could/might＋have p.p.

在這種句型裡，也可以把 if 去掉，had 放在子句句首。

➲ If we **had had** more time, we **could have visited** more places.
如果我們以前有更多時間，就可以參觀更多地方了。

➲ If he **had not broken** his leg, he **would have come** along.
如果他的腿沒斷，他就之前就會來了。

(左側旁註)
去事實的假設，與事實相反（我們以有很多時間），動用過去完成式。

實際狀況是他腿斷而且他當時也沒有

### 用 wish 表達對過去和現況的願望

## I wish I had been able to negotiate a better deal with the supplier.
**但願我可以跟供應商談到更好的交易價。**

對過去和現在的事實用動詞 wish 提出假設時，代表「事與願違」的希望，後面常接用 that 引導的名詞子句，子句的動詞變化往前推一格如下：

1. 對現況的願望 → 動詞用「過去式」，be 動詞一律用 were

   wish (＋that) ＋S＋were/Ved

2. 對過去的願望 → 動詞用「過去完成式」

   wish (＋that) ＋S＋had＋p.p.

➲ The poor man said, "I **wish** (**that**) I **had** a lot of money."
這個窮人說：「我希望有很多的錢。」

➲ Monica **wishes** she **had been** with her parents when the accident **happened**.
莫妮卡真希望意外發生時，她和父母在一起。

(左側旁註)
況的願望，事實是窮人沒有很多錢。

去的願望，事實是她沒有和父母在一

## Level 1 挑戰多益 *450*

**請從 (A)、(B)、(C)、(D) 中選出一個最適合的答案。**

□ *1.* If you _____ right now, you could catch the last train.
(A) leave
(B) left
(C) had left
(D) leaving

□ *2.* We will go hiking _____ the weather is good tomorrow.
(A) if
(B) when
(C) for
(D) wish

□ *3.* If I _____ you, I wouldn't go in there.
(A) were
(B) was
(C) am
(D) are

□ *4.* I wish I _____ in New York City right now.
(A) were
(B) was
(C) could be
(D) had been

□ *5.* Alicia _____ she _____ gone on the trip with her friends.
(A) wishes ; should
(B) wishes ; could have
(C) wishes ; should have
(D) wishes ; is

*1.* 如果你現在離開，你還可以趕上末班火車。

解析 主要子句用過去式助動詞 could 來和 if 子句搭配，表示「與現在事實相反」的假
設，所以 if 子句動詞要用過去式，答案為 (B)。這句話的言外之意表示：現在並沒
有要離開。如果選 (A) 的現在式，則表「可能發生的事」，主要句子的助動詞須改
為 will。

● train [tren] (n./v.) 火車；訓練，培養

*2.* 如果明天天氣好，我們就去健行。

解析 兩句中間需要連接詞，根據語意判斷，「假如明天天氣好」應該是「去健行」的條
件，故應選表假設的連接詞 if。對「未來可能發生的事」作假設時，if 子句動詞用
現在式（is），主要子句動詞則用未來式（will go hiking）。

● go hiking 去遠足，去健行

*3.* 如果我是你，我就不會進去那裡。

解析 主要子句用「would＋動詞現在式」來搭配 if 子句，代表「與現在事實相反」的假
設，而 be 動詞為固定用法，無論人稱為何都必須用 were，故選 (A)。

*4.* 我希望我現在在紐約。

解析 wish 後面接子句表「事與願違」的希望。從句尾的 right now 可知本句為對「現
況」許下的希望，be 動詞一律用 were，故選項 (A) 為正確答案。

*5.* 艾莉西亞希望她跟朋友一起去旅行了。

解析 wish 接的子句要表達「與現在事實相反」，應該用過去式；要表達「與過去事實
相反」，應該用過去完成式。由題目中的過去分詞 gone 可推測前面應搭配「完成
式」助動詞 have，只有 (B)、(C) 有可能，但 (C) 選項的 should（應該）不合語
意，故正確答案為選項 (B)。

● trip [trɪp] (n./v.) 旅行

**答案** 1.(B) 2.(A) 3.(A) 4.(A) 5.(B)

6. I wish I _____ there when you graduated.
   (A) have been
   (B) had been
   (C) were
   (D) was

7. If she _____ a little older, she would understand things better.
   (A) were
   (B) was
   (C) had been
   (D) has been

8. A: We will go to the park if it is fine.
   B: And if it _____ will we do?
   (A) isn't, what
   (B) rains what
   (C) doesn't rain, how
   (D) will

9. Do you ever wish _____ be someone else?
   (A) you should
   (B) them could
   (C) you could
   (D) you can

10. You could have become a queen if you _____ married the elder prince.
    (A) would
    (B) should
    (C) have
    (D) had

*6.* 我希望你畢業時我有出席。

解析 從 when you graduated 可知道是過去的事情，wish 表「與過去事實相反」的假設句，必須用「過去完成式」，所以選 (B) had been。

• graduate [`grædʒʊˌet] (v./n.) 畢業；畢業生

---

*7.* 如果她年紀稍長一點，她就會更懂事了。

解析 主要子句用過去式助動詞 would 來與 if 子句搭配，可知是陳述「與現在事實相反」的事情，假設句須用「過去式」，be 動詞恆用 were，不可用 was，因此答案為選項 (A)。

• understand [ˌʌndəˋstænd] (v.) 懂得，理解

---

*8.* A：如果天氣好，我們就去公園。

B：那如果不好，我們要做什麼呢？

解析 A 句說的是如果「天氣好」要做的事，因此 B 句問的應該是如果「天氣不好」的計畫，空格若填選項 (C) doesn't rain 也表示「天氣好」，語意矛盾，不可選。選項 (A) it isn't (fine) 和 (B) it rains 都表示「天氣不好」，但 if 子句在句首時，必須用逗號與主要句子隔開，所以選項 (B) 錯誤，答案為選項 (A)。

---

*9.* 你曾經希望你可以成為其他人嗎？

解析 wish 後面接子句，表達「與現在事實相反」的希望，助動詞及動詞一律要用「過去式」，所以選項 (D) 不對。再從語意上判斷，選項 (C) 為最適當的答案。

---

*10.* 如果妳當初嫁給了較年長的那個王子，妳可能已經是皇后了。

解析 主要子句用「could have＋過去分詞」來搭配 if 子句，表示「與過去事實相反」的假設，所以 if 子句必須用過去完成式「had＋過去分詞」，因此選項 (D) 才是正確的助動詞。

• elder [ˋɛldə] (adj.) 年齡較大的　　　　• prince [prɪns] (n.) 王子

答案 6.(B) 7.(A) 8.(A) 9.(C) 10.(D)

# Level **2**　挑戰多益 *650*

請從 (A)、(B)、(C)、(D) 中選出一個最適合的答案。

☐ **1.** _____ I you, I _____ it.
(A) Were ; will buy
(B) Were ; would buy
(C) Was ; would have bought
(D) was ; will buy

☐ **2.** I wish that I had _____ more money so that I could have bought the better model.
(A) have
(B) been
(C) had
(D) to have

☐ **3.** I wish you _____ have _____ on time, but you are always late, aren't you?
(A) better ; come
(B) can ; arrived
(C) could ; been
(D) can ; been arrived

☐ **4.** I think we _____ stayed together. It would have been safer.
(A) should
(B) should have
(C) had
(D) had better

☐ **5.** If you _____ ask me now, I _____ say no.
(A) will ; would
(B) were ; should
(C) were to ; would
(D) are ; am

**1.** 如果我是你，我就買了。

解析 這題是省略 if、將 be 動詞置於句首的假設語氣倒裝用法。表示「與現在事實相反」的假設，假設子句的 be 動詞恆用 were，故不可選 (C) 或 (D)，主要子句用法為「should/would/...＋動詞原形」，所以答案為選項 (B)。Were I you... = If I were you...。

**2.** 我希望我有更多錢，那麼我就可以買較好的車款。

解析 從子句中 could have bought 知道陳述的是過去的事情，所以 wish 接的子句必須用「過去完成式」，刪除選項 (A) 和 (D)。從語意上判斷，正確答案為 (C) had（動詞 have「有」的過去分詞）。

- model [`mɑdl] (n.) 模型，雛型 (adj.) 模範的，榜樣的

**3.** 我原本希望你可以準時，不過你老是遲到，對吧？

解析 從 you are always late 知道要對方準時是不可能的，因此用 wish 表「事與願違」的希望。要表示「與現在事實相反」的願望，子句的動詞必須用「過去式」；要表示「與過去事實相反」的願望，子句的動詞則用「過去完成式」。根據題目中已有的助動詞 have，可知前面應加上助動詞，後面應接過去分詞，必須選 (C) 形成過去完成式 could have been on time。

- on time 準時

**4.** 我覺得我們那時應該待在一起的。那樣就會安全一點了。

解析 從第二個句子 would have been 知道是希望發生但沒有發生的事情，所以選 (B) 形成 should have stayed together，表「遺憾、後悔」之意。選項 (A) should 和 (D) had better 後面都必須接動詞原形，表「義務」與「建議」。選 (C) 構成過去完成式 had stayed 表示過去確實發生過，語意不符。

- safe [sef] (adj.) 安全的

**5.** 如果你現在問我，我會說不。

解析 以 if 子句表達「與現在事實不符」的用法為：「If＋主詞＋過去式，主詞＋should/ould...＋動詞原形」，所以刪除選項 (A) 和 (D)。if 子句的 be 動詞恆用 were，(B) 和 (C) 均可考慮，但若選擇選項 (B)，if 子句會出現兩個動詞：were 和 ask，應把 ask 改成 asking，故答案選 (C)。

答案 1.(B) 2.(C) 3.(C) 4.(B) 5.(C)

253

6. If you _____ the cheaper compact car tomorrow, you _____ a lot of money.
   (A) buy ; could have saved
   (B) had bought ; would have saved
   (C) buy ; will save
   (D) buy ; saved

7. If you had been more responsible in your job, you _____ be involved in a lawsuit now.
   (A) can't
   (B) shouldn't
   (C) weren't
   (D) wouldn't

8. We can assemble this batch on time only if everyone _____ to work overtime.
   (A) has agreed
   (B) will agree
   (C) agrees
   (D) agreed

9. _____ Sherry _____ enough money, she would have bought the dress.
   (A) Had ; had
   (B) Had ; not
   (C) Has ; got
   (D) If ; had

10. To tell you the truth, I wouldn't want to be your business partner _____ you were the richest man in the world!
   (A) should
   (B) could
   (C) even if
   (D) even

*6.* 如果你明天買較便宜的小車，你會省很多錢。

解析 有時間點 tomorrow，表示是對未來的假設，if 子句用現在式，主要子句用未來式，故選 (C)。

● compact [kəm`pækt] (adj.) 小型的，緊實的 (v.) 壓緊

---

*7.* 假如你之前在工作上更負責一點，你現在就不會身陷官司。

解析 本題兩個子句發生的時間不同，If you had been... 代表的是「假如你那時候……」，而主要子句 you...now 指的是「那你現在就……」，所以此處須搭配過去式助動詞 wouldn't，來做與現在事實相反的假設。

● responsible [rɪ`spɑnsəbl] (adj.) 負責的 ● be involved in... 涉及，被捲入
● law suit 法律訴訟，官司

---

*8.* 唯有每個人都同意加班，我們才能準時組裝好這批貨。

解析 題目給的是表示結果的子句，且時態為現在式 can assemble，這是第一種的假設語氣句型，故 if 所接的條件子句要用現在簡單式，選項 (C) agrees 是正確答案。

● assemble [ə`sæmbl] (v.) 組裝 ● batch [bætʃ] (n.)（一批）貨
● overtime [`ovə͵taɪm] (adv.) 加班地

---

*9.* 如果 Sherry 當時有足夠的錢，她就會買下洋裝了。

解析 主要子句的「would have＋過去分詞」搭配 if 子句，表示「與過去事實相反」，if 子句必須用過去完成式「had＋過去分詞」，選項 (D) 的 had 表示一般動詞的過去式，所以錯誤。選項 (A) 是省略 if 的倒裝句用法：「Had＋主詞＋過去分詞」，原句為 If Sherry had had enough money...。

---

*10.* 老實告訴你，就算你是全世界最有錢的人，我也不想當你的生意夥伴。

解析 To tell you the truth 是「插入語」，經常放句首，相當於副詞 Honestly。本句中由 be 動詞 were 可看出此為「假設語氣」，因此前面須使用連接詞 if，而加入 even 則代表「強調」，意思是「即使，就算」。

● to tell you the truth 老實告訴你 ● partner [`pɑrtnə] (n.) 夥伴

答案 6.(C) 7.(D) 8.(C) 9.(A) 10.(C)

# 形容詞子句

### 形容詞子句概述

● 形容詞子句用來修飾主要子句中的某個名詞，即「先行詞」。

● 形容詞子句由一個關係代名詞／副詞（who、whom、which、that、when、where 等）引導出來，放在要修飾的名詞後面。

**用商務英文
學多益句型**

## 形容詞子句　必考重點句

**先行詞為「人」的形容詞子句**

## Is there someone who can help me return this item?

**有沒有人可以幫我退還這項物品？**

先行詞是「人」，關係代名詞在主格位置：用 who 或 that，但一般情形下，比較習慣用 who，較少用 that 來代替主詞為「人」的先行詞。

先行詞是「人」，關係代名詞在受格位置：用 whom，但比較常用 who 或 that 取代，甚至可以省略。

先行詞 a friend 是「人」，關係代名詞在主格位置，用 who/that。who 較常見，that 較少見。

○ Mr. Peterson has **a friend** who/that is a successful lawyer.
　彼得森先生有個朋友，是位成功的律師。

先行詞 a friend 是「人」，關係代名詞在受格位置，用 whom/who/that。直接省略／who/that 較常見，whom 較正式。

○ Mr. Peterson has **a friend** whom/who/that he met at a conference in Norway.
　彼得森先生有個朋友，是在挪威的會議上遇到的。

**先行詞為「物」的形容詞子句**

## Is this the digital camera that's on sale for $199?

**這是那台特價 199 美元的數位相機嗎？**

先行詞是「物」，關係代名詞不論是在主格／受格位置，皆可用 that 或 which，但一般較常用 that。which 雖然在文法上也通，但實則非常少見。受格位置的 that 或 which 也可直接省略。

先行詞 the money 是「物」，關係代名詞在主格位置，用 that/which。that 較常見，which 較少見。

○ Did you see **the money** that was on the table?
　你有看到桌子上的錢嗎？

⊃ I can't find **the book** (that) Linda lent me last week.
我找不到琳達上禮拜借我的書。

行詞 the book 是
勿」，關係代名詞在受
位置，用 that 或直
省略。

---

### 先行詞是「時間或地點」

## The boutique where I bought this blouse is having a sale today.

**我買這件上衣的那家精品店今天正在打折。**

先行詞是「時間或地點」：用關係副詞 when 或 where 來帶出形容詞子句。
關係副詞可以用「**介系詞＋which**」來取代：此時的 which 不可換成 that，也
不能省略。介系詞要看先行詞為何而定。

行詞 the day 是「時
，用關係副詞 when
整個形容詞子句。

⊃ I still remember **the day** when my daughter was born.
= I still remember **the day** on which my daughter was born.
我還記得我女兒出生的那一天。

行詞 the restaurant
「地點」，用關係副
where 引導整個形容
句。

⊃ **The restaurant** where I had my last birthday party has moved to a
different location.
= **The restaurant** at which I had my last birthday party has moved
to a different location.
我上次辦生日派對的那家餐廳已經搬到別的地點了。

---

### 用 which/as 代替前面的句子

## There are lots of great stores and restaurants at the mall, which is why I go there so often.

**那家賣場有很多不錯的商店和餐廳，這就是我為何這麼常去那兒的原因。**

關係代名詞 which 所引導的子句可以代替前面的句子，要放在主要句子後
面，以逗號與前面句子分隔。若是用 as 引導的子句，則可以放在主要子句之
前或之後。

s 來引導句子
也可寫做 As we
ow, he can talk
y with anyone he
s.

⊃ **He can talk easily with anyone he meets**, which/as we all know.
他和任何人碰面都可以輕鬆交談，這是我們都知道的。

n 用來指 he was
ys late 整件事。

⊃ **He was always late**, which is why he got fired.
他總是遲到，這是他被炒魷魚的原因。

## Would the shopper whose car is blocking the entrance please move it now?
車輛擋住出口的顧客，麻煩現在將車移開。

若先行詞是「人」，而形容詞子句裡的主詞是「先行詞的所有物」：用代表所有格的 whose 來連接。先行詞是「物」時，也可使用所有格 whose，或用 of which 來連接。

- **The man** whose wallet was stolen is talking to the police.
  皮夾被偷的男人正在和警察談話。

- **The girl** whose cell phone I found is our new classmate.
  那位我找到她手機的女孩是我們的新同學。

- **The house** whose door is red is mine.
  = **The house** of which the door is red is mine.
  紅色門的那棟房子是我的。

## It's the bags on the top shelf that are on sale.
是上層櫃子的袋子在打折。

強調語氣句型為 It is/was＋名詞或代名詞＋形容詞子句 (that/who...)。無論先行詞為人或物，無論做主格或受格，關係代名詞都用 that。但當先行詞為人作主格用時，關係代名詞也可用 who。

- **It's** the students **that/who** should talk more in the class, not the teacher.
  在班上應該多說話的人是學生，不是老師。

- **It is** the light **that** makes the photographs so special.
  是光線讓照片這麼特別的。

what/whatever/whoever/whichever 引導的名詞子句

## Whatever you buy can be exchanged or returned if you're not satisfied.

**無論你買什麼，如果不滿意，都可以換貨或退貨。**

複合關係代名詞 = 先行詞＋關係代名詞，即複合關係代名詞前沒有先行詞：

1. **what** = the＋名詞＋that（或 all that）

2. **whatever** = anything that/no matter what（無論什麼）

3. **whoever** = anyone who；**whomever** = anyone whom（無論誰）

4. **whichever** = anyone that（無論哪一個）

➲ **What** (= **All that**) is mine is yours, and what is yours is mine.
我的都是你的，你的都是我的。

➲ You need to get along with **whomever** (= **anyone whom**) you're working with.
你必須跟每個和你一起工作的人好好相處。

➲ **Whatever** (= **No matter what**) we say to him, he won't change his mind.
不管我們跟他說什麼，他都不會改變心意的。

# Level 1 　挑戰多益 450

**請從 (A)、(B)、(C)、(D) 中選出一個最適合的答案。**

1. I really like the gift _____ you bought for me.
   (A) that
   (B) where
   (C) what
   (D) who

2. Who is the lady _____ an umbrella?
   (A) where holding
   (B) that is holding
   (C) which is holding
   (D) what is holding

3. She is the most beautiful woman _____ I have ever seen.
   (A) whom
   (B) that
   (C) which
   (D) what

4. Is that the man _____ you met on the subway?
   (A) who
   (B) whom
   (C) that
   (D) all of the above

5. Is this the best wine _____ you have?
   (A) which
   (B) what
   (C) that
   (D) if

**1.** 我真的很喜歡你買給我的禮物。

解析 形容詞子句的先行詞為物（the gift），關係代名詞必須使用 that，答案為選項
(A)。

● gift [gɪft] (n.) 禮物

**2.** 拿著雨傘的那位小姐是誰？

解析 先行詞是 the lady，這裡的關係代名詞需要 who 或 that，才能接動詞 is holding，
但為避免與句首的疑問詞 Who 重複，關係代名詞應用 that，所以選 (B)。

● umbrella [ʌmˋbrɛlə] (n.) 雨傘

**3.** 她是我見過最美麗的女人。

解析 本題的形容詞子句先行詞為人（woman），而且使用最高級形容詞 the most
beautiful 修飾，因此只可以用 that 引導，答案為選項 (B)。

**4.** 那是你在地鐵遇到的那名男子嗎？

解析 先行詞 the man 為人，需要的關係代名詞在子句中是作為受格，(A)、(B)、(C) 三
個選項的 who/whom/that 皆可用，因此答案為選項 (D)。

● subway [ˋsʌb‚we] (n.) 地下鐵

**5.** 這是你們最好的葡萄酒嗎？

解析 這題的形容詞子句中前面有先行詞 the best wine，故不可選複合關係代名詞
what。先行詞為物，關係代名詞原本可用 which 或 that，但是這個先行詞中有最高
級 the best，因此只能用 that，答案為 (C)。

● wine [waɪn] (n.) 葡萄酒

答案 1.(A) 2.(B) 3.(B) 4.(D) 5.(C)

**6.** _____ is the letter addressed to?
  (A) Whose
  (B) Whom
  (C) To whom
  (D) What

**7.** I think it was John _____ was late yesterday.
  (A) who
  (B) whom
  (C) which
  (D) of whom

**8.** Is this the desk _____ found on the street?
  (A) you
  (B) what you
  (C) whom you
  (D) who you

**9.** It is the sauce _____ makes the food so special.
  (A) that
  (B) what
  (C) who
  (D) where

**10.** Do you know _____ car is parked in my spot?
  (A) who
  (B) whom
  (C) who's
  (D) whose

**6.** 這封信是寄給誰的？

解析 這個問句在句尾已經有介系詞 to，故不可選 (C)。要填入的疑問代名詞是受格，故用 Whom，也可用 Who 代替，答案為選項 (B)。

● address [əˋdrɛs] (v./n.) 地址；寄信給…；對…說話

**7.** 我想昨天遲到的那個人是約翰。

解析 本句的形容詞子句用來修飾 John，先行詞為人，在形容詞子句中作為主詞用，因此關係代名詞可用 who 或 that，答案為選項 (A)。「It is/was＋人或物＋that 形容詞子句」的句型為表強調的用法。

**8.** 這是你在街上找到的那張桌子嗎

解析 空格後所有的字若要構成形容詞子句，需要關係代名詞 which/that 和主詞 you 引導。因為關係代名詞的功能為 found 的受詞，所以可以省略，只留下 you，故答案為 (A)。

● find [faɪnd] (v.) 發現；尋找

**9.** 是醬料讓食物這麼特別的。

解析 先行詞為物品 sauce，關係代名詞為 that，故答案為 (A)。「It is/was＋人或物＋that 形容詞子句」的句型為表強調的用法。

● sauce [sɔs] (n.) 醬料

**10.** 你知道是誰的車停在我的位置嗎？

解析 四個選項都和「誰」有關，但空格後接的是名詞 car，應該用代表「某人的」所有格 whose，故選項 (D) 為正確答案。本句的 whose car is parked in my spot 為 wh-疑問詞所引導的名詞子句，作為 Do you know 的受詞。

● spot [spɑt] (n.) 空位

答案 6.(B) 7.(A) 8.(A) 9.(A) 10.(D)

請從 (A)、(B)、(C)、(D) 中選出一個最適合的答案。

C **1.** The books _____ pages are torn must be replaced.
    (A) with
    (B) that
    (C) whose
    (D) which

B **2.** The man _____ you met on the subway was my tennis coach.
    (A) which
    (B) whom
    (C) what
    (D) where

A **3.** Patricia didn't get the job _____ really surprised her friends.
    (A) ,which
    (B) which
    (C) that
    (D) that

D **4.** The place _____ she lives is located in a beautiful river valley with pine trees all around.
    (A) that
    (B) which
    (C) what
    (D) where

C **5.** _____ shoes are these green ones?
    (A) Who's
    (B) Whom's
    (C) Whose
    (D) Who

**1.** 書籍頁面破損者必須更換。

解析 此句出現兩個動詞 are torn 和 be replaced，需要關係代名詞來連接，不可選 (A) with。先行詞為 the books，子句中的 pages，是「先行詞的所有物」，故需要所有格 whose 來引導，答案為選項 (C)。

- tear [tɛr] (v./n.) 撕開，扯破（過去分詞為 torn）
- replace [rɪˋples] (v.) 放回原處；更換

**2.** 你在地鐵遇到的那個男人就是我的網球教練。

解析 先行詞 the man 為人，不可用 which、where 或 what 引導形容詞子句。由於關係代名詞在子句中是作為受格，應用 whom，也可用 who 或 that 代替，因此答案選 (B)。

- coach [kotʃ] (n./v.) 教練；訓練

**3.** 派翠西沒有得到那份工作，這讓她的朋友感到震驚。

解析 從句意可得知，從空格後一直到句點應該都是要補述 Patricia didn't get he job 這一件事情。在所有的關係代名詞中，只有 which 可以這樣用，而且前方必須有逗點，不能用 that 取代，答案選 (A)。

**4.** 她住的地方坐落於美麗的河谷，四周松樹環繞。

解析 形容詞子句的動詞 live 表示（居住），後面需要介系詞表居住在某地，本句沒有，所以需要關係副詞 where（＝in which）來引導，答案為選項 (D)。

- valley [ˋvælɪ] (n.) 山谷

**5.** 這雙綠色的鞋子是誰的？

解析 本題是疑問句，主詞為 these green ones，動詞為 are，空格需要所有格 whose，加上一般名詞 shoes 作為受詞，意思是「誰的鞋子？」，答案為選項 (C)。注意：whose 可作所有格或所有代名詞，本句也可說 Whose are these green shoes?，其中的 whose 則為所有代名詞。

答案 1.(C) 2.(B) 3.(A) 4.(D) 5.(C)

**A** **6.** Is she the girl _____ were telling me about?
   (A) you
   (B) that
   (C) which
   (D) whom

**B** **7.** The person to _____ you should speak is Martha. She's an expert on the Asian market.
   (A) which
   (B) whom
   (C) who
   (D) that

B **C** **8.** Do you know the factory _____ this particular model is made?
   (A) which
   (B) in which
   (C) at where
   (D) in that

**A** **9.** The hotel _____ the convention will be held is conveniently located.
   (A) at which
   (B) which
   (C) that
   (D) at where

**C** **10.** It's the parents _____ should be held responsible for their children's bad behavior.
   (A) whose
   (B) who's
   (C) who
   (D) which

**6.** 她就是你跟我說的那個女孩子嗎？

解析 本句的 the girl 為子句的先行詞，空格後的動詞為 were telling，與先行詞不一致，可推知子句中的主詞另有他人，如選項 (A) 的 you。而修飾 the girl 的關係代名詞則作受格，可用 whom/who/that，也可以省略，故答案為選項 (A)。

**7.** 你應該和瑪莎這個人談一談。她是亞洲市場的專家。

解析 The person 指的是人，且空格前有介系詞 to，故應選受格的關係代名詞 whom，答案為 (B)。本題的介系詞 to 若移到 speak 之後，則 (C) 或 (D) 亦可選，句子變為 The person whom/who/that you should speak to is Martha.
• expert [`ɛkspɚt] (n.) 專家　　　　• market [`mɑrkɪt] (n.) 市場

**8.** 你知不知道做這個特定款式的工廠？

解析 空格明顯指的是 factory，也就是 model 製作的地方，應選用表示地點的關係副詞 where 或其相同用法 in which，不能單用 which。where 是副詞，本身已包含 in、at 等介系詞的含意，不能再加介系詞，故 (C) 為錯誤選項。that 則不能放在介系詞之後，故 (D) 也不可選。
• particular [pɚ`tɪkjəlɚ] (adj.) 特別的

**9.** 即將舉行大會的飯店地裡位置很方便。

解析 本題的 hotel 是 convention 即將被舉辦的地方，應選用表示地點的關係副詞 where 或其相同用法 in/at which，不能單用 which 或 that，不可選 (B)、(C)。where 是副詞，本身已包含 in、at 等介系詞的含意，不能再加介系詞，故 (D) 為錯誤選項。答案應選 (A)。
• convention [kən`vɛnʃən] (n.) （某職業、政黨的）大會，集會

**10.** 孩子行為不矩該追究的人是他們的父母親。

解析 先行詞 the parents 是人，不能用 which 來修飾，因此不可選 (D)。本題關係代名詞後直接接動詞 should be held...，因此須用主格的 who 或 that 來引導，故答案為 (C)。「It is/was＋人或物＋形容詞子句」的句型為表強調的用法，語氣會比 The parents should be held responsible for their children's bad behavior. 強烈。
• hold sb. responsible for sth.：要求某人為某事負責
• behavior [bɪ`hevjɚ] (n.) 行為

答案 6.(A) 7.(B) 8.(B) 9.(A) 10.(C)

### 限定與非限定用法概述

- 形容詞子句修飾先行詞可分限定與非限定兩種用法。
- 限定子句：前方沒有逗點，用來修飾不明確的普通名詞。
- 非限定子句：前面有逗點，若在整句話中間，則後面也要有逗點。它用來修飾明確的人事物或專有名詞。

**用商務英文學多益句型**　**限定與非限定用法** 必考重點句

**限定子句基本用法**

## The CPA who does my taxes charges reasonable rates.

**處理我的稅務的會計師收費合理。**

當形容詞子句為一個句子的必要資訊時，可稱此形容詞子句為「限定子句」，先行詞與關係代名詞之間沒有逗號。限定子句所修飾的一定都是普通名詞，如 the woman、the book 等。

who is sitting on the bench 用來說明先行詞 the man 是哪一位男人

○ **The man** who is sitting on the bench is my teacher.
　這個坐在長凳上的男人是我的老師。

> 若少了 who is sitting on the bench 這個資訊，整個句子剩下 The man is my teacher.，文法上雖沒有錯誤，但句意不明確。

who lost her family in the flood 用來說明先行詞 the woman

○ We visited **the woman** who lost her family in the flood.
　我們探望了在水災中喪失了家人的女人。

> 如果沒有 who lost her family in the flood 這個子句的話，We visited the woman. 就變成是一個令人困惑的句子，因為聽者或讀者會不知道到底是哪個女人，所以這個形容詞子句提供的是必要資訊。

**非限定子句基本用法**

## The auditor, who works for a large CPA firm, is coming tomorrow.

**這位稽核員服務在一家大型註冊會計事務所，他明天要過來。**

1. 當形容詞子句只是一個句子的補充資訊時，可稱此為「非限定子句」。在這樣的補述用法中，關係代名詞前面要以逗號與主要子句分開。補述用法可用在主格和受格 who、whom 和 which 以及所有格 whose。補述用法的關係代名詞均不可用 that 代替，受格代名詞也不可省略。

2. 非限定子句修飾的一定都是專有名詞（如人名、地名）或是明確的人事物（如 my sister、the U.S. president、John's car），因為像這樣的名詞不需要加以解釋說明，別人就已知道是哪一個。

容詞子句 who teaches
conomics 用來說明先
詞 Professor Adams

⊃ **Professor Adams**, **who teaches economics**, is one of the committee members.

亞當教授是其中一位委員，他教經濟學。

> 由於先行詞 Professor Adams 是個明確、獨一無二的名字，所以就算少了這個資訊，Professor Adams is one of the committee members. 也是一個句意完整的句子。

which 開頭的子句即
形容詞子句，用來說
Taipei 101。

⊃ We visited **Taipei 101**, **which was the tallest building in the world at that time**.

我們參觀了台北 101，它是當時最高的建築物。

> We visited Taipei 101 是個意思很清楚的句子，至於它當時是否為世界上最高的建築物，對於理解 We visited Taipei 101 這個句子沒有任何影響，所以這個形容詞子句所提供的只是補充資訊。

### 「介系詞＋whom/which」只能用在限定子句

## Are you the accountant to whom I spoke yesterday?
### 你是我昨天交談過的會計師嗎？

限定子句句尾有介系詞時，可以把介系詞移到 whom、which 的前面。非限定用法的關係代名詞前方不會有介系詞。

「介系詞＋關係代名
」的用法中，關代只
用 whom/which。

⊃ That is the house that Mark Twain was born **in**.
= That is the house **in which** Mark Twain was born.
那就是馬克吐溫出生的房子。

⊃ What is the source of the statistics that you are referring **to**?
= What is the source of the statistics **to which** you are referring?
你指的資料來源出處是哪裡？

# Level ① 挑戰多益 *450*

請從 (A)、(B)、(C)、(D) 中選出一個最適合的答案。

**1.** The Japanese singer, _____ just released his new album, is known all around the world.
(A) who
(B) whom
(C) whose
(D) who is

**2.** I'm not sure of _____ you are speaking.
(A) who
(B) whom
(C) that
(D) whose

**3.** _____ am I speaking?
(A) Whom
(B) Who
(C) With whom
(D) Whose

**4.** Sherry _____ lost both of her parents when she was little, is very independent young woman.
(A) that
(B) who
(C) who
(D) that

**5.** The report, _____ needs to be revised by 4:00 p.m., is on your desk.
(A) that
(B) which
(C) what
(D) where

*1.* 這位日本歌手全球知名，他才剛發了新專輯。

解析 兩個逗號之間的子句為「非限定用法」，用來補充先行詞 the Japanese singer 的資訊。本子句中關係代名詞為主格用法，故答案選 (A) who。

● album [`ælbəm] (n.) 專輯；相片簿

*2.* 我不確定你說的是誰。

解析 I'm not sure 後面要接名詞，這裡是省略了先行詞 the person。子句的部分為 of (the person) you are speaking，乃是將 speak of 的 of 移到句首的用法，先行詞在受格位置，關代只可以用受格 whom，故答案為選項 (B)。

*3.* 我在跟誰說話？

解析 speak 後面要接介系詞 to/with，才能再接受詞「人」。本題句尾沒有介系詞，表示介系詞前移至疑問詞之前，故應選 (C) With whom。With whom am I speaking to? = Whom am I speaking with? 這句話是常用的電話用語，用來確認來電者是誰。

*4.* 雪莉是一位很獨立的女性，她從小就失去了雙親。

解析 由空格到逗號的部分是形容詞子句。Tina is a very independent young woman 是個意思很清楚的句子，所指的人也很明確，所以可以判斷中間的形容詞子句是非限定用法，前後要用逗號隔開。先行詞為「人」時，在非限定用法中關代只能用 who，不可用 that 代替，因此答案選 (B)。

*5.* 報告在你桌上，下午四點前要改好。

解析 兩個逗號之間是一個形容詞子句，用來修飾 report。空格應填入的字詞為子句的主詞，且因為 report 後有逗號，是「非限定用法」，因此關係代名詞要用 (B) which，不能用 (A) that。

● revise [rɪ`vaɪz] (v.) 修改

答案 1.(A) 2.(B) 3.(C) 4.(B) 5.(B)

**6.** The cashier _____ I talked refused to issue me a refund.
(A) who
(B) whom
(C) to whom
(D) which

**7.** The new DVD, _____ is sitting on the table over there, won't play in your DVD player.
(A) that
(B) which
(C) where
(D) whose

**8.** The English newspaper, _____ is available online for free, costs NT$15 at the newsstand.
(A) that
(B) which
(C) what
(D) when

**9.** The man in the gray suit, _____ is talking to Professor James, is a world-renowned economist.
(A) whom
(B) that
(C) which
(D) who

**10.** Are you familiar with the person _____ this letter is addressed?
(A) that
(B) which
(C) to whom
(D) who

**6.** 和我交涉的收銀員拒絕退錢給我。

解析 本句關係代名詞明顯是 I 談話的對象,「與……談話」應用動詞片語 talk to,介系詞 to 不能省略,但原句中的 talked 後並沒有 to,應將 to 移至關係代名詞前,後面只能接受格的 whom,(C) 為正確答案。

● cashier [kæˋʃɪə] (n.) 收銀員　　　　　● refund [rɪˋfʌnd] (n.) 退款

---

**7.** 放在那邊桌子上的新 DVD 用你的放影機不能播放。

解析 先行詞為物(DVD),形容詞子句需要主詞,但子句前用逗號與主要子句隔開,表「非限定用法」,不可使用選項 (A) that。故應選 which 作引導,答案為 (B)。

● player [ˋpleə] (n.) 放映機器;玩遊戲的人;演奏者;球員

---

**8.** 這份英文報提供線上免費閱讀,在報攤上買要台幣十五元。

解析 兩逗號間是一形容詞子句,空格應填入子句的主詞。選項 (D) when 不可以在形容詞子句中作主詞,故不可選。子句前有先行詞 (the English newspaper),故不可選 (C) what (= 先行詞＋關係代名詞)。由於子句與先行詞以逗號分隔,屬「非限定用法」,不可使用 (A) that 作引導,故正確答案為選項 (B) which。

● available [əˋveləbl] (adj.) 可取得的;可利用的

---

**9.** 穿灰色西裝的男子,也就是正在和詹姆士教授說話的人,是全球知名的經濟學家。

解析 這裡的空格雖然在物品 suit 後面,但子句中和教授說話的是「人」,所以不可選 which。本題關係代名詞在子句中是主詞,且子句與先行詞以逗號分隔,屬「非限定用法」,不可使用 that,故選項 (D) who 為正確答案。

● world-renowned [wɜd rɪˋnond] (adj.) 全球知名的

● economist [ɪˋkɑnəmɪst] (n.) 經濟學家

---

**10.** 你跟這封信的收件者熟嗎?

解析 空格後面引導的是一形容詞子句,修飾 person,故不可選 (B) which。子句中的主詞是 this letter,後面接被動用法的動詞 is addressed,意思是「這封信是寫給……」,後面還欠缺介系詞 to,可見 to 被前移至關係代名詞之前,因此應選 (C) to whom。形容詞子句 to whom this letter is addressed = whom/that this letter is addressed to。

● be familiar with... 與…熟識;熟悉…

● address [əˋdrɛs] (n./v.) 地址;致函;向…說話

---

答案 6.(C) 7.(B) 8.(B) 9.(D) 10.(C)

# Level 2　挑戰多益 *650*

**請從 (A)、(B)、(C)、(D) 中選出一個最適合的答案。**

☐ **1.** My _____ lives in _____ a teacher. My other son is a dentist.
(A) son who ; New York is
(B) son, who ; New York, is
(C) son who ; New York, is
(D) son, that ; New York is

☐ **2.** The new _____ was hired last _____ give a speech tomorrow.
(A) CEO, that ; week, will
(B) CEO, who ; week, will
(C) CEO, who ; week will
(D) CEO who ; week will

☐ **3.** To _____ photo are you pointing?
(A) whom
(B) who's
(C) whose
(D) that

☐ **4.** Our professor had us read the novel _____ the author is best known.
(A) for what
(B) for which
(C) that
(D) when

☐ **5.** The man _____ house the stolen goods were found was arrested.
(A) in which
(B) in who's
(C) whose
(D) in whose

**1.** 我那個住在紐約的兒子是老師。另一個兒子是牙醫。

解析 這題考限定或非限定用法，由於後面句子出現 my other son，可知不只一個兒子，應用「限定用法」明確指出哪一個兒子，形容詞子句前後不可加逗號，因此答案必須選 (A)。

● dentist [ˋdɛntɪst] (n.) 牙醫

---

**2.** 新執行長上週剛受聘，明天將發表演講。

解析 公司的新 CEO 是明確的人物，不須用限定用法加以解釋說明，別人就知道是誰，因此本題用「非限定用法」，形容詞子句前後均加逗號，且關係代名詞不可以用 that，故答案選 (B)。

---

**3.** 你在指誰的照片？

解析 這是一句疑問句，是將動詞 point to 當中的介系詞移到句首的變化形。一般名詞 photo 前面需要所有格 whose，這個句子還原後應該是 Whose photo are you pointing to?，答案為選項 (C)。

---

**4.** 我們教授要我們讀那本該作者最出名的小說。

解析 空格後面引導的是一形容詞子句，修飾 novel，可考慮用關係代名詞 which 或 that，但子句中的動詞 is best known 後面還欠缺介系詞 for，說明該作者是「以那本小說最為人所知」，可見 for 被前移至關係代名詞之前，因此應選 (B) for which。形容詞子句 for which the author is best known = which/that the author is best known for。

● be known for... 因⋯出名，以⋯著稱

---

**5.** 房子裡被搜出失竊貨品的那個人被逮捕了。

解析 先行詞 the man 和子句裡的 house 是所有格的關係，關係代名詞應用 whose，但子句中 whose house 的功用是作為地方副詞，指失竊的貨品被找到的地方，因此還加入表地點的介系詞 in，故應選 (D)。

● goods [gʊdz] (n.) 商品，貨物　　● arrest [əˋrɛst] (v./n.) 逮捕

答案 1.(A) 2.(B) 3.(C) 4.(B) 5.(D)

**6.** Our accounting department, _____ is located on the 11th floor, will provide you with the documents you need.
(A) that
(B) which
(C) where
(D) there

**7.** My _____ worked at the _____ laid off last week.
(A) wife who ; mall was
(B) wife who's ; mall was
(C) wife, who; mall, was
(D) wife, who ; mall was

**8.** The _____ wearing the black _____ my boss, not the one wearing the brown hat.
(A) man who's ; hat is
(B) man whose; hat is
(C) man, who's ; hat, is
(D) man, whose ; hat, is

**9.** The factory _____ they worked was dark and dirty.
(A) in where
(B) in which
(C) which
(D) in that

**10.** My favorite _____ new book is on the bestseller _____ having a book signing at a local bookstore.
(A) author, who's ; list, will be
(B) author whose ; list will be
(C) author, who ; list, will be
(D) author, whose ; list, will be

*6.* 我們位在十一樓的會計部會提供你需要的文件。

解析 「會計部」是明確的部門,因此用「非限定用法」來修飾,關係代名詞前面有逗點,
且不能用 that,故選項 (B) which 為正確答案。

- accounting [əˈkauntɪŋ] (n.) 會計
- department [dɪˈpɑrtmənt] (n.) 部門
- document [ˈdɑkjumənt] (n.) 文件

*7.* 我老婆在那家賣場上班,上週被解雇了。

解析 my wife 是明確、僅有的一人,因此不必用限定用法來修飾,只要用「非限定用
法」補充資訊。非限定子句前面有逗點,且關係代名詞不能用 that,若子句在整個
句子中,則後面也要加逗號,故選項 (C) 為正確答案。

*8.* 那位戴黑色帽子的人是我老闆,不是戴棕色帽子那位。

解析 由於後面句子出現 not the one wearing the brown hat,可知當場不只一個戴帽子的
人,必須用「限定用法」來明確指出所描述的對象,形容詞子句前後不可加逗號,
不可選 (C)、(D)。此外,子句中關係代名詞後面接現在分詞 wearing,前面還缺 be
動詞,因此關係代名詞應選 who's,答案必須選 (A)。

*9.* 他們工作的那家工廠又暗又髒。

解析 本題先行詞 the factory 是地點,即他們所工作的地方,關係代名詞前還須加介系詞
in,不能單用 which,因此選 (B) in which,等於關係副詞 where。where 是副詞,
本身已包含 in、at 等介系詞的含意,不能再加介系詞,故 (A) 為錯誤選項。that 則
不能放在介系詞之後,故 (D) 也不可選。

*10.* 我最喜愛的作者的新書登上暢銷書排行榜,他正在本地一家書店舉辦簽名會。

解析 先行詞 my favorite author 是明確的人,只須用「非限定用法」來補充資訊,所以
子句前後要加逗號。而 author 和子句裡的 new book 是所有格的關係,關係代名詞
應用 whose,故應選 (D)。

- bestseller [bɛstˈsɛlɚ] (n.) 暢銷書
- book signing 簽書會

答案 6.(B) 7.(C) 8.(A) 9.(B) 10.(D)

# 名詞子句

### 名詞子句種類

● 所謂「名詞子句」，顧名思義就是把一個句子當作名詞，用在另一個句子裡。

● 名詞子句可在另一個句子裡當主詞、受詞或補語。

● 名詞子句原本可能是個疑問句或直述句。

用商務英文
學多益句型

## 名詞子句　必考重點句

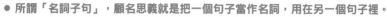

#### if/whether 所引導的名詞子句

### We need to decide if/whether we're going to participate in the trade show.

**我們需要決定是否參加那場貿易展。**

if/whether 所引導的名詞子句表示「是否」，是由 yes/no 問句改變而來的名詞子句，句型為：「if/whether＋S＋be 動詞……」或「if/whether＋S＋還原為正確時態的一般動詞……」。

if/whether 子句作為 Do you know 的受詞

➲ Do you know? Is **Mark** coming to the party?
　→ Do you know **if/whether** Mark **is coming** to the party?
　　你知道馬克會不會來派對嗎？

John 為第三人稱單數主詞，if/whether 子句中動詞應還原為 has。

➲ I don't care. Does John have a lot of money?
　→ I don't care **if/whether** John **has** a lot of money.
　　我不在意約翰是否有很多錢。

#### 疑問詞所引導的名詞子句

### Do you know when the computer show will be held this year?

**你知道今年電腦展什麼時候舉辦嗎？**

將 why/when/how/where 等疑問句改為名詞子句時，應將主詞和動詞位置對調，句型為：「疑問詞＋S＋be 動詞」或「疑問詞＋S＋還原為正確時態的一般動詞……」。

why 所引導的子句作為 Do you know 的受詞

➲ Do you know? Why isn't Jack at work today?
　→ Do you know **why** Jack **isn't** at work today?
　　你知道傑克為什麼今天沒有來上班嗎？

wh- 疑問句為過去
，改為名詞子句時動
應還原為過去式 left

o 本身為 wh- 疑問句
主詞，改為名詞子句
後面直接接動詞

⊃ Could you tell me? When did David leave?
　→ Could you tell me **when** David **left**?
　你可以告訴我大衛什麼時候會離開嗎？

⊃ I have no idea. Who took my cell phone?
　→ I have no idea **who took** my cell phone.
　我不知道誰拿走了我的手機。

### that 引導的名詞子句作為補語的用法

## What the organizer said is (that) our booth should be set up by next Monday.
**主辦單位說的是我們必須在下週一之前把攤位設置好。**

直述句要改為名詞子句，須用 that 引導。that 引導的名詞子句，常作為補語
來補充說明前述項目的內容，此時 that 也可省略。

⊃ **The fact** is **(that)** I don't trust you.
　事實是我不信任你。

⊃ The most important **thing** is **(that)** you're alive.
　最重要的事情是你還活著。

### 一般動詞＋that 名詞子句

## We didn't realize (that) our main competitor would also be participating in the book fair.
**我們不知道我們的主要競爭對手也要參加這次書展。**

動詞後面可接 that 子句作受詞，常見的動詞有：think、believe、know、
understand、realize、learn、hear、find out、notice、hope、dream、
forget、remember、decide、feel 等。子句作受詞用的時候，that 也可省略。

⊃ I **think** **(that)** the red dress looks better.
　我覺得紅色洋裝比較好看。

⊃ You don't **believe** **(that)** he is ninety years old?
　你不相信他已經九十歲了嗎？

形容詞＋that 名詞子句

## I'm confident (that) having a booth at the trade show will help us attract new business.

**我相信在貿易展裡有個攤位可以幫我們招攬新客戶。**

情緒形容詞後面可接 **that** 子句，常見的有：sure、sorry、aware 和 surprised、afraid、glad 等。

➲ I'm not **sure** **(that)** they'll like you.
我不確定他們會喜歡你。

➲ The teacher was **surprised** **(that)** Jeff was early this morning.
老師很驚訝傑夫今天早上竟然早到了。

**Level 1**　挑戰多益 *450*

請從 (A)、(B)、(C)、(D) 中選出一個最適合的答案。

**1.** I didn't know _____ were a skydiver.
(A) which
(B) that you
(C) that
(D) whether

**2.** The teacher asked the students _____ movie they wanted to see most.
(A) what
(B) where
(C) that
(D) who's

**3.** If you know _____ junk food is bad for you, then why do you eat it?
(A) if
(B) what
(C) that
(D) why

**4.** The president didn't like _____ Jack said about the company's main product.
(A) who
(B) what
(C) that
(D) which

**5.** I hear _____ you want to attend university overseas.
(A) that
(B) where
(C) which
(D) when

**1.** 我不知道你是一位跳傘選手。

解析 主要子句的動詞 know 為及物動詞，需要受詞，that 與 whether 均可引導名詞子句作受詞，但本句中的名詞子句還欠缺主詞（you），故答案為選項 (B)，其中 that 也可以省略。

● skydiver [`skaɪ͵daɪvɚ] (n.) 跳傘選手

**2.** 老師問學生他們最想看的電影是哪一部。

解析 主要動詞 ask 的用法為「ask sb. sth.」，因此空格要填一字引導名詞子句，作為 ask 的受詞。從語意上來判斷，老師問的應該是他們最想看「什麼電影」，因此答案為選項 (A) what。如果 (D) 改為 whose 也正確，意思為他們最想看「誰的電影」。

**3.** 如果你知道垃圾食物對你不好，那你為什麼還吃？

解析 主要動詞 know 後面需要子句作受詞，if「是否」、wh- 疑問詞和 that 均可引導名詞子句，但本題 know 後面接的是完整直述句，只有選項 (C) that 合乎語意，故為正確答案。

● junk food 垃圾食物

**4.** 董事長不喜歡傑克對公司主要產品所說的事情。

解析 主要子句的動詞 like「喜歡」需要受詞（the things）、形容詞子句則缺少了關係代名詞 that，所以空格內需要填入 the things that，也就等於 what，答案選 (B)。

● product [`prɑdʌkt] (n.) 產品

**5.** 我聽說你想要就讀國外的大學。

解析 主要動詞 hear 後面要接名詞子句作為受詞，空格後為完整直述句，只有選項 (A) that 合乎語意，為正確答案。

● attend [ə`tɛnd] (v.) 出席；前往就學

答案 1.(B) 2.(A) 3.(C) 4.(B) 5.(A)

**6.** I couldn't believe _____ won the lottery.
(A) I
(B) me
(C) myself
(D) my

**7.** This is a study on _____ small and medium enterprises can reduce costs.
(A) what
(B) who
(C) how
(D) that

**8.** I heard that _____.
(A) you two are getting married
(B) you said yesterday
(C) the couple who got married
(D) they are going with

**9.** The lady seems overly nice. _____ we say to her, she always agrees.
(A) What
(B) Which
(C) Whatever
(D) Whenever

**10.** Tom said that _____ could drive a car.
(A) his
(B) him
(C) he
(D) himself

**6.** 我不敢相信我中了樂透。

解析 主要動詞 believe 後面要接受詞，需要 that 引導的名詞子句，而且 that 可以省略。這題的子句部份還缺少主詞，故應選 (A)。

- believe [bɪˋliv] (v.) 相信

---

**7.** 這是一份關於中小企業如何能減少開支的研究。

解析 a study on... 指的是「一份有關……的研究」，on 後面應接名詞子句。以句意而言，指的應該是「如何」節省開支，故正確答案為表示「方式」的 (C) how。把名詞子句還原為疑問句，就會比較好理解，該研究的主題應為：How can small and medium enterprises reduce costs?

- enterprise [ˋɛntəˌpraɪz] (n.) 企業
- reduce [rɪˋdus] (v.) 減少

---

**8.** 我聽說你們兩個人要結婚了

解析 主要動詞 heard 後面需要受詞，that 引導名詞子句作受詞，而子句必須是完整句子，只有選項 (A) 正確。

- married [ˋmærɪd] (adj.) 已婚的

---

**9.** 這位女士似乎人太好了，無論我們跟她說什麼，她都會同意。

解析 say sth. to sb. 表示「向某人說某事」，本題的 sth. 放在句子最前面表強調，空格前沒有先行詞，所以不可選 (B) Which；但即使選 (A) What ( = The thing that; all that) 依舊不符語意，因為 What we say to her 當主詞，後面應接動詞才對。從 she always agrees 的句意上推論應該選 (C) Whatever ( = No matter what)，表示「無論任何事」。Whatever 子句後面有逗號，形成表「讓步」的副詞子句，修飾主要子句。

- overly [ˋovəlɪ] (adv.) 過度地

**10.** 湯姆說他會開車。

解析 主要動詞 said 後面接 that 引導的名詞子句，that 也可以省略。子句一定要有主詞和動詞，因此空格內須填入主格人稱代名詞，答案為 (C)。

答案 6.(A) 7.(C) 8.(A) 9.(C) 10.(C)

請從 (A)、(B)、(C)、(D) 中選出一個最適合的答案。

**1.** What was she doing _____ the teacher didn't approve of?
(A) who
(B) what
(C) that
(D) where

**2.** Look at _____ dog with pink fur! Who would ever do _____ to a dog?
(A) that ; that
(B) which ; that
(C) that ; what
(D) whose ; which

**3.** If we get lost, the most important thing _____ we stay together.
(A) will be
(B) is that
(C) which
(D) what

**4.** _____ the bank approves our loan application or not won't affect our decision.
(A) How
(B) If
(C) Whether
(D) What

**5.** Did you _____ that all the trees in this area are dying?
(A) look
(B) saw
(C) notice
(D) knew

**1.** 她在做什麼老師不允許的事情？

解析 疑問詞 What 為 doing 的受詞，因構成疑問句而移到句首，實際上空格以後的文字所形成的子句，是要修飾 what，因此只有以關係代名詞 that 引導的形容詞子句才正確，答案為選項 (C)。

● approve [əˋpruv] (v.) 允許；贊成

**2.** 看看那隻毛是粉紅色的狗！誰會對一隻狗做那種事啊？

解析 兩個空格後面都沒有動詞，所以不是子句，答案為選項 (A)，第一個 that 為指示形容詞，修飾 dog，指「那隻狗」；第二個 that 為指示代名詞，意思為「那件事」，作 do 的受詞。

● fur [fɜ] (n.)（動物的）毛

**3.** 如果我們迷路了，最重要的事情是我們在一起。

解析 主要句子的 the most important thing 與空格後的 we stay together 為主詞與補語的關係，中間需要動詞 is 和引導名詞子句的連接詞 that，故答案為選項 (B)。

**4.** 銀行是不是會核准我們的貸款申請病不會影響我們的決定。

解析 這題的動詞有兩個：approves 和 affect，可以推測 won't affect... 前方應是一個名詞子句當作整句的主詞。前方的子句結尾有 or not，判斷句首應為 whether「是否」來引導整個名詞子句。注意，由 yes/no 疑問句變成的名詞子句若當主詞，只能用 whether 而不能用 if，因此答案選 (C)。

**5.** 你注意到這地區所有的樹都快死了嗎？

解析 這個句子有主詞 you，以及作受詞用的名詞子句 that all the trees...area，但缺少及物動詞，只有選項 (C) 為時態正確的及物動詞，為正確答案。

● dying [ˋdaɪɪŋ] (a.) 垂死的

答案 1.(C) 2.(A) 3.(B) 4.(C) 5.(C)

**6.** Please tell _____ you didn't lock the keys _____ the house!
(A) that ; in
(B) me ; that in
(C) me ; in
(D) mine ; in

**7.** I saw _____ girl _____ short hair.
(A) that ; with
(B) the ; that has
(C) that the ; had
(D) All of the above

**8.** Ralph _____ that his parents wouldn't discover _____ he had broken the vase.
(A) knows ; why
(B) hoped ; that
(C) thought ; which
(D) saw ; what

**9.** _____ were a brave soldier is not being questioned.
(A) That you
(B) You
(C) If you
(D) If

**10.** Marketing experts had a hard time figuring out _____ the product was so successful.
(A) which
(B) what
(C) that
(D) why

**6.** 請告訴我你沒有把鑰匙鎖在房子裡！

解析 動詞 tell 的句型為 tell sb. sth.，所以第一空格應填入人稱代名詞 me。主要句子為祈使句 Please tell me...，後面接 that 子句作受詞，也可以省略 that。第二空格中應填介系詞 in，所以選項 (C) 正確。

- lock [lɑk] (v./n.) 鎖上；鎖

**7.** 我看到那個短髮的女孩子。

解析 選項 (A) 構成的句子為 I saw that girl with short hair.，that girl 為受詞，with short hair 為介系詞片語修飾 that girl，所以是正確句子。選項 (B) 構成的句子為 I saw the girl that has short hair.，the girl 為受詞，that has short hair 為形容詞子句，修飾 the girl，也正確。(A) 和 (B) 兩個句子意思相同。選項 (C) 構成的句子為 I saw that the girl had short hair. 意思稍有不同，表示「我看到那個女孩有短頭髮。」that the girl had short hair 為名詞子句，作 saw 的受詞。

**8.** 賴夫希望他的父母不會發現他打破了花瓶。

解析 第一個空格後為 that 所引導的名詞子句，子句為過去式 wouldn't discover，所以第一個空格的主要動詞必須是為過去式，因此選項 (A) 錯誤。第二個空格後面為完整直述句，因此需要 that 所引導的名詞子句作 discover 的受詞，正確答案為選項 (B)。

- discover [dɪs`kʌvɚ] (v.) 發現

**9.** 你是一位勇敢的軍人這件事是不容懷疑的。

解析 本句出現兩個動詞 were 和 is，需要子句來連接，從語意上來判斷，That you... 比較適當，答案為選項 (A)。注意，that 引導的名詞子句作主詞用時，that 絕對不可省略，故選項 (B) 錯誤。

- brave [brev] (adj.) 勇敢的
- soldier [`soldʒɚ] (n.) 士兵
- question [`kwɛstʃən] (v./n.) 質疑；問題

**10.** 行銷專家們搞不太懂這個產品為什麼會這麼成功。

解析 以句意判斷，應該是搞不懂產品成功的原因，故選項 (D) why 為正確答案。在解題時可把名詞子句還原為疑問句來看，有助理解句意。原疑問句應為：Why was the product so successful?

- expert [`ɛkspɚt] (n.) 專家
- figure out 想出；算出

答案 6.(C) 7.(D) 8.(B) 9.(A) 10.(D)

# 間接問句

## 間接問句的定義

● 間接問句是把一個問句變成「名詞子句」後，併入「主要子句」構成。整個句子的句意仍然是在「詢問資訊」、「表達質疑」，或「轉述問題」，但因為它不是一個直接的問句 (如：What do you do for a living?/Where is she?)，所以不見得是句尾會是問號。

● 多數人會把上一課教到的 I don't know where she is. 這一類的句子誤認為是間接問句。這類句子只是含有名詞子句 where she is，但其實並沒有「詢問資訊、表達質疑」的意涵，所以並不算是間接問句。

用商務英文
學多益句型

**間接問句**　必考重點句

### Wh- 疑問句改為間接問句

## Can you tell me where the admissions desk is?
**你可以告訴我櫃台在哪裡嗎？**

間接問句的句型是「主要子句＋疑問句」。而疑問詞 (how/where/when/what/who/which) 引導的疑問子句，主詞和動詞的位置同直述句：

主要子句＋疑問詞＋主詞＋be 動詞

主要子句＋疑問詞＋主詞＋適當形式的一般動詞

主要子句＋疑問詞＋主詞＋助動詞 (can/will/should)＋原形動詞

つ Do you know **where the restrooms are**?
　你知道廁所在哪裡嗎？

つ Could you tell me **who that girl in red is**?
　你可以告訴我那個穿紅衣服的女孩是誰嗎？

つ May I ask **how many hours you work a day**?
　我可以問你一天工作幾個小時嗎？

つ Who knows **how fast he can run**?
　誰知道他能跑多快？

### Yes/No 問句改為間接問句

## Do you know if/whether my insurance will cover this procedure?
**你知道我的保險是否會給付這項手術嗎？**

此種間接問句是由主要子句和從 yes/no 問句演變來的 **if/whether** 子句組合而成。

> ➲ Do you know **if/whether** <u>Jim is married</u>?
> 你知道喬是否已婚嗎？

> ➲ Can you ask Cathy **if/whether** <u>she likes me</u>?
> 你可以問凱西她喜不喜歡我嗎？

> ➲ How should I know **if/whether** <u>he is telling</u> the truth?
> 我們怎麼知道他說的是不是實話？

**間接問句的省略寫法**

## Do you know how to call an ambulance?
### 你知道怎樣叫救護車嗎？

間接問句如果含有一般動詞，子句可以改成「how/who/what ＋ to 原形動詞」，例如：how to...。但由 Yes/No 疑問句變成的名詞子句則不能縮減。

> ➲ Do you know **how to get to** the post office?
> 你知道該怎麼去郵局嗎？

> ➲ Could you tell me **who to contact** about this matter?
> 你可以告訴我這件事應該跟誰聯繫嗎？

> ➲ Does she know **what to do** if there's an earthquake?
> 她知道如果有地震該怎麼辦嗎？

**間接問句的結尾是問號還是句號？**

## Sharon asked me if she should get a free flu shot.
### 雪倫問我她是不是該去打免費的流感預防針。

間接問句句尾可能是問號、也可能是句號，但句意上都是在詢問資訊，或是轉述他人的問題。

子句 can you tell me
句，故用問號。

> ➲ Can you tell me **where <u>Karen went</u>**?
> 你可以告訴我凱倫去了哪裡嗎？

子句 I wonder 為敘
，則用句號。

> ➲ I wonder **where <u>Karen went</u>**.
> 我想知道凱倫去了哪裡。

請從 (A)、(B)、(C)、(D) 中選出一個最適合的答案。

☐　*1.* Do you know _____ time _____?
　　(A) what ; is
　　(B) what ; it is
　　(C) what ; is it
　　(D) the ; is what

☐　*2.* Guess who _____.
　　(A) am I
　　(B) is me
　　(C) I am
　　(D) me is

☐　*3.* Does anyone know _____?
　　(A) where is Joe
　　(B) where Joe is
　　(C) Joe is where
　　(D) is Joe where

☐　*4.* I wonder if anyone knows _____ here last night.
　　(A) what happened
　　(B) what happens
　　(C) had happened
　　(D) None of the above

☐　*5.* Can you tell me what _____?
　　(A) should I do
　　(B) should do I
　　(C) I should do
　　(D) should to do

**1.** 你知道現在幾點嗎？

解析 動詞後面接疑問詞引導的名詞子句，原來的問句為：What time is it?，疑問詞為 what time，主詞是 it。改為名詞子句句型：「疑問詞＋主詞＋be 動詞」，即 what time it is，讓整句形成一個間接問句，選項 (B) 正確。

**2.** 猜猜我是誰。

解析 「我是誰？」問句為 Who am I?，放在動詞 guess 的後面作受詞，應改為名詞子句，句型為：「疑問詞＋主詞＋be 動詞」，即 who I am，答案為選項 (C)。
- guess [gɛs] (v./n.) 猜測

**3.** 有人知道喬在哪裡嗎？

解析 原問句應為 Where is Joe?，放在動詞 know 後面應改為名詞子句，即 where Joe is，故選項 (B) 正確。

**4.** 我在想有沒有人知道昨晚這裡發生了什麼事。

解析 動詞 know 後面不可選另一個動詞 (C) had happened。這裡需要名詞子句作 know 的受詞，句型為：「疑問詞＋主詞＋一般動詞（適當形式）」。從時間副詞 last night 判斷，名詞子句中需要過去式的動詞，而疑問詞 what 本身作主詞，答案為選項 (A)。
- happen [`hæpən] (v.) 事情發生

**5.** 你可以告訴我該怎麼做嗎？

解析 Can you tell me 後面應用名詞子句作受詞，句型為「疑問詞＋主詞＋should＋原形動詞」。答案選 (C)。注意，名詞子句 what I should do 可以改為不定詞 what to do，選項 (D) 用法錯誤。

答案 1.(B) 2.(C) 3.(B) 4.(A) 5.(C)

**6.** Do you want me to show you _____ write it?
(A) how to
(B) how should
(C) how
(D) to how

**7.** Could you tell me why he _____ his job?
(A) leaves
(B) left
(C) did leave
(D) had left

**8.** I want to know why _____ at home.
(A) isn't he
(B) he isn't
(C) is he
(D) he not

**9.** _____ you remember what you _____ last week?
(A) Do ; did
(B) Can ; had done
(C) Would ; done
(D) Did ; have done

**10.** Could you please tell me _____ ?
(A) when to start
(B) when start
(C) when should I start
(D) I should start when

**6.** 你要我示範給你看怎麼寫嗎？

解析 本題名詞子句部份為 how you should write it，可縮減為「疑問詞＋to＋原形動詞」的形式，即 how to write it，選項 (A) 正確。

**7.** 你可以告訴我什麼他會離開他的工作嗎？

解析 Could you tell me 後面應接名詞子句，句型為「疑問詞＋主詞＋V（適當形式）」。從語意上得知，動詞必須用過去式 left 的形式，答案為選項 (B)。

● leave [liv] (v./n.) 離開

**8.** 我想知道他為什麼不在家。

解析 這題原疑問句為 Why isn't he at home?/Why is he not at home?，改為名詞子句，即 why he isn't/is not at home，選項 (B) 為正確答案。

**9.** 你記得你上星期做了什麼事嗎？

解析 從句尾的時間副詞判斷，第二個空格須用過去式，只有選項 (A) 正確。

**10.** 我想知道什麼時候開始。

解析 本題名詞子句為 when I should start，當主要句子與 wh- 引導的名詞子句的主詞相同時，名詞子句可以省略主詞，改成「疑問詞＋to＋原形動詞」，選項 (A) 正確。

答案 6.(A) 7.(B) 8.(B) 9.(A) 10.(A)

# Level 2　挑戰多益 *650*

請從 (A)、(B)、(C)、(D) 中選出一個最適合的答案。

**1.** Could you tell me what _____ for a living?
(A) you do
(B) do you
(C) do you do
(D) you doing

**2.** I wonder _____ every night.
(A) where does he go
(B) where he goes
(C) where does he
(D) where he does go

**3.** Do you know when _____ off work?
(A) he does get
(B) he gets
(C) will he get
(D) does he get

**4.** I'm going to Hong Kong on business. Can you tell me _____ for the airport?
(A) when I leaving
(B) when to leave
(C) when should leave
(D) when I leave

**5.** I'm new here, Joe. Can you tell me _____ this photocopier?
(A) how to operate
(B) to operate
(C) how operate
(D) how to operating

*1.* 你可以告訴我你是如何維持生計的嗎？

解析 疑問詞問句句型為「疑問詞＋do/does/did＋主詞＋V（原形）？」，改成間接問句句型為「主要子句＋疑問詞＋主詞＋V（適當形式）」。本題原問句為 What do you do for a living?，改寫第一步是刪除助動詞 do，第二步要判斷動詞 do 的形式應為現在式，主詞 you 後面接原形的 do，故間接問句為 what you do for a living，答案為選項 (A)。

*2.* 我在想他每天晚上到哪裡去了。

解析 I wonder 後面應接間接問句作受詞，句型為「主要子句＋疑問詞＋主詞＋V（適當形式）」。從句尾的時間副詞 every night 知道應搭配現在式，所以原問句為 Where do you go every night?，改寫為名詞子句的第一步是刪除助動詞 do，第二步為判斷動詞 go 的形式，第三人稱單數主詞 he 後面接 goes，故名詞子句為 where he goes every night，答案為選項 (B)。

*3.* 你知道他什麼時候下班嗎？

解析 從語意上了解，疑問句可以用現在式表一般情況、用未來式表未來動作，所以本題原疑問句可為 When does he get off work? 或 When will he get off work?，改為名詞子句則為 when he gets off work 或 when he will get off work，答案為選項 (B)。

*4.* 我要去香港出差。你能告訴我何時要前往機場嗎？

解析 本句是由名詞子句簡化而來。原本的間接問句應該是 when I should leave for the airport，名詞子句中的主詞如果與句中所指的人一樣，並且有助動詞，那麼可將主詞和助動詞省略簡化子句，變成「疑問詞＋to＋原形動詞」，也就是 when to leave for the airport。

• leave for 前往

*5.* 我是新來的，喬。你可以告訴我如何操作這台影印機嗎？

解析 本句是由名詞子句簡化而來。原本的間接問句應該是 how I can operate this photocopier，名詞子句中的主詞如果與句中所指的人一樣，並且有助動詞，便可將主詞和助動詞省略簡化子句，變成「疑問詞＋to＋原形動詞」的句型，也就是 how to operate the photocopier，所以答案選 (A)。

• operate [`ɑpə͵ret] (v.) 運作，操作

答案 1.(A) 2.(B) 3.(B) 4.(B) 5.(A)

6. I'd like to know _____ read Chinese. Could you ask him?
   (A) if Alex can
   (B) can Alex
   (C) Alex can
   (D) if can Alex

7. The tourists asked the Boy Scout how _____ the ferry terminal.
   (A) they got to
   (B) should get to
   (C) to get to
   (D) get to

8. Would you like to know _____?
   (A) how much is it
   (B) it is how much
   (C) how much it is
   (D) is it how much

9. A: What _____?
   B: You don't know what _____?
   (A) happened to him ; to him happened
   (B) happened to him ; happened to him
   (C) to him happened ; happened to him
   (D) has happened to him ; did happen to him

10. A: What _____ about this problem?
    B: I don't know what _____.
    (A) can we do ; can we do
    (B) we can do ; we can do
    (C) can we do ; we can do
    (D) we can do ; can we do

**6.** 我想知道艾力克斯能不能讀中文，你可以問他嗎？

解析 I'd like to know 後面需要受詞，所以空格處需要的字必須包括可以形成名詞子句的 if（= whether），刪除選項 (B) 和 (C)。名詞子句中的主詞要在助動詞之前，所以答案為選項 (A)。

---

**7.** 旅客們問男童子軍要怎麼到渡輪站。

解析 疑問詞 how 可引導名詞子句，用法為：how they should get to...，選項 (B) 缺少主詞、選項 (A) 還原為問句為 How did they get to...，不合語意。名詞子句簡化為不定詞的用法為 how to get to...，選項 (C) 正確。

- ferry [`fɛrɪ] (n.) 渡船
- Boy Scout 童子軍
- terminal [`tɝmən!] (n.) 航站；終點

---

**8.** 你想知道這個多少錢嗎？

解析 「這個多少錢？」原疑問句為 How much is it?，放在 know 後面作受詞，應用名詞子句，即 How much it is，選項 (C) 為正確答案。

---

**9.** A：他發生什麼事了？

B：你不知道他發生什麼事了嗎？

解析 第一個句子為直接問句，選項 (C) 用法錯誤，刪除。第二個句子整個語氣為間接問句，原問句為 What (has) happened to him?，主詞為 What，改為名詞子句字序不變，選項 (B) 正確。

---

**10.** A：關於這個問題我們可以怎麼做呢？

B：我不知道我們可以怎麼做。

解析 第一個句子為直接問句，助動詞 can 放在主詞 we 的前面；第二個句子為間接問句，在 what 引導的名詞子句中助動詞 can 會放在主詞 we 的後面，所以答案為選項 (C)。

---

答案 6.(A) 7.(C) 8.(C) 9.(B) 10.(C)

# 子句的簡化

## 子句簡化的種類

- 子句是一組包含至少一個主詞和一個動詞的完整句,當子句與主要句有重複的主詞出現時,可進行簡化。
- 根據子句的功能,可分為三類:形容詞子句、名詞子句、副詞子句,有不同的簡化方式。
- 子句的簡化:通常是省略主詞(子句的主詞與主要句子相同時)與 be 動詞。

**用商務英文學多益句型**

## 子句的簡化  必考重點句

**形容詞子句的簡化**

**The bus that goes to the airport is usually on time.**
**= The bus going to the airport is usually on time.**
**往機場的公車通常準時。**

當主要子句和形容詞子句有相同的主詞時,可以將形容詞子句簡化:

| 形容詞子句動詞型態 | 子句的簡化方法 |
| --- | --- |
| 1. 進行式 | 省略主詞與 be 動詞,剩下 Ving。 |
| 2. 非限定用法 | 省略主詞與 be 動詞,剩下 adj./n.。 |
| 3. 主動語態 | 省略主詞,把動詞改成 Ving。 |
| 4. 被動語態 | 1. 省略主詞與 be 動詞,剩下 p.p.。<br>2. 被動完成式 have been p.p.,have 改成 having。 |
| 5. 含情態助動詞 | 簡化成不定詞片語 (to V)。 |

○ **The athlete** who is preparing to dive represents Canada.
  = **The athlete** preparing to dive represents Canada.
  正在準備跳水的那位運動選手代表加拿大。

○ **Obama**, who is an African-American, was elected as the 44th
  U.S. president.
  = **Obama**, an African-American, was elected as the 44th U.S.
  president.
  歐巴馬是一位非裔美國人,當選為第四十四屆美國總統。

○ **Anyone** who wants to go is welcome.
= **Anyone** wanting to go is welcome.
任何想參加的人都歡迎。

○ **The man** that was wounded in the accident was sent to the hospital.
= **The man** wounded in the accident was sent to the hospital.
在意外中受傷的那個人被送往醫院了。

○ I think this model is **the one** that you should buy.
= I think this model is **the one** to buy.
我認為這一款是你應該買的款式。

---

**分詞構句：副詞子句的簡化**

## Before exiting the train, please make sure you have all your belongings.
離開火車之前，請確認您拿妥所有行李。

1. 分詞構句的目的是將副詞子句簡化，使整個句子變得比較簡潔。原句的連接詞若是表因果關係的 because、as、since 或表時間的 when、while，且兩個子句的主詞相同，則可將副詞子句的主詞與連接詞省略。但如果原句的連接詞是「對先後順序」會有影響的連接詞（如 before、after），則須將副詞子句的連接詞保留。

2. 接著，再把副詞子句中的動詞改成分詞形態，若子句為主動語態，要將動詞改成 Ving。若句子為被動語態，則動詞改成 p.p.。

○ **Before** Hank moved to a small town, he lived in a crowded city.
= **Before** moving to a small town, Hank lived in a crowded city.
在搬到小鎮之前，漢克原本住在擁擠的大都市裡。

before 引導的副詞子句改為分詞構句時，before 需保留。Before Hank move to... 是主動語態，改成分詞構句時動詞要用 Ving。

○ The man committed suicide **because** he was depressed by his wife's death.
= **Depressed** by his wife's death, the man committed suicide.
因妻子過世而抑鬱寡歡，那個人結果自殺了。

because he was depressed... 為被動語態，改為分詞構句時動詞要用 p.p.，並將此句放到句首。

# Not having a ticket, the passenger was removed from the train.

**因為沒有車票，那位乘客被請出火車。**

上一個句型的原句皆為肯定句，但若原句是否定句，改為分詞構句的句型會稍有不同：

1. 改為分詞構句的句子為主動語態：直接將 not 放在分詞 Ving 的前面。

2. 句子原本為被動語態：保留 be 動詞，把 not 放在由 be 動詞演變來的現在分詞 being 的前面。

➲ She **didn't know** what to do, so she called her mother for advice.
= **Not knowing** what to do, she called her mother for advice.
因為不知道該怎麼辦，她打電話給母親請求建議。

➲ Jeff **wasn't invited to Rick's party**, so he decided to throw his own.
= **Not being invited** to Rick's party, Jeff decided to throw his own.
因為沒收邀參加瑞克的派對，傑夫決定自己辦一個。

# Having taken the overnight bus, we arrived in Berlin early in the morning.

**因為搭了通霄巴士，我們一大早抵達柏林。**

若要將完成式句子改為分詞構句，有下列兩種狀況：

1. 完成式的句子若為主動語態：將完成式的助動詞 have/has/had 改為分詞 having，後面接原本完成式裡的 p.p.。

2. 原本句子為完成式的被動語態：仍先將完成式的助動詞 have/has/had 改為分詞 having，後面接 been＋p.p.。

➲ She **had eaten** a big meal, so she didn't feel like having any dessert.
= **Having eaten** a big meal, she didn't feel like having any dessert.
她已經吃了一頓大餐，所以不想吃任何甜點。

➲ I **had been told** to arrive early, so I left home at 6:00 a.m.
= **Having been told** to arrive early, I left home at 6:00 a.m.
因為事先被告知要早到，所以我早上六點就出門了。

名詞子句簡化成「疑問詞＋to V」

## Do you know where I can buy ferry tickets? = Do you know where to buy ferry tickets?
**你知道哪裡可以買渡輪票嗎？**

由疑問詞 what/who/when/how/which 等引導，且含「助動詞 should、could、can＋原形動詞」的名詞子句，可將子句部分簡化成「疑問詞＋to V」。

➲ I'm not sure **which way** **I should go**.
   = I'm not sure **which way** **to go**.
   我不確定要往哪個方向走。

➲ I don't know **how** **I can get to the train station**.
   = I don't know **how** **to get to the train station**.
   我不知道要怎麼去火車站。

# Level 1　挑戰多益 *450*

請從 (A)、(B)、(C)、(D) 中選出一個最適合的答案。

**1.** After _____ the man's financial activities for a year, the court found him guilty of insider trading.
(A) investigate
(B) investigating
(C) investigated
(D) to investigate

**2.** _____ of tax evasion, the company's manager was sentenced to a lengthy prison term.
(A) Convict
(B) Convicting
(C) To convict
(D) Convicted

**3.** Once _____, the Great Wall of China is not easily forgotten.
(A) see
(B) to see
(C) saw
(D) seen

**4.** The man _____ ready to sing is known for his beautiful voice.
(A) getting
(B) to get
(C) gets
(D) gotten

**5.** You should stop and ask for directions if you're not sure which way _____.
(A) go
(B) to go
(C) went
(D) going

**1.** 調查了這個人的財務狀況一年之後，法庭認為他的內線交易罪名成立。

解析 從屬連接詞的句型之中，如果主詞與主要子句相同，可以省略副詞子句的主詞，將動詞改為分詞形式；動詞主動用「現在分詞」，動詞被動用「過去分詞」。這裡兩子句的主詞都是 the court，可省略前句主詞，因為動詞主動所以分詞構句用 investigating。

● insider trading 內線交易

---

**2.** 被說服去逃稅，這家公司的經理被判了很長的監獄刑期。

解析 這題前半句的原句應該是說 Because he was convinced of tax evasion，從屬連接詞的句型之中，可以省略主詞和連接詞，並將動詞改為分詞，動詞主動用「現在分詞」，動詞被動用「過去分詞」。本句主詞是 the company's manager，根據句意，是指經理「被說服」逃漏稅，因此分詞構句應用過去分詞 convinced。

● tax evasion 逃稅

---

**3.** 只要見過中國長城，就很難忘懷。

解析 逗號後有完整句子，逗號前的結構必須是副詞子句或改為分詞構句，又因為主詞「長城」是「物」，應搭配被動語態，所以需要過去分詞，答案為 (D)。分詞構句 Once seen,... 可還原成副詞子句 = Once it is seen,...。

● the Great Wall 長城

---

**4.** 準備唱歌的那個人以美聲聞名。

解析 be 動詞 is 前面整段為主詞，空格前已有名詞 the man，因此需要子句或分詞片語作後位形容詞修飾。因為空格前的名詞為「人」，為主動，所以用現在分詞，答案為 (A) getting。現在分詞片語 getting ready to sing 可還原成形容詞子句 who is getting ready to sing。

---

**5.** 如果你不確定要走哪一條路，你應該停下來問路。

解析 you're not sure 後面需接名詞子句或簡化為「疑問詞＋to V」來使文意完整。名詞子句應寫成 which way you should go，簡化為不定詞片語則為 which way to go，故答案為 (B)。

● direction [dɪ`rɛkʃən] (n.) 方向

---

答案 1.(B) 2.(D) 3.(D) 4.(A) 5.(B)

6. _____ to his new classical CD, Bernard drifted off to sleep.
   (A) Listen
   (B) Listening
   (C) To listen
   (D) Listened

7. The airplane _____ on the runway has been cleared for takeoff.
   (A) sitting
   (B) sat
   (C) is sitting
   (D) sits

8. _____ that it was snowing outside, all the children ran to the window to look.
   (A) Hear
   (B) To hear
   (C) Hearing
   (D) Heard

9. The teacher read several poems _____ by a famous poet to the class.
   (A) was written
   (B) wrote
   (C) written
   (D) had written

10. Government leaders from all over the world are meeting to discuss what _____ about global warming.
   (A) to do
   (B) they do
   (C) should do
   (D) are doing

**6.** 聽著新買的古典樂 CD，伯納德漸漸睡著了。

解析 逗號後面為主要句子，前面需要連接詞引導子句，如 While he was listening to...，或是將子句簡化為分詞構句，即 While listening to...，因省略連接詞不影響聽者對句意的理解，故可進一步簡化成 Listening to...，因此答案為 (B)。注意，句首不定詞 To V 的用法表示「目的」（= In order to V），在此句意不合。

---

**7.** 停在跑道上的飛機已經獲准起飛。

解析 本題主要子句為 The airplane has been cleared for takeoff.，主詞 the airplane 後面接的是形容詞子句或分詞片語作後位修飾。飛機停在跑道上的動作 sit 為主動，所以用現在分詞，答案為 (A) getting。現在分詞片語 sitting on the runway 可還原成形容詞子句 that/which is sitting on the runway。

- clear [klɪr] (v.) 清除障礙；批准（飛機、船隻等）離境或入境
- takeoff [`tek͵ɔf] (n.) 起飛

**8.** 聽到外面下雪了，所有的孩童都跑到窗戶往外看。

解析 本句是分詞構句，原句是 When all (of) the children heard that it was snowing outside, they ran to the window to look。省略副詞子句中相同的主詞 all (of) the children 和連接詞之後，可形成分詞構句，原句的動作是主動狀態，所以要用現在分詞，故選 (C)。

---

**9.** 老師在課堂上讀了幾首名詩人寫的詩。

解析 poems 後面接的是形容詞子句或分詞片語作後位修飾，由空格後面的「by＋人」可推知此處是被動，形容詞子句應用 which/that were written by a famous poet，可省略關係代名詞和 be 動詞，簡化為分詞片語 written by a famous poet，答案為 (C)。

- poem [`poəm] (n.) 詩　　　　　　　　　　• poet [`poət] (n.) 詩人

---

**10.** 全球領袖群聚在一起討論如何處理全球暖化。

解析 動詞 discuss 後面需接名詞子句作受詞，或將其簡化為「疑問詞＋to V」的結構。名詞子句應寫成 what they should do，簡化為不定詞片語則為 what to do，故答案為 (A)。

- global warming 全球暖化

答案 6.(B) 7.(A) 8.(C) 9.(C) 10.(A)

請從 (A)、(B)、(C)、(D) 中選出一個最適合的答案。

**1.** _____ if she wanted to borrow the book, she reminded him that she was the one _____ it.
(A) When asked ; who bought
(B) When asking ; who's buying
(C) When asked ; bought
(D) When asks ; who buys

**2.** _____ met him a few times before, I'm sure I'll be able to recognize him if I see him again.
(A) To have
(B) Have
(C) Having
(D) I will have

**3.** I didn't hear all of the performers, but I did hear the man _____ the violin.
(A) which played
(B) playing
(C) whom is playing
(D) who will have played

**4.** _____ up to her ears in paperwork, Marcia had no choice but to work overtime for several days.
(A) Was
(B) Had been
(C) Being
(D) To be

**5.** According to the news report, one of the teams _____ in the tournament has been disqualified for cheating.
(A) competes
(B) has competed
(C) is competing
(D) competing

**1.** 被問到她是否想借那本書時，她提醒他，買那本書的人是她。

解析 選項中皆有連接詞「When＋分詞」，可知本題為分詞構句。根據句意，原句應是 When she was asked...，因為後句主詞也是 she，所以可以省略主詞 she 與 be 動詞 was，構成 When asked...。後句中 the one who... 是關係代名詞的一個常見的用法，意思是「那個……的人」的意思，本句時態為過去式，所以子句動詞用 bought，故選 (A)。

**2.** 之前見過他幾次，我確信以後再見到他我能夠認得出來。

解析 本題是完成式的分詞構句型態，原句是 I have met him a few times before, so I'm sure I'll be able to recognize him if I see him again. 因為主詞相同，省略相同的主詞 I 和連接詞 so，再將完成式的助動詞 have 轉變成 having，故選 (C)。
- recognize [ˋrɛkəɡ͵naɪz] (v.) 認出；認識

**3.** 我聽不到所有演奏者的演出，但是我的確聽到小提琴手的演奏。

解析 the man 後面應接形容詞子句作後位修飾，the man who played the violin 是「那個拉小提琴的人」的意思。也可以用分詞片語簡化形容詞子句，因人演奏樂器的動作為主動，所以動詞改為現在分詞 playing the violin.，故答案選 (B)。

**4.** 深陷在文書作業之中，瑪莎別無選擇只能好幾天都加班。

解析 這題前半句的原句應該是說 Because she was up to her ears in paperwork，才符合下一句所說的「她只好加班好幾天」。因前後子句主詞相同（she, Marcia），可以省略連接詞和主詞，將動詞改為分詞。在這裡的 be 動詞沒有被動意思，因此改成現在分詞的 being，故選 (C)。
- be up to one's ears 深陷於…，埋頭於…，忙於…
- have no choice but to V 沒有選擇，只好

**5.** 根據新聞報導，聯賽的競賽隊伍之一因為舞弊已被取消資格。

解析 句首的 According to... 為介系詞片語，本詞為 one of the teams，後面要接形容詞子句或分詞片語作修飾。選項中無關係代名詞，所以應用分詞。隊伍競賽的動作 compete 為主動，因此用現在分詞 competing，故選 (D)。
- according to 根據…
- tournament [ˋtɝnəmənt] (n.) 錦標賽，聯賽
- disqualify [dɪsˋkwɑləˌfaɪ] (v.) 取消資格

答案 1.(A) 2.(C) 3.(B) 4.(C) 5.(D)

6. _____ the deadline for the project, Roger decided to finish it as soon as possible just in case.

(A) Not knowing

(B) Didn't know

(C) Because

(D) Not knows

7. I just spoke to the man _____ to give a speech at tomorrow's conference, and he said he won't be able to make it.

(A) who schedules

(B) scheduling

(C) scheduled

(D) is scheduled

8. _____ all of the proposals for the new project, I've decided to choose David and Anne's idea.

(A) Have heard

(B) Having to hear

(C) Have hear

(D) Having heard

9. Peter Finch, _____ actor to win an Oscar after his death, was given the Academy Award for Best Actor in 1977.

(A) was the only

(B) the only

(C) is the only

(D) only

10. It _____ a national holiday, the product launch was postponed until the following week.

(A) be

(B) being

(C) was

(D) is

**6.** 因為不知道這項計畫的截止日期，羅傑決定盡快完成以防萬一。

解析 題目應該是要說 Roger「因為不知道」截止日期，所以決定盡快完成。前半句原本應該是 Because Roger didn't know the deadline，兩子句的主詞一樣，可以省略主詞和連接詞，將動詞以分詞形式出現。這裡的動詞為主動所以用 knowing，因為句意本身有否定，所以將 not 放在句首。故答案選 (A)。

● as soon as possible 盡快　　　● just in case 以防萬一

**7.** 我剛跟那位預定在明天的會議上演講的人談過話，他說他沒有辦法來。

解析 the man 後面應接形容詞子句作後位修飾，動詞 schedule 是「為⋯⋯安排時間」之意，根據句意，這個人是被安排在明天來演講的人，所以子句應用被動語態 the man who is scheduled to...，也可以用分詞片語簡化形容詞子句，因動詞為被動，所以省略關係代名詞和 be 動詞，只留下過去分詞片語作修飾，故答案選 (C)。

● make it 準時到達；能夠到場　　　● schedule [`skɛdʒul] (n./v.) 日程安排；預定

**8.** 聽了這項新計畫的所有提議之後，我決定選擇大衛和安的想法。

解析 這題前半句的原句應該是說 I have heard all of the proposals for the new project，兩子句主詞相同，可以省略主詞和連接詞，並將動詞改為分詞。在這裡用到的完成式 have heard，因此改成分詞的形式 having heard。

**9.** 彼得芬奇，唯一在去世後贏得奧斯卡獎的演員，在一九七七年獲頒最佳男演員獎。

解析 「非限定用法」的形容詞子句可省略關係代名詞與 be 動詞，只保留補語當作同位語，故答案選 (B)。the only actor to win an Oscar after his death 還原為形容詞子句則為 who is the only actor to win an Oscar after his death。

● Academy Award 奧斯卡金像獎（亦稱 Oscar）

**10.** 因為這天是國定假日，產品發表會被延到下一周。

解析 這題前半句的原句應該是說 Because it was a national holiday，才符合下一句所說的「發表會延期」的意思。從屬連接詞的句型之中，如果省略連接詞（必須是省略後仍看得出句意），必須將動詞改為分詞，動詞主動用「現在分詞」，動詞被動用「過去分詞」。本題從屬子句的主詞（It，指時間）與主要子句不同，因此必須保留。在這裡的 be 動詞沒有被動意思，因此分詞構句用現在分詞 It being...。

● product launch 產品發表會

答案 6.(A) 7.(C) 8.(D) 9.(B) 10.(B)

311

New
TOEIC

第1次就考好

# 新多益文法
# 全真模擬試題

# 多益文法模擬考　第一回

**單句填空** ▶ 請從 (A)、(B)、(C)、(D) 中選出一個最適合的答案。

**1.** The inspection team will meet you _____ the corner of First Street and Market Street.
(A) at
(B) in
(C) over
(D) next to

**2.** This advertising jingle is great! I _____ like it!
(A) very
(B) really
(C) many
(D) hardly

**3.** I'm afraid that's out of the question! We _____ have enough money to cover our costs, let alone give everybody raises.
(A) almost
(B) barely
(C) nearly
(D) sometimes

**4.** It doesn't matter how you do your work, just as long as you get it finished _____.
(A) sometimes
(B) overtime
(C) on time
(D) anytime

**5.** It's so difficult to find work these days, even though I check the classified ads _____ day.
(A) sometimes
(B) once
(C) most of
(D) every

6. You're _____ not paying attention, Laura. I said he's guilty of "insider trading" not "insider training."
   (A) observing
   (B) obvious
   (C) obviously
   (D) obviousness

7. I'd like to compliment you on your _____ work, Harry. You negotiated that contract really _____.
   (A) well ; well
   (B) good ; good
   (C) good ; well
   (D) well ; good

8. How _____ money do I need to start a business, Uncle Henry?
   (A) much
   (B) many
   (C) some
   (D) a lot

9. New Zealand exports a lot of wool because there _____ sheep there.
   (A) is very much
   (B) are very much
   (C) is many
   (D) are many

10. I'm going to the supply room, Jay. How _____ and how _____ do you need?
    (A) many paper ; many pens
    (B) much paper ; much pens
    (C) many paper ; much pens
    (D) much paper ; many pens

**11.** We've done some research, and we've found that the average American drinks 3.4 _____ of coffee per day.

(A) cups
(B) pounds
(C) bottles
(D) buckets

**12.** I don't think Mr. Sanders' missing the meeting was an accident. I think he did it _____ purpose.

(A) for
(B) with
(C) to
(D) on

**13.** The Harrington Company specializes in designing, developing, and manufacturing _____ wear.

(A) woman
(B) women
(C) women's
(D) womens

**14.** Your product is extremely good. But to be honest with you, the name _____ the product is a bit strange. I suggest that you change it.

(A) of
(B) to
(C) in
(D) by

**15.** Because of downsizing, some of our employees _____ going to be laid off.

(A) is
(B) are
(C) will
(D) has

**16.** I'm going to take Lionel to court! That invention wasn't his idea, it was _____!
(A) his
(B) my
(C) mine
(D) my's

**17.** I'm not sure why our product isn't catching on. It's _____ too expensive _____ it's of insufficient quality.
(A) both ; and
(B) either ; or
(C) much ; than
(D) neither ; or

**18.** I've been working as an economist for several years, and I still feel it's impossible _____ the market accurately.
(A) predict
(B) to predict
(C) prediction
(D) predicting

**19.** I think we have a bad connection, Ms. Lee. I can't understand _____ saying.
(A) what are you
(B) what you are
(C) what you
(D) your

**20.** I know you have a lot of cash now, Mr. Herbert. But I think it's _____ invest in hedge funds at this time.
(A) too risky
(B) risky
(C) too risky to
(D) too risky for

21. Don't call Dr. Finster after 9:00 p.m. He will have _____ to bed by that time.
(A) went
(B) go
(C) going
(D) gone

22. The Wallingford Company was originally going to set up a factory in Indonesia, but they just didn't have _____ invest in the project.
(A) enough capital to
(B) many capital for
(C) enough capital
(D) capital enough

23. Do you know how to get in touch with John, the guy _____ for the consulting firm? I need to contact him right away.
(A) who working
(B) who works
(C) works
(D) worked

24. Our main office is _____ in the southern suburbs of the city. Feel free to visit anytime.
(A) been
(B) finding
(C) building
(D) located

25. The mistake has been made, and there's nothing we can do about it. There's no use in crying over _____ milk.
(A) spill
(B) spills
(C) to spill
(D) spilt

**26.** I saw Jim _____ with the client in his office yesterday. Does that mean he's going to reconsider our offer?
(A) to talk
(B) talked
(C) talking
(D) talks

**27.** The schedule of events had been _____ and sent to each of the participants two weeks before the campaign was launched.
(A) copy
(B) copied
(C) copying
(D) copies

**28.** I realize that it's a dog-eat-dog world out there, but I still feel that _____ to one's customers is bad for business.
(A) lie
(B) lying
(C) lain
(D) lies

**29.** Would you _____ checking these sales figures for me, Joe? I'm not sure if they're accurate.
(A) mind
(B) understand
(C) bother
(D) forget

**30.** The only reason Don got promoted is because he's really good _____ currying favor.
(A) of
(B) at
(C) to
(D) for

**31.** I feel I would be perfect for the job because I'm very _____ finance.
(A) interesting about
(B) interesting in
(C) interested in
(D) interested on

**32.** After _____ with the advertising executives for six hours, a promotional campaign was finally agreed upon.
(A) to meet
(B) met
(C) meeting
(D) of meeting

**33.** During the negotiations, Kyle rambled on for an hour before _____ to the point.
(A) came
(B) coming
(C) comes
(D) come

**34.** Government representatives will be at the meeting, so please be _____ time!
(A) at
(B) on
(C) in
(D) of

**35.** How _____ is it from home to your office, Peter?
(A) far
(B) farther
(C) farthest
(D) very far

**36.** It's _____ difficult to break into that market! There are _____ many trade barriers.

(A) so ; much

(B) much ; so

(C) so ; too

(D) only ; not

**37.** That conference call was a complete waste of time. I could barely _____ what anybody else was saying.

(A) see

(B) talk

(C) listen

(D) hear

**38.** Many _____ have called us to complain about our new product. They claim that it is defective.

(A) person

(B) people

(C) peoples

(D) people's

**39.** The fall in stock prices caught everyone by surprise. _____ was expecting it at all.

(A) Everyone

(B) Someone

(C) No one

(D) I

**40.** The Holger Company has a really state-of-the-art inventory system. I wish we had _____ too.

(A) some

(B) one

(C) ones

(D) any

**Questions 1~4 refer to the following article.**

According to the latest statistics, Taiwan is currently in a _____

1. (A) worsened
   (B) worsen
   (C) worsening
   (D) worst

recession. Due to the economic downturn, many unemployed or laid off
workers have no choice but _____ the public service examination

2. (A) took
   (B) to take
   (C) taking
   (D) taken

in order to support their _____. As a result of the general economic

3. (A) homes
   (B) houses
   (C) household
   (D) families

situation, companies are being forced to cut their staffs and increase the
number of workers on unpaid leave. What's even worse, the New Taiwan
dollar has hit a record low against the greenback. _____ more and

4. (A) Nevertheless
   (B) Although
   (C) In spite of
   (D) Despite

more people are losing their jobs, looking for new jobs or taking pay
cuts, they still hope that an economic recovery is just around the corner.

## Questions 5~8 refer to the following article.

Long one of the world's richest men (ranked no. 1 in 14 of the past 16 years), Gates announced that he was leaving his day-to-day duties as Microsoft chairman in June 2006 to devote more time _____

    5. (A) to
       (B) in
       (C) on
       (D) at

philanthropy. The Bill and Melinda Gates Foundation, which Gates heads along with his wife Melinda and close friend Warren Buffet, is the largest charitable organization in the world. Each year, the foundation funds projects focused on combating disease, _____ educational

    6. (A) raising
       (B) progressing
       (C) elevating
       (D) improving

opportunities, and enhancing information technology both at home and abroad. It should come as no surprise that Gates, _____ was so

    7. (A) which
       (B) whose
       (C) who
       (D) that

successful in earning money in his first career, has proven equally good at giving it away in his second. His generosity continues _____ the world.

    8. (A) change
       (B) will change
       (C) changes
       (D) to change

**A** *1.* The inspection team will meet you _____ the corner of First Street and Market Street.

視察小組會在第一街和市場街的轉角跟你碰面。

(A) at      (B) in      (C) over      (D) next to

觀念   介系詞

解析   在某處（如兩條街道）的轉角是用「at the corner of＋地方」的用法。如果是指室內的角落，就會用「in the corner of＋地方」。

• inspection [ɪnˋspɛkʃən] (n.) 檢查，視察

---

**B** *2.* This advertising jingle is great! I _____ like it!

這首廣告歌真棒！我好喜歡喔！

(A) very      (B) really      (C) many      (D) hardly

觀念   副詞

解析   前一句說「廣告歌很棒」，下一句應是強調非常喜歡這首歌，要選修飾 like 的副詞。very 修飾名詞，如果要用來修飾動詞，應改成 very much 並放在句尾。really 副詞「相當地」修飾動詞，有強調語氣的用法。many 修飾名詞。hardly「幾乎不」與文意不符。答案選 (B)。

• advertising jingle 廣告歌

---

**B** *3.* I'm afraid that's out of the question! We _____ have enough money to cover our costs, let alone give everybody raises.

我認為這根本不可能！我們幾乎沒有足夠的錢來負擔我們的支出，更別提要給大家加薪！

(A) almost      (B) barely      (C) nearly      (D) sometimes

觀念   副詞

解析   根據前後文可推知，說話者應該是要表示「幾乎沒有足夠的錢來負擔支出」，更別提要給大家加薪。所以本題應選帶有否定意味的 barely「幾乎不」才符合句意。答案選 (B)。

• out of the question 不可能的      • let alone＋子句：更不用說⋯

C  **4.** It doesn't matter how you do your work, just as long as you get it finished _____.

你怎麼做你的工作都無所謂，只要能準時完成就好。

(A) sometimes　　(B) overtime　　(C) on time　　(D) anytime

**觀念** 副詞片語

**解析** 前半句提到「你怎麼做你的工作都無所謂」，所以下一句應是要說「準時完成就好」，這樣前後句意才順暢。sometimes（有時候）和 overtime（超時），這兩個選項與句意不符。anytime（任何時刻）放進句中會跟第一句要暗示的意思不相符。因此，答案選 (A)（準時）。

● it doesn't matter＋子句：不論…，不管…

---

D  **5.** It's so difficult to find work these days, even though I check the classified ads _____ day.

現在真的好難找工作，儘管我每天都看分類廣告。

(A) sometimes　　(B) once　　(C) most of　　(D) every

**觀念** 形容詞

**解析** 這題後面有 day，表示前面要選修飾 day 的形容詞，且句子的意思是就算「每天都看分類廣告」，工作還是很難找。sometimes 是（有時候），once 是（曾經），most of 是（大部分……），這三個選項都不能直接加上 day，只有選項 (D) 才合適。

● these days 如今，而今　　　　● classified ads 分類廣告

---

C  **6.** You're _____ not paying attention, Laura. I said he's guilty of "insider trading" not "insider training."

蘿拉，很明顯妳根本沒有專心。我說是他因「內線交易」有罪，而不是「內部訓練」。

(A) observing　　(B) obvious　　(C) obviously　　(D) obviousness

**觀念** 副詞

**解析** 這題要選擇修飾動詞的副詞。題目的位置是要去修飾 paying attention（專心），因此要選擇副詞 obviously（明顯地）。observing（正在觀察），與題意不符。形容詞 obvious 和名詞 obviousness 則與本句文法不符。

● insider trading 內線交易

C 7. I'd like to compliment you on your _____ work, Harry.
You negotiated that contract really _____.

我要來稱讚一下你優良的工作表現,哈利。你那項合約的洽談非常成功。

(A) well ; well　　(B) good ; good　(C) good ; well　　(D) well ; good

**觀念** 形容詞與副詞

**解析** 修飾名詞要用形容詞,而修飾動詞則要用副詞。前半句修飾名詞 work(工作),要選形容詞 good。後半句修飾動詞 negotiated(洽談),要選副詞 well。

● compliment [`kɑmpləmənt] (v./n.) 讚美,恭維;讚美的話

---

A 8. How _____ money do I need to start a business, Uncle Henry?

亨利叔叔,我需要多少錢才能創業?

(A) much　　(B) many　　(C) some　　(D) a lot

**觀念** how many/how much 的用法

**解析** 本題考的是修飾不可數名詞的用法。money 不可數,所以要用 much 來修飾;many 則修飾可數複數名詞。some 修飾可數與不可數名詞,但是這裡問的是「多少」,因此不會選 some。a lot 是副詞,修飾動詞並且強調語氣,通常位於句尾。

● start a business 創業

---

D 9. New Zealand exports a lot of wool because there _____ sheep there.

紐西蘭出口很多羊毛,因為那裡有很多綿羊。

(A) is very much　　　　　　(B) are very much
(C) is many　　　　　　　　(D) are many

**觀念** 集合名詞

**解析** 本題考的是 sheep 的用法。sheep 意思是「綿羊」,是一個集合名詞,單複數都是 sheep。這裡指的紐西蘭有很多綿羊,所以答案要選複數的 be 動詞,以及修飾複數可數名詞的 many。

● wool [wʊl] (n.) 羊毛

D **10.** I'm going to the supply room, Jay. How _____ and how _____
do you need?

我要去供應室，杰你要多少紙和多少隻筆？

(A) many paper ; many pens      (B) much paper ; much pens
(C) many paper ; much pens      (D) much paper ; many pens

觀念   可數 / 不可數名詞

解析   paper 不可數，所以用 how much 修飾；pen 為可數名詞，所以用 how many 修
飾。如果要確切說「多少張紙」，應該以單位來說明，例：How many pieces of
paper do you need?

● supply room 供應室

A **11.** We've done some research, and we've found that the average American
drinks 3.4 _____ of coffee per day.

我們做了一些研究，而且發現美國人平均一天喝 3.4 杯的咖啡。

(A) cups      (B) pounds      (C) bottles      (D) buckets

觀念   名詞單位化

解析   這裡要能夠選擇出正確的單位，一天應該是喝 3.4「杯」的咖啡，所以答案選
(A)。pound 是「磅」，bottle 是「瓶子」，bucket 是「桶子」。

● average [ˋævərɪdʒ] (n./adj./v.) 平均；平均的；算出…的平均數

D **12.** I don't think Mr. Sanders' missing the meeting was an accident. I think
he did it _____ purpose.

我不認為桑德先生錯過這個會議是一個意外。我想他是故意這麼做的。

(A) for      (B) with      (C) to      (D) on

觀念   副詞片語

解析   前句說不認為「錯過這個會議是一個意外」，也就表示後句要說這麼做是「故
意」的。「故意」的副詞片語是 on purpose，所以答案選 (D)。

● accident [ˋæksədənt] (n.) 意外，交通事故

**C** *13.* The Harrington Company specializes in designing, developing, and manufacturing _____ wear.

海靈頓公司專門從事設計、發展、和製造女性的服飾。

(A) woman      (B) women      (C) women's      (D) womens

觀念 所有格

解析 woman 是「女性」的單數，這裡的「女性服飾」要用到統稱「女性」的複數形 women，還要用所有格來表示「服飾」是屬於「女性的」，因此答案選 (C)。

● specialize [`spɛʃə‚laɪz] (v.) 專攻，專門從事

---

**A** *14.* Your product is extremely good. But to be honest with you, the name _____ the product is a bit strange. I suggest that you change it.

你的產品非常好。但是說實話，這個產品的名字實在有點奇怪。我建議你換一下。

(A) of      (B) to      (C) in      (D) by

觀念 所有格

解析 題目要說的是「產品的名字」，無生命的所有格會用 of，例：「這間房子的窗戶」the windows of the house。因此答案要選 (A)。

● to be honest with you 老實跟你說（此表達經常放句首）

---

**B** *15.* Because of downsizing, some of our employees _____ going to be laid off.

由於公司要縮減開支，我們的一些員工將被解雇。

(A) is      (B) are      (C) will      (D) has

觀念 不定代名詞、現在進行式代替未來式

解析 後半句的主詞為 some of our employees，從 some 這裡可以知道主詞為複數。而且，句子有 going to，前面應該是接上 be 動詞，表示「即將要」的意思，因此答案選 (B)。

● downsizing [`daun‚saɪzɪŋ] (n.) 縮減開支      ● lay off 解雇

C **16.** I'm going to take Lionel to court! That invention wasn't his idea, it was _____!

我會讓萊昂內爾上法院！這個發明根本不是他的想法，是我的！

(A) his        (B) my        (C) mine        (D) my's

觀念   所有格代名詞

解析   原本的句子應該是 it's my idea，這裡用所有格代名詞 mine 來代替 my idea，這樣才符合第一句說到的要讓 Lionel 上法院的原因。

● take sb. to court 帶某人上法院（對他進行訴訟）

---

B **17.** I'm not sure why our product isn't catching on. It's _____ too expensive _____ it's of insufficient quality.

我不知道為何這個產品不受歡迎。它不是太貴，就是品質不好。

(A) both ; and      (B) either ; or      (C) much ; than    (D) neither ; or

觀念   連接詞

解析   前一句提到產品銷售不好，所以下一句應該是提出原因。選項 (A) 的 both...and... 是表示「兩者都……」的意思，選項 (D) 用到的 neither 是否定的意思，與前一句意思不符。選項 (C) 應搭配的用法是「much 比較級 than...」，也不符合題目的句型。選項 (B) 的 either...or... 表示「要不……就是……」，符合前後文。

● catch on 受歡迎

---

B **18.** I've been working as an economist for several years, and I still feel it's impossible _____ the market accurately.

我當一名經濟學家非常多年，但我仍然覺得要正確地預測市場走向是不可能的。

(A) predict       (B) to predict       (C) prediction       (D) predicting

觀念   it 當虛主詞

解析   句子的意思是「正確地預測市場走向」這件事是不可能的，以虛主詞 it 開頭，後面加上不定詞 to V，to predict the market accurately 即為後句真正的主詞，所以答案選 (B)。

● economist [ɪˋkɑnəmɪst] (n.) 經濟學家      ● predict [prɪˋdɪkt] (v.) 預測

**B** **19.** I think we have a bad connection, Ms. Lee. I can't understand _____ saying.

我想我們彼此電話的通訊不是很好，李小姐。我聽不懂你在說什麼。

(A) what are you　(B) what you are　(C) what you　　(D) your

**觀念** 名詞子句

**解析** 句子要表達聽不懂「你在說什麼」，必須要用到「名詞子句」，因為題目有 saying，所以原本的問句應該是 what are you saying。放在句中做名詞子句，原本倒裝的 are 要改為直述的方式，也就是放在主詞之後，變成 what you are saying，因此答案選 (B)。

● bad connection 接觸不良，通訊不好

---

**C** **20.** I know you have a lot of cash now, Mr. Herbert. But I think it's _____ invest in hedge funds at this time.

我知道你現在手上有很多現金，赫伯特先生。但我認為現在不適合投資對沖基金，太冒險了。

(A) too risky　　(B) risky　　　(C) too risky to　(D) too risky for

**觀念** too...to... 的用法

**解析** 本句用到的是 too...to... 的句型，表示「太……以致於不能……」，句型是「too ＋adj./adv.＋to V」。選項 (D) 的 for 是加上人，表示「對某人而言太……」。因此答案選 (C)。

● hedge funds 對沖基金，避險基金

---

**D** **21.** Don't call Dr. Finster after 9:00 p.m. He will have _____ to bed by that time.

晚上九點後別打電話給芬斯特先生。他那時將已經就寢了。

(A) went　　　(B) go　　　　(C) going　　　(D) gone

**觀念** 未來完成式

**解析** 「by＋未來時間」常與未來完成式連用，表示「在未來該時間點以前已完成的動作」。本句中 by that time 意即 by 9:00 p.m.，表示 Dr. Finster 到九點時將已經上床睡覺了。

● go to bed 上床睡覺

**A** **22.** The Wallingford Company was originally going to set up a factory in Indonesia, but they just didn't have _____ invest in the project.

沃靈福德公司原本要在印尼設廠，但他們沒有足夠的資金投注在這項計畫中。

(A) enough capital to　　　　　(B) many capital for
(C) enough capital　　　　　　(D) capital enough

觀念　enough...to V 的用法

解析　前一句說「要設廠」，後一句以轉折語氣的連接詞 but 開頭，表示後句應該是說「資金不夠到能夠投資」。enough 如果當形容詞接名詞的話，句型是「enough ＋N＋to V」，因此答案應該選 (A)。capital「資金」是不可數名詞，不能用選項 (B) 的 many 來修飾。

• set up 設立

**B** **23.** Do you know how to get in touch with John, the guy _____ for the consulting firm? I need to contact him right away.

你知道要如何連繫到約翰，那個在顧問公司工作的男生？我必須馬上聯絡到他。

(A) who working　(B) who works　　(C) works　　　(D) worked

觀念　關係代名詞引導形容詞子句

解析　題目是要去解釋是「哪一個」John，所以用關代引導出形容詞子句，來修飾做為 John 的同位格的 the guy。先行詞為人，關代用 that 或者是 who，引導出的子句動詞依照句中的時態而變化。這裡指在顧問公司「工作」，使用現在式，the guy 為第三人稱單數，因此答案選 (B)。

• get in touch with sb. 聯絡…

**D** **24.** Our main office is _____ in the southern suburbs of the city. Feel free to visit anytime.

我們主要的辦公室位於本市南面郊區。歡迎隨時來訪。

(A) been　　　　(B) finding　　　　(C) building　　　　(D) located

觀念　被動語態

解析　locate意思是「把……設置在」，要指某場所「位於……」，則必須以被動的形式 be located in... 呈現。

• suburb [ˋsʌbɝb] (n.) 郊區　　　　　　• feel free to (do something) 隨意，不要客氣

D 25. The mistake has been made, and there's nothing we can do about it. There's no use in crying over _____ milk.

錯誤已經造成了，我們也做不了任何事去彌補。覆水難收，哭也沒有用。

(A) spill　　　　(B) spills　　　　(C) to spill　　　　(D) spilt

觀念 動詞變化

解析 這題的句意是說為了「潑出去的」牛奶哭泣是沒有用的。這裡的動作是被動的用法，因為牛奶是被灑出去的，所以要選擇以過去分詞形式表示被動的形容詞，也就是 spilt，這個字也可拼成 spilled。

● no use in＋Ving 做…沒有用

---

C 26. I saw Jim _____ with the client in his office yesterday. Does that mean he's going to reconsider our offer?

我看到吉姆昨天跟客戶在他的辦公室說話。這意味著他願意重新考慮我們的提議嗎？

(A) to talk　　　　(B) talked　　　　(C) talking　　　　(D) talks

觀念 感官動詞

解析 這題要看到「感官動詞」saw，並且了解「感官動詞」後面加上動詞的用法。「感官動詞」後面的動詞通常為「原形」或者是「進行式」，本題強調看到「正在談話」的動作，因此答案選 (C)。

● reconsider [ˌrikən`sɪdɚ] (v.) 重新考慮

---

B 27. The schedule of events had been _____ and sent to each of the participants two weeks before the campaign was launched.

活動的行程已經複印好，並已在活動開始前兩周送到各個參加者手上。

(A) copy　　　　(B) copied　　　　(C) copying　　　　(D) copies

觀念 被動語態

解析 本題的主詞 the schedule of events 為事物，不會主動進行 copy 和 send 的動作，動詞應以被動語態呈現，因此答案應該選 copy 的過去分詞，也就是 (B)。此外，這兩個動作均發生在活動開始之前，為了區分時間點，便將先作的動作以過去完成式的形式表現，所以整個句子的動詞寫成 had been＋p.p. 的形式。

● participant [pɑr`tɪsəpənt] (n./adj.) 參與者；參與的

332

**B** **28.** I realize that it's a dog-eat-dog world out there, but I still feel that
_____ to one's customers is bad for business.

我發現外面真是個人吃人的世界，但我仍然認為欺騙顧客對生意是不好的。

(A) lie       (B) lying       (C) lain       (D) lies

觀念 動名詞

解析 本題的重點是以「動名詞」做主詞的句型。後半句的主詞為「欺騙顧客」，在英文中，若要以動作做為主詞，動詞必須以「動名詞」或者是「不定詞」呈現，選項中只有「動名詞」，所以答案選 (B)。「欺騙」的動詞變化為 lie→lied→lied，分詞是 lying。

- dog-eat-dog 狗咬狗，引伸為人吃人、弱肉強食

---

**A** **29.** Would you _____ checking these sales figures for me, Joe?
I'm not sure if they're accurate.

你介意幫我檢查一下這些銷售數字嗎，朱歐？我不太確定它們是不是正確的。

(A) mind       (B) understand       (C) bother       (D) forget

觀念 動名詞

解析 本句要看到題目中的 checking 的變化。mind「介意」後面碰到動詞時，動詞要變成 Ving 的形式。將 mind 的選項代入，也符合前後句意，故選 (A)。understand「了解」和 forget「忘記」，均與句意不符。bother「花費精力做……」，後面的動詞要變成 to V，與題目不符。

- sales figures 銷售數字       • accurate [`ækjərɪt] (adj.) 正確的

---

**B** **30.** The only reason Don got promoted is because he's really good
_____ currying favor.

唐升官唯一的原因就是他很會拍馬屁。

(A) of       (B) at       (C) to       (D) for

觀念 介系詞

解析 本句要看得懂句子要表達的是 Don「很擅長」拍馬屁，所以一開始才會說這是他升官的唯一原因。「擅長」的用法是「be good at＋N./Ving」，因此答案選 (B)。

- curry favor (with) 討好，巴結，拍馬屁

C **31.** I feel I would be perfect for the job because I'm very _____ finance.
我認為我很適合這個工作，因為我對金融非常感興趣。

(A) interesting about          (B) interesting in

(C) interested in            (D) interested on

**觀念** 情緒形容詞

**解析** 後半句要說的是「對……感興趣」。在這裡用「動詞」轉換為「形容詞」的用法，如果是「某人對某件事感到……」，動詞以「過去分詞」形式表達。如果是「某件事令人感到……」，動詞以「現在分詞」形式表達。本句是表示「對……感興趣」，所以將 interest 加上 ed，在文法中 be interested 搭配的介系詞是 in，所以答案選 (C)。

• finance [`faɪnæns] (n.) 財政，金融

---

C **32.** After _____ with the advertising executives for six hours, a promotional campaign was finally agreed upon.
跟廣告主管開了六小時的會之後，終於擬定了促銷活動的舉辦。

(A) to meet     (B) met     (C) meeting     (D) of meeting

**觀念** 介系詞接動名詞

**解析** 本句開頭的 after 是介系詞，後面必須接「名詞」或「動名詞」當受詞，所以選 (C)。

• promotional campaign 促銷活動

---

B **33.** During the negotiations, Kyle rambled on for an hour before _____ to the point.
在談判中，在進入重點之前，凱爾一直漫無目的地談了一小時。

(A) came     (B) coming     (C) comes     (D) come

**觀念** 從屬連接詞

**解析** before 是從屬連接詞。從屬連接詞連接的句子如果主詞一樣，可以省略從屬子句的主詞，將動詞以分詞形式呈現。動詞主動用「現在分詞」，被動用「過去分詞」。句中要說的「進入重點」，這個動作應該是主動的，所以選 (B) coming。

• ramble on 漫談下去

**B** **34.** Government representatives will be at the meeting, so please be
_____ time!

政府代表會出席這次的會議，所以請務必準時！

(A) at　　　　　(B) on　　　　　(C) in　　　　　(D) of

**觀念**　介系詞

**解析**　從前半句可推測，後半句是「請大家準時」，「準時」的用法是 be on time，所以答案選 (B)。另外，很容易搞混的是「及時」be in time。其他兩個選項都沒有直接加上 time 的用法。

• representative [rɛprɪˋzɛtətɪv] (n./adj.) 代表，典型；有代表性的

---

**A** **35.** How _____ is it from home to your office, Peter?

彼得，從你家到辦公室有多遠？

(A) far　　　　　(B) farther　　　　(C) farthest　　　(D) very far

**觀念**　形容詞

**解析**　題目是問「從你家到辦公室有多遠？」問「多遠」，用 how far，不需要用到比較級 farther 或最高級 farthest。far 的另外一組比較級和最高級 further 和 furthest 則是指較抽象的概念。如：Do you have further questions?「你有進一步的問題嗎？」

• how long （時間）多久

---

**C** **36.** It's _____ difficult to break into that market! There are _____ many trade barriers.

打進那個市場實在是太困難了！那裡有太多的貿易壁壘。

(A) so ; much　　(B) much ; so　　(C) so ; too　　(D) only ; not

**觀念**　副詞

**解析**　本題要選擇配合文意的副詞。so 修飾形容詞，並且做強調語氣，表示「那麼的」。much 修飾不可數名詞，表示「很多」。too 用於形容詞與副詞前，表示「太……」。參照前後句意，前句提到「打進市場」以及形容詞「困難」，必需用 so 修飾。而根據句意，後句應該是指「太多貿易壁壘」，需用 too。答案應選 (C)。

• trade barrier 貿易壁壘（限制國際貿易的政策或規定）

**D** *37.* That conference call was a complete waste of time. I could barely _____ what anybody else was saying.

那個電話會議完全是浪費時間。我幾乎無法聽到其他人在說什麼。

(A) see          (B) talk          (C) listen          (D) hear

**觀念** 動詞

**解析** 本題要考對字彙和動詞用法的了解。conference call 是「電話會議」，所以 see 和句意不符。第二句的子句是「其他人在說什麼」，表示是幾乎「聽不到」，因此也不能選 talk。hear 是「聽到」，listen 是「專心聽」，要加上 to 才能接受詞，例：listen to music。所以答案選 (C)。

• conference [ˋkɑnfərəns] (n.) 會議

---

**B** *38.* Many _____ have called us to complain about our new product. They claim that it is defective.

很多人打電話來抱怨我們的新產品。他們說這個產品有瑕疵。

(A) person        (B) people        (C) peoples        (D) people's

**觀念** 集合名詞

**解析** 題目用 many，表示修飾複數可數名詞，從選項中可知，要選具有複數形的集合名詞 people。person 為單數，people 指「人們」的時候不加 s。

• defective [dɪˋfɛktɪv] (adj.) 有缺陷的，不完美的

---

**C** *39.* The fall in stock prices caught everyone by surprise. _____ was expecting it at all.

股價的下跌讓每個人都很震驚。沒有人想到會發生。

(A) Everyone       (B) Someone       (C) No one       (D) I

**觀念** 代名詞

**解析** 前句說到股價下跌讓大家「很震驚」，所以後句應該是說「沒有人」想到會發生。本句有 not...at all 的句型，而題目並沒有否定字，所以要選有否定意味的代名詞選項，符合句意和文法的，就是選項 (C)。

• catch sb. by surprise 令某人驚訝，出其不意

B **40.** The Holger Company has a really state-of-the-art inventory system.
I wish we had _____ too.

霍格公司有一個非常先進的庫存系統。我真希望我們也有一個。

(A) some        (B) one        (C) ones        (D) any

觀念    不定代名詞

解析    這裡的題目是指 a state-of-the-art inventory system，並沒有特定指哪一種，只是要說明也想要有「一個」，在這種情況下就會使用不定代名詞，單數用 one，複數用 ones。

● state-of-the-art 最先進的，最高級的        ● inventory [ˋɪnvənˌtorɪ] (n.) 存貨清單，庫存

**Questions 1~4 refer to the following article.**

According to the latest statistics, Taiwan is currently in a ___**C**___

1. (A) worsened
   (B) worsen
   (C) worsening
   (D) worst

recession. Due to the economic downturn, many unemployed or laid off workers have no choice but ___**B**___ the public service examination

2. (A) took
   (B) to take
   (C) taking
   (D) taken

in order to support their ___**D**___. As a result of the general economic

3. (A) homes
   (B) houses
   (C) household
   (D) families

situation, companies are being forced to cut their staffs and increase the number of workers on unpaid leave. What's even worse, the New Taiwan dollar has hit a record low against the greenback. ___**B**___ more and

4. (A) Nevertheless
   (B) Although
   (C) In spite of
   (D) Despite

more people are losing their jobs, looking for new jobs or taking pay cuts, they still hope that an economic recovery is just around the corner.

**問題 1～4 請參考以下文章。**

根據最新的數據，台灣現今處在越來越來惡化的經濟衰退。因為經濟不景氣，許多失業或是被裁員的人只好準備公職考試以維持家計。受到大環境衝擊，企業被迫縮編人員和增加放無薪假的員工。更糟的是，新台幣兌美元已創下新低點。雖然有越來越多人口正在失去工作，找尋新的工作和面臨減薪的情況，大家還是希望經濟很快就會復甦。

1. 觀念 分詞當形容詞

   解析 此處欠缺的是形容詞，用來修飾 recession 一字。worsen 是動詞「使……惡化」， worsening 為其現在分詞，作形容詞用時表「主動、進行」，有「越來越惡化」之意；worsened 為其過去分詞，作形容詞用時則表「被動、完成」，意思為「更加惡化的」。根據句意，經濟衰退的狀況還在持續進行中，所以應以 worsening 來修飾。

   • statistics [stə`tɪstɪks] (n.) 統計，統計學　• recession [rɪ`sɛʃən] (n.) 經濟衰退

2. 觀念 不定詞

   解析 have no choice but... 指「除了……外別無選擇」，後面接動詞時必須以 to V 的形式呈現，所以本題應說 have no choice but to take...。

   • unemployed [ˌʌnɪm`plɔɪd] (adj.) 失業的　• take an exam 參加考試

3. 觀念 集合名詞

   解析 family 表示「家人」時，做為集合名詞，不加 s。如果指的是「家庭」或「家族」，就是可數名詞，兩個家庭以上加 s。本題中指的是許多家庭，因此應用 families。household 的用法則與 family 相同。

   • support one's family 養家活口
   • household [`haus`hold] (n.) 一家人；同住一房子的人

4. 觀念 連接詞

   解析 前半句「正在失去工作，找尋新的工作和面臨減薪」與後半句「希望很快經濟就會復甦」有明顯的轉折語氣，所以此處應選具有轉折語氣的連接詞。本題四個選項皆具轉折語氣，但以詞性來判斷，只有 although 是連接詞，故選 (B)。nevertheless 是副詞，且應放在兩個轉折語氣子句中間；in spite of 和 despite 皆為介系詞，後面須接名詞，而非子句。

   • recovery [rɪ`kʌvərɪ] (n.) 復甦，復原　• around the corner 在附近；即將來臨

**Questions 5~8 refer to the following article.**

Long as one of the world's richest men (ranked no. 1 in 14 of the past 16 years), Gates announced that he was leaving his day-to-day duties as Microsoft chairman in June 2006 to devote more time ____A____

5.(A) to
  (B) in
  (C) on
  (D) at

philanthropy. The Bill and Melinda Gates Foundation, which Gates heads along with his wife Melinda and close friend Warren Buffet, is the largest charitable organization in the world. Each year, the foundation funds projects focused on combating disease, ____D____ educational

6.(A) raising
  (B) progressing
  (C) elevating
  (D) improving

opportunities, and enhancing information technology both at home and abroad. It should come as no surprise that Gates, ____C____ was so

7.(A) which
  (B) whose
  (C) who
  (D) that

successful in earning money in his first career, has proven equally good at giving it away in his second. His generosity continues ____D____ the world.

8.(A) change
  (B) will change
  (C) changes
  (D) to change

**問題 5～8 請參考以下文章。**

長期是全球最有錢的人之一（過去十六年有十四年名列第一），蓋茲在二○○六年六月宣布卸下微軟董事長的日常責任，以便投入更多時間於慈善事業。以蓋茲和妻子梅琳達和摯友華倫巴菲特為首的「比爾及梅琳達蓋茲基金會」是世界最大的慈善組織。每一年，基金會都會資助國內外著眼於對抗疾病、提升教育機會和改善資訊科技的計畫。毫不意外地，在生涯第一階段賺錢賺得如此成功的蓋茲，已在第二階段證明他同樣擅長捐錢。他的慷慨將繼續改變這個世界。

5. 觀念 介系詞

解析 devote 是「奉獻；投入」之意，與介系詞 to 連用。

- day-to-day 每天的；例行的
- philanthropy [fɪˋlænθrəpɪ] (n.) 博愛；（常複數）慈善事業

---

6. 觀念 動詞

解析 projects focused on... 是「著眼於……的計畫」，後面所接的三個動名詞「對抗疾病、提升教育機會和改善資訊科技」皆為其受詞。四個選項中以 improving 語意最適合接 educational opportunities，即「提升、改善教育機會」之意。其他選項 raise 指「增加、提高（數量）」，elevate 指「提高（位置）」，progress 則是「（隨著時間）進展；進步」之意。

- combat [ˋkɑmbæt] (n./v.) 戰鬥；與…搏鬥 • enhance [ɪnˋhæns] (v.) 提高；增強

---

7. 觀念 關係代名詞

解析 此處要選關係代名詞修飾前面的 Gates，修飾人的關代可用 who 或 that，但此處關代前有逗號，為「補述」用法，不能用 that。所謂「補述」用法，即先行詞很明確，通常為人名（比如本句的 Gates）或僅有的一人，此時的關代子句是為補充說明先行詞的資訊，這種用法關代前會有逗號；至於「限定」用法則不加逗號，目的是要在很廣的範圍中加以限制以明確指出對象。

- come as no surprise 意料之中；不令人奇怪

---

8. 觀念 不定詞與動名詞

解析 continue 後面可以接不定詞或動名詞，指「繼續做某事」。兩者的些微差異在於 continue doing something 指「繼續做原本已在做的事」，而 continue to do something 則是「完成原本的動作，接著做另一件事」。

- generosity [dʒɛnəˋrɑsətɪ] (n.) 慷慨

# 多益文法模擬考　第二回

單句填空 ▶ 請從 (A)、(B)、(C)、(D) 中選出一個最適合的答案。

☐ **1.** Ladies and gentlemen, you'll find the annual reports _____ the table in front of you. Please feel free to look through them.
(A) on
(B) in
(C) around
(D) from

☐ **2.** I'll be in Taiwan on business for seven days. I'll be heading _____ on the 18$^{th}$.
(A) up
(B) house
(C) home
(D) to home

☐ **3.** Whew! I _____ spilled correction fluid all over the carpet. It would have left quite a stain!
(A) almost
(B) most
(C) very
(D) never

☐ **4.** Shirley's presentation was _____ difficult _____ understand. It was so complicated!
(A) so ; too
(B) to ; too
(C) too ; to
(D) so ; so

☐ **5.** I'm really excited about this chance to tour the factory in Shenzhen, Mr. Li. I've _____ been to China before.
(A) never
(B) used to
(C) ever
(D) always

6. The factory is _____ the freeway, so transportation is very convenient.

(A) at

(B) near

(C) close

(D) next

7. Mr. Simms hired his nephew to be the manager of our branch office, but most of us feel he's _____ qualified for the position.

(A) hardly

(B) almost

(C) too

(D) very

8. Don't worry, Mr. Lewis. The shipment will be arriving in only a few _____ time.

(A) day's

(B) day

(C) days

(D) days'

9. How _____ does your company do OEM manufacturing, Ms. Tyler?

(A) many

(B) sometimes

(C) often

(D) can

10. I'd like to work at that company, but there _____ job openings right now.

(A) isn't any

(B) is no

(C) aren't any

(D) are none

**11.** Ron is very punctual. He _____ gets to work on time.
(A) always
(B) sometimes
(C) never
(D) once

**12.** Yvonne, you're so lazy! I _____ do your work for you ever again!
(A) didn't.
(B) won't
(C) will
(D) can

**13.** A: You'll be meeting with Roger at 3:00 p.m. tomorrow, won't you?
B: _____
(A) Yes, at 4:00 p.m.
(B) Yes, I will.
(C) No, I'm meeting him at 3:00 p.m.
(D) No, I don't.

**14.** The invoice wasn't _____ very clearly, so we had to rewrite it.
(A) write
(B) writes
(C) written
(D) to write

**15.** _____ you do me a favor? Make 20 copies of this document for me.
(A) Couldn't
(B) Could
(C) Please
(D) Pardon

**16.** There is a lot of pressure to finish this project on time. I _____
I didn't have to work overtime.
(A) hope
(B) wish
(C) wished
(D) wishing

**17.** A: You really wish you'd gone to business school instead of art school,
don't you?
B: _____
(A) Yes, I do.
(B) No, I didn't.
(C) Yes, I wished.
(D) No, I didn't wish.

**18.** Yes, the manager is _____ today, but you need to make an
appointment first.
(A) inside
(B) up
(C) outside
(D) in

**19.** The Barstow Company performed _____ better than we did in the
fourth quarter.
(A) more
(B) many
(C) much
(D) very

**20.** Miss Jones, I'm quite surprised by your report. You _____ do a
good job on them, but this one is full of typos and grammatical errors.
(A) once
(B) occasionally
(C) sometimes
(D) usually

**21.** Many companies use the possessive apostrophe in the name of their company, such as Macy's, while others don't, such as _____.
(A) Starbuck's
(B) Starbucks
(C) Starbuck
(D) Starbucks'

**22.** Thank you for your applause everyone, but the real credit goes to Tom and Nancy. They're the _____ who came up with the idea in the first place.
(A) some
(B) anybody
(C) one
(D) ones

**23.** For all her efforts to secure the Henderson account, Maria _____ a raise of 10% of her current salary.
(A) was taken
(B) was requested
(C) was given
(D) was approved

**24.** Mr. Muller will be arriving to negotiate a new contract _____ six days, so we need to make arrangements quickly.
(A) from
(B) in
(C) under
(D) of

**25.** Congratulations, Mark! I think the client _____ liked your presentation.
(A) quietly
(B) true
(C) quite
(D) real

**26.** This company treats its female employees very well. For instance, they _____ provide paid maternity leave.
(A) never
(B) used to
(C) always
(D) seldom

**27.** There aren't _____ investors now, so we don't have _____ capital.
(A) much ; much
(B) much ; many
(C) many ; many
(D) many ; much

**28.** A: Will you take the recent economic problems into consideration when you prepare your proposal?
B: _____
(A) Yes, I did.
(B) Yes, I can.
(C) Yes, I was.
(D) Yes, I will.

**29.** Mr. and Mrs. Jackson _____ tomorrow to submit their letter of credit.
(A) are arriving
(B) were arriving
(C) arriving
(D) to arrive

**30.** It _____ like our client will not renew his contract with us next year.
(A) hears
(B) listens
(C) sees
(D) looks

**31.** I have to let you go, Kevin, as I heard you _____ to our competitor.
(A) giving information
(B) trading commodities
(C) delivering clothes
(D) singing songs

**32.** We met with the shipping company this morning and asked them _____ the shipment by next Friday.
(A) to complete
(B) completing
(C) completed
(D) will complete

**33.** There's cause for alarm because the price of raw materials _____ go up next year.
(A) are
(B) might
(C) was
(D) is

**34.** A job interview is serious business. You'd _____ not wear jeans and a T-shirt.
(A) better
(B) shouldn't
(C) can't
(D) won't

**35.** The entire shipment was damaged. I really _____ we'd had it insured.
(A) want
(B) said
(C) wish
(D) think

**36.** _____ our production can't meet the demand, we may go out of business.
(A) Where
(B) Should
(C) Could
(D) If

**37.** The position at that company will be filled quickly. If I were you, I'd _____ for it right away.
(A) announce
(B) campaign
(C) fill
(D) apply

**38.** We don't have _____ capital to begin a project like that any time soon.
(A) much as
(B) every
(C) many
(D) enough

**39.** I'm afraid I can't offer you the position, Mr. Collins. You are _____ work for our company.
(A) not enough experience to
(B) not experienced enough to
(C) no experience to
(D) very experienced to

**40.** In order to break into the China market, we're _____ to have to do some research.
(A) going
(B) will
(C) should
(D) need

段落填空 ▶ 請從 (A)、(B)、(C)、(D) 中選出一個最適合的答案。

**Questions 1~4 refer to the following article.**

A pre-dawn blaze at a popular five-star hotel last Saturday killed 15 people, including guests, employees and firefighters. Most of the guests were sleeping or resting when the blaze _____. While firefighters

    1.(A) broke out
      (B) breaks out
      (C) broken out
      (D) was breaking out

were trying hard to put out the fire, all of the people _____ in the

    2.(A) stayed
      (B) caught
      (C) lived
      (D) seized

hotel were fleeing in panic. In this tragic incident, several victims _____ severely injured and taken to the hospital for emergency

3.(A) find
  (B) found
  (C) were found
  (D) finding

treatment. After a _____ inspection, smoke inhalation was found to

    4.(A) through
      (B) thorough
      (C) though
      (D) thoroughly

be the main cause of death.

## Questions 5~8 refer to the following article.

_____ a recent poll, about 60 percent of Americans think the nation

5. (A) According
   (B) According to
   (C) According with
   (D) In accordance

could be heading for another depression. To be sure, the disturbing
events of recent months—a _____ credit crisis, failures of banks

6. (A) deepened
   (B) deepen
   (C) deepening
   (D) deepens

and Wall Street brokerages, and major declines in stock markets around
the world—are cause for concern. But at the same time, most people's
everyday reality is nothing like that during the Great Depression, when
millions of families were _____ poverty. There is no doubt that

7. (A) driven in
   (B) driven into
   (C) driven onto
   (D) driven at

damage to the financial _____ has been severe, with the collapse

8. (A) sector
   (B) section
   (C) department
   (D) division

of major financial institutions and rising unemployment.

**A** 1. Ladies and gentlemen, you'll find the annual reports _____ the table in front of you. Please feel free to look through them.

女士先生們，你們會看到放在你們桌子前的年度報告書。不用客氣，請隨意翻閱。

(A) on        (B) in        (C) around        (D) from

**觀念** 介系詞

**解析** 題目的意思應該是告訴來賓他們會「看到放在你們桌子前的年度報告書」，因為下一句說「請隨意翻閱」。on the table 是「在桌子上」；in the table 是「在桌子裡」；around the table 是「在桌子周圍」；from the table 是「從桌子那裡」。報告書是放在桌子上的，所以選 (A)。

● annual [ˋænjʊəl] (adj./n.) 年度的；年刊，年鑑

● feel free (to do sth.) 表示允許，隨意，不用拘束…

---

**C** 2. I'll be in Taiwan on business for seven days. I'll be heading _____ on the 18th.

我要去台灣出差七天，將在十八號回家。

(A) up        (B) house        (C) home        (D) to home

**觀念** 介系詞

**解析** 第一句「要去台灣出差」，下一句應該是說「要在十八號回家」。head 在這裡指的是「前往」。home、here、there 等副詞前面不加任何介系詞，所以回家直接說 head home 即可。不選 (B) 的原因是 house 通常指「房子」，也就是整個建築物本身，在英文「家」是用 home。

● on business 出差

---

**A** 3. Whew! I _____ spilled correction fluid all over the carpet. It would have left quite a stain!

好險！我差一點把修正液弄翻在地毯上。它可能會留下一個大污點呢！

(A) almost        (B) most        (C) very        (D) never

**觀念** 副詞

**解析** 此處要選擇修飾動詞、並配合文意的副詞。第二句說「可能會留下一個大污點」，表示前一句應該是「差點弄翻」。almost 是副詞「幾乎」，並符合文意，故選 (A)。

● correction fluid 修正液

C 4. Shirley's presentation was _____ difficult _____ understand. It was so complicated!

Shirley的報告實在是困難到無法了解。真是有夠複雜！

(A) so ; too     (B) to ; too     (C) too ; to     (D) so ; so

**觀念** 副詞

**解析** 從第二句「有夠複雜」推斷出第一句是說報告太難以致於無法理解。「太……以致於無法……」的句型為「too＋形容詞／副詞＋to＋V」。如果要用 so 來修飾 difficult，句子要改成「so＋形容詞／副詞＋that＋子句」，例：so difficult that I can't understand it。正確答案為 (C)。

● complicated [ˋkɑmpləˏketɪd] (adj.) 複雜的，難懂的

A 5. I'm really excited about this chance to tour the factory in Shenzhen, Mr. Li. I've _____ been to China before.

林先生，我很興奮這次有機會能去參觀深圳的工廠。我以前從未到過中國。

(A) never     (B) used to     (C) ever     (D) always

**觀念** 副詞

**解析** 第二句應是說「從未到過中國」，第一句才會說對於這次的參觀機會感到很興奮。used to 是「過去習慣……」，ever 是「曾經」，always 是「總是」，這三個選項與句意不符。因此，答案選 (A)「從未」。

B 6. The factory is _____ the freeway, so transportation is very convenient.

這個工廠就在高速公路附近，所以運輸交通非常便利。

(A) at     (B) near     (C) close     (D) next

**觀念** 介系詞

**解析** 後半句說「所以運輸交通非常便利」，可以推測前半句應該是指工廠離高速公路不遠。類似的意思可以用 near、next to、close to，選項 (C) 和 (D) 都少了 to。at the freeway 是「工廠就在高速公路上」，這樣的說法不妥。答案選 (B)。

● freeway（美式用語）高速公路     ● transportation [ˏtrænspɚˋteʃən] (n.) 運輸

**A** **7.** Mr. Simms hired his nephew to be the manager of our branch office, but most of us feel he's _____ qualified for the position.

西姆斯先生雇用他的姪子來當我們分公司的經理,但是大部分的人都覺得他不夠資格坐這個位置。

(A) hardly      (B) almost      (C) too      (D) very

**觀念** 副詞

**解析** 後半句以 but 開頭,表示口氣上有轉折,應該是覺得經理「不夠資格」,要選擇有否定意味的副詞來修飾 qualified。hardly(幾乎不),有否定意味。almost(幾乎),too(太……),very(非常),這三個都與文意不符,故答案選 (A)。

● branch office 分公司

---

**D** **8.** Don't worry, Mr. Lewis. The shipment will be arriving in only a few _____ time.

不用擔心,路易斯先生。貨物在幾天的時間之內就會送達。

(A) day's      (B) day      (C) days      (D) days'

**觀念** 所有格

**解析** 題目中的 a few(一些,幾個),用來修飾可數複數名詞,因此可知 day 應該為複數。複數名詞的所有格,是在最後加上「'」,因此答案選 (D)。

● shipment [`ʃɪpmənt] (n.) 裝運,裝載的貨物

---

**C** **9.** How _____ does your company do OEM manufacturing, Ms. Tyler?

你的公司多常做代工製造,泰勒小姐?

(A) many      (B) sometimes      (C) often      (D) can

**觀念** 副詞

**解析** 這裡要了解以 how 開頭的問句型式,how many(多少)修飾可數複數名詞,用來詢問「數量」;how often(多久、多長)用來詢問「頻率與次數」。選項 (A) 和選項 (D) 都沒有直接用 how 加上去的疑問形式,答案選 (C) 最合適。

● OEM (original equipment manufacturing) 代工製造

C 10. I'd like to work at that company, but there _____ job openings right now.

我想在那家公司工作,但那裡現在沒有任何職缺。

(A) isn't any     (B) is no     (C) aren't any     (D) are none

觀念 可數 / 不可數名詞

解析 本題考的是修飾可數名詞的用法。job openings 是可數複數名詞,所以 be 動詞要用 are。選項 (D) 要改成 are not,而選項 (A) 和 (B) 則是文法單複數錯誤。選項 (C) 的 any 常放在疑問句和否定句,這裡的意思是說「沒有任何職缺」。

• job openings 工作職缺

---

A 11. Ron is very punctual. He _____ gets to work on time.

榮恩非常準時。他總是準時上班。

(A) always     (B) sometimes     (C) never     (D) once

觀念 副詞

解析 前半句說「榮恩非常準時」,所以下一句應該是「他總是準時上班」。sometimes（有時候）、never（從未）、once（曾經）,這三個選項都與句意不符。因此,答案選 (A)「總是」。

• punctual [`pʌŋktʃʊəl] (adj.) 準時的     • on time 準時

---

B 12. Yvonne, you're so lazy! I _____ do your work for you ever again!

依凡,你好懶!我再也不會幫你做你的工作了!

(A) didn't.     (B) won't     (C) will     (D) can

觀念 未來簡單式

解析 由話說話者抱怨的語氣,可推知他以後將不會為 Yvonne 做她份內的工作,因此時態應用未來式「助動詞 will＋原形動詞」。而根據句意,此處應用否定助動詞 will not,縮寫為 won't。此外,助動詞 will 除了表「未來」之外,也表「意願」,因此 won't...ever again 帶有強烈的「不願意」語氣。

• not...ever again 再也不…

**B** *13.* A: You'll be meeting with Roger at 3:00 p.m. tomorrow, won't you?

B: _____

A：你明天下午三點將會跟羅傑碰面，對不對？

B：對，我會。

(A) Yes, at 4:00 p.m.        (B) Yes, I will.

(C) No, I'm meeting him at 3:00 p.m.        (D) No, I don't.

觀念   未來進行式、附加問句

解析   本句是「未來進行式＋附加問句」的句子，回答時與一般的未來進行式無異，肯定簡答說 Yes, I will.，否定簡答則說 No, I won't.。

● meet with 與⋯碰面

---

**C** *14.* The invoice wasn't _____ very clearly, so we had to rewrite it.

這張發票沒有寫得很清楚，所以我們必須重開。

(A) write        (B) writes        (C) written        (D) to write

觀念   被動語態

解析   invoice（發票）是事物，不會主動做 write 的動作，因此須用被動語態 wasn't written。

● invoice [`ɪnvɔɪs] (n.) 發票；發貨單        ● rewrite [ri`raɪt] (v.) 重寫；修改

---

**B** *15.* _____ you do me a favor? Make 20 copies of this document for me.

你可以幫我一個忙嗎？這份文件幫我印二十份。

(A) Couldn't        (B) Could        (C) Please        (D) Pardon

觀念   情態助動詞

解析   本句為疑問句，所以不能選 (C) 或 (D)。而根據句意，此處應用肯定的情態助動詞 Could 來引導。注意 Could 在此並不是過去式，而是用來表達比 Can 更「委婉、客氣」的請求。

● do...a favor 幫⋯一個忙

● copy [`kɑpɪ] (n.) 副本；（文件、書報等）份、冊

**B** **16.** There is a lot of pressure to finish this project on time. I _____ I didn't have to work overtime.

要準時完成這個案子壓力很大。我好希望我不必加班。

(A) hope      (B) wish      (C) wished      (D) wishing

觀念 假設語氣

解析 hope 和 wish 皆表示「希望」，後面均可接 that 子句。但 hope 是指「希望某事發生」，如：I hope (that) I will pass the exam.（我希望我會通過考試。）而 wish 是指「與現在事實相反或不太可能發生的願望」，屬「假設語氣」，子句中動詞須用「過去式」。本題由子句中的過去式助動詞 didn't 可推知前面應用 wish。

• pressure [ˋprɛʃɚ] (n.) 壓力

---

**A** **17.** A: You really wish you'd gone to business school instead of art school, don't you?

     B: _____

     A：你真的希望你念的是商業學校而不是藝術學校，是不是？

     B：是啊，我是。

(A) Yes, I do.               (B) No, I didn't.

(C) Yes, I wished.        (D) No, I didn't wish.

觀念 假設語氣、附加問句

解析 本題在假設語氣的陳述句後加上附加問句 don't you?，答題時直接根據附加問句回答即可，肯定簡答說 Yes, I do.，否定則說 No, I don't.。

• instead of 代替

---

**D** **18.** Yes, the manager is _____ today, but you need to make an appointment first.

沒錯，經理今天在公司，但你必須先預約。

(A) inside      (B) up      (C) outside      (D) in

觀念 介系詞

解析 後半句說「但你必須先預約」，表示前半句應該是指「經理在公司」，但還是要先「預約」。「sb.＋be＋in」表示某人在家裡或者在工作單位；inside/outside 是指地點的「裡」和「外」；the manager is up 則是「經理已經起床」，不合適。答案選 (D)。

• make an appointment 預約

• appointment [əˋpɔɪntmənt] (n.) (尤指正式的)約會，約定

**C** *19.* The Barstow Company performed _____ better than we did in the fourth quarter.

巴斯托公司在第四季表現得比我們好得多了。

(A) more      (B) many      (C) much      (D) very

**觀念** 副詞

**解析** 本題要選擇修飾比較級 better 的副詞。「more＋形容詞原級」＝形容詞比較級，這裡已經有比較級 better，所以 (A) 不可選。many 修飾可數複數名詞。much 可修飾形容詞比較級，much better 意思是「好很多」。very 修飾形容詞原級。答案選 (C)。除了 much 之外，far、a little、even 等也可修飾形容詞比較級。

• quarter [`kwɔtə] (n.) 四分之一；季度

---

**D** *20.* Miss Jones, I'm quite surprised by your report. You _____ do a good job on them, but this one is full of typos and grammatical errors.

瓊斯小姐，我對你的報告還滿驚訝的。你通常都做得很好，但這次的報告卻充滿著錯字和文法錯誤。

(A) once      (B) occasionally    (C) sometimes    (D) usually

**觀念** 副詞

**解析** 前句說對報告「很驚訝」，選擇後句的「頻率副詞」時，還要再考慮到第二句後半部分說的「但這次的報告卻充滿著錯字和文法錯誤」。從前後文意可知，應該是她「通常」寫得很好，但這次卻做不好。once（曾經）、occasionally（偶爾）和 sometimes（有時候），這三個選項都不會導致一開始說的「很驚訝」。因此答案選 (D)「通常」。

• typo [`taɪpo] (n.) 打字排印錯誤

---

**B** *21.* Many companies use the possessive apostrophe in the name of their company, such as Macy's, while others don't, such as _____.

很多公司都用所有格撇號做為公司的名稱，例如 Macy's 百貨，然而其他的公司則沒有，例如 Starbucks 星巴克。

(A) Starbuck's    (B) Starbucks    (C) Starbuck    (D) Starbucks'

**觀念** 所有格

**解析** 前句提到一些公司用「所有格撇號」作為名稱，下一句用到具有轉折語氣的連接詞 while，表示這裡的舉例應該跟前句相反，所以選擇沒有撇號的選項，也就是選項 (B)。

• possessive apostrophe 所有格撇號

D **22.** Thank you for your applause everyone, but the real credit goes to Tom and Nancy. They're the _____ who came up with the idea in the first place.

謝謝你們大家的鼓勵，但應該真正歸功於湯姆和南西，他們才是一開始想到這個想法的人。

(A) some　　　　(B) anybody　　(C) one　　　　(D) ones

觀念　不定代名詞

解析　在第二句空格的位置是要代替「當初想到這個想法的人」，並不是特定指某個人，因此要用不定代名詞，they 是複數，所以用 ones。

● applause [əˋplɔz] (n.) 鼓掌，喝采　　　● come up with sth. 想到…，想出…

---

C **23.** For all her efforts to secure the Henderson account, Maria _____ a raise of 10% of her current salary.

聽了這項新計畫的所有提議之後，我決定選擇大衛和安的想法。

(A) was taken　　　　　　(B) was requested
(C) was given　　　　　　(D) was approved

觀念　被動語態

解析　raise 當名詞指「加薪」，request a raise 是「要求加薪」，give a raise 則是「給……加薪」。本句中的 Maria 是員工，而所有選項均為被動語態，故應說 Maria was given a raise（瑪麗亞被加薪）。

● secure [sɪˋkjʊr] (v.) 使安全；替……弄到　　● account [əˋkaunt] (n.) 帳戶；客戶

---

B **24.** Mr. Muller will be arriving to negotiate a new contract _____ six days, so we need to make arrangements quickly.

木樂先生將在六天之後抵達來協商新的合約，所以我們必須趕快做好相關安排。

(A) from　　　　(B) in　　　　(C) under　　　(D) of

觀念　介系詞

解析　題目表示是未來時態，表示「未來」的時間，要用介系詞 in。from 是「從……」；under 是「在……之下」；of 是「屬於……的」。答案選 (B) 表示「六天之後」。

● negotiate [nɪˋgoʃɪͺet] (v.) 談判，協商

● arrangement [əˋrendʒmənt] (n.) 安排，準備工作

C **25.** Congratulations, Mark! I think the client _____ liked your presentation.

馬克，恭喜你！我想顧客挺喜歡你的報告的。

(A) quietly      (B) true      (C) quite      (D) real

**觀念** 副詞

**解析** 這題要選擇修飾「喜歡」（動詞）的副詞。quietly 副詞「安靜地」，與句意不符。true 形容詞「真正的」，要改為副詞 truly。quite 副詞「相當」。real 形容詞「真實的」，要改為副詞 really。因此答案選 (C)。

• congratulations [kən͵grætʃəˋleʃənz] (n.) 祝賀，恭喜

---

C **26.** This company treats its female employees very well. For instance, they _____ provide paid maternity leave.

這間公司對女員工的福利很好。例如，他們都會提供有給職的產假。

(A) never      (B) used to      (C) always      (D) seldom

**觀念** 副詞

**解析** 前半句提到「對女員工的福利很好」，下一句舉例說到的「有給職的產假」公司應該是會提供。never（從未）和 seldom（很少），這兩個選項與句意不符。used to 是「過去習慣……」，如果說公司女員工福利很好，那麼舉例就不會舉過去曾做、現在卻沒有做的事。因此，答案選 (C) always（總是）。

• maternity leave 產假

---

D **27.** There aren't _____ investors now, so we don't have _____ capital.

現在沒有太多投資者，所以我們手邊沒有太多的資金。

(A) much ; much    (B) much ; many    (C) many ; many    (D) many ; much

**觀念** many/much 的用法

**解析** 本題考的是修飾可數和不可數名詞的用法。many 和 much 都是表示「很多」的意思。investors「投資者」是可數複數名詞，要用 many 修飾。capital「資金」是不可數名詞，要用 much 修飾。

• capital [ˋkæpət!] (n.) 首都，資本，大寫字母

**D** *28.* A: Will you take the recent economic problems into consideration when you prepare your proposal?

B: _____

A：當你準備提案時，你會將最近的經濟問題列入考慮嗎？

B：是的，我會。

(A) Yes, I did.　　(B) Yes, I can.　　(C) Yes, I was.　　(D) Yes, I will.

觀念　　未來簡單式

解析　　本題為未來簡單式的疑問句，以助動詞 Will 引導。肯定簡答應說 Yes, I will.，否定簡答則說 No, I won't.。

- take...into consideration 把…列入考慮　　• proposal [prə`pozl] (n.) 建議；提案

---

**A** *29.* Mr. and Mrs. Jackson _____ tomorrow to submit their letter of credit.

傑克森夫婦明天將來提交他們的信用狀。

(A) are arriving　　(B) were arriving　(C) arriving　　(D) to arrive

觀念　　未來簡單式

解析　　來去動詞如 come（來）、go（去）、arrive（抵達）、leave（離開）等，可用「現在進行式」代替「未來簡單式」，來表達事件「即將發生」。

- submit [səb`mɪt] (v.) 提交，遞出　　• letter of credit 信用狀

---

**D** *30.* It _____ like our client will not renew his contract with us next year.

看起來我們的客戶明年將不會跟我們續約。

(A) hears　　(B) listens　　(C) sees　　(D) looks

觀念　　連綴動詞

解析　　see 和 look 都有「看」的意思，但 see（看見）後面直接接受詞，不會接 like。look 則可當「連綴動詞」，句型為「look＋形容詞（看起來……）」或「look like＋名詞（看起來像……）」。此外，「look at＋名詞」意思則是「注視」。

- renew [rɪ`nju] (v.) 更新；（契約）續約；（證件）更換

**A** *31.* I have to let you go, Kevin, as I heard you _____ to our competitor.

我必須讓你走，凱文，因為我聽到你提供情報給我們的對手。

(A) giving information      (B) trading commodities

(C) delivering clothes      (D) singing songs

觀念 感官動詞

解析 heard 是「感官動詞」hear（聽見；聽到）的過去式，常用的感官動詞還有 see、watch、feel 等，句型為「感官動詞＋受詞＋原形動詞／現在分詞」。本題中說話者表示必須讓 Kevin 離職，可推知他做了圖利競爭對手的事，因此選 giving information（提供情報）。

- information [ˌɪnfəˈmeʃən] (n.) 資訊；情報   • competitor [kəmˈpɛtətə] (n.) 競爭對手
- commodity [kəmˈmɑdətɪ] (n.) 商品

---

**A** *32.* We met with the shipping company this morning and asked them _____ the shipment by next Friday.

我們今天早上跟貨運公司碰面，請他們在下週五前完成送貨。

(A) to complete      (B) completing      (C) completed      (D) will complete

觀念 不定詞

解析 動詞 ask 意思是「要求；請求」，句型為「ask＋人＋不定詞（to V）」；如果要表示「請人不要做某事」則說「ask＋人＋not＋不定詞（to V）」。

- complete [kəmˈplit] (v.) 完成

---

**B** *33.* There's cause for alarm because the price of raw materials _____ go up next year.

有理由要警覺，因為原料價格明年可能上漲。

(A) are      (B) might      (C) was      (D) is

觀念 情態助動詞

解析 在動詞 go 之前不能加 be 動詞，而應加入情態助動詞。情態助動詞 may 與 might 意思均為「可能；可以」，而 might 的語氣比 may 更委婉。

- cause [kɔz] (n.) 原因；理由      • raw material 原料

**A** **34.** A job interview is serious business. You'd _____ not wear jeans and a T-shirt.

求職面試是件嚴肅的事。你最好別穿牛仔褲和T恤。

(A) better (B) shouldn't (C) can't (D) won't

**觀念** 情態助動詞

**解析** 情態助動詞 should、can、will 等必須直接放在主詞後，兩者之間不會再插入縮寫的 'd，所以 (B)、(C)、(D) 均不可選。You'd better 為 You had better 的縮寫，意思是「你最好（做某事）」，其用法同情態助動詞，句型為「had better (not) ＋原形動詞」。注意 had better 為固定的詞組，不可改為 have/has better。

• interview [`ɪntɚˌvju] (n.) 面試；採訪 • serious [`sɪrɪəs] (adj.) 嚴肅的

**C** **35.** The entire shipment was damaged. I really _____ we'd had it insured.

整批運送的貨物都受損了。我真希望我們有為它買保險。

(A) want (B) said (C) wish (D) think

**觀念** 假設語氣

**解析** we'd had it insured 是「過去完成式」，須與 wish 搭配，表示「與過去式事實相反」的願望，「我真希望我們有為它買保險」代表的事實是 we didn't have it insured，而說話者現在非常後悔。此外，have it insured 是「使役動詞＋受詞＋過去分詞」的用法，意思是「讓它被保險」。

• damage [`dæmɪdʒ] (v.) 損壞，毀損 • insure [ɪn`ʃʊr] (v.) 為…投保

**D** **36.** _____ our production can't meet the demand, we may go out of business.

假如我們的產品無法符合要求，我們可能會關門大吉。

(A) Where (B) Should (C) Could (D) If

**觀念** 從屬連接詞

**解析** 本題在逗號前後分別為兩個子句，故需要一個從屬連接詞，將兩個子句連接起來。從屬連接詞 If 意思為「假如」，指「現在或未來可能發生的假設」時，If 子句的動詞時態須用「現在式」。

• demand [dɪ`mænd] (v./n.) 要求，請求；需求

• out of business 停業；歇業

D 37. The position at that company will be filled quickly. If I were you,
I'd _____ for it right away.

那家公司的職缺很快就會沒了。要是我是你，我會立刻申請。

(A) announce     (B) campaign     (C) fill     (D) apply

**觀念** 假設語氣

**解析** If I were you（假如我是你）是「與事實相反的假設」，故動詞用 were。If I were you 經常用來表示「建議，忠告」，句型為「If I were you, I would＋原形動詞...」。本題中適合選填的動詞為 apply（申請），與介系詞 for 連用。

● position [pə`zɪʃən] (n.) 職缺；位置     ● apply for... 申請⋯

---

D 38. We don't have _____ capital to begin a project like that any time soon.

我們近期內沒有足夠的資本去進行那樣的計畫。

(A) much as     (B) every     (C) many     (D) enough

**觀念** 形容詞

**解析** 本題要選擇配合文意的用法。句子以否定開頭，可推斷應是說「沒有足夠的資本去進行那樣的計畫」。much as「雖然，儘管」，去掉 as 就可修飾不可數名詞 capital。

● capital [`kæpət!] (n.) 首都；資本；大寫字母 ● not...any time soon 近期內⋯無法

---

B 39. I'm afraid I can't offer you the position, Mr. Collins. You are _____ work for our company.

我恐怕無法提供你這項職位，科林先生。你的經驗不夠到能在我們公司工作。

(A) not enough experience to     (B) not experienced enough to
(C) no experience to     (D) very experienced to

**觀念** 副詞

**解析** 本題要選擇配合文意 enough「夠⋯⋯」（副詞）的用法。前句提到「無法提供你這項職位」，表示 Collins 無法在這個公司上班，因此，可推測後句應該是說「經驗不夠到能在我們公司工作」。experienced 在這裡做表「被動」的形容詞，意思是「有經驗的」，enough「夠⋯⋯去做⋯⋯」的句型為「形容詞＋enough＋to V」，否定則為「not＋形容詞＋enough＋to V」。答案選 (B)。

● work for 為⋯工作

A **40.** In order to break into the China market, we're _____ to have to do some research.

為了搶進中國市場，我們要做點調查。

(A) going        (B) will        (C) should        (D) need

觀念　未來簡單式

解析　未來簡單式的句型為「will/be going to＋原形動詞」，本句題目中已有 be 動詞，所以答案必須選 going。

● break into 闖入                  ● research [rɪˋsɝtʃ] (n.) 調查，研究

**Questions 1~4 refer to the following article.**

A pre-dawn blaze at a popular five-star hotel last Saturday killed 15 people, including guests, employees and firefighters. Most of the guests were sleeping or resting when the blaze _____A_____. While firefighters

1.(A) broke out
　(B) breaks out
　(C) broken out
　(D) was breaking out

were trying hard to put out the fire, all of the people _____B_____ in the

2.(A) stayed
　(B) caught
　(C) lived
　(D) seized

hotel were fleeing in panic. In this tragic incident, several victims _____C_____ severely injured and taken to the hospital for emergency

3.(A) find
　(B) found
　(C) were found
　(D) finding

treatment. After a _____B_____ inspection, smoke inhalation was found to

4.(A) through
　(B) thorough
　(C) though
　(D) thoroughly

be the main cause of death.

**問題 1~4 請參考以下文章。**

上週六，某家著名五星級飯店發生凌晨大火，奪去 15 條人命，其中包括房客、員工及消防隊員。大火發生時，大部分的房客都在睡覺或休息。當消防員在努力撲滅大火時，受困在旅館裡的民眾驚慌失措地逃離。在這場悲慘的事件中，幾個嚴重受傷的受害者被尋獲後，就被送去醫院做緊急治療。在完整調查之後，發現濃煙吸入是死亡主因。

1. 觀念 過去簡單式

   解析 在過去時間裡，某動作正在進行中，而有另一動作突然插入時，第一個進行中的動作須用「過去進行式」，而第二個瞬間插入的動作則用「過去簡單式」，且經常與 when 連用。本題中大火發生是一瞬間的事，因此用過去簡單式。動詞 break 的三態為 break-broke-broken，所以答案選 broke out。

   ● blaze [blez] (n./v.) 大火；熊熊燃燒　　● break out 爆發

2. 觀念 動詞、形容詞子句簡化

   解析 注意本句題目中已有動詞 were fleeing，所以這裡要選的是修飾 people 的分詞，根據句意應選過去分詞 caught「被困在旅館裡的」。此為形容詞子句的簡化，原句為 all of the people who were caught in the hotel...。此外，「住在旅館裡」的動詞應用 stay，而非 live。但此處不可選過去式動詞 stayed，應將其改為現在分詞 staying 才對，表「正住在旅館中的」。

   ● flee [fli] (v.) 逃跑　　● panic [`pænɪk] (n./v.) 恐慌；使驚慌

3. 觀念 被動語態

   解析 受傷者是「被尋獲」然後「被送往醫院」，因此動詞應以「被動語態」呈現，故選 were found。

   ● tragic [`trædʒɪk] (adj.) 悲傷的　　● emergency [ɪ`mɝdʒənsɪ] (n.) 緊急情況
   ● incident [`ɪnsɪdənt] (n.)（犯罪、事故、襲擊等）事件

4. 觀念 形容詞

   解析 本題的四個選項拼法類似，考的是字彙的熟悉度。through 是介系詞「穿越，透過」，thorough 是形容詞「徹底的，完整的」，though 是連接詞「雖然」，thoroughly 則是 thorough 的副詞形「徹底地，完整地」。根據文意應選 (B)。

   ● inspection [ɪn`spɛkʃən] (n.) 調查　　● inhalation [ɪnhə`leʃən] (n.) 吸入

## Questions 5~8  refer to the following article.

_____**B**_____ a recent poll, about 60 percent of Americans think the nation
5.(A) According
  (B) According to
  (C) According with
  (D) In accordance

could be heading for another depression. To be sure, the disturbing
events of recent months—a _____**C**_____ credit crisis, failures of banks
            6.(A) deepened
              (B) deepen
              (C) deepening
              (D) deepens

and Wall Street brokerages, and major declines in stock markets around
the world—are cause for concern. But at the same time, most people's
everyday reality is nothing like that during the Great Depression, when
millions of families were _____**B**_____ poverty. There is no doubt that
          7.(A) driven in
            (B) driven into
            (C) driven onto
            (D) driven at

damage to the financial _____**A**_____ has been severe, with the collapse
          8.(A) sector
            (B) section
            (C) department
            (D) division

of major financial institutions and rising unemployment.

**問題 5～8 請參考以下文章。**

根據最近一項民意調查，有百分之六十左右的美國人認為美國可能正面臨著另一次
經濟大蕭條。正確來說，近幾個月發生了數起令人惶惶不安的事件——信用危機加
劇、銀行和華爾街經濟業務一敗塗地，以及全球股市暴跌——這些的確值得擔心。
但在此同時，多數人的日常現實與經濟大蕭條時期截然不同，當時，有數百萬個家
庭被迫落入貧窮。毋庸置疑地，隨著大型金融機構崩解、失業率節節上升，金融部
門已受到重創。

5. 觀念 介系詞片語

   解析 片語 according to 指「根據……」，也可替換為 in accordance with。
   - poll [pol] (n.) 民調
   - head for 朝…邁進
   - depression [dɪ`prɛʃən] (n.) 消沉；蕭條

6. 觀念 分詞當形容詞

   解析 此處要選可修飾 credit crisis 的形容詞。deepen 是動詞「使……加深、加劇」，deepening 為其現在分詞，作形容詞用時表「主動、進行」，有「越來越加劇的」之意；deepened 為其過去分詞，作形容詞用時則表「被動、完成」，意思為「已經變糟的」。根據句意，信用危機還在持續進行中，所以應以 deepening 來修飾。
   - disturbing [dɪs`tɜbɪŋ] (adj.) 引起煩惱的
   - brokerage [`brokərɪdʒ] (n.) 經濟業務
   - decline [dɪ`klaɪn] (n.) 衰退

7. 觀念 動詞片語

   解析 drive...into... 是「使……陷入（某困境）」，此處用被動語態表示「數百萬個家庭被迫落入貧窮」。
   - poverty [`pɑvətɪ] (n.) 貧窮
   - The Great Depression 指 1929-1933 年間全球性的經濟大蕭條

8. 觀念 名詞

   解析 本題考的是字彙熟悉度。這四個選項的中文皆有「部門」之意，但只有 sector 用來指「一國經濟的各部門、領域或行業」，如：public/private sector「公營部門 / 私營部門」、semiconductor sector「半導體業」。另外三字則近似，department 指「（企業 / 行政機關內部的）部、司、局、科、系」等；division 為其同義字，但也可泛指「某個分部或分公司」；section 則泛指「部門、處、科」等。
   - collapse [kə`læps] (n.) 崩潰
   - institution [ˌɪnstə`tjuʃən] (n.) 機構
   - severe [sə`vɪr] (adj.) 十分嚴重的；極為惡劣的

# 多益文法模擬考　第三回

**單句填空 ▶** 請從 (A)、(B)、(C)、(D) 中選出一個最適合的答案。

**1.** Kim has been voted "Employee of the Month" for _____ everyone in the company to do their best.
(A) encourage
(B) encouraged
(C) encouraging
(D) encourages

**2.** Never _____ eye contact during an interview. The interviewer will think you lack confidence.
(A) to avoid
(B) avoiding
(C) avoid
(D) avoided

**3.** The part I like best about my job _____ to potential customers about our line of products.
(A) is talk
(B) are talking
(C) is talking
(D) to talk

**4.** The board of directors decided _____ several departments to increase efficiency.
(A) downsize
(B) will downsize
(C) downsizing
(D) to downsize

**5.** _____ up to her ears in paperwork, Marcia had no choice but to work overtime for several days.
(A) Was
(B) Had been
(C) Being
(D) To be

**6.** It's obvious that our warehousing procedure is not cost effective.
I _____ recommend we adopt a different one.
(A) hardly
(B) worriedly
(C) badly
(D) strongly

**7.** I like working for Bill. He's the kind of guy _____ his employees
and doesn't treat them like underlings.
(A) who respecting
(B) who respect
(C) who respects
(D) who is respected

**8.** I'm new here, Joe. Can you tell me _____ this photocopier?
(A) how to operate
(B) operate how
(C) how operate
(D) how to operating

**9.** My financial advisor told me _____ in treasury bonds at this time.
He thinks it would be better to wait a few months.
(A) not invest
(B) not to investing
(C) no invest
(D) not to invest

**10.** Yvonne's Boutique is having a going-out-of-business sale. _____
item in the store _____ on sale.
(A) All ; are
(B) All ; was
(C) Some ; is
(D) Every ; is

**11.** Your idea for increasing sales isn't going to work, Peter. _____ the price reduction _____ the repackaging will be enough to convince consumers to buy our product.

(A) Either ; or

(B) Neither ; nor

(C) Both ; and

(D) Never ; sometimes

**12.** You have to remember that this is a family company. The vice president is the _____ brother-in-law, and he obviously wasn't hired because of his qualifications.

(A) boss

(B) boss's

(C) bosses

(D) bossy

**13.** *The Wall Street* Journal is a very influential _____ published in the United States.

(A) street

(B) TV show

(C) newspaper

(D) program

**14.** We are the chief importer of Chateau le Rouge, one of the finest _____ in the world.

(A) wine

(B) winery

(C) wines

(D) wineries

**15.** Year-end bonuses for employees have been _____ reduced because of huge losses in sales. You should feel lucky you still have a job.

(A) greatly

(B) wonderfully

(C) mutually

(D) lively

16. It's not a good idea to set up a factory in that area because labor and resources are _____.
    (A) scarce
    (B) scarcely
    (C) seldom
    (D) shortage

17. The Nocturna Company never accepts our offers. They _____ think our rates are too high.
    (A) once
    (B) never
    (C) always
    (D) used to

18. Rice production _____ Taiwan is profitable because it can be grown year-round.
    (A) at
    (B) over
    (C) from
    (D) in

19. Thank you, Mr. Zimmerman. It's been a pleasure _____ with you.
    (A) to work
    (B) works
    (C) worked
    (D) work

20. That mistake has ruined your business career, Eugene. But it's _____ start a new career in another field.
    (A) not too late to
    (B) later than to
    (C) never later to
    (D) not later than

**21.** I prefer to invest in certificates of deposit, _____ a less risky form of investment.
(A) which are
(B) which being
(C) which is
(D) which can

**22.** The Project Manager was disappointed with the brainstorming team. He didn't like _____ of their ideas at all.
(A) all
(B) any
(C) some
(D) none

**23.** Karen was so nervous during her presentation that her hands _____ as she spoke.
(A) to tremble
(B) tremble
(C) trembled
(D) trembling

**24.** _____ letters by hand is too time-consuming—practically everyone writes e-mails nowadays.
(A) Written
(B) Write
(C) For writing
(D) Writing

**25.** I don't want you to make any conclusions without _____ some market research first.
(A) you're conducting
(B) conducting
(C) conduct
(D) to conduct

**26.** _____ today's meeting, does anyone have anything else to
suggest?
(A) Before finishing
(B) Before finished
(C) Before has finished
(D) Before we finished

**27.** The unfinished product is suspended _____ the floor so the worker
can more easily work on it.
(A) on
(B) around
(C) at
(D) above

**28.** John _____ on the phone for an hour already.
(A) talks
(B) is talking
(C) has been talking
(D) talking

**29.** The warehouse just called, and they said the shipment _____ just
arrived.
(A) has
(B) can
(C) are
(D) did

**30.** We won't have any final sales reports concerning our online sales
_____ next month, so we'll just have to wait.
(A) over
(B) until
(C) in
(D) at

**31.** A: Trudy, will you cross-reference the inventory lists to make sure all goods are accounted for?

B: Yes, I _____.

(A) could

(B) won't

(C) can

(D) will

---

**32.** I _____ my boss would give me a raise or a promotion.

(A) want

(B) hope

(C) wish

(D) like

---

**33.** If you make a deal with us now, we'll _____ you free shipping on your first order.

(A) offered

(B) offering

(C) to offer

(D) offer

---

**34.** The financial statements _____ by the top executives of the company.

(A) issued

(B) is issued

(C) were issued

(D) can be issued

---

**35.** Our company will hold its annual year-end party on Friday, the _____ of January.

(A) eight

(B) eightieth

(C) eighth

(D) eighty

**36.** You've been working on your market forecast report for two weeks now. Aren't you finished _____?

(A) yet

(B) soon

(C) then

(D) with

**37.** Our accountant will have the proper documents _____ for you by tomorrow afternoon.

(A) prepare

(B) preparing

(C) prepared

(D) will be prepared

**38.** The contract _____ yet.

(A) is signed

(B) hasn't been signed

(C) will be signed

(D) can sign

**39.** I found the missing documents! They _____ stored in John's computer.

(A) was

(B) be

(C) have

(D) were

**40.** Be quiet everybody! _____ comes the new CEO, and he doesn't look happy.

(A) There

(B) This

(C) That

(D) Here

段落填空 ▶ 請從 (A)、(B)、(C)、(D) 中選出一個最適合的答案。

**Questions 1~4 refer to the following article.**

In the advanced countries, most working adults have credit cards.
_____ credit cards are replacing banknotes and coins, they

1.(A) Due to
   (B) Because
   (C) Even if
   (D) While

_____ a kind of "plastic money." However, huge amounts of bad

2.(A) have become
   (B) had become
   (C) became
   (D) become

debt due to the rapid increase in credit card users and delayed payments
have triggered a financial crisis. Take the United States for example:
credit card debt has exceeded a trillion dollars and is rising _____.

3.(A) hasty
   (B) fastly
   (C) rapid
   (D) rapidly

Although credit cards provide convenience, society as a whole has to
pay a _____ price in the long run.

4.(A) heavy
   (B) critical
   (C) strong
   (D) intense

## Questions 5~8 refer to the following article.

Most people don't have enough cash in the bank to pay for large purchases up front. _____, it's common practice for buyers of

5. (A) Rather
   (B) Instead
   (C) Otherwise
   (D) Except

expensive things like homes and cars _____ purchases using credit.

6. (A) making
   (B) to make
   (C) make
   (D) will make

Buying something on credit is essentially borrowing money from a bank, credit card company or other financial institution. The loan is used to pay for the purchase, and the buyer is then indebted to the lender for the _____ of the purchase plus interest. The interest rate of the loan is

7. (A) number
   (B) quantity
   (C) amount
   (D) figure

calculated using the borrower's credit history, _____ it has a large

8. (A) and
   (B) but
   (C) if
   (D) or

effect on the total amount of money the person will need to pay.

**C** **1.** Kim has been voted "Employee of the Month" for _____ everyone in the company to do their best.

金姆被選為「本月員工」，因為他鼓勵公司裡的每個人表現出最好的一面。

(A) encourage　　(B) encouraged　　(C) encouraging　　(D) encourages

觀念　介系詞接動名詞

解析　本句的介系詞 for 有「因為」的意思，for 後面接的是一整件事，以「動名詞」的形式呈現，正確答案應該寫成 for encouraging everyone in the company to do their best。

● do one's best 竭盡全力

---

**C** **2.** Never _____ eye contact during an interview. The interviewer will think you lack confidence.

面試時不要去迴避眼神接觸。面試官會認為你缺乏自信。

(A) to avoid　　　(B) avoiding　　　(C) avoid　　　(D) avoided

觀念　動詞

解析　本句的用法是「祈使句」的命令口吻，「祈使句」的句型是以 you 當主詞，但省略 you，所以「動詞」都作原形。開頭的 never 是「決不」的意思，表示要對方決不要做某件事，因為是祈使句命令句型，所以用「動詞」原形 avoid。

● eye contact 眼神接觸

---

**C** **3.** The part I like best about my job _____ to potential customers about our line of products.

我最喜歡我工作的地方就是跟我們的潛在客戶說明我們的產品線。

(A) is talk　　　(B) are talking　　　(C) is talking　　　(D) to talk

觀念　動名詞

解析　本句要說明的是工作中最喜歡的部分，所以主詞後面要先接 be 動詞再接「名詞」。在這裡用的「名詞」是由「動詞」轉換而來，在這種情況下，會用「動名詞」或「不定詞」來呈現。本題的主詞「我的工作中我最喜歡的部分」是單數，所以「be 動詞」也作單數形，因此答案選 (C)。(D) 選項中的不定詞前面因為欠缺 be 動詞，所以不能選。

● line of products 產品線

D **4.** The board of directors decided _____ several departments to increase efficiency.

董事會決議要縮編部門，增加公司效益。

(A) downsize　　(B) will downsize　(C) downsizing　　(D) to downsize

觀念　不定詞

解析　這題的動詞 decide 後面加上另一個動詞時，會以不定詞 to V 的形式來呈現。因此答案選 (D)。

• board of directors 董事會　　　　　　　• downsize [ˋdɑʊn͵sɑɪz] (v.) 縮減開支

---

C **5.** _____ up to her ears in paperwork, Marcia had no choice but to work overtime for several days.

深陷在文書作業之中，瑪西亞別無選擇只加班個幾天。

(A) Was　　　　(B) Had been　　(C) Being　　　(D) To be

觀念　從屬連接詞的省略

解析　這題前半句的原句應該是說 Because she was up to her ears in paperwork，才符合下一句所說的她只好加班好幾天。從屬連接詞的句型之中，如果前後主詞相同，可以省略連接詞和主詞，將動詞改為分詞，動詞主動用「現在分詞」，動詞被動用「過去分詞」。在這裡的 be 動詞沒有被動意思，因此改成現在分詞的 being。

• be up to one's ears 深陷於⋯，埋頭⋯，忙於⋯

• have no choice but to 沒有選擇，只好

D **6.** It's obvious that our warehousing procedure is not cost effective. I _____ recommend we adopt a different one.

很明顯的我們的倉儲程序並不符合成本效益。我強烈地建議我們應該採取不同的方式。

(A) hardly　　　(B) worriedly　　(C) badly　　　(D) strongly

觀念　副詞

解析　這裡要選修飾動詞 recommend（建議）的副詞。而且，前句說「倉儲程序並不符合成本效益」，表示後句應該是「強烈地」建議採取不同方式。hardly（幾乎不）、worriedly（擔心地）和 badly（糟糕地），均與句意不符。答案應選 strongly（強烈地）。

• warehousing [ˋwɛr͵hɑʊzɪŋ] (n.) 倉儲　　• procedure [prəˋsidʒə] (n.) 程序，常規

• cost effective 有成本效益的，划算的

C 7. I like working for Bill. He's the kind of guy _____ his employees and doesn't treat them like underlings.

我很喜歡為比爾工作。他是那種會尊重員工，不會把他們當作下屬看待的人。

(A) who respecting      (B) who respect

(C) who respects      (D) who is respected

**觀念** 關係代名詞引導形容詞子句

**解析** 題目是要去解釋是 Bill 是怎樣的人，所以用關代引導出形容詞子句來修飾 the kind of guy，也就是 Bill。先行詞為人，關代用 that 或者是 who，引導出的子句動詞依照該有的變化，這裡指「尊重」他的員工，使用現在式，the kind of guy 為第三人稱單數，因此答案選 (C)。

● underling [ˋʌndəlɪŋ] (n.)（貶義）部下，下屬

A 8. I'm new here, Joe. Can you tell me _____ this photocopier?

我是新來的，喬。你可以告訴我如何操作這台影印機嗎？

(A) how to operate      (B) operate how

(C) how operate      (D) how to operating

**觀念** 名詞子句的簡化

**解析** 本句是由間接問句形式的名詞子句簡化而來。原本的間接問句應該是 how I can operate this photocopier，間接問句中的主詞如果與句中所指的人一樣，並且有助動詞，便可將主詞和助動詞省略簡化子句，變成「疑問詞＋to＋V」的句型，也就是 how to operate the photocopier，所以答案選 (A)。

● operate [ˋɑpəˌret] (v.) 運作，操作

D 9. My financial advisor told me _____ in treasury bonds at this time. He thinks it would be better to wait a few months.

我的財務顧問跟我說不要在這個時候投資國債。他認為最好再等幾個月。

(A) not invest      (B) not to investing

(C) no invest      (D) not to invest

**觀念** 不定詞

**解析** 因為第二句說「他認為最好再等幾個月」，可知第一句要表達「不要去做某事」。「告訴某人不要去做某事」的句型是「tell＋人＋not to V...」，因此答案選 (D)。

● treasury bonds 國債

D 10. Yvonne's Boutique is having a going-out-of-business sale. _____ item in the store _____ on sale.

伊芳精品店正在結束營業大拍賣。店裡每個東西都有打折。

(A) All ; are      (B) All ; was      (C) Some ; is      (D) Every ; is

觀念 不定代名詞

解析 這裡要看到句子裡面的 item，在這裡做單數形。all 和 some 不應該接在單數可數名詞之前。every 接的是單數可數名詞，be 動詞也要用單數形。因此答案選 (D)。

● going-out-of-business 結束營業大拍賣

---

B 11. Your idea for increasing sales isn't going to work, Peter. _____ the price reduction _____ the repackaging will be enough to convince consumers to buy our product.

你增加銷售的想法行不通的，彼得。價格降低和重新包裝都無法說服顧客來購買我們的產品。

(A) Either ; or              (B) Neither ; nor
(C) Both ; and             (D) Never ; sometimes

觀念 連接詞

解析 前一句提到這個想法不好，所以以下一句應該是說這兩項建議都不會有用。選項 (A) 的 either...or... 表示「要不……就是……」與前一句的意思不符。選項 (C) 的 both...and... 表示「兩者都」，也與前句不符。選項 (B) 的 neither...nor... 表示「兩者皆否」，有承接到前句，因此選 (B)。

● repackage [riˋpækədʒ] (v.) 重新包裝

---

B 12. You have to remember that this is a family company. The vice president is the _____ brother-in-law, and he obviously wasn't hired because of his qualifications.

你必須要了解這是個家族企業。副總裁是老闆的姊夫，而很明顯他並不是因為他的能力被雇用的。

(A) boss      (B) boss's      (C) bosses      (D) bossy

觀念 所有格

解析 題目應該是說「副總裁是老闆的姊夫」，這樣前文所說的「家族企業」才能承接。因此，這裡要選名詞的所有格，也就是在最後加上 's，因此答案選 (B)。bossy 是形容詞，表示像老闆一樣「頤指氣使」。

● family company 家族企業
● brother-in-law / sister-in-law （姊夫、妹夫等 / 嫂嫂、小姨子等）姻親

C **13.** *The Wall Street Journal* is a very influential _____ published in the United States.

華爾街日報是美國一份非常有影響力的報紙。

(A) street      (B) TV show      (C) newspaper      (D) program

觀念 名詞

解析 看到題目用到斜體，就要知道與某種出版品有關，而且 journal 有「報紙、雜誌」的意思，因此答案選 (C)。題目中出現的 published，是過去分詞，以被動形式修飾前面的名詞。

- influential [ˌɪnfluˈɛnʃəl] (adj.) 有影響的；有權勢的

---

C **14.** We are the chief importer of Chateau le Rouge, one of the finest _____ in the world.

我們是世界上最好的葡萄酒之一，紅堡的主要進口商。

(A) wine      (B) winery      (C) wines      (D) wineries

觀念 可數 / 不可數名詞

解析 wine 指「酒的種類」時，屬於可數名詞。「one of＋可數複數名詞」意思是「……之一」，所以要選 wines。如果 wine 是單純指「酒」這個液體，則為不可數名詞，會用單位來指稱，例：a glass of wine。winery 是「酒廠」，複數為 wineries，這裡不會是說進口「酒廠」，所以不能選 (D)。

- importer [ɪmˈportɚ] (n.) 進口商

---

A **15.** Year-end bonuses for employees have been _____ reduced because of huge losses in sales. You should feel lucky you still have a job.

因為業績大量損失，員工的年終獎金被大幅刪減。你應該感到很幸運還有工作。

(A) greatly      (B) wonderfully      (C) mutually      (D) lively

觀念 副詞

解析 句子中說到業績「大量損失」，表示年終獎金應該也是遭到「大量地」刪減，所以下一句才會說有工作就很幸運。wonderfully（很棒地）、mutually（相互地）和 lively（很有活力地），這三個選項都與句意不符。答案應該選 greatly（大量地）。

- year-end bonuses 年終獎金

**A** *16.* It's not a good idea to set up a factory in that area because labor and resources are _____.

在那區建造工廠不是個好主意，因為勞工和資源都很缺乏。

(A) scarce      (B) scarcely      (C) seldom      (D) shortage

**觀念** 形容詞

**解析** 根據前面的子句可知，說話者認為「在那個區域建造工廠不是個好主意」，所以可推測「勞工和資源」很缺乏，選項應填修飾名詞 labor 和 resources 的形容詞。scarce 是形容詞「很少的」，本身帶有否定意味。scarcely 是副詞「幾乎不」，與句意不符。seldom 是副詞「很少」。shortage 是名詞「短缺」。答案選 (A)。

- labor [ˋlebɚ] (n.) 勞工
- resource [rɪˋsɔrs] (n.) 資源

**C** *17.* The Nocturna Company never accepts our offers. They _____ think our rates are too high.

那托納公司從沒接受我們的報價。他們總是覺得我們的價碼太高了。

(A) once      (B) never      (C) always      (D) used to

**觀念** 副詞

**解析** 前半句是這個公司「從沒接受我們的報價」，所以下一句應該是他們「總是」認為「我們的價碼太高」。once 是「一次、曾經」，never 是「從未」，這兩個選項與句意不符。used to 是「過去習慣……」，如果說是「過去認為我們的價碼太高」，第一句就不會出現現在式的 accepts。因此，答案選 (C)「總是」。

- offer [ˋɔfɚ] (v./n.) 提供；提議，報價
- rate [ret] (n.) 比率；速度；價格

**D** *18.* Rice production _____ Taiwan is profitable because it can be grown year-round.

在台灣稻米的產值很高，因為這裡稻米一年四季都能生長。

(A) at      (B) over      (C) from      (D) in

**觀念** 介系詞

**解析** 指較大的地點，例如本題的台灣，要用介系詞 in。如果是較小的地點，例如學校，就會用介系詞 at。

- profitable [ˋprɑfɪtəb]] (adj.) 有利潤的，有好處的
- year-round 全年的

**A** **19.** Thank you, Mr. Zimmerman. It's been a pleasure _____ with you.

謝謝你，齊默曼先生。跟你工作真是我的榮幸。

(A) to work　　　(B) works　　　(C) worked　　　(D) work

**觀念** 不定詞

**解析** 這裡的句型是it is...＋to V...，以虛主詞 it 來開啟句子，主要主詞是 to 之後接的動作，to 之後做的動詞為原形，所以答案選 (A)。句子的意思是「跟你工作」這件事，真是我的榮幸。

● pleasure [`prɛʒɚ] (n.) 榮幸；愉快

---

**A** **20.** That mistake has ruined your business career, Eugene. But it's _____ start a new career in another field.

這失誤已毀了你的事業，尤金。但在另一個領域重新開啟新事業也不算太遲。

(A) not too late to　　　　　(B) later than to
(C) never later to　　　　　(D) not later than

**觀念** too...to... 的用法

**解析** 前一句說生意失敗，後一句加上有轉折語氣的 but，所以接下來的句子應該是說「不會太遲……」。選項 C 要改成 never too late to，其他的選項都與句意不符。答案只能選 (A) 的句型，「not too＋adj./adv.＋to＋V」表示「做……不會太……」。

● field [fild] (n.) 原野；運動場；領域

---

**A** **21.** I prefer to invest in certificates of deposit, _____ a less risky form of investment.

我偏好以定存做投資，它是風險較低的投資方式。

(A) which are　　(B) which being　　(C) which is　　(D) which can

**觀念** 關係代名詞引導形容詞子句

**解析** 題目是要去解釋是 certificates of deposit「定期存款」，用關代引導出形容詞子句來去解釋。先行詞為物，關代用 that 或者是 which，引導出的子句動詞因為 certificates 是複數所以用複數的 be 動詞，因此答案選 (A)。

● prefer to... 偏好（做）…

**B** *22.* The Project Manager was disappointed with the brainstorming team. He didn't like _____ of their ideas at all.

專案經理對這個商討小組感到失望。他一點也不喜歡他們提出的任何一個想法。

(A) all      (B) any      (C) some      (D) none

觀念    不定代名詞

解析    前句提到經理感到「失望」，所以他應該是一點也不喜歡這個小組的想法。本句是用否定句，因此要選可以放在否定句的不定代名詞，也就是 any。

• brainstorming [ˋbrɛnˌstɔrmɪŋ] (n.) 集體研討

---

**C** *23.* Karen was so nervous during her presentation that her hands _____ as she spoke.

凱倫在報告期間實在是太緊張了，她講話時手一直發抖。

(A) to tremble      (B) tremble      (C) trembled      (D) trembling

觀念    動詞

解析    由前半句的 was 可知這題的時態是過去式，因此後半句的動詞應該也是用過去式，所以答案選 (C)。

• presentation [ˌprɪzɛnˋteʃən] (n.) 演出；介紹；報告

---

**D** *24.* _____ letters by hand is too time-consuming—practically everyone writes e-mails nowadays.

用手寫信實在太花時間了──尤其是現在大家都用電子郵件。

(A) Written      (B) Write      (C) For writing      (D) Writing

觀念    動名詞

解析    本題的重點是以「動名詞」開頭做主詞的句型。主詞為「用手寫信」，在英文中，若要以動作做為主詞，動詞必須以「動名詞」或者是「不定詞」呈現，選項中只有「動名詞」，所以答案選 (D)。

• time-consuming 耗費時間的

**B** **25.** I don't want you to make any conclusions without _____ some market research first.

我不希望你在沒有做市場調查之前就先下結論。

(A) you're conducting　　(B) conducting

(C) conduct　　(D) to conduct

觀念　介系詞接動名詞

解析　without「沒有」是介系詞，用法是「without＋N./Ving」，在這裡是接動詞，所以答案應該寫成 without conducting some market research「沒有做任何市場調查」。

● conduct [kən`dʌkt] (v.) 執行；帶領；表現　● market research 市場調查

---

**A** **26.** _____ today's meeting, does anyone have anything else to suggest?

在結束今天的會議之前，有沒有還有任何提議的？

(A) Before finishing　　(B) Before finished

(C) Before has finished　　(D) Before we finished

觀念　介系詞接動名詞

解析　本句開頭的before 是介系詞，後面必須接「名詞」或「動名詞」當受詞，所以選 (A)。before 也可當從屬連接詞，後面須接子句，選項 (D) 的時態若改成 Before we finish 就可選。

● before we wrap up 在我們結束之前

---

**D** **27.** The unfinished product is suspended _____ the floor so the worker can more easily work on it.

這個尚未完成的產品被掛離地面，這樣工人才比較容易在上面工作。

(A) on　　(B) around　　(C) at　　(D) above

觀念　介系詞

解析　floor 在這裡指「地板」，句子要說的是這個產品 (product) 跟地板的位置，而且這個位置是讓「工人才比較容易在上面工作」。on「在……上面」，表示直接在地板上；around 指「在……周圍」；at 指「在……的位置」。從句意上來看，懸掛在地板之上比較合適，故選 (D) above「在……之上」。

● unfinished [ʌn`fɪnɪʃt] (adj.) 未完成的　● suspend [sə`spɛnd] (v.) 懸掛；暫停

C 28. John _____ on the phone for an hour already.

約翰已經講了一個小時的電話。

(A) talks　　　　(B) is talking　　　(C) has been talking (D) talking

觀念　現在完成進行式

解析　for an hour already 意思是「已經持續一小時了」，須與現在完成式連用。本句的 has been talking 為現在完成進行式，表示動作從過去某時刻持續到現在，且仍然進行中，強調持續性。

● talk on the phone 講電話

A 29. The warehouse just called, and they said the shipment _____ just arrived.

倉庫剛才打電話來，他們說貨物剛剛運到了。

(A) has　　　　(B) can　　　　(C) are　　　　(D) did

觀念　現在完成式

解析　just 意思是「剛」，與現在完成式「have/has＋過去分詞」連用，表示某動作剛完成。句尾 arrived 即為過去分詞，故主詞 the shipment 後只須補上表現在完成式的助動詞 has。

● warehouse [`wɛr͵haʊs] (n.) 產品　　　● shipment [`ʃɪpmənt] (n.) 運送的貨物

B 30. We won't have any final sales reports concerning our online sales _____ next month, so we'll just have to wait.

我們要到下個月才會有線上銷售的最終銷售報表，所以我們現在只能等。

(A) over　　　　(B) until　　　　(C) in　　　　(D) at

觀念　介系詞

解析　後半句 we'll just have to wait 代表說話者正在等最終銷售報表，可推知「要到下個月才會有報表」，因此應使用 not...until...（直到⋯⋯才⋯⋯）句型。

● sale report 銷售報表

**D** *31.* A: Trudy, will you cross-reference the inventory lists to make sure all goods are accounted for?

B: Yes, I _____.

A：楚笛，你可以對照一下存貨清單確認所有的貨品都對嗎？

B：好的，我會做。

(A) could      (B) won't      (C) can      (D) will

觀念    未來簡單式

解析    「will＋原形動詞」為未來簡單式，本題題目問句由 will 引導，故答句也應用 will 回答。但 will 除了表示未來式之外，還帶有「承諾、意願」的意思，如本題中的 I will (cross-reference...) 便是表達「我會去做；我正要去做」的意思。

- cross-reference [`krɔs`rɛfərəns] (v.) 相互參照
- account [ə`kaʊnt] (v.)（數量上）佔
- inventory [`ɪnvən.tɔrɪ] (n.) 存貨清單；財產目錄

---

**C** *32.* I _____ my boss would give me a raise or a promotion.

要是我老闆能給我加薪或升職就好了。

(A) want      (B) hope      (C) wish      (D) like

觀念    假設語氣

解析    「hope＋to V / that 子句」是「希望現在或未來會發生的事」，其中的時態搭配現在式或未來式。而本題中的時態搭配過去式助動詞 would，屬「假設語氣」用法，應選 wish，代表「事與願違」的希望，I wish my boss would give me a raise... 其實是指 my boss won't give me a raise...。

- raise [rez] (n./v.) 加薪；抬起；升高

---

**D** *33.* If you make a deal with us now, we'll _____ you free shipping on your first order.

假如你現在跟我們成交，我們將提供首批訂單免運費服務。

(A) offered      (B) offering      (C) to offer      (D) offer

觀念    從屬連接詞

解析    If you make a deal with us now 是「從屬子句（條件子句）」，子句裡的動詞時態用的是「現在式」，但主要子句 we'll _____ you free shipping 則必須用「未來式」，所以助動詞 will 後應接原形的 offer。

- make a deal 做交易；成交

**C** **34.** The financial statements _____ by the top executives of the company.

財務報表是由公司的高層主管簽發。

(A) issued　　(B) is issued　　(C) were issued　(D) can be issued

觀念　被動語態

解析　動詞 issue（核發；發佈）的行為者應為「人」，而本題是以「物」the financial statements 當主詞，故動詞應使用「被動語態」were issued，後面的介系詞 by 則引導出真正的行為者 the top executives of the company。

● financial statement 財務報表　　　● issue [`ɪʃjʊ] (v.) 核發；發佈；發行

● executive [ɪɡˋzɛkjʊtɪv] (n.) 執行者；高級官員；業務主管

**C** **35.** Our company will hold its annual year-end party on Friday, the _____ of January.

我們公司將於一月八日星期五舉行一年一度的年終尾牙餐會。

(A) eight　　(B) eightieth　　(C) eighth　　(D) eighty

觀念　序數

解析　序數可用來表達「日期」，如：the eighth of January = January eighth（一月八日）。

● hold [hold] (v.) 舉辦　　　● year-end party 年終尾牙

**A** **36.** You've been working on your market forecast report for two weeks now. Aren't you finished _____?

那份市場預估報告你已經做了兩個禮拜了。你還沒做完嗎？

(A) yet　　(B) soon　　(C) then　　(D) with

觀念　副詞

解析　Are you finished? 意思是「你做完了嗎？」，而本句是以否定句呈現，故須搭配副詞 yet，意思變成「你還沒做完嗎？」。

● forecast [`forˏkæst] (n.) 預測；預報

**C** **37.** Our accountant will have the proper documents _____ for you by tomorrow afternoon.

我們的會計師明天下午以前會幫你準備好需要的文件。

(A) prepare                      (B) preparing

(C) prepared                   (D) will be prepared

| 觀念 | 使役動詞 |
|---|---|

| 解析 | have 在此當「使役動詞」，句型為「have＋人＋原形動詞」及「have＋物＋過去分詞」。前者的意思是「叫人做某事」，後者的過去分詞表「被動」，意思是「讓某事被做好」，所以 have the proper documents prepared 就是「讓所需的文件被準備好」的意思。 |
|---|---|

- accountant [ə`kauntənt] (n.) 會計師；會計人員

---

**B** **38.** The contract _____ yet.

這份合約還沒有簽訂。

(A) is signed                     (B) hasn't been signed

(C) will be signed               (D) can sign

| 觀念 | 現在完成式、被動語態 |
|---|---|

| 解析 | 主詞 contract 為事物，無法主動進行簽約的動作，因此須用被動語態 be signed；句尾的 yet 意思為「還（沒）」，用於完成式的否定句，因此整句須寫成現在完成式被動語態 hasn't been signed。 |
|---|---|

- contract [`kɑntrækt] (n.) 合約          • sign [saɪn] (v.) 簽字，簽約

---

**D** **39.** I found the missing documents! They _____ stored in John's computer.

我找到遺失的文件了！它們存在約翰的電腦裡。

(A) was          (B) be          (C) have          (D) were

| 觀念 | 被動語態 |
|---|---|

| 解析 | 第二句的主詞 They 指的是前句的 documents（文件），文件為事物，無法主動自行 store（儲存），因此須用被動語態「be 動詞＋過去分詞」。本句主詞為複數，故 be 動詞選 were。 |
|---|---|

- missing [`mɪsɪŋ] (adj.) 遺失的         • store [stor] (v.) 儲存

**D** *40.* Be quiet everybody! _____ comes the new CEO, and he doesn't look happy.

大家安靜！新的CEO過來了，而且他臉色不好看。

(A) There      (B) This      (C) That      (D) Here

觀念 介系詞

解析 「Here＋動詞＋主詞」的用法中，動詞需隨主詞變化。如果主詞是代名詞，如 you，主詞和動詞位置需對調：「Here＋主詞（代名詞）＋動詞」。

• CEO (chief executive officer) 首席執行官，總裁

## Questions 1~4 refer to the following article.

In the advanced countries, most working adults have credit cards.
_____**B**_____ credit cards are replacing banknotes and coins, they

1.(A) Due to
  (B) Because
  (C) Even if
  (D) While

_____**A**_____ a kind of "plastic money." However, huge amounts of bad

2.(A) have become
  (B) had become
  (C) became
  (D) become

debt due to the rapid increase in credit card users and delayed payments
have triggered a financial crisis. Take the United States for example:
credit card debt has exceeded a trillion dollars and is rising _____**D**_____.

3.(A) hasty
  (B) fastly
  (C) rapid
  (D) rapidly

Although credit cards provide convenience, society as a whole has to
pay a _____**A**_____ price in the long run.

4.(A) heavy
  (B) critical
  (C) strong
  (D) intense

## 問題 1～4 請參考以下文章。

在先進國家，大部份有工作的成年人都有信用卡。由於信用卡漸漸取代了紙鈔和硬幣，它們已成為一種「塑膠貨幣」。然而，信用卡使用人數的快速增加和延遲繳款造成的巨額呆帳，已引發了金融危機。以美國為例，信用卡債的金額已超過一兆美金，並且正急速攀升。信用卡雖然提供一時的便利，但長期來說，整個社會必須付出慘痛代價。

1. **觀念** 從屬連接詞

   **解析** 此處要選連接詞連接前後兩個子句。根據語意判斷，「信用卡漸漸取代了紙鈔和硬幣」是造成「它們成為一種塑膠貨幣」的原因，所以應選表「因果關係」的連接詞 Because。選項中的 Due to 也表原因，但只能接名詞，須改成 Due to the fact that 才能接子句。

   - replace [rɪˋples] (v.) 取代
   - banknote [ˋbæŋknot] (n.) 鈔票
   - coin [kɔɪn] (n.) 硬幣

2. **觀念** 現在完成式

   **解析** 指「過去到現在為止已經發生的事」，用現在完成式，過去式則常與「過去時間」連用。此外，現在完成式還表示「事件發生的影響持續到現在」，過去式則僅單純敘述單一事件。本句中「信用卡成為塑膠貨幣」的狀況到目前為止是持續存在的，所以應用「現在完成式」have become。

   - plastic money 塑膠貨幣

3. **觀念** 副詞

   **解析** 此處要選修飾動詞 is rising 的副詞，指「急速」應用副詞 rapidly。fast 也指「快速」，其副詞與形容詞同形，應用 fast 才對。hasty 則是形容詞「倉促；勿忙」，語意不合。

   - take...for example 以…為例
   - exceed [ɪkˋsid] (v.) 超過；超越
   - trillion [ˋtrɪljən] (n.) （美）兆；（英）百萬兆

4. **觀念** 形容詞

   **解析** 本句的 price 指「代價」，應選 heavy「沉重的」來修飾。其他選項 critical「關鍵的」、strong（強壯的）與 intense（密集的）則與語意不合。

   - convenience [kənˋvinjəns] (n.) 方便；便利之事
   - in the long run 最終；從長遠來看

## Questions 5~8 refer to the following article.

Most people don't have enough cash in the bank to pay for large purchases up front. _____**B**_____, it's common practice for buyers of

5.(A) Rather
(B) Instead
(C) Otherwise
(D) Except

expensive things like homes and cars _____**B**_____ purchases using credit.

6.(A) making
(B) to make
(C) make
(D) will make

Buying something on credit is essentially borrowing money from a bank, credit card company or other financial institution. The loan is used to pay for the purchase, and the buyer is then indebted to the lender for the _____**C**_____ of the purchase plus interest. The interest rate of the loan is

7.(A) number
(B) quantity
(C) amount
(D) figure

calculated using the borrower's credit history, _____**A**_____ it has a large

8.(A) and
(B) but
(C) if
(D) or

effect on the total amount of money the person will need to pay.

## 問題 5～8 請參考以下文章。

多數人在銀行並沒有足夠的現金可以預先付清所有大筆消費,買家購買如房子和汽車等昂貴物品的常見做法反而是:利用信用來購買。以信用購物基本上就是向銀行、信用卡公司或其他金融機構借錢。貸款是用來支付購物消費,於是方便賒欠貸方購物的金額加利息。貸款利率的計算是視借方的信用記錄而定,這會大大影響借方必需支付的總金額。

5. 　觀念　副詞

　解析　上一句說「多數人在銀行並沒有足夠的現金可以預先付清所有大筆消費」，而本句卻提到「買家購買昂貴物品的常見做法」，所以此處應選 Instead 表示「反而；替代」的轉折語氣。rather 指「寧願」，不放句首，應放句中以 would rather...than... 句型呈現，如：I would rather pay by cash than use a credit card.（我寧願付現而不使用信用卡。）otherwise 放句首時指「除此之外；在其他方面」；except「除……之外」是介系詞，不能單獨放句首，語意也不合。

● purchase [`pɜtʃəs] (n.) 購買之物　　● up front 預付

6. 　觀念　it 虛主詞的用法

　解析　指「做某事對某人是……的」應用句型「It's...for＋人＋to V」，所以本題選 to make。在此句型中 to make purchases using credit 這件事才是真主詞，意指「利用信用來購買」。

● practice [`præktɪs] (n.) 通常的作法；常規；慣例

7. 　觀念　不可數名詞

　解析　此處指的是 the purchase plus interest 的「加總」，也就是 buyer「買方」賒欠 lender「貸方」的「總額」，應選 amount 一字。其他選項 number 泛指「數量；數字」，quantity 指「數量」，figure 則是明確的「數字」。

● indebt [ɪn`dɛt] (v.) 使負債；使受惠

8. 　觀念　對等連接詞

　解析　前半句說「貸款利率的計算是視借方的信用記錄而定」，後半句接「這會大大影響借方必需支付的總金額」，前後語意相承，故選對等連接詞 and 順接即可。

● interest rate 利率　　● credit history 信用記錄
● have an effect on... 對…產生影響

# 多益文法模擬考　第四回

**單句填空** ▶ 請從 (A)、(B)、(C)、(D) 中選出一個最適合的答案。

**1.** We won't be able to make a profit because the customer wants us _____ the price by another 10%.
(A) to reduce
(B) to increase
(C) to expand
(D) to demand

**2.** From this chart, we _____ that the dollar has fallen against most major currencies.
(A) can see
(B) can seeing
(C) seeing
(D) were seeing

**3.** I've been out of work for months! I sure wish the economy would _____!
(A) get worse
(B) improved
(C) better
(D) improve

**4.** We'll offer you a discount of 10% _____ you order more than 100,000 units.
(A) why
(B) could
(C) if
(D) would

**5.** I'm so disappointed in you! If you had worked harder, we _____ have won the contract!
(A) would
(B) will
(C) won't
(D) wouldn't

**6.** Shirley! Have those faxes _____ yet? My client is waiting for them.
(A) been sent
(B) being sent
(C) were sent
(D) sent

**7.** We are all _____ to have this opportunity to do business with you, Mr. Reed.
(A) exciting
(B) excite
(C) be excited
(D) excited

**8.** Please take the elevator up to the _____ floor.
(A) seven
(B) seventh
(C) seventy
(D) basement

**9.** You shouldn't worry about losing your job, William. You still have thousands of dollars in your bank _____.
(A) ATM card
(B) account
(C) withdrawal
(D) teller

**10.** We bought stocks in that company before the recession, and now that the market has declined they're hardly _____ anything now.
(A) value
(B) amount
(C) cost
(D) worth

**11.** We need to import these special instruments from _____ before we can begin production.
(A) German
(B) Germany
(C) Germania
(D) Germanese

**12.** I lived in _____ for two years before moving to France.
(A) English
(B) Brittany
(C) Britain
(D) British

**13.** I'm sorry. Ms. Chang is _____ of the office right now. May I take a message?
(A) away
(B) out
(C) outside
(D) inside

**14.** We've been doing business in the Far East for _____ 30 years now.
(A) more
(B) close
(C) much
(D) almost

**15.** We're _____ awaiting your reply to our letter dated March 17, 2009.
(A) anxiously
(B) excited
(C) lively
(D) anticipate

**16.** The client called and said _____ we sent them are of inferior quality.

(A) the products

(B) products

(C) product

(D) production

**17.** We've been losing a lot of our investors lately. What kind of _____ can you offer us on how to prevent them from leaving?

(A) kindness

(B) advice

(C) friendship

(D) honesty

**18.** This laptop computer does not belong to the company. It's _____ personal property.

(A) Mandy

(B) Mandys

(C) Mandy's

(D) Mandys'

**19.** I'm sorry to tell you this, but this pink slip isn't mine. It's _____. Good luck finding a new job.

(A) you

(B) your

(C) your's

(D) yours

**20.** You seem like a nice person and your academic record is outstanding. But you don't seem to have _____ work experience.

(A) a

(B) many

(C) one

(D) any

21. There's no need _____, Mr. Johnson. We should be able to win the copyright infringement case easily.
   (A) of worry
   (B) worry
   (C) to worrying
   (D) to worry

22. Several employees have accused you of selling company secrets to our competitors. Do you have _____ to say in your defense?
   (A) what
   (B) any
   (C) anything
   (D) some

23. We'd like to enter the publishing industry, but it's _____ feasible at this time.
   (A) no
   (B) not
   (C) not to
   (D) never

24. Marty is going to _____ the annual budget tomorrow.
   (A) prepares
   (B) finish preparing
   (C) preparing
   (D) got prepared

25. Our company's specialty _____ helping clients to invest profitably in the stock market.
   (A) is
   (B) is to
   (C) are to
   (D) be

**26.** The trade commission is suing us for _____ to fulfill our end of the bargain.

(A) fail

(B) failed

(C) have failed

(D) failing

**27.** Harry _____ finish the assignment on time, so it was given to someone else.

(A) could

(B) wasn't

(C) can

(D) couldn't

**28.** To expand our facilities, we need to _____ several thousand dollars from the bank.

(A) lend

(B) borrow

(C) give

(D) donate

**29.** They complained about the quality of the goods? I don't believe it! It _____ be true!

(A) can't

(B) can

(C) should

(D) would

**30.** How I wish I hadn't _____ in the stock market last year. Now I'm broke!

(A) divested

(B) invested

(C) investigated

(D) enrolled

**31.** Our award-winning advertising campaign was created _____ the Sutter & Parsons Advertising Agency.

(A) of

(B) from

(C) by

(D) to

---

**32.** Thank you all for your support with the product launch! I couldn't have done it _____ your help!

(A) for

(B) without

(C) with

(D) outside

---

**33.** The company's promotional posters at the festival _____ the strong winds.

(A) were blown away by

(B) was blown away to

(C) were blown away from

(D) was blown away with

---

**34.** The economic slowdown has resulted in thousands of workers being _____.

(A) laid off

(B) hired

(C) given raises

(D) complimented

---

**35.** Kent tried to negotiate with the client over the price, but was _____ to make any progress.

(A) unwilling

(B) unsatisfied

(C) unable

(D) undeniable

**36.** My father advised me to invest in _____ or other precious metals.
(A) golden
(B) goldy
(C) golds
(D) gold

**37.** Michael is _____ to graduate from university and start his career.
(A) eager
(B) earnest
(C) urgent
(D) wishful

**38.** We won't be able to broadcast our commercial on the day we wanted. _____ of the prime-time TV slots _____ already taken.
(A) All ; are
(B) None ; are
(C) Any ; are
(D) All ; is

**39.** You haven't returned my phone calls and messages. I'm _____ to look for someone a little more responsible.
(A) have
(B) will
(C) going
(D) gone

**40.** The company usually _____ year-end bonuses to its employees, but this year they'll be withheld because of the bad economy.
(A) give
(B) giving
(C) given
(D) gives

段落填空 ▶ 請從 (A)、(B)、(C)、(D) 中選出一個最適合的答案。

**Questions 1~4 refer to the following article.**

The downtown branch of a major bank was robbed by two armed robbers yesterday. The security guard at the bank was shot in the shoulder and taken to the hospital for treatment _____ the robbers left.

1. (A) just before
   (B) right after
   (C) while
   (D) since

The police _____ confirmed that the two robbers were released

2. (A) was
   (B) were
   (C) has
   (D) have

from prison just last month. One of the robbers _____ by the police

3. (A) had been wanted
   (B) has been wanted
   (C) has wanted
   (D) were wanted

for two years before his last arrest. This is the third time the bank has been robbed in the past two years. The manager will be brought _____ for questioning by the police next week.

4. (A) at
   (B) in
   (C) on
   (D) to

## Questions 5~8 refer to the following article.

When most people think of working holidays, Australia is usually the first
country that _____ mind. Australia was the first country to offer

      5. (A) comes up
         (B) comes on
         (C) comes to
         (D) comes at

working holiday program visas—its working holiday program was
established in 1975—and it's still the most popular destination. Originally
_____ to young people from Great Britain, the Republic of Ireland

6. (A) free
  (B) open
  (C) vacant
  (D) public

and Canada, the visa is now available to young people from 18
countries, and the list keeps _____. Over the years, many other

      7. (A) thriving
         (B) boosting
         (C) raising
         (D) growing

countries _____ Australia's lead. From Argentina to Australia, from

      8. (A) have followed
         (B) follow
         (C) are following
         (D) had followed

Singapore to Switzerland, 26 countries around the world now offer
working holiday visas.

**A** **1.** We won't be able to make a profit because the customer wants us _____ the price by another 10%.

由於顧客要我們把價格再降百分之十，我們將無法獲利。

(A) to reduce　　(B) to increase　　(C) to expand　　(D) to demand

觀念　不定詞

解析　動詞 want 意思是「想要」，用法與 ask 相同，受詞後面的動詞須以不定詞（to V）呈現。這兩個動詞意思雖然與「使役動詞」have、make、let 等相近，但用法不同，使役動詞在受詞後面是接「原形動詞」，注意勿混淆。

• reduce [rɪ`djus] (v.) 降低　　　　　• demand [dɪ`mænd] (v.) 要求，請求

---

**A** **2.** From this chart, we _____ that the dollar has fallen against most major currencies.

從這張圖表上，我們可以看見美元兌大多主要貨幣走貶。

(A) can see　　(B) can seeing　　(C) seeing　　(D) were seeing

觀念　情態助動詞

解析　本句中的 that 子句為名詞用法，作為動詞 see 的受詞。而情態助動詞 can 後面必須接原形動詞，因此答案選 can see。

• chart [tʃɑrt] (n.) 圖表　　　　　　• major [`medʒɚ] (adj.) 主要的
• currency [`kɜənsɪ] (n.) 貨幣

---

**D** **3.** I've been out of work for months! I sure wish the economy would _____!

我已經失業好幾個月了！我真的希望經濟能好轉。

(A) get worse　　(B) improved　　(C) better　　(D) improve

觀念　假設語氣

解析　說話者已失業好幾個月，當然希望經濟能好轉，但此處用 wish 一字即可知這個願望不太可能實現。而助動詞 would 後應接原形動詞，故本題選 improve，也可用 get better 代換。

• out of work 失業　　　　　　　　• improve [ɪm`pru] (v.) 改善

C **4.** We'll offer you a discount of 10% _____ you order more than 100,000 units.

假如你訂超過十萬組，我們將提供你九折優惠。

(A) why      (B) could      (C) if      (D) would

觀念 從屬連接詞

解析 本題在空格前後分別為兩個子句，而分析兩子句關係可知「我們將提供你九折優惠」的條件是「你訂超過十萬組」，所以此處須用從屬連接詞 if（假如）連接。if 子句也稱為「條件子句」，子句的動詞時態須用「現在式」，但主要子句 We'll offer you... 裡的動詞則用「未來式」。

● offer [ˋɔfə] (v.) 提供      ● discount [ˋdɪskaʊnt] (n.) 折扣

---

A **5.** I'm so disappointed in you! If you had worked harder, we _____ have won the contract!

我對你好失望！假如你有更努力一點，我們就會贏得那份合約！

(A) would      (B) will      (C) won't      (D) wouldn't

觀念 假設語氣

解析 If 用來指「與過去事實相反的假設」時，句型為「If＋主詞＋had＋過去分詞...，主詞＋would/could have＋過去分詞...」。本題 If you had worked harder, we would have won the contract! 代表的事實是 You didn't work harder, so we didn't win the contract.。

● disappointed [ˌdɪsəˋpɔɪntɪd] (adj.) 失望的

---

A **6.** Shirley! Have those faxes _____ yet? My client is waiting for them.

雪莉！那些傳真傳過去了沒有？我的客戶在等。

(A) been sent      (B) being sent      (C) were sent      (D) sent

觀念 被動語態

解析 faxes（傳真）不會自己主動傳過去，所以動詞要用「被動語態」。句首的 Have 表示本句為完成式疑問句，所以被動語態寫成 Have...been sent。

● fax [fæks] (n.) 傳真

**D** **7.** We are all _____ to have this opportunity to do business with you, Mr. Reed.

瑞德先生，能有機會跟您做生意，我們大家都感到興奮。

(A) exciting     (B) excite     (C) be excited     (D) excited

**觀念** 現在分詞與過去分詞

**解析** excite 是動詞，意思是「使……興奮」，被動語態「人＋be excited」指的是「某人（被某事物影響而）感到興奮」，所以過去分詞 excited 作形容詞用時指的是「（人）感到興奮的」；反之，現在分詞 exciting 則指「（事物）令人興奮的」。如：Everybody is excited about the news. = The news is exciting to everybody.。

● opportunity [ˌɑpəˋtjunətɪ] (n.) 機會

---

**B** **8.** Please take the elevator up to the _____ floor.

請搭電梯上七樓。

(A) seven     (B) seventh     (C) seventy     (D) basement

**觀念** 序數

**解析** 要表達「樓層」須使用序數，「七樓」應說 the seventh floor。序數前面須加上定冠詞 the 或所有格，如：This is my first job.「這是我的第一份工作。」在拼法上，除了個位數字為「一、二、三」時拼成first、second、third外，其它序數字尾均為 th，「二十、三十」等字尾為 ty 者則改成 ieth。

● elevator [ˋɛləˌvetə] (n.) 電梯     ● basement [ˋbesmənt] (n.) 地下室

---

**B** **9.** You shouldn't worry about losing your job, William. You still have thousands of dollars in your bank _____.

威廉，你不用擔心丟掉工作。你的銀行戶頭裡還有好幾千美元。

(A) ATM card     (B) account     (C) withdrawal     (D) teller

**觀念** 名詞

**解析** 本題須掌握與銀行相關的名詞字義，其中的 ATM 是Automatic Teller Machine（自動提款機）的縮寫，withdrawal（提款）的相反詞為 deposit（存款），而 teller 則是「出納員」。

● withdrawal [wɪðˋdrɔ] (n.) 提款；撤回     ● withdrawal/deposit slip 提／存款單

● teller [ˋtɛlə] (n.) 出納員

D 10. We bought stocks in that company before the recession, and now that the market has declined they're hardly _____ anything now.

我們在經濟蕭條前買了那家公司的股票，而現在既然市場已經衰退，它們幾乎已經不值錢了。

(A) value      (B) amount      (C) cost      (D) worth

觀念　形容詞

解析　now that 是「既然；因為」的意思，根據句意，既然市場已經衰退，股票就幾乎不值錢了。選項中的 value（價值）是名詞，cost（價值；花費）是動詞，均不適合放在 be 動詞之後，只有 worth（有……價值的）可以與 be 動詞連用，如：This house is worth ten million dollars.「這棟房子值一千萬元。」

- recession [rɪ`sɛʃən] (n.) 蕭條
- decline [dɪ`klaɪn] (v.) 衰退
- hardly [`hɑrdlɪ] (adv.) 幾乎不

---

B 11. We need to import these special instruments from _____ before we can begin production.

在我們開始生產之前，必須先從德國進口這些特別的儀器。

(A) German      (B) Germany      (C) Germania      (D) Germanese

觀念　名詞

解析　介系詞 from 後面應接地名 Germany，指「德國」；至於 German 則可當名詞或形容詞，指「德國人（的），德語」。

- instrument [`ɪnstrə,mənt] (n.) 儀器，器具

---

C 12. I lived in _____ for two years before moving to France.

我在搬到法國前曾住在英國兩年。

(A) English      (B) Brittany      (C) Britain      (D) British

觀念　名詞

解析　英國的全名是 the United Kingdom of Great Britain and Northern Ireland，簡稱 the UK，也可說 Britain 或 England。而 English 則是「英國人（的），英語」，也可用 British 一字。至於 Brittany 則是「不列塔尼」，是法國西北部的一地區。

- Britain [`brɪtən] (n.) 英國
- British [`brɪtɪʃ] (adj./n.) 英國人（的），英國英語

**B** *13.* I'm sorry. Ms. Chang is _____ of the office right now. May I take a message?

不好意思，張小姐現在不在辦公室。可以讓我幫您留言嗎？

(A) away      (B) out      (C) outside      (D) inside

觀念　介系詞

解析　題目一開始說「不好意思」，下一句又說「可以幫您留言嗎？」因此，可以推測張小姐應該是「不在辦公室」。選項 (A) 要改成 away from the office。out of the office 是「不在辦公室」。out of 有脫離的意思，表示她「不在辦公室，外出」。outside of the office 是「在辦公室外面」，並不是特別指外出。答案應選 (B)。

- take a message 幫對方留言　　　　　• leave a message 自己留言給對方
- out of work 失業　　　　　　　　　• out of date 過時的

---

**D** *14.* We've been doing business in the Far East for _____ 30 years now.

我們在遠東地區做生意將近三十年了。

(A) more      (B) close      (C) much      (D) almost

觀念　副詞

解析　這裡要選擇修飾時間「三十年」的副詞。more 要加上 than，才能指「超過三十年」。close 形容詞、副詞同形，指「接近、親密」，修飾距離或人際關係。much「很多」修飾不可數名詞。almost 副詞「幾乎」，修飾時間、程度、距離等。除了 almost 外，nearly 也是修飾時間的副詞。

- Far East 遠東地區（尤指中國、日本、或是在東亞的國家）

---

**A** *15.* We're _____ awaiting your reply to our letter dated March 17, 2009.

我們正在焦急地等待您對我們在2009年三月十七日給您的信件的回覆。

(A) anxiously      (B) excited      (C) lively      (D) anticipate

觀念　副詞

解析　這裡要選修飾動詞 awaiting「等待」的副詞。此外，因為在等待信件回覆，所以不會是 lively「精力充沛地」。excited 是形容詞「興奮的」，anticipate 是動詞「期望」，與文法不符。因此答案選 anxiously「焦急地」。

- lively [`laɪvlɪ] (adj./adv.) 精力充沛的；活潑地
- anticipate [æn`tɪsə‚pet] (v.) 預期

[A] **16.** The client called and said _____ we sent them are of inferior quality.

客戶打電話來說我們寄的產品品質不良。

(A) the products　(B) products　　(C) product　　(D) production

觀念　可數 / 不可數名詞

解析　本題要說的應該是所寄去「產品」，production 是「製作」，語意不符。此外，這裡要用定冠詞 the 來指稱所寄去的那批產品。product 為可數名詞，答案應該為 the products。

● inferior [ɪnˋfɪrɪə] (adj.) 次等的　　　● quality [ˋkwɑlətɪ] (n.) 品質

---

[B] **17.** We've been losing a lot of our investors lately. What kind of _____ can you offer us on how to prevent them from leaving?

我們最近一直在失去投資者。你能提供怎樣的建議給我們，讓他們不要離開？

(A) kindness　　(B) advice　　　(C) friendship　　(D) honesty

觀念　名詞

解析　前一句說「一直在失去投資者」，所以下一句應該是問有沒有什麼「建議」可以 prevent them from leaving。因此答案應該選 advice「建議」。kindness 是「好意」，friendship 是「友情」，honesty 是「誠實」，這三個選項都與句意不符。

● prevent...from＋Ving：預防…不要做某事

---

[C] **18.** This laptop computer does not belong to the company. It's _____ personal property.

這台筆記型電腦不屬於公司。它是曼蒂的個人財產。

(A) Mandy　　(B) Mandys　　(C) Mandy's　　(D) Mandys'

觀念　所有格

解析　前句提到這台電腦「不屬於」公司，所以下一句應該是說它是「Mandy 的」財產。人名的所有格須在人名之後加上 's，所以答案選 (C)。

● property [ˋprɑpətɪ] (n.) 財產；所有物

**D** **19.** I'm sorry to tell you this, but this pink slip isn't mine. It's _____.
Good luck finding a new job.

很抱歉要跟你說，這個解雇通知單不是我的。它是你的。祝你找新工作順利。

(A) you      (B) your      (C) your's      (D) yours

**觀念** 所有格代名詞

**解析** 題目應該是指 it's your pink slip，為了避免重複，如同前一句也用到的 mine，這裡應用所有格代名詞，以 yours 代替 your pink slip。

● pink slip （美式）解雇通知單

---

**D** **20.** You seem like a nice person and your academic record is outstanding. But you don't seem to have _____ work experience.

你似乎是個很不錯的人，而且你的學業成績也非常優秀。但你似乎沒有任何工作經驗。

(A) a      (B) many      (C) one      (D) any

**觀念** 不定代名詞

**解析** 從第二句的 but 可以看到這裡應該有轉折語氣，而且句中也有否定的意味。因此可以猜測到應該是說對方「沒有工作經驗」。做否定的單數代名詞會用 any，不會用 a 或者是 one。如果要選 (B) 的話，題目的 work experience 應該要複數。

● academic record 學業成績

---

**D** **21.** There's no need _____, Mr. Johnson. We should be able to win the copyright infringement case easily.

不需要擔心，強森先生。我們應該能輕易地贏得這項版權侵害官司。

(A) of worry      (B) worry      (C) to worrying      (D) to worry

**觀念** 不定詞

**解析** 這裡的 need 作名詞，表示「需要」，「沒有需要去做某事」的句型就是 there's no need to V...。因此答案選 (D)「不需要擔心」。

● copyright infringement 版權侵害

**C** **22.** Several employees have accused you of selling company secrets to our competitors. Do you have _____ to say in your defense?

許多員工都指控你盜賣公司機密給我們的競爭者。你有沒有任何話想說來為自己辯駁？

(A) what          (B) any          (C) anything          (D) some

**觀念** 代名詞

**解析** 句子要表達的意思是是否有「任何話」想說，應該要用代名詞的形式出現。any 和 some 都應該在後面加上 words 等名詞，讓答案有名詞的形式。正確答案是可以放在疑問句和否定句的代名詞 anything。

● defense [dɪˋfɛns] (n./v.) 防禦，辯護；抵禦

---

**B** **23.** We'd like to enter the publishing industry, but it's _____ feasible at this time.

我們想要進入出版業，但現在這個時機行不通。

(A) no          (B) not          (C) not to          (D) never

**觀念** 副詞

**解析** 前一句說「想要進入出版業」，後一句加上有轉折語氣的 but，所以接下來的句子應該是說「行不通」。feasible 是形容詞，表示「行得通的」，如果要符合前後句意，應該要選擇否定的意思。以形容詞造句表示否定意味，直接在 be 動詞後面加上 not，因此答案選 (B)。

● feasible [ˋfizəbl] (adj.) 可行的

---

**B** **24.** Marty is going to _____ the annual budget tomorrow.

瑪緹明天將準備完年度預算案。

(A) prepares          (B) finish preparing
(C) preparing          (D) got prepared

**觀念** 未來簡單式

**解析** 未來簡單式的助動詞除了用 will 外，也可以用 be going to，兩者後面都應接「原形動詞」，所以本題應選 finish preparing，其中的 finish 為原形動詞，後面的 preparing 則為動名詞，做為 finish 的受詞。

● annual [ˋænjuəl] (adj.) 年度          ● budget [ˋbʌdʒɪt] (n.) 預算

**A** **25.** Our company's specialty _____ helping clients to invest profitably in the stock market.

我們公司的專長就是幫助顧客在股票市場上投資獲利。

(A) is          (B) is to          (C) are to          (D) be

**觀念** 動名詞

**解析** 本句首先要看到主詞「我們公司的專長」是單數形，所以要選單數的「be 動詞」is。後面接的是「名詞」形式的補語，也就是題目中的 helping，是由動詞轉換而來的「動名詞」，前面不須再加上 to，所以應選 (A) 而不選 (B)。

- specialty [ˋspɛʃəltɪ] (n.) 專長

---

**D** **26.** The trade commission is suing us for _____ to fulfill our end of the bargain.

貿易委員會因我們沒有履行承諾而提告。

(A) fail          (B) failed          (C) have failed          (D) failing

**觀念** 介系詞接動名詞

**解析** 本句的介系詞 for 有「因為」的意思，for 後面加的是代表一整件事，以「動名詞」的形式呈現，也就是選項 (D) 的答案。選項 (C) 的答案必須將 have 改為 having，讓它所表現的動作也有動名詞的形式。

- fulfill/do one's end of the bargain 履行 / 實現諾言（通常指商業上）

---

**D** **27.** Harry _____ finish the assignment on time, so it was given to someone else.

哈利無法準時完成這項任務，所以被指派給別人。

(A) could          (B) wasn't          (C) can          (D) couldn't

**觀念** 情態助動詞

**解析** 後半句的 be 動詞指出時態為過去簡單式，因此前半句的情態助動詞也要用過去式；而根據句意「任務被指派給其他人」可推知「哈利無法準時完成任務」，所以此處的助動詞應用否定的 couldn't。

- assignment [əˋsaɪnmənt] (n.)（指派的）任務；工作
- on time 準時

**B** *28.* To expand our facilities, we need to _____ several thousand dollars from the bank.

我們必須向銀行借幾千美元來擴增我們的設施。

(A) lend         (B) borrow        (C) give        (D) donate

觀念   不定詞

解析   need（必須）當動詞時，後面接不定詞（to V）。根據句意，此處應選的動詞為 borrow（借入），搭配介系詞 from指「向……借」；其相反詞為 lend（借出），搭配介系詞 to 指「借給……」。

• expand [ɪk`spænd] (v.) 擴大，擴展      • borrow [`bɑro] (v.) 借入

• donate [`donet] (v.) 捐贈

---

**A** *29.* They complained about the quality of the goods? I don't believe it! It _____ be true!

他們抱怨商品的品質？我不相信！這不可能是真的。

(A) can't        (B) can        (C) should        (D) would

觀念   情態助動詞

解析   表「推測」的情態助動詞可用 must、can/could、may/might 等，其中以 must（一定）語氣最為肯定，如：You must be new here.（你一定是新來的。）而 could 和 might 的語氣則最保守。若要表示「否定推測」，則以 can't（不可能）語氣最強烈。注意 mustn't 意思是「不准」，表「強烈禁止」，不能用於推測。

• complain [kəm`plen] (v.) 抱怨      • quality [`kwɑlətɪ] (n.) 品質

---

**B** *30.* How I wish I hadn't _____ in the stock market last year. Now I'm broke!

我多麼希望我去年沒投資股市。現在我破產啦！

(A) divested      (B) invested      (C) investigated      (D) enrolled

觀念   假設語氣

解析   wish 如果是指過去的事，則是表示「希望某事沒發生（但卻已發生了）」，動詞時態應搭配過去完成式（had＋過去分詞）。說話者現在破產了，可知他有多希望去年沒投資股市，動詞應搭配 invest，其他 divest（賣出）、investigate（調查）、enroll（註冊）均與題意不符。

• invest [ɪn`vɛst] (v.) 投資      • broke [brok] (adj.)（口語）破產的

**C** *31.* Our award-winning advertising campaign was created _____ the Sutter & Parsons Advertising Agency.

我們得獎的廣告宣傳活動是由舒特＆派森廣告公司設計的。

(A) of        (B) from        (C) by        (D) to

觀念   被動語態

解析   was created 是「被動語態」用法，要引出真正的行為者時，要接介系詞 by（由……）。

● award-winning [əˋwɔrd͵wɪnɪŋ] (adj.) 獲獎的

● campaign [kæmˋpen] (n.)（具社會、商業或政治目的的）運動，活動

---

**B** *32.* Thank you all for your support with the product launch! I couldn't have done it _____ your help!

謝謝你們大家對產品發表的支持！沒有你們的幫忙，我是做不到的。

(A) for        (B) without        (C) with        (D) outside

觀念   介系詞

解析   介系詞 with 代表「有」，without 則代表「沒有」。根據句意，本題應選 without。句型 not...without... 意思是「沒有……就不能（就沒有）……」。如：I can't work without the Internet.（我沒有網際網路就不能工作。）

● launch [lɔntʃ] (n./v.)（產品）上市

---

**A** *33.* The company's promotional posters at the festival _____ the strong winds.

公司在慶祝活動上的促銷宣傳海報被大風吹走了。

(A) were blown away by        (B) was blown away to

(C) were blown away from        (D) was blown away with

觀念   被動語態

解析   本句主詞為複數的 posters，所以被動語態應用 were blown down，而後面的介系詞則應接 by，引出「吹散海報的行為者」the wind。

● poster [ˋpostɚ] (n.) 海報

● festival [ˋfɛstəvl] (n.) 節慶；慶祝活動；音樂／戲劇節

**A** *34.* The economic slowdown has resulted in thousands of workers being

_____.

經濟衰退已經造成好幾千名工人被解雇。

(A) laid off      (B) hired      (C) given raises    (D) complimented

觀念   動詞

解析   根據語意，可推知經濟衰退造成工人被 laid off（解雇），原形為 lay off。其他選項 hire（雇用）、give raises（加薪）、compliment（稱讚）則與句意不符。

- slowdown [ˋsloˏdaʊn] (n.) 減速；衰退

**C** *35.* Kent tried to negotiate with the client over the price, but was _____ to make any progress.

肯特試著跟客戶議價，但無法獲得任何進展。

(A) unwilling      (B) unsatisfied      (C) unable      (D) undeniable

觀念   形容詞

解析   對等連接詞 but 代表肯特要議價卻無法有進展，所以此處的形容詞應選 unable（無法）。其他像 unwilling（不願意）、unsatisfied（不滿意）、undeniable（無法否認的）均不符句意。

- negotiate [nɪˋgoʃɪˏet] (v.) 協商      • make progress 獲得進展
- be unable to＋原形動詞：無法（做某事）

**D** *36.* My father advised me to invest in _____ or other precious metals.

我父親建議我投資黃金或其他貴重金屬。

(A) golden      (B) goldy      (C) golds      (D) gold

觀念   名詞

解析   介系詞 in 後面應接名詞，gold 當名詞為不可數名詞，不可加 s，指「黃金；金色」，golden 則是形容詞「金色的，金製的」。

- advise [ədˋvaɪz] (v.) 建議      • precious [ˋprɛʃəs] (adj.) 珍貴的

**A** **37.** Michael is _____ to graduate from university and start his career.

麥可急著從大學畢業，展開他的職業生涯。

(A) eager      (B) earnest      (C) urgent      (D) wishful

**觀念** 形容詞

**解析** be eager to... 是「渴望／急切想要……」，be earnest in/about... 是「對……很認真」。至於 urgent 則是「緊急的」，用來形容事物，而 wishful 則帶有「一廂情願」的意味。

• be eager to＋原形動詞：渴望做…      • graduate [`grædʒʊˌet] (v.) 畢業

• career [kə`rɪr] (n.) 生涯；職業

---

**A** **38.** We won't be able to broadcast our commercial on the day we wanted. _____ of the prime-time TV slots _____ already taken.

我們沒辦法在我們要的日期播出我們的廣告。所有電視台的黃金時段都已經滿了。

(A) All ; are      (B) None ; are      (C) Any ; are      (D) All ; is

**觀念** 不定代名詞

**解析** 前一句說「沒辦法在我們要的日期播出我們的廣告」，就表示下一句要說的是廣告時段都滿了。prime-time TV slots 是可數名詞，因此要用複數的 be 動詞。從句意上來看，要選 (A)。any 要放在疑問句和否定句，這裡是肯定句，所以不能選。

• prime-time 黃金時段

---

**C** **39.** You haven't returned my phone calls and messages. I'm _____ to look for someone a little more responsible.

你沒有回我的電話和簡訊。我打算另找一個比較負責任的人。

(A) have      (B) will      (C) going      (D) gone

**觀念** 未來簡單式

**解析** 「be going to＋原形動詞」為未來簡單式，本題題目已有 be 動詞和 to，故中間只須加入 going。一般而言，be going to 和 will 皆可相互替換，但 be going to 多用在表達「計畫、意向、可以預見馬上要發生的事」，如本題中的 I'm going to look for someone... 便是表達「另外找人的打算」。

• return [rɪ`tɜn] (v.) 歸還；回覆      • message [`mɛsɪdʒ] (n.) 訊息，留言

D **40.** The company usually _____ year-end bonuses to its employees, but this year they'll be withheld because of the bad economy.

這家公司通常會發給員工年終獎金,不過由於今年經濟狀況不好,他們將不發放獎金。

(A) give        (B) giving        (C) given        (D) gives

觀念   現在簡單式

解析   本題主詞 the company 後面欠缺動詞,故應選 gives。現在簡單式用來表現在的「習慣、事實」,usually gives year-end bonuses 代表這家公司有發年終獎金的慣例。

• year-end bonus 年終獎金        • withhold [wɪθˋhold] (v.) 保留;抑制

**Questions 1~4 refer to the following article.**

The downtown branch of a major bank was robbed by two armed robbers yesterday. The security guard at the bank was shot in the shoulder and taken to the hospital for treatment _____**B**_____ the robbers left.

1.(A) just before
(B) right after
(C) while
(D) since

The police _____**D**_____ confirmed that the two robbers were released

2.(A) was
(B) were
(C) has
(D) have

from prison just last month. One of the robbers _____**A**_____ by the police

3.(A) had been wanted
(B) has been wanted
(C) has wanted
(D) were wanted

for two years before his last arrest. This is the third time the bank has been robbed in the past two years. The manager will be brought _____**B**_____ for questioning by the police next week.

4.(A) at
(B) in
(C) on
(D) to

**問題 1~4 請參考以下文章。**

一家大銀行位於市中心的分行在昨日被兩名持槍搶匪所搶。該銀行的警衛肩膀中槍,在搶匪離開後立刻被送往醫院治療。警方已證實這兩名搶匪是上個月剛被釋放出獄的。其中一名搶匪在上次被捕前,被警方通緝達兩年。這已是該銀行在過去兩年中第三次被搶。該銀行經理下周將被警方約談。

*1.* 觀念 從屬連接詞

解析 根據語意，警衛應該是在搶匪離開後被送往醫院治療，故選 right after。

● treatment [`tritmənt] (n.) 治療　　　　● robber [`rɑbɚ] (n.) 搶匪

---

*2.* 觀念 現在完成式

解析 警方是動詞 confirm 的行為人，應用「主動語態」。本句為現在完成式，主詞
the police 為「集合名詞」，視為複數，所以選 have。

● release [rɪ`lis] (v.) 釋放；發行

---

*3.* 觀念 過去完成式

解析 本句的時間點是 before his last arrest「在他上次被捕前」，在此過去時間點之
前已經發生的事，應用「過去完成式」。而 want 在此指「通緝」，以搶匪當主
詞則應接「被動語態」be wanted，所以本句的動詞整體以「過去完成式被動語
態」had been wanted 呈現。

● want [wɔnt] (v.) 緝拿，追捕　　　　● arrest [ə`rɛst] (v./n.) 逮捕；拘留

---

*4.* 觀念 動詞片語

解析 指「警方將某人帶至警察局訊問」應用 bring somebody in，本句主詞 the
manager 為被偵訊的對象，故動詞用「被動語態」be brought in。

bring in something 則指「產生，賺進（利潤）」。此外，bring 也常和介系詞
to 連用構成片語，如 bring somebody to 指「使某人恢復知覺」；bring to light
指「揭露」；bring to a stop 則指「使終止」等。

● question [`kwɛstʃən] (v./n.) 訊問；問題

## Questions 5~8 refer to the following article.

When most people think of working holidays, Australia is usually the first
country that ____C____ mind. Australia was the first country to offer

        5.(A) comes up
          (B) comes on
          (C) comes to
          (D) comes at

working holiday program visas—its working holiday program was
established in 1975—and it's still the most popular destination. Originally
____B____ to young people from Great Britain, the Republic of Ireland

6.(A) free
  (B) open
  (C) vacant
  (D) public

and Canada, the visa is now available to young people from 18
countries, and the list keeps ____D____. Over the years, many other

        7.(A) thriving
          (B) boosting
          (C) raising
          (D) growing

countries ____A____ Australia's lead. From Argentina to Australia, from

    8.(A) have followed
      (B) follow
      (C) are following
      (D) had followed

Singapore to Switzerland, 26 countries around the world now offer
working holiday visas.

## 問題 5〜8 請參考以下文章。

大多數的人一想到打工度假，第一個想到的國家通常是澳洲。澳洲是第一個提供打
工簽證的國家——它的打工度假方案早在一九七五年就成立——而且至今仍是最受
歡迎的地方。原本只開放給英國、愛爾蘭及加拿大的年輕人，如今已經擴增為十八
個國家，且名單仍繼續增加中。這些年來，其他許多國家也跟隨澳洲的腳步。從阿
根廷到奧地利，從新加坡到瑞士，目前世界上共有二十六個國家提供打工度假簽
證。

**5.** 觀念 動詞片語

解析 指「想到，浮現在腦海」要用片語 something comes to mind，所以本題選 (C)。

- working holiday 打工度假

---

**6.** 觀念 形容詞

解析 指「名額開放給……」應用 open to...。其他選項 free 指「自由的，免費的」，vacant 指「（職位，位置）空缺的」，public 指「公共的」，皆與語意不合。

- available [ə`veləbḷ] (adj.) 可獲得的；可找到的

---

**7.** 觀念 動詞

解析 本題要選適合語意的動詞，指「名單持續增加」應用 grow 一字，有「名單的長度不斷變長」之意。其他選項中文亦可指「成長」，但須分辨其原本的英文字義。thrive 指「茂盛成長」，boost 指「使增長；使興旺」，raise 指「提高」，均不適用於 list。

- thrive [θraɪv] (v.) 茂盛成長
- raise [rez] (v./n.) 提高；舉起；增加
- boost [bust] (v./n.) 使增長；使興旺；推進，促進

---

**8.** 觀念 現在完成式

解析 lead 在此為名詞，指「榜樣」。Over the years 指「這些年來」，表從打工度假制度開始實施以來到現在，時態應搭配「現在完成式」，因此選 have followed。

- follow one's lead 跟隨某人的腳步

# 多益文法模擬考　第五回

**單句填空 ▶** 請從 (A)、(B)、(C)、(D) 中選出一個最適合的答案。

☐ **1.** Help me _____ a pen, will you? I need to leave a memo for Doris.
(A) write
(B) find
(C) sharpen
(D) sell

☐ **2.** We _____ think this deal over carefully before we commit ourselves. We might lose a lot of money.
(A) shouldn't
(B) can't
(C) don't
(D) should

☐ **3.** If I _____ a rich man, I wouldn't have to work for this silly company.
(A) were
(B) could
(C) be
(D) am

☐ **4.** Sarah has been _____ by the Society of Marketing Professionals to speak at their annual meeting.
(A) invite
(B) invited
(C) inviting
(D) invites

☐ **5.** The Sanborn Corporation reported significant profits during the _____ quarter.
(A) one
(B) number three
(C) fifth
(D) first

**6.** Your idea for a new product line is quite unique, Tom, but I'm _____ the board of directors won't like it.
(A) afraid
(B) feared
(C) upset
(D) troubled

**7.** Our company wants to import feta cheese from Greece, but none of our staff speaks _____.
(A) Greece
(B) Grecian
(C) Greekish
(D) Greek

**8.** The _____ weather has resulted in floods, which have caused a rise in agricultural prices.
(A) sunny
(B) cold
(C) rainy
(D) windy

**9.** I thought Lionel's presentation was very informative. He's always _____.
(A) well prepared
(B) well preparing
(C) good prepared
(D) good preparing

**10.** Because the order wasn't received before the deadline, we _____ be able to process your order until next month.
(A) can't
(B) won't
(C) are
(D) should

**11.** Norman usually punches in before 8:00 a.m., but today for some reason he _____ at 10:30.
(A) punches in
(B) punched in
(C) punching in
(D) punch in

**12.** Commodity prices were quite low last winter, but this spring they _____ to rise.
(A) were expected
(B) are expected
(C) can expected
(D) will expecting

**13.** The economy is not expected to improve until _____ year, so this year we'll just have to grin and bear it.
(A) last
(B) this
(C) next
(D) that

**14.** Thomas decided to sell his stocks two years _____ and invested in treasury bonds instead.
(A) then
(B) from
(C) until
(D) ago

**15.** Exports to Brazil had always been profitable, but _____ last year we've been experiencing major losses.
(A) at
(B) ago
(C) since
(D) for

**16.** A: Have you ever led a marketing team before?

B: No, I _____ have, but I'm willing to learn.

(A) never

(B) always

(C) not

(D) didn't

**17.** Your progress reports and self-evaluations will be due _____ Friday, so get busy!

(A) this

(B) from

(C) last

(D) to

**18.** Consumers in that country can hardly keep up with _____ inflation.

(A) rapidly fallen

(B) rapidly risen

(C) rapidly rising

(D) rapidly fell

**19.** Special packaging is required because the product is made out of

_____.

(A) wood

(B) woody

(C) wooden

(D) woods

**20.** This kind of product may appeal to French people, but _____ people probably won't think it's anything special.

(A) Taiwan

(B) Taiwanese

(C) Taiwaner

(D) Taiwan of

**21.** Our company's website needs to _____ every day.
  (A) updated
  (B) be updated
  (C) update
  (D) updating

**22.** You should have recorded the serial numbers. If you _____,
we would be able to claim insurance on the missing items.
  (A) can
  (B) will
  (C) had
  (D) were

**23.** The boss is unhappy that our bid wasn't accepted. He thinks we should
have _____ harder.
  (A) accepted
  (B) tried
  (C) listened
  (D) run

**24.** I've been so _____ this week that I haven't had time to finish the
report.
  (A) busy
  (B) restless
  (C) tired
  (D) bored

**25.** With the economy doing so poorly, it's getting _____ to make a
profit in business these days.
  (A) easier
  (B) simpler
  (C) harder
  (D) more possible

26. The shipment was _____ late, so the clients are a bit upset about the delay.
    (A) arrived
    (B) sent
    (C) ordered
    (D) paid

27. We'd better sell our stocks now, because by this time tomorrow their value will have _____.
    (A) increased
    (B) measured
    (C) decreased
    (D) expanded

28. The stock market will be _____ at 9:00 a.m. on Tuesday, so we should be there by 8:45.
    (A) to open
    (B) opening
    (C) has open
    (D) opens

29. When _____ the shipment scheduled to arrive?
    (A) will
    (B) can
    (C) is
    (D) are

30. Mr. Kent, your plane _____ at 7:20, so we'll have to get you to the airport early.
    (A) left
    (B) can leave
    (C) was leaving
    (D) leaves

**31.** The products come off the line here and are stored in the warehouse over _____.

(A) this

(B) there

(C) that

(D) from

---

**32.** Unfortunately, the infrastructure of that country is _____ to support an advanced communication network like ours.

(A) too developed enough

(B) not developed enough

(C) too developed

(D) developed very much

---

**33.** Many _____ in the USA are owned by the Gannett Company.

(A) newspaper

(B) paper

(C) newspapers

(D) news

---

**34.** You got to work on time today, but unfortunately you forgot to punch _____. You're therefore considered late.

(A) out

(B) on

(C) in

(D) up

---

**35.** Did you hear the way Tom spoke to the boss? I could _____ believe my ears!

(A) hardly

(B) hard

(C) really

(D) almost

**36.** I'm not sure if this kind of product will sell. We manufactured one just like it _____ before, and it was a total flop.

(A) for

(B) once

(C) ever

(D) one

**37.** I've really enjoyed my visit to your company, Mr. Edwards. Thank you for your _____.

(A) kindness

(B) kind

(C) kindnesses

(D) kinds

**38.** This is a very important project, Marjorie! _____ in the company is counting on it being successful!

(A) Everything

(B) Everybody

(C) No one

(D) None

**39.** The client has refused to speak to us, and says there _____ no further negotiations.

(A) won't be

(B) will be

(C) wasn't

(D) can't be

**40.** By the time new energy sources are developed, worldwide petroleum supplies will have _____ out.

(A) run

(B) used

(C) broken

(D) sent

段落填空 ▶ 請從 (A)、(B)、(C)、(D) 中選出一個最適合的答案。

## Questions 1~4 refer to the following article.

Taiwan is bigger than Singapore, but _____ smaller than most

          1. (A) many
             (B) more
             (C) very
             (D) much

countries in Asia. Taiwan is one of the richest and _____ countries

          2. (A) modernist
             (B) modernest
             (C) most modern
             (D) modern

in Asia. Living expenses in Taiwan are also higher than in most Asian
countries. Nowadays, Taiwan has stronger _____ ties with China

          3. (A) economic
             (B) economical
             (C) economy
             (D) economically

than with Japan. The reasons are that Taiwan is closer to China than to
Japan, and that China has a larger _____ than Japan.

          4. (A) population
             (B) citizenship
             (C) people
             (D) society

**Questions 5~8 refer to the following article.**

30 St Mary Axe is one of Europe's first green skyscrapers. It opened in 2004 in London's financial district, and at 40 stories high it dominates the city's skyline. _____ like a giant glass bullet, the skyscraper's

5. (A) To shape
   (B) Shape
   (C) Shaped
   (D) Shaping

green design _____ it to use 50 percent less energy than most

6. (A) allows
   (B) makes
   (C) lets
   (D) has

buildings its size. Gaps in each floor create six huge shafts that serve _____ a natural ventilation system, with gardens on every sixth

7. (A) to
   (B) in
   (C) with
   (D) as

floor to purify the air. The shafts move hot air out of the building in the summer, and use solar energy to heat the building in the winter. All of this is done, amazingly, _____ electric heaters or fans. The shafts

8. (A) without
   (B) except
   (C) aside from
   (D) besides

also allow sunlight to pass through the building, creating a pleasant working environment and keeping lighting costs down.

**B** *1.* Help me _____ a pen, will you? I need to leave a memo for Doris.

幫我找支筆，好嗎？我需要留張紙條給朵莉絲。

(A) write　　　　(B) find　　　　(C) sharpen　　　　(D) sell

觀念　不定詞

解析　help（幫忙）的句型是「help＋人＋不定詞（to V）」，但此處的 to 經常省略，故可說 help me find a pen（幫我找支筆）。

● sharpen [`ʃɑrpən] (v.) 使銳利　　　　● memo [`mɛmo] (n.) 備忘錄

---

**D** *2.* We _____ think this deal over carefully before we commit ourselves. We might lose a lot of money.

在我們做出承諾前，應該仔細把這項交易考慮清楚。我們可能會損失很多錢。

(A) shouldn't　　(B) can't　　(C) don't　　(D) should

觀念　情態助動詞

解析　第二句話指出「可能會損失很多錢」，根據句意可回推第一句應用情態助動詞 should（應該），用來表「義務；建議」等。

● think over 仔細考慮　　　　● commit [kə`mɪt] (v.) 做出保證

---

**A** *3.* If I _____ a rich man, I wouldn't have to work for this silly company.

假如我是有錢人，我就不必為這家蠢公司工作。

(A) were　　　　(B) could　　　　(C) be　　　　(D) am

觀念　假設語氣

解析　If 用來指「與現在事實相反的假設」時，屬「假設語氣」，動詞時態須搭配「過去式」，句型為「If＋主詞＋過去式動詞，主詞＋would＋原形動詞」。而過去式動詞如果是使用 be 動詞，不論主詞為哪個人稱，一律搭配 were。

● rich [rɪtʃ] (adj.) 富有的　　　　● silly [`sɪlɪ] (adj.) 愚蠢的

B  **4.** Sarah has been _____ by the Society of Marketing Professionals to speak at their annual meeting.

莎拉曾經被行銷專家協會邀請在他們的年會上演講。

(A) invite　　　　(B) invited　　　　(C) inviting　　　　(D) invites

觀念　被動語態

解析　由 be 動詞與介系詞 by 可明顯看出此處應用「被動語態（be 動詞＋過去分詞＋ by...）」，所以答案選 invited。

• invite [ɪn`vaɪt] (v.) 邀請

---

D  **5.** The Sanborn Corporation reported significant profits during the _____ quarter.

桑柏恩公司第一季財報獲利亮眼。

(A) one　　　(B) number three　(C) fifth　　　(D) first

觀念　序數

解析　quarter 一字是「四分之一」，因此 quarter 可指一年的四分之一，就是「一季（三個月）」，而一年只有四季，所以不可能有 the fifth quarter。

• profit [`prɑfɪt] (n.) 利潤　　　　　• quarter [`kwɔrtɚ] (n.) 四分之一；季（三個月）

---

A  **6.** Your idea for a new product line is quite unique, Tom, but I'm _____ the board of directors won't like it.

湯姆，你對新產品線的的想法很獨特，但是我怕董事會不會喜歡。

(A) afraid　　　(B) feared　　　(C) upset　　　(D) troubled

觀念　形容詞

解析　「I'm afraid＋that 子句」意思是「恐怕……；害怕……」；fear（害怕）是動詞，句型則為「人＋fear＋that 子句」，這兩個句型中的 that 都可以省略，答案選 (A)。upset（心煩的）與 troubled（煩惱的）則與本句語意不合。

• unique [ju`nik] (adj.) 獨特的　　　　　• board of directors 董事會

**D** 7. Our company wants to import feta cheese from Greece, but none of our staff speaks _____.

我們公司想要進口希臘羊乳酪，但我們的員工沒有任何人會說希臘語。

(A) Greece      (B) Grecian      (C) Greekish      (D) Greek

觀念    名詞

解析    Greece 是國名「希臘」，Greek 則是「希臘人（的）；希臘語」。通常當國籍的形容詞也可以當名詞，指該國籍的人或該國語言，如：Japanese 是「日本人（的）；日語」、Spanish 是「西班牙人（的）；西班牙語」、Italian 是「義大利人（的）；義大利語」等。

● staff [stæf] (n.) 全體員工

---

**C** 8. The _____ weather has resulted in floods, which have caused a rise in agricultural prices.

多雨的天氣造成水災，使得產品價格上漲。

(A) sunny      (B) cold      (C) rainy      (D) windy

觀念    形容詞

解析    四個選項都是描述天氣的形容詞，但只有「多雨的」天氣才會造成水災，故選 rainy。

● floods [flʌdz] (n.)（複數）水災；洪水      ● agricultural [ˋæɡrɪˋkʌltʃʊəl] (adj.) 農業的

---

**A** 9. I thought Lionel's presentation was very informative. He's always _____.

我覺得李奧納的簡報資訊非常豐富。他總是準備充分。

(A) well prepared            (B) well preparing

(C) good prepared          (D) good preparing

觀念    形容詞、現在分詞與過去分詞

解析    過去分詞 prepared 可當形容詞，指人「準備好的」，而要修飾形容詞則必須用副詞 well。此兩字也可連成一字構成複合形容詞 well-prepared。

● informative [ɪnˋfɔrmətɪv] (adj.) 提供有用資訊的

**B** *10.* Because the order wasn't received before the deadline, we _____ be able to process your order until next month.

因為訂單沒有在截止期限前收到，所以我們要到下個月才能處理你的訂單。

(A) can't      (B) won't      (C) are      (D) should

**觀念** 未來簡單式

**解析** not...until... 意思是「不到……無法……；直到……才……」，所以本句應選 won't。此外，也可說 we can't process your order until next month。

- deadline [`dɛd,laɪn] (n.) 截止期限      • process [`prɑsɛs] (v.) 處理，辦理

---

**B** *11.* Norman usually punches in before 8:00 a.m., but today for some reason he _____ at 10:30.

諾曼通常都在上午八點半以前打卡上班，但今天不知為了什麼原因他十點半才打卡。

(A) punches in      (B) punched in      (C) punching in      (D) punch in

**觀念** 過去簡單式

**解析** 現在簡單式用來表現在的「習慣、事實」，如題目中的 Norman usually punches in before 8:00 a.m. 便是他的習慣。但單單今天，他卻十點半才打卡，此一發生在過去時間的單獨事件則應用「過去簡單式」，故選 punched in。

- punch in/out 打卡上 / 下班

---

**B** *12.* Commodity prices were quite low last winter, but this spring they _____ to rise.

商品價格去年冬天相當低，但今年春天預估會上漲。

(A) were expected      (B) are expected
(C) can expected      (D) will expecting

**觀念** 被動語態

**解析** expect（預期；期待）的行為者為「人」，當主詞為事物 Commodity prices 時，則應用「被動語態」。而本題時間是 this spring，故動詞應選 are expected。

- expect [,ɪk`spɛkt] (v.) 預期；期待

C **13.** The economy is not expected to improve until _____ year, so this year we'll just have to grin and bear it.

經濟狀況預估要到明年才會好轉，所以今年我們只能咬緊牙忍受。

(A) last      (B) this      (C) next      (D) that

觀念   介系詞

解析   「月份；年份」前面通常須搭配介系詞 in，但如果有 this/that（這個 / 那個）或 last/next（上一個 / 下一個）等形容詞時則不加介系詞。

• grin and bear it 苦笑著忍受；默默忍受

---

D **14.** Thomas decided to sell his stocks two years _____ and invested in treasury bonds instead.

湯瑪仕兩年前決定賣掉他的股票，改投資於公債。

(A) then      (B) from      (C) until      (D) ago

觀念   副詞

解析   本句為過去簡單式，two years 須加上 ago（兩年前）才能當成句子的時間副詞。如果題目中無 two years，則時間可搭配 then（那時候）。

• treasury bonds 國庫債券

---

C **15.** Exports to Brazil had always been profitable, but _____ last year we've been experiencing major losses.

對巴西的出口以前一向獲利不錯，不過從去年起我們就一直遭受重大損失。

(A) at      (B) ago      (C) since      (D) for

觀念   介系詞、現在完成進行式

解析   現在完成進行式 we've been experiencing major losses，表示「從過去某一時間開始到現在」我們都持續在面臨重大損失，而此一時間起點必須用介系詞 since（自從……起）來引導。

• profitable [ˋprɑfɪtəbl̩] (adj.) 有利潤的      • experience [ɪkˋspɪrɪəns] (v.) 經歷

**A** *16.* A: Have you ever led a marketing team before?

B: No, I _____ have, but I'm willing to learn.

A：你帶領過行銷團隊嗎？

B：沒有，我從來沒有過，不過我很願意學。

(A) never      (B) always      (C) not      (D) didn't

觀念 副詞

解析 頻率副詞 ever、never、always 等的位置一般在「be 動詞／助動詞之後」或「一般動詞之前」，但在簡答時，則一律放在「be 動詞／助動詞之前」，所以本題回答應說 No, I never have...。

● lead [lid] (v.) 領導        ● be willing to＋原形動詞：願意（做某事）

---

**A** *17.* Your progress reports and self-evaluations will be due _____ Friday, so get busy!

你們的進度報告和自我評鑑本週五要交，所以趕快去忙吧！

(A) this      (B) from      (C) last      (D) to

觀念 介系詞

解析 「星期幾；日期；特定日子」前面通常須搭配介系詞 on，但如果有 this/that（這個／那個）或 last/next（上一個／下一個）等形容詞時則不加介系詞。

● evaluation [ɪˌvæljʊˋeʃən] (n.) 評鑑      ● due [dju] (adj.) 到期的

---

**C** *18.* Consumers in that country can hardly keep up with _____ inflation.

該國消費者幾乎趕不上迅速攀升的通貨膨脹。

(A) rapidly fallen    (B) rapidly risen    (C) rapidly rising    (D) rapidly fell

觀念 形容詞、現在分詞與過去分詞

解析 「副詞＋現在分詞／過去分詞」也可構成複合形容詞，通常與現在分詞連用代表「主動；正在進行」，而與過去分詞連用則代表「被動；完成」。本題中的 inflation（通貨膨脹）是正在攀升中的事物，故用 rapidly rising 來修飾。

● rapidly [ˋræpɪdlɪ] (adv.) 迅速地      ● inflation [ɪnˋfleʃən] (n.) 通貨膨脹

A 19. Special packaging is required because the product is made out of
_____.

特殊包裝是必須的，因為這個產品是木製品。

(A) wood      (B) woody      (C) wooden      (D) woods

觀念　名詞

解析　介系詞 of 後面必須接名詞，故選 wood（木材）。至於 woods（樹林）、woody（茂密的）則與句意不符，而 wooden（木製的）則詞性不合。

● package [`pækɪdʒ] (v./n.) 包裝　　　● be made of... 由⋯做成（成品仍看得出原料）

● be made from... 由⋯做成的（原料性質已改變）

---

A 20. This kind of product may appeal to French people, but _____
people probably won't think it's anything special.

這種產品可能對法國人有吸引力，但是台灣人可能不會覺得它有什麼特別之處。

(A) Taiwan      (B) Taiwanese      (C) Taiwaner      (D) Taiwan of

觀念　形容詞

解析　people 前應接形容詞 Taiwanese（台灣的），本字也可直接當「台灣人」使用，所以 Taiwanese people = Taiwanese。

● appeal to＋人　對⋯有吸引力；訴諸，求助

---

B 21. Our company's website needs to _____ every day.

我們公司的網站需要每日更新。

(A) updated      (B) be updated      (C) update      (D) updating

觀念　被動語態

解析　website（網站）是「事物」，不會主動 update（更新），故應使用「被動語態」。而 need to 後面必須接原形動詞，故答案選 be updated。

● website [`wɛbˌsaɪt] (n.) 網站　　　● update [ʌp`det] (v.) 更新；使⋯合乎時代

**C** *22.* You should have recorded the serial numbers. If you _____, we would be able to claim insurance on the missing items.

你應該要把序號記錄下來的。如果你有做，我們就可以請求遺失品項的保險理賠。

(A) can      (B) will      (C) had      (D) were

**觀念** 假設語氣

**解析** should have recorded 意思是「應該要記錄，但事實卻未記錄」，表示對過去事件的「指責、懊悔」之意。所以其後的 If 子句也表示「與過去事實相反的假設」，應說 If you had recorded the serial numbers...，可省略為 If you had。

● serial number 序號      ● claim [klem] (v.) （根據權利）要求；索取

---

**B** *23.* The boss is unhappy that our bid wasn't accepted. He thinks we should have _____ harder.

老闆不高興我們的出價沒被接受。他覺得我們應該要更努力爭取才是。

(A) accepted      (B) tried      (C) listened      (D) run

**觀念** 情態助動詞

**解析** 第一句道出老闆不高興的理由是 our bid wasn't accepted，可推知「老闆認為我們應該更努力爭取、但我們卻沒有」，因此應用 we should have tried harder (but we didn't) 來表達老闆的責備之意。

● accept [ə`sɛpt] (v.) 接受      ● hard [hɑrd] (adv.) 努力地；艱苦地

---

**A** *24.* I've been so _____ this week that I haven't had time to finish the report.

我這週一直很忙，以至於我沒有時間寫完報告。

(A) busy      (B) restless      (C) tired      (D) bored

**觀念** 副詞

**解析** 副詞 so 意思是「如此；這麼地」，句型「so＋形容詞／副詞＋that 子句」意思是「如此……以至於……」。本句由 that 子句中的語意可推知說話者「忙到沒有時間寫完報告」，所以選 busy。

● restless [`rɛstlɪs] (adj.) 焦躁不安的

C 25. With the economy doing so poorly, it's getting _____ to make a profit in business these days.

由於經濟狀況很差，近來做生意要賺錢變得更難了。

(A) easier      (B) simpler      (C) harder      (D) more possible

觀念   形容詞比較級

解析   With the economy doing so poorly 是「分詞構句」，意思是「隨著經濟狀況惡化」，因此後半句應接 it's getting harder to make a profit。此處的 getting harder 是「比較級」的用法，表示「愈來愈難了」。

- economy [ɪ`kɑnəmɪ] (n.) 經濟      • poorly [`purlɪ] (adv.) 貧窮地；糟地
- make a profit 獲利；賺錢

---

B 26. The shipment was _____ late, so the clients are a bit upset about the delay.

貨物送得有點遲，所以客戶對於延誤有點生氣。

(A) arrived      (B) sent      (C) ordered      (D) paid

觀念   被動語態

解析   shipment 是「運送的貨物」，搭配動詞 arrive（抵達）時，應以主動語態呈現，如：The shipment has just arrived.「貨物剛運到。」但若搭配動詞 send（寄送），則須以「被動語態」呈現，因為進行寄送動作的行為者是人。此外，選項 (C) 與 (D) 意思是「（客戶）指定送貨／付款的時間太遲」，均與後半句的語意不合。

- a bit 有點

---

C 27. We'd better sell our stocks now, because by this time tomorrow their value will have _____.

我們最好現在把我們的股票賣掉，因為到明天的這個時候它們的價值就已經下跌了。

(A) increased      (B) measured      (C) decreased      (D) expanded

觀念   未來完成式

解析   by this time tomorrow 意思是「到明天的這個時候」，在此時間點以前已經發生的事必須用未來完成式。根據句意，說話者認為最好現在就賣股票，表示他預測在明天以前股票價格會「下跌」，因此動詞須選 decreased，相反詞為 increased。

- value [`vælju] (n.) 價值；價格      • decrease [dɪ`kris] (v.) 減少

**B** *28.* The stock market will be _____ at 9:00 a.m. on Tuesday, so we should be there by 8:45.

股市星期二上午九點將會開始交易，所以我們應該在八點四十五分以前到那兒。

(A) to open      (B) opening      (C) has open      (D) opens

觀念 未來進行式

解析 要表達未來的事件或安排，可以用未來簡單式「will/be going to＋原形動詞」或未來進行式「will be＋現在分詞」，本句題目中已出現 will be，因此後面應該接現在分詞 opening。

- stock market 股票市場
- by [baɪ] (prep.) 不遲於…；在…之前

---

**C** *29.* When _____ the shipment scheduled to arrive?

貨物預計何時送達？

(A) will      (B) can      (C) is      (D) are

觀念 現在簡單式

解析 schedule 當名詞時是「時間表；行程表」，而當動詞則是「將……排入行程表」。片語 be scheduled to 則是指主詞「被安排要……；預定要……」，後面接原形動詞。本題的主詞為 the shipment，be 動詞應搭配 is。

- be scheduled to＋原形動詞：預定，安排於

---

**D** *30.* Mr. Kent, your plane _____ at 7:20, so we'll have to get you to the airport early.

肯特先生，你的飛機七點二十分起飛，所以我們必須早點送你到機場。

(A) left      (B) can leave      (C) was leaving      (D) leaves

觀念 未來簡單式

解析 當未來的事件、行為是確定的計劃或時程表時，可以用「現在簡單式」來代替「未來簡單式」。如本句的飛機起飛時刻即是確定的行程，因此動詞只須說 leaves 即可。常搭配「時間表、節目表」的動詞有 leave（離開）、arrive（抵達）、start/begin（開始）、end/finish（結束）、open（開門）、close（關門）等。

- leave [liv] (v.) 離開；動身
- airport [`ɛr͵port] (n.) 機場

**B** *31.* The products come off the line here and are stored in the warehouse over _____.

這些產品是在這裡完成，然後儲存在那裏的倉庫。

(A) this        (B) there        (C) that        (D) from

觀念    介系詞

解析    come off the line 表示離開生產線，也就是「完成製造」的意思，stored in the warehouse 則是「儲存在倉庫」。前一句說產品在這裡完成，後一句應該也是說明儲存貨物的地點，over there 就是表示倉庫「在那裏」。

● come off 與…分離

● warehouse [`wɛr, haʊs] (n./v.) 倉庫；把…存入倉庫

---

**B** *32.* Unfortunately, the infrastructure of that country is _____ to support an advanced communication network like ours.

很不幸地，那個國家的基礎建設，並沒有發展到足以支持像我們國家一樣進步的通訊網絡。

(A) too developed enough        (B) not developed enough

(C) too developed        (D) developed very much

觀念    副詞

解析    本題要選擇配合文意 enough「夠……」的用法。unfortunately 是「不幸地」，含有轉折語氣，因此下一句應該是說「發展不夠到可以去……」。developed 在這裡是表「被動」的形容詞，意思是「已開發的」。enough「夠……去做……」的句型為「形容詞＋enough＋to V」，否定則為「not＋形容詞＋enough＋to V」。答案選 (B)。

● infrastructure [`ɪnfrəs, trʌktʃə] (n.) 基礎建設，公共建設

---

**C** *33.* Many _____ in the USA are owned by the Gannett Company.

美國的很多報社都是賈耐特公司所有。

(A) newspaper      (B) paper        (C) newspapers   (D) news

觀念    可數 / 不可數名詞

解析    newspaper 指「報社」時為可數名詞。選項 (B) 的 paper 也可以指報紙，但是必須加上 s。選項 (D) 的 news 指的是新聞，與文意不符。答案選 (C)。

● own [on] (v.) 擁有

C **34.** You got to work on time today, but unfortunately you forgot to punch _____. You're therefore considered late.

你今天有準時上班,但是很可惜的是你忘記打卡了。所以你仍被認為遲到。

(A) out      (B) on      (C) in      (D) up

**觀念** 介系詞

**解析** 前半句說「你今天上班有準時」,下一句則說「很可惜你忘記做某件事,所以還是被認為遲到」。由前後文可以猜測出應該是忘記「打卡」。上班打卡的美式英文是 punch in,所以答案選 (C)。

- on time 準時
- unfortunately [ʌnˋfɔrtʃənɪtlɪ] (adv.) 不幸地,遺憾地
- punch [pʌntʃ] (v.) 用力擊,用力按
- clock in (英式英文)打卡
- be considered (to be)+n./adj. 被認為⋯

---

A **35.** Did you hear the way Tom spoke to the boss? I could _____ believe my ears!

你有沒有聽到湯姆跟老闆說話的樣子?我實在無法相信我的耳朵!

(A) hardly      (B) hard      (C) really      (D) almost

**觀念** 副詞

**解析** 根據第一句的說法,可以推測後句是指「無法相信」。hardly 意思是「幾乎不」,本身帶有否定意味。hard 是「困難的;努力的」,形容詞、副詞同形。really 是「真地」,與句意不符。almost 是「幾乎」,與句意不符。答案選 (A)。

---

B **36.** I'm not sure if this kind of product will sell. We manufactured one just like it _____ before, and it was a total flop.

我不確定這種商品會賣得出去。我們曾經製造過一個跟這個一樣的,結果完全失敗。

(A) for      (B) once      (C) ever      (D) one

**觀念** 副詞

**解析** 第一句對這個產品沒信心,下一句說「曾經」做過一樣的,但賣得不好。這樣的句意才順,要選擇表示「曾經」的副詞。這裡的「曾經」是表示「次數」的 once,與強調時間、放在動詞之前的 ever 不同。

- manufacture [ˌmænjəˋfæktʃɚ] (v.) 製造

**A** **37.** I've really enjoyed my visit to your company, Mr. Edwards. Thank you for your _____.

愛得華先生，到你公司參觀讓我非常開心。謝謝你的好意。

(A) kindness　　(B) kind　　　　(C) kindnesses　　(D) kinds

觀念　名詞

解析　Thank you for your... 後面應該要接名詞形，所以選 kindness。這裡的 kindness 指的是參觀公司這件事，所以以單數形式呈現即可。kind 當形容詞是「仁慈的」，kind＋s 指的是名詞「種類」的複數。

● thank you for＋N./Ving 感謝你做某事

---

**B** **38.** This is a very important project, Marjorie! _____ in the company is counting on it being successful!

這是一個很重要的計畫，瑪喬麗！公司的每一個人都指望它可以成功！

(A) Everything　　(B) Everybody　　(C) No one　　　(D) None

觀念　代名詞

解析　前句說到這個計畫「很重要」，所以後句應該是說「每個人」都希望它可以成功。因此選項 (C) 和 (D) 就不符合句意。Everything 指的是物，在這裡不合適。所以答案選 (B)「每一個人」。

● count on sth. 指望…，依靠…

---

**B** **39.** The client has refused to speak to us, and says there _____ no further negotiations.

客戶拒絕跟我們對話，而且說不會有進一步的協商了。

(A) won't be　　(B) will be　　(C) wasn't　　(D) can't be

觀念　未來簡單式

解析　根據前半句句意，客戶拒絕對話，可推知將不會有進一步的協商，所以後半句應用否定句。但句中已有表否定的 no 一字，所以此處應說 there will be no further negotiations，也可代換為 there won't be any further negotiations。

● refuse [rɪˋfjuz] (v.) 拒絕　　　　　● further [ˋfɝðɚ] (adj.) 進一步的

● negotiation [nɪˌgoʃɪˋeʃən] (n.) 協商

**A** **40.** By the time new energy sources are developed, worldwide petroleum supplies will have _____ out.

在新能源開發出來之前，全球石油供應將已經枯竭了。

(A) run         (B) used         (C) broken         (D) sent

觀念    未來完成式

解析    「by＋未來時間」常與未來完成式連用，指在未來某個時間點或期限之前，將已經發生或完成的事。本句的未來期限是「新能源開發出來時」，說話者推測石油的供應不夠撐到那時候，因此動詞片語要選 run out（耗盡）。

● energy [ˈɛnədʒɪ] (n.) 能源        ● petroleum [pəˈtrolɪəm] (n.) 石油
● run out 被用完，被耗盡

**Questions 1~4 refer to the following article.**

Taiwan is bigger than Singapore, but ____D____ smaller than most

1.(A) many
(B) more
(C) very
(D) much

countries in Asia. Taiwan is one of the richest and ____C____ countries

2.(A) modernist
(B) modernest
(C) most modern
(D) modern

in Asia. Living expenses in Taiwan are also higher than in most Asian

countries. Nowadays, Taiwan has stronger ____A____ ties with China

3.(A) economic
(B) economical
(C) economy
(D) economically

than with Japan. The reasons are that Taiwan is closer to China than to

Japan, and that China has a larger ____A____ than Japan.

4.(A) population
(B) citizenship
(C) people
(D) society

**問題 1～4 請參考以下文章。**

台灣比新加坡大，但卻比亞洲大部份的國家小許多。台灣是亞洲最富裕、最現代化
的國家之一。台灣的生活消費也比亞洲大部份的國家高。目前台灣和中國的經濟關
係比和日本密切。原因是台灣離中國較離日本近，且中國的人口大於日本。

1. 觀念 副詞

   解析 修飾形容詞比較級應用副詞 much，much smaller 意思是「小多了」；very「很；非常」則只用來修飾原級。至於 many「許多」則只能當形容詞，修飾複數可數名詞，而 more 則是 many 和 much 的比較級。

   • not any＋比較級：沒有比較…     • even＋比較級：甚至還要更…

2. 觀念 形容詞最高級

   解析 the richest 是形容詞最高級，對等連接詞 and 後面也應使用 modern 的最高級。最高級的構成方式為：單音節形容詞加 -est，雙音節以上為 most 加原級，所以本題選 most modern。如果是雙音節但字尾為 y 者則去 y 加 -iest，如：happy → happiest。此外，形容詞最高級一定要搭配定冠詞 the 或所有格使用。

   • the＋最高級＋in / of... 某地 / 某群體中最…的

3. 觀念 形容詞

   解析 名詞 tie 在此指「聯繫；關係」，前面應用形容詞來修飾。選項中的形容詞有 economic 和 economical，這兩個字拼法相似但意義不同。economic 指「經濟上的；與經濟有關的」，如：economic growth「經濟成長」、economic policies「經濟政策」。economical 則指「經濟實惠的；節省的」，如：an economical car「一輛經濟實惠的車子」、an economical housewife「一個節儉的家庭主婦」。

   • economic tie 經濟聯繫

4. 觀念 集合名詞

   解析 本題要選合乎語意的名詞。根據前後文推斷，此處應選 population「人口」。population 為集合名詞，指「一國、一地整體的人口」，視為單數，經常搭配定冠詞 the 或 a population of 來表示。如：The population of China is around 1.3 billion. = China has a population of around 1.3 billion.（中國的人口約為十三億。）

   • citizenship [ˋsɪtəzṇʃɪp] (n.) 公民身分     • society [səˋsaɪətɪ] (n.) 社會

**Questions 5~8 refer to the following article.**

30 St Mary Axe is one of Europe's first green skyscrapers. It opened in 2004 in London's financial district, and at 40 stories high it dominates the city's skyline. _____C_____ like a giant glass bullet, the skyscraper's

        5.(A) To shape
           (B) Shape
           (C) Shaped
           (D) Shaping

green design _____A_____ it to use 50 percent less energy than most

      6.(A) allows
        (B) makes
        (C) lets
        (D) has

buildings its size. Gaps in each floor create six huge shafts that serve _____D_____ a natural ventilation system, with gardens on every sixth

7.(A) to
  (B) in
  (C) with
  (D) as

floor to purify the air. The shafts move hot air out of the building in the summer, and use solar energy to heat the building in the winter. All of this is done, amazingly, _____A_____ electric heaters or fans. The shafts

        8.(A) without
          (B) except
          (C) aside from
          (D) besides

also allow sunlight to pass through the building, creating a pleasant working environment and keeping lighting costs down.

**問題 5～8 請參考以下文章。**

倫敦聖瑪利府街三十號是歐洲第一批綠色摩天大樓之一。它於二○○四年在倫敦金融區啟用，樓高四十層，高聳於這座城市的天際線。這座外形宛如巨型玻璃子彈的摩天樓拜綠線設計之賜，使用的能源只有大多數同等大小建築的一半。每一樓層的間隙形成六座巨大的通風井，作為天然的通風系統。每六層樓還闢有花園來淨化空氣。這些通風井會在夏天把熱空氣排出大樓，冬天則用太陽能來暖化整棟建築。令人驚奇的是，以上功能完全不需電熱器或風扇。通風井也讓陽光得以穿透大樓，創造宜人的工作環境並降低照明成本。

5. 觀念 過去分詞

解析 本題逗號前的結構為前導的「修飾語」，用來修飾主詞 the skyscraper。shape 當動詞是「使成形」的意思，要修飾 skyscraper 此一「事物」，應用表「被動」的過去分詞 shaped，意思是「被塑造成……造型」，故選 (C)。至於選項 (A) 則為不定詞片語，放在句首的 To V 通常是 In order to 的簡化，表示「目的」，與本題的語意不符。

- skyscraper [`skaɪ`skrepɚ] (n.) 摩天大樓

6. 觀念 動詞

解析 allow 意思是「允許；使……可能」，句型為「allow＋受詞＋to V」，所以本句的 allow it to use 50 percent less energy... 就是「讓它可以少用一半的能源」。其他選項 make、let、have 等也有「允許；讓」之意，但這三個字均為「使役動詞」，句型為「make/let/have＋受詞＋原形動詞」。

- energy [`ɛnədʒɪ] (n.) 能源；精力

7. 觀念 動詞片語

解析 serve 在此是「作為……之用」，句型為「serve as＋名詞」或「serve＋to V」。本句中所接的是名詞 a natural ventilation system，因此本題選 as。

- gap [gæp] (n.) 間隙
- shaft [ʃæft] (n.) 通風井
- ventilation [ˌvɛntl̩`eʃən] (n.) 通風

8. 觀念 介系詞

解析 本題要表達的是「沒有用到電熱器或風扇」，所以應選 without「沒有……；不……」。其他三個選項中文意思均是「除……之外」，但實際意義卻不同。besides 是「除……之外還有」，亦即「包含其後的名詞」；except (for) 是「除去」，亦即「不包含後面的名詞」；aside from 則兼具 besides 和 except (for) 之意，須看前後文判別語意。

- heater [`hitɚ] (n.) 電熱器
- fan [fæn] (n.) 風扇

# 文法規則列表 Grammar Bank

## 名詞的複數形變化

| 一般狀況：**名詞後加 s** | | |
|---|---|---|
| girl → girls | dog → dogs | rose → roses |
| 單字字尾是 s、z、sh、ch、x：**名詞加上 es** | | |
| glass → glasses | buzz → buzzes | dish → dishes |
| 單字字尾是子音＋y：**去 y 加上 ies** | | |
| city → cities | baby → babies | cherry → cherries |
| 單字字尾是 o：**加上 s/es** | | |
| zoo → zoos | photo → photos | piano → pianos |
| 單字字尾是 f/fe：**加上 s，或是去掉 f/fe 加上 ves** | | |
| roof → roofs | chief → chiefs | leaf → leaves |

## 人稱代名詞

| | 人稱 | 主格 | 所有格 | 受格 | 所有代名詞 | 反身代名詞 |
|---|---|---|---|---|---|---|
| 單數 | 第一人稱 | I | my | me | mine | myself |
| | 第二人稱 | you | your | you | yours | yourself |
| | 第三人稱 | he | his | him | his | himself |
| | | she | her | her | hers | herself |
| | | it | its | it | its | itself |
| 複數 | 第一人稱 | we | our | us | ours | ourselves |
| | 第二人稱 | you | your | you | yours | yourselves |
| | 第三人稱 | they | their | them | theirs | themselves |

# 不定代名詞

• **下列不定代名詞可作形容詞，後面接名詞**

| some, any, all<br>few, less, more, most<br>much, many, plenty, several | + | 名詞 |

• **下列不定代名詞的動詞要用單數**

anybody, anyone, anything
everybody, everyone, everything
somebody, someone, something
nobody, no one (none), nothing
one, another, the other

• **下列不定代名詞的動詞要用複數**

few, many, plenty, several,
more, most, all, both

• **下列不定代名詞的動詞要視替代名詞的單複數而定**

some, any, each, either, neither

## 第三人稱單數動詞字尾變化規則

| 一般狀況：**在動詞字尾加 s** | | |
| --- | --- | --- |
| open → opens | look → looks | sit → sits |
| 單字字尾是 s、z、sh、ch、x：**動詞加上 es** | | |
| teach → teaches | wash → washes | watch → watches |
| 單字字尾是子音＋y：**去 y 加上 ies** | | |
| hurry → hurries | carry → carries | study → studies |
| 不規則變化 | | |
| have → has | do → does | |

## Ving 字尾變化規則

| 一般狀況：**在動詞字尾加 ing** | | |
| --- | --- | --- |
| say → saying | speak → speaking | watch → watching |
| 單字字尾是不發音的 e：**去掉 e 加上 ing** | | |
| stare → staring | celebrate → celebrating | come → coming |
| 單字字尾是「子音＋母音＋子音」：**先「重覆字尾」，再加 ing** | | |
| sit → sitting | run → running | stop → stopping |

# 過去分詞字尾變化

| 一般狀況：**直接在動詞後面加上 ed** | | |
|---|---|---|
| enjoy → enjoy**ed** | practice → practic**ed** | clean → clean**ed** |
| 字尾是子音＋y：**去 y 再加 ied** | | |
| study → stud**ied** | try → tr**ied** | cry → cr**ied** |
| 字尾是短母音＋子音：**重複字尾再加 ed** | | |
| plan → plan**ned** | drop → drop**ped** | stop → stop**ped** |
| 不規則變化 | | |
| bring → brought | think → thought | write → written |

# 動詞三態變化規則

| | 原形 | 過去式動詞 | 過去分詞 |
|---|---|---|---|
| 一般狀況：**加上 ed** | play | play**ed** | play**ed** |
| 字尾是 e：**直接加 d** | live | liv**ed** | liv**ed** |
| 字尾是子音＋y：**去 y 再加 ied** | cry | cr**ied** | cr**ied** |
| 字尾是短母音＋子音：**重複字尾再加 ed** | stop | stop**ped** | stop**ped** |

# 常見的不規則動詞變化

| 原形 | 過去式 | 過去分詞 |
|---|---|---|
| do | did | done |
| take | took | taken |
| run | ran | run |
| see | saw | seen |
| read | read | read |
| put | put | put |
| come | came | come |
| go | went | gone |
| spoil | spoilt | spoilt |
| spend | spent | spent |
| find | found | found |

# 副詞的形成規則

| 一般狀況：**直接在形容詞字尾加上 ly** | | |
|---|---|---|
| quick → quick**ly** | sad → sad**ly** | beautiful → beautiful**ly** |
| 形容詞字尾是子音＋ y：**先去掉字尾 y，之後再加 ily** | | |
| happy → happ**ily** | angry → angr**ily** | lucky → luck**ily** |
| 形容詞字尾是 ble：**先去掉字尾 e，再加 y** | | |
| comfortable → comfortab**ly** | | possible → possib**ly** |
| 形容詞和副詞同形 | | |
| early | fast | late |
| 形容詞和副詞完全不同 | | |
| good → well | | |

## 副詞、形容詞比較級和最高級的字尾變化

| |
|---|
| 兩個音節以內:**比較級字尾加 er,最高級字尾加 est** |
| old → older → oldest　　　fast → faster → fastest |
| 發音為「子音+短母音+子音」:**重複字尾,比較級加 er,最高級加 est** |
| big → bigger → biggest |
| 兩音節以內,字尾為「子音+y」:**去掉 y,比較級加 ier,最高級加 iest** |
| easy → easier → easiest |
| 超過兩個音節:**比較級字前加 more,最高級字前加 most** |
| expensive → more expensive → most expensive |
| 「名詞+固定字尾」的形容詞:**比較級字前加 more,最高級字前加 most** |
| carefully → more carefully → most carefully |
| 加 er 較不好唸的形容詞:**比較級字前加 more,最高級字前加 most** |
| boring → more boring → most boring<br>modern → more modern → most modern |

**Unit 17** 常見介系詞片語

| 動詞片語 | | | |
|---|---|---|---|
| bring back | 帶回來 | call up | 打電話 |
| cheer up | 使高興 | cross out | 刪掉 |
| figure out | 找出答案 | fill in | 填寫（表格） |
| fill up | 裝滿 | find out | 找出問題 |
| get over | 復原 | give back | 歸還 |
| look up | 查字典 | pick out | 找出、挑出 |
| put off | 延遲 | put out (the trash) | 拿（垃圾）出去 |
| put on | 穿上 | take out (the dog) | 帶（狗）出去 |
| throw away | 丟掉 | turn off (a light) | 關（燈） |
| turn on (a light) | 開（燈等電器用品） | write down | 寫下 |
| call on (sb.) | 拜訪（某人） | come over (place) | 拜訪某人的家 |
| get over (illness) | 從（病）復原 | look for | 尋找 |
| run into (sb.) | 遇到某人 | get along with (sb.) | 與人友善交往 |
| come up with | 想出 | put up with (sb.) | 容忍某人 |
| look down on (sb.) | 看不起某人 | stay away from | 避開 |
| run out of (sth.) | 用完 | | |

## 形容詞片語

| kind of | 一點兒 | good at | 精通，擅長 |
|---|---|---|---|
| late for | 遲到 | afraid of | 害怕 |
| sorry for | 為……而抱歉 | supposed to | 應該 |
| filled with | 充滿 | rich in | 富含…… |
| crowded with | 擠滿了 | full of | 充滿 |

## 「介系詞＋名詞」片語

| **at** | | | |
|---|---|---|---|
| at table | 在吃飯 | at school | 求學 |
| at present | 現在 | at a glance | 一瞥 |
| at first | 起初 | at last | 最後 |
| **by** | | | |
| by accident | 意外地 | by any chance | 萬一 |
| by chance | 偶然地 | by heart | 默記 |
| **from** | | | |
| from now on | 從現在開始 | from then on | 從那時開始 |
| from time to time | 時常 | from door to door | 挨家挨戶 |
| **in** | | | |
| in one's youth | 某人年輕時 | in a minute | 一會兒 |
| in one's absence | 在某人不在時 | in the beginning | 起初，最初 |
| in the meantime | 同時，在此期間 | in the end | 最後 |
| in honor of | 對……表達敬意 | in pursuit of | 追求 |

| of | | | |
|---|---|---|---|
| of courage | 有勇氣的 | of importance | 重要的 |

| on | | | |
|---|---|---|---|
| on occasion | 隨時 | on the spot | 當場 |
| on average | 平均 | on duty | 上班；值勤中 |
| on sale | 廉售；拍賣 | on one's way to... | 在……途中 |

| out of | | | |
|---|---|---|---|
| out of date | 過時的 | out of the ordinary | 不平常的 |
| out of question | 不可能的 | | |

| under | | | |
|---|---|---|---|
| under control | 在……控制下 | under age | 未成年的 |
| under fire | 遭受攻擊的 | under suspicion | 受到懷疑的 |

| with | | | |
|---|---|---|---|
| with an eye on | 考慮到 | with efficiency | 有效率地 |
| with care | 小心地 | with regret | 遺憾地 |

國家圖書館出版品預行編目資料

第一次就考好 New TOEIC 文法 / EZ 叢書館編輯部作.
-- 初版 . -- 臺北市：日月文化，2011.07
464 面，17×23 公分（EZ 叢書館）
ISBN：978-986-248-164-6（平裝）
1. 多益測驗　2. 文法
805.1895　　　　　　　　　　　　　100007160

## EZ 叢書館

# 第一次就考好 New TOEIC 文法

作　　者：EZ 叢書館編輯部
執行顧問：陳思容
副 總 編：葉瑋玲
英文編審：Judd Piggott
中文編審：陳慧萍
文字編輯：李佳真
執行編輯：賴建豪
美術設計：管仕豪
排版設計：健呈電腦排版股份有限公司

董 事 長：洪祺祥
法律顧問：建大法律事務所
財務顧問：高威會計師事務所

出　　版：日月文化集團　日月文化出版股份有限公司
製　　作：EZ 叢書館
地　　址：台北市大安區信義路三段 151 號 9 樓
電　　話：(02)2708-5509
傳　　真：(02)2708-6157
網　　址：www.ezbooks.com.tw

總 經 銷：高見文化行銷股份有限公司
電　　話：(02)2668-9005
傳　　真：(02)2668-6220
印　　刷：禹利電子分色有限公司
初　　版：2011 年 7 月
二　　刷：2011 年 12 月
定　　價：380 元
I S B N：978-986-248-164-6